A FATAL FEAST AT BRAMSFORD MANOR

Books by Darci Hannah

A Beacon Bakeshop Mystery

MURDER AT THE BEACON BAKESHOP

MURDER AT THE CHRISTMAS COOKIE
BAKE-OFF

MURDER AT THE BLUEBERRY FESTIVAL

MURDER AT THE PUMPKIN PAGEANT

MURDER AT THE BLARNEY BASH

A Food & Spirits Mystery

A FATAL FEAST AT BRAMSFORD MANOR

Published by Kensington Publishing Corp.

A FATAL FEAST AT BRAMSFORD MANOR

A FOOD & SPIRITS MYSTERY

DARCI HANNAH

Kensington Publishing Corp.
www.kensingtonbooks.com

Dedication
For my brothers, Randy & Ron Hilgers
For a rich and blessed childhood, and a love that endures.
With love, Darci

KENSINGTON BOOKS are published by

Kensington Publishing Corp.
900 Third Avenue
New York, NY 10022

All Kensington titles, imprints, and distributed lines are available at special quantity discounts for bulk purchases for sales promotion, premiums, fundraising, educational, or institutional use. Special book excerpts or customized printings can also be created to fit specific needs. For details, write or phone the office of the Kensington Special Sales Manager: Attn. Special Sales Department, Kensington Publishing Corp., 900 Third Avenue, New York, NY 10022. Phone: 1-800-221-2647.

Library of Congress Control Number: 2024936509

ISBN: 978-1-4967-4744-0
First Kensington Hardcover Edition: September 2024

ISBN: 978-1-4967-4746-4 (ebook)

10 9 8 7 6 5 4 3 2 1

Printed in the United States of America

Acknowledgments

Years ago, when I sat down to write my first novel, I never intended to add paranormal elements to my story. I was simply telling a tale the way I saw it. However, before long, I realized that somehow paranormal elements snuck in, elevating my story to a place I was not only intrigued by but happy with. Whether a ghostly echo from the past, a twist in time, an angelic visit, or the spirit of a lighthouse captain still on duty, these elements began to come alive in the stories I wrote. Honestly, I never considered them strange or paranormal. In fact, I considered them possible. I blame that on my active imagination and the fact that my younger brother, Ron, was a paranormal investigator. He and his wife were also big foodies. Ron told me many spooky and fascinating stories, and I believed him!

Ten years ago, I came up with the premise for this book, only back then I imagined it as a pitch for a reality tv show for my brother. He loved watching ghost hunting shows on cable television. I found them not only creepy, but often farcical. However, I realized they were hugely popular. I also realized that many cable channels had one, except for my favorite channel, Food Network, and with good reason. However, that didn't stop me from calling him one day with my great idea. I said something like, "Hey, we should pitch a ghost hunting show to Food Network and call it 'Food & Spirits.' It'll be a food-baiting ghost hunting show based on the old Celtic tradition of the Dumb Supper. I think it'll be hilarious." He thought it sounded great too, so I wrote it up and stuck it in my desk drawer.

In the fall of 2022 my wonderful editor at Kensington, John Scognamiglio, asked me for ideas for another cozy mystery series. I was thinking very hard over this when I heard my brother's voice in my head saying, "Food and Spirits. What are you waiting for? Pull it out, dust it off, and send it over." I should probably tell you that my brother Ron passed away in 2020. But he did have a point. It was an idea.

As fate would have it, of the three ideas I pitched to John, Food & Spirits was the winner. For many reasons, the thought of writing it terrified me. However, the longer I thought about it the more I realized that this was a journey I was meant to take, if not for my sake, then for the sake of my brother's memory. I'm happy I did.

I would like to thank the amazing John Scognamiglio for choosing Food & Spirits and encouraging me to write it. And a huge thanks to Larissa Ackerman, Rebecca Cremonese, and the rest of the amazing team at Kensington Publishing.

I would also like to thank my dear friend and agent extraordinaire, Sandy Harding, for her wisdom, encouragement, and for helping me navigate the very tricky world of publishing.

To the love of my life, John, and our children, Dan, Matt, Jim, and daughter-in-law Allison. Love you all so very much. You fill my heart with joy and our home with laughter. We are blessed.

To my wonderful parents, Jan and Dave Hilgers. My love and gratitude are immeasurable. And to my brothers, Randy and Ron Hilgers, for a lifelong friendship filled with love, teasing, giggles, and adventures. Best brothers ever. Love you!

Chapter 1

❦

Food, to a people-pleaser like Bridget "Bunny" MacBride, was a powerful medium. It helped that she was a naturally gifted cook. It also helped that she had grown up with nature's bounty literally on her doorstep, having been raised on a farm in the United Kingdom. To Bunny's way of thinking, it was hard for someone to dislike you when you offered them a lovingly crafted slice of the most decadent, triple-layer chocolate cake. A cake like that ignited the taste buds in the most pleasing way. It was also hard to stay glum when offered a homecooked meal. This Bunny had learned from her mother. At the tender age of ten, under her mother's loving guidance, Bunny had made the most esthetically pleasing and delicious tomato tart her mother had ever seen, using fresh tomatoes and herbs grown in the family garden. Her mother was so proud of her and her tomato tart that she told Bunny to bring a slice to her father, who was in his office grumbling over the account books. Davie MacBride loved farming, but he always grumbled over the account books. Bunny had tiptoed into his office, placed the colorful and aromatic slice of tomato tart in front of him, then stood back and watched the magic happen. In just one bite her father had gone from glum to grinning. After two bites his face was beaming with delight as he looked at her. The confounding numbers which were causing such misery had faded away, replaced by, well, joy. Tasting something delightful had that kind of effect on people. It was remarkable. It was powerful. It made Bunny realize that with a little effort and good ingredients, she could not only win smiles but maybe even make a difference in the world in some small way.

That humble tomato tart and her father's broad smile stuck with Bunny, carrying her from the humble shores of Scotland to the hustle and bustle of New York City and its cutting-edge food scene, where a young Bridget MacBride studied and honed her culinary skills. She had quickly climbed the culinary ladder and at twenty-nine, Bridget "Bunny" MacBride found herself working as a menu developer and guest chef on *Mary Stobart's Memorable Meals* at the home studio in Connecticut. Mary, as Bunny well knew, had been America's number-one foodie and lifestyle expert for over forty years. She was also the star of the show and one of the co-founders of the Mealtime Network. Bunny's culinary skills had worked their magic on the aging foodie, prompting a job offer. However, as Bunny's popularity on the show began to rise, she detected a tinge of resentment, and even regret on occasion from Mary. She suspected that so many decades in front of the camera touting the latest trends in food, gardening, and home decorating ideas had taken its toll on the woman. As Bunny well knew, the professional world of food was a competitive game. There were even whispers in the kitchens and hallways of the studio that perhaps it was time to put the old mare out to pasture. Such talk made Mary Stobart not only particularly grumpy, but also cunning. Bunny, for her part, stayed out of it. She was still very grateful for the opportunities Mary had given her.

However, the fact remained that grumpy old Mary Stobart was getting harder to please. Yet Bunny, with her infectious optimism, still believed that the iconic foodie could be coaxed into a smile by the right dish.

Therefore, with the beautifully prepared plate in her hands, Bunny approached the large corner office. As usual, she gave a soft knock before opening the door. Mary, as usual, was sitting behind her desk, reading the script for the morning's shoot, while Jasmine from makeup was still fussing with her hair. Bunny marveled at how at eighty Mary's perfectly styled hair had not one speck of gray in it. It was often the topic of discussion between Bunny, her mother, Maggie, and Granny MacBride, who faithfully streamed the cooking show in the UK. Her mother claimed it was the product of good genetics. Granny MacBride leaned on the side of witchcraft. Bunny surmised it was a little of both.

"Good morning, Mary," Bunny said in her bright, cheerful manner—with just a hint of her Scottish accent shining through. "I've brought the dish I've been preparing for my weekly spot." Mary's milk-chocolate brown eyes peered over the script, then went right back to reading. The eye contact, however brief, was Bunny's signal. She set the plate on the desk, laid the fork between the dark green skin of the roasted acorn squash and the still warm muffin slathered with honey-butter, and nudged it in front of her boss.

And then she waited.

Mary turned the page and continued reading.

Jasmine's hairbrush stilled in her hand as her eyes fell to the plate on the desk. "Whoo-y!" she proclaimed with delight. "That looks delicious, Bunny. It smells even better. My tum-tum is grumbling at the sight of it. I'm about ready to snatch that dish up if Mary doesn't stop reading." Even through the threat, Mary, amazingly, kept on reading. Jasmine cast an apologetic look Bunny's way and set down her brush. She then arranged a rogue strand of hair, stepped back to admire her work, and declared, "I'm done. You look stunning as usual, Mary. Call me if you need me."

A grumble that might be interpreted as "Thank you" came from behind the script as the stylist left the office.

Although Bunny had yet to be acknowledged by her boss, she knew that the tantalizing aroma wafting from the humble plate would work its magic, eventually.

Patience was a virtue Bunny had learned in the kitchen. As every good cook knows, a pot of water boils when it's ready to, and not a moment before that. To Bunny, Mary Stobart was akin to that obstinate pot of water. Bunny, enjoying the aroma of her festive, fall dish, folded her hands and waited a moment longer. Then, without ever removing her eyes from the script, Mary picked up the fork and selected a bite of food. Bunny watched patiently as the older woman chewed. Then, suddenly, the fork turned and pointed at her. Mary released her grip on the papers, letting them fall on the desk. Since Mary was still chewing and seemed incapable of forming words, she just kept jabbing her fork in Bunny's direction. Bunny thought that the aging foodie was about to say something, but she didn't. She took another bite instead. This time, however, Mary closed her eyes and made a little sound that to Bunny might indicate one of several things. She kept her eyes glued to Mary's face. Unfortunately, unlike most women in their eighties, Mary's face had been ironed out by one of Hollywood's finest plastic surgeons. The man had a gift, and Mary looked fifty if she was a day. However, her face had been nipped and tucked so well that all micro-expressions—those tiny lifts, dips, and twinges of the face that mirrored one's innermost thoughts ever so subtly—had essentially been eradicated. Yet even through the surgically taut skin, Bunny could tell that an expression was beginning to form. The suspense was galling, but in the end, Mary smiled.

"Pleasant. Very pleasant. If autumn had a taste, this would be it. Let me try the muffin."

Bunny waited until Mary had taken a bite before she described her dish.

"As you see, I wanted to create something that used the flavors of the season. It's early September, and so many bonnie vegetables are in season. This," she began, pointing to the colorful creation on the plate, "is a pan-fried pork chop sautéed with yellow onions and tart apples and with a hint of fresh rosemary. Once the pork chop is fully cooked, and the apples and onions are tender, the pork chop is cut from the bone, sliced, and tossed with the apples and onions. A hearty scoop of the mixture is then put into half of a roasted acorn squash that's been baked with a cinnamon-brown butter glaze. The whole thing is then topped with a sprinkling of brown sugar, a crumble of Danish blue cheese, and baked an additional fifteen minutes. The muffin is a cornbread muffin with a hint of sweetness and topped with whipped honey-butter."

"The muffin is rather tasty and moist. I was afraid it would be dry. Cornbread can be so dry. As you know, the world has no room for dry, crumbly muffins." Mary took another bite just to be certain.

Bunny had the grace and experience to understand that this was a high compliment from her boss. As Mary aged, she grew stingy with her compliments. Part of this, Bunny knew, was a desperate grasp to remain on top. Bunny couldn't help the fact that not only was she young, beautiful, talented, and had a head full of light ginger curls that were better suited to an Irish dancer rather than a television chef with a five-minute guest spot on America's favorite cooking show. In other words, Bunny looked good on camera and was popular with the viewers, a fact the old foodie was having a hard time grappling with.

"I haven't had breakfast," Mary told her. "Leave this with me . . . and be ready to prepare it live on Bunny's Culinary Corner tomorrow. Then I want you to start thinking spooky. Got it? Halloween is one of my favorite holidays. It's just around the corner, and I want you to create clever, tasty, spooky treats for kids."

Bunny forced a smile. "Spooky? I don't really embrace spooky, Mary. What about cute? Kids love treats that are bright and appealing." For some reason Mary's lips puckered and bent into what appeared to be a frown. Bunny didn't understand.

"Cute? It's Halloween, Bunny. It's the season to embrace your inner witch. Didn't you celebrate Halloween in Scotland?" Mary narrowed her eyes as she asked this.

Inner witch? No thank you, Bunny thought. Halloween and all things spooky were not to her liking. She disliked old buildings. She *really* disliked derelict, crumbling old buildings. And she had a very hard time tolerating those black-clad yahoos and wannabe witches who poured into the old Scottish villages on Samhain—or Halloween—on a mission to drum up the ghosts of the past. The truth was, although she had come to America to pursue her culinary ambitions, it wasn't the only reason she had left her home in Scotland. Bunny, quite simply, had run from the ghosts of her own past. And, truth be told, she was still running. Embracing the spooky side of Halloween would not only be a huge mistake, but it was something she wasn't about to do—even for *Mary Stobart's Memorable Meals*.

"Aye, they celebrate Halloween in Scotland," Bunny answered. "It's a spooked-up holiday, to be sure, but I've never been a fan of it."

"That's not a good reason. We run a cooking show that prides itself on innovative foods and festive ideas. I want delicious cupcakes in any flavor you choose, even pumpkin if you wish, but I want them to be scary. I want mini graveyards, with little tombstones, fake blood, killer spiders, ghouls, and spooky ghosts. Got it?"

"Well now, why would anyone want to give those gruesome fairy cakes to innocent children? I should think children have enough worries without eating sweets that look like death and all manner of evil. What about a pumpkin patch instead? Children love pumpkins."

"I want graveyards! Make them for adults, then. I don't care. Adults love graveyards."

"Do they, now? I should think that eating a fairy cake . . . or a cupcake as you call them, decorated like a grave, might make a person reflect on their own mortality. Nobody wants to be reminded of that on a holiday. It sends the wrong message. . . . Or maybe that is the message. Eat enough of these fat-laden, sugary wee cakes and that tombstone will be yours. That's not fun, Mary. That's morbid."

"You're really having a hard time with this, aren't you?"

Bunny hated to admit it, but she was. However, she also believed she had the perfect solution. Flashing her winning smile, she offered, "I have a better idea. Let Sherry make the spooky treats. She's not only artistic, but she's also clever and very good at decorating cakes and cookies. I have something better in mind. I've been working on a light, velvety smooth pumpkin cheesecake with a warm caramel topping and a sprinkling of toasted pecans. I know fans of the show will love that."

Mary studied her for a moment through narrowed eyes before finally giving her nod of approval.

Little did Bunny know that although she had successfully dodged making spooky treats for the Halloween show, she wasn't out of the woods yet. In fact, thanks to her reluctance to embrace "spooky," what she had really done was give Mary the one ingredient she'd been looking for to put the spotlight back on Mary Stobart once again.

Chapter 2

"Bunny MacBride, it's your lucky day!" Tommy announced, thrusting his head inside the doorway of the studio's prep-kitchen. "The boss is requesting your presence in the big office."

"The big office? Why does that sound more foreboding than lucky?" Sherry remarked, grasping her loaded frosting bag with a little more aggression than she had meant to. Thick chocolate buttercream oozed out the tip as she cast a concerned look Bunny's way.

"What's this about, Tommy?" Tommy Allan was Mary Stobart's personal assistant and had been for the last ten years. Tommy, now in his early forties, was also a huge gossip. Bunny cast him a scrutinizing gaze while holding her chef's knife in what might be construed as a slightly threatening manner, prompting a look of amused surprise from the man. In her defense, Bunny had been slicing myriad colorful vegetables for a segment she was doing on ratatouille. Sherry, the other sous chef and menu developer in the kitchen, was working on the Halloween cupcakes that Bunny had passed on two weeks ago.

"If you must know, Bunny, it's all good. *Really good*," Tommy emphasized. "Word on the street, kid, is that you're getting your own show."

"No way," Sherry said, just before Bunny uttered the same phrase. Both women exchanged a look, letting the news sink in. Then Bunny, wisely, set down her knife and took off her apron.

"I don't know if I believe you, Tommy, but lead the way."

As Bunny and Tommy walked down the maze of hallways that led to the corner office, Tommy assured her, "Believe me, it's true. Why else would Jerry Goldstein from the head office pop around for a visit? Wait. Don't answer that. We all know that Mary and Jerry have a thing going on. But Bunny," he said, looking at her pretty face that was now clouded by pensive thought, "all your hard work in the prep kitchen and your short but fascinating guest segments have finally paid off. So young! So talented! And with an *It* factor that our dear old Mary Stobart is envious of! We all know it's the reason you're back in the prep-kitchen most of the time and not doing another segment on the show." She cast him a nervous glance before he continued. "Look, everyone likes to take jabs at Mary from time to time. It's part of the price one pays when they're at the pinnacle of their profession and have been for decades. However, I've worked for Mary long enough to know that although she might have an envious streak from time to time regarding up-and-coming talent, she's also very generous. She knows that you deserve your own show, yet she's wise enough not to put you in direct competition with what she has created here. Also, by discovering you and helping to launch a show of your own, she can claim some of the credit. It's a win-win for everyone."

Bunny stopped before Mary's door and turned to Tommy. "I don't believe this. You really are serious, aren't you?" Tommy gave a gentlemanly nod. "I really am getting my own show?" He nodded again, causing a sudden attack of butterflies to swarm and pummel her stomach. Nerves took her, and she feared that her knees would buckle before Tommy could open the door.

Her own cooking show!

Was she ready for this?

Before she could answer that, Tommy put one hand on the door handle and the other on Bunny's shoulder. "Look, you're going to be fine. Remember, you deserve this." He then opened the door and gave her a little push, propelling her into Mary Stobart's office.

"Hello," Bunny said by way of announcement as she stumbled into the room. Mary was standing so close to Mr. Goldstein that their noses were nearly touching. She startled them in mid-laugh, a fact which caused her face to flush. Jerry Goldstein, an imposing man in his early seventies, looked at her as the laugh on his lips faded. So did Mary.

The trouble with having porcelain fair skin, Bunny mused, was that when embarrassment struck, there was no graceful way to hide it. With a face as bright red as a stop sign, Bunny cleared her throat and offered a polite, "You asked to see me?"

"We did," Mary said, nervously smoothing her smart, cashmere sweater. "Have a seat."

Professionalism settled once again in the head office. The plasticine face of Mary Stobart split into a generous smile. "Bridget, I have some very good news for you. Jerry called me a week ago to tell me that Mealtime Network has signed a contract for a new type of cooking show. Isn't that right, Jerry?" Jerry, sitting a tad too close to Mary, nodded. Mary continued. "It's a travel cooking show, requiring the host chef to be able to think on their feet as they create a special meal to represent the country and the place the show takes them. When Jerry came to me with news of this new show, he asked me if I had anyone in mind that would fit these requirements, and I immediately thought of you."

A FATAL FEAST AT BRAMSFORD MANOR   11

Bunny inhaled. She was blushing again, but she didn't care, she was so honored. "Crivens, Mary . . . I can't believe this. I'm chuffed. I'm honored. Thank you."

"Bridget . . . Bunny, is it alright if I call you Bunny?" Bunny nodded at the executive. "This is a groundbreaking show. When we met with the creator and learned of the unique angle this cooking show would take, I couldn't help thinking of you and that popular segment you have on Mary's show. Your look, your slight English accent—"

"Scottish," Bunny corrected.

"Right, Scottish," he said breezily, waving a hand as if they were the same thing. Clearly, the man had no clue. With another smile, Jerry continued. "I called Mary straightaway. Of course, your segment is popular, and a staple on *Mary Stobart's Memorable Meals*. But in the end, I got her to confirm my gut instinct. Which is that you would be perfect for this new show. What I'm saying, Bunny, is that this would be the opportunity of a lifetime for you. Mary tells me that you're single, which is also a bonus, due to the travel." Jerry leaned forward. "You wouldn't have a problem with travel, would you?"

To Bunny the entire conversation was surreal, and she was mentally pinching herself, trying to stay focused. "Travel?" she uttered. Her mind was reeling. Travel was every young woman's dream, including Bunny's. With her busy schedule, she rarely made it back home to Scotland, or out of Connecticut for that matter. Oh, the exotic destinations! Visions of sunny Caribbean islands with their unique spices, exotic fruits, and bare-chested men were swirling in her head until she realized that they were both staring at her. "I love travel. That won't be a problem at all. It might be a problem for Mr. Wiggles, but I'll see if my neighbor's daughter would like to take care of him while I'm gone."

"And what exactly is a Mr. Wiggles?" Jerry asked, looking both puzzled and a little frightened.

"My pet rabbit. He's a Holland Lop." The thought of Mr. Wiggles and his soft floppy ears and little puff-ball tail never failed to bring a smile to Bunny's face.

"Never heard of it, but now I know why your nickname is Bunny." That caused him to chuckle.

"Aye, it might be one of the reasons," Bunny admitted. "I have a long, complicated history with bunnies and rabbits. I like dogs too, but no woman wants to be called Dog. However, I once made an Easter cake on the show to resemble Mr. Wiggles. It wasn't only delicious, but adorable as well. It went viral, and I was then dubbed Bunny Cakes. Since I'm a chef and not a stripper, I felt it best to drop the 'cakes' and embrace the 'bunny.'" It pleased her to see that both Jerry and Mary had chucked at her little joke. "I didn't mind, of course," she continued. "Bunny's been my nickname since I was a wee girl."

"I like it." Jerry said, as if it was up for debate. "I say we keep it. 'Bunny MacBride, host of *Food and Spirits.*' It has a nice ring to it. Doesn't it, Mary?"

"That's the name of the show?" Bunny liked the sound of it too. However, the name *Spirits* gave her pause. She was fair at mixing drinks, but by no means an expert.

"It is. What do you think?" Mary asked as her plasticine face pinched into a grin again. "Although don't be alarmed by the spirit angle of the show. According to Jerry, there are two other hosts of the show as well. You'll be responsible for the food. The other two will handle the spirits. Regarding the contract Jerry brought in, I've looked it over and sent it off to Bernard Buckley's office this morning, purely because we're old friends and we both want what's best for you. We've negotiated a salary I think you'll be happy with. He's fine with everything else, but don't take my word. Call him if you'd like."

Bunny was amazed. Bernard Buckley was her agent, recommended by Mary herself when she was offered the job at *Mary Stobart's Memorable Meals*. She didn't know back then that she needed an agent to work on the show but was grateful for the heads-up from Mary. "Thank you, but if you and Bernard have already looked this over, I'm sure it's sound," she said, her head still swimming from this unexpected offer. She then thought to ask, "And the salary?"

Mary flipped through the contract, found the Compensation Agreement page, and pushed it under her nose. Bunny couldn't believe her eyes. "Is this a mistake?"

"Not at all. We believe in you, and you'll be one of the stars of the show. That's for the first season with room to negotiate depending on how well the show does. Well, Bunny, are you in?"

With her heart tripping like a techno drum in her chest, *BA-BA-BA-BA-BA*, she blurted, "Aye! Oh, yes, I'm in!"

Jerry handed her his golden pen and pointed to the place she was to sign.

In the time it took her to write, *Bridget "Bunny" MacBride,* Bunny had successfully ended her contract with Mary Stobart and was now the host of her own travel food show on Mealtime Network. She was chuffed. She really couldn't believe her good fortune.

Chapter 3

❧

Still reeling with excitement, Bunny made her way to the network's headquarters in New York City. It had been a busy few days since the signing of her new contract. After filming her last Bunny's Culinary Corner segment for *Mary Stobart's Memorable Meals*, which had been surprisingly bittersweet, Bunny had said her goodbyes to her coworkers, and had thanked Mary profusely for the opportunity. She then packed up her knives and left the studio.

Her collection of cooking knives were the tools of her trade. Every chef worked with their own set, and they were responsible for keeping them sharp and in excellent condition. Bunny's knife set had been given to her by her parents as a gift the day before she left for America. She was touched by her family's generosity and their belief in her skills. The beautiful knives, with their razor-sharp blades, had made her cry. Bunny, like most professional chefs, cherished her knives. They were now sitting in her Connecticut condo, rolled in their leather carrier and ready to travel.

The moment she had left the set of *Memorable Meals*, Bunny had phoned her family, sharing the good news. Of course, her mother and father were thrilled for her. Granny MacBride was too, but she had asked some pointed questions that Bunny hadn't known the answers to.

"Where will you be traveling to first?" her grandmother had asked. "Will you be in Scotland ever? I think that you will be." Granny MacBride was nearly certain of it, which was a tad unsettling. This was because, as everybody in their village knew, Granny MacBride had the second sight on occasion. In America, they called it clairvoyance, or, more correctly, just a hunch. Bunny had assured her that she really didn't know. "Who are these other chefs you'll be working with? Do you think they'll be chefs at all? When are you leaving?" Bunny loved her grandmother, but at times the woman could be exhausting. What she had done, in fact, was to illustrate to Bunny, and her parents, just how little Bunny knew about the new cooking show she'd be hosting.

"Look, when I find out all the details, I'll be sure to let you know. However, Gran, I doubt they'll be sending me to Scotland. No offense, but Scottish cuisine is hardly noteworthy." When that statement was met with dead silence on the other end, she added, "... To a primarily American audience. But maybe I can convince the producers otherwise."

As Bunny stood before the door of the large building that housed the headquarters of Mealtime Network, she paused a moment to watch the steady stream of busy New Yorkers walk on by, with the same frenetic energy and focus as a swarm of ants. She had to pinch herself once again, acknowledging that Bridget MacBride of Inverary, Scotland, was here, in this great city, about to embark on the dream of a lifetime, her own cooking show. She took a deep breath, adjusted her purse, and marched through the stream of people, heading for the door. She might not know all the little details regarding *Food & Spirits* yet, but once the meeting was over, she was certain she'd be able to answer all of Granny Mac's burning questions.

The moment Bunny entered the production meeting she was met with a warm greeting by the show's producer, Trig Gunderson. "Bridget, what a pleasure," he said, standing up from the conference table. Bunny had met Trig before. Tall, thin, and with a slightly receding hairline that revealed more of his pleasant face than he would have liked, Trig was one of the top producers working at the network. The fact that he was producing her show was a good sign. She noticed that there were only four others at the table, all of them men. Just as she was about to think that odd, her eyes settled on one of the men in question. She was rendered a wee breathless by his classic all-American good looks, a fact which made her blush. *Crivens*, she berated herself. *Stop blushing, Bunny!* She was certain her face was as bright as the mating feathers of a tropical bird. Then, to make matters worse, the gorgeous man's eyes were on her. They just had to be that robin's-egg shade of blue too! Those eyes with that lush blond hair were akin to kryptonite to her. Why was he smiling at her? Her face was practically burning from the rush of blood. She then turned her mind to the process of gutting a fish. Gutting fish was disgusting. It made her go pale at the thought, which was the point. *Fish guts*, she thought as she returned the smile to the handsome man.

"Sorry I'm late," she said, then waved a hand in front of her hot face to pretend she'd been running. "I hustled all the way from Grand Central Station. This city!" She rolled her eyes then quickly took her seat.

"Bridget," Trig began, then asked, "or do you prefer Bunny?"

"Bunny's fine." After she said this, she covertly glanced around the table. Of the three men, the blond looked slightly familiar. Had she met him before? Did he work in the kitchen of a famous restaurant? *Doubtful*, she thought. *If he did, I'd remember him.*

"Bunny, let me introduce you to the guys," Trig said, grabbing her attention once again. "Sitting on your left is Cody Jenkins, a top-notch cameraman and video editor who will also handle most of the technical gear."

Bunny gave a little wave in greeting to the youngish man, somewhere in his thirties, with the chocolate-brown hair and light brown eyes.

"To your right is another top-notch cameraman and video editor, Ed Franco," Trig continued.

Again, Bunny waved at Ed, another man in his midthirties with meticulously styled thick black hair and a chin dimple. Ed waved back with a grin.

"Next to Ed is Mike Miller, who'll also be working a camera, or a boom as needed."

Bunny waved to Mike, who had dark blondish hair and hazel eyes. She noted that he was the same age as the rest of the men.

"And directly across from you is one of your two cohosts of *Food and Spirits*, Mr. Brett Bloom. Brett is the creator of the show and pitched the idea to us a few months ago. After banging it around for a while, it was finally given the green light. We couldn't be happier."

"I'm impressed," Bunny told Brett sincerely. "I must say, the title just grabs you. *Food and Spirits*. Very nice. I'm so honored to be a part of this new show. I'm told I'm the food in this cast. I take it you're the mixologist, you know, the spirits?"

For some reason this made all the men, particularly the man sitting across the conference table from her, exchange looks as smiles slowly appeared on their faces. Brett was still smiling as he said, "Nope. Not a mixologist, although I'm told I make a mean cherry martini and a brandy old-fashioned, but that's the extent of my abilities. I'm a ghost hunter."

"Come again?" This time as Bunny stared at him, she

knew that she wasn't in any danger of combusting. In fact, due to the way the hair was prickling on the back of her neck she was fairly certain her face was as colorless as clotted cream.

"Ghost hunter," Brett repeated, narrowing his eyes in a suspicious manner.

Bunny gave a quick shake of her head, as if to erase the word. "You just said it again. Ghost hunter. I don't understand. Are you saying that you don't have any experience cooking food or mixing drinks?"

"Professional experience?" Cody offered, grinning unseemly. "Brett can cook. Although you might not always want to eat what he makes. Sometimes it's unholy."

Ed laughed at this. Brett, Bunny noticed, exchanged a look with Trig, before asking,

"Are you pulling our legs, Bunny, or do you really not understand what this show is about?"

Although her heart clenched painfully in her chest, she valiantly powered through it as she said, "I was told that *Food and Spirits* is a travel cooking show . . ." Yet here she petered to a stop, thinking for a moment. That was all she was told. In fact, in her meeting with Mary Stobart and Jerry Goldstein, the spirits part of the show had never really been addressed. All she knew was that two others would be handling the "spirits" part of the show. Crivens, she was a dunderhead! She had never asked. She had never pressed them on the facts. She had merely assumed that her cohosts would be mixing drinks. She looked across the table again at the seriously handsome man as a feeling of doom began to prickle her toes. "So, this travel show isn't about food and drink?"

Pointed looks and suggestive glances circled the table as the men let her question sink in. Trig, taking a deep breath, attempted to explain. "Bunny, let me put your mind at ease.

This show is about food. After all, it's on the Mealtime Network. There will also, undoubtedly, be mixology as well, but that will mostly fall to you. Brett, here, was the former host of the hit show, *Ghost Guys*, on Travel Channel. He came to us with an innovative show that combines ghost hunting with food. We've never heard anything like it before and thought it would be perfect for the nine p.m. time slot."

"That's right," Brett continued, softening his voice and expression a measure. "This is a ghost-hunting show inspired by the ancient Celtic belief that the souls of the dead, enticed by the aroma of beloved foods and the joy of a gathering, are thought to revisit their homes during certain feast days and celebrations."

"I'm well aware of the Dumb Supper or spirit supper, or whatever they call it. It's an old Samhain tradition, meaning that it usually takes place during Halloween."

"You know about this?" Brett looked impressed. Bunny wrinkled her nose at him, indicating what she thought of the practice. Oblivious to her look, Brett sallied forth. "We'd like to put that to the test. As a renowned chef and menu developer, you'll create a meal meant to entice the local spirits to the table."

Alarm bells were going off in her head as he spoke. He was so enthusiastic that she had no wish to break his spirit, even if she thought the very notion was akin to a child playing with fire. With a kind smile pinned on her face, Bunny said, "I can see you've given this much thought. It is a mysterious and compelling ancient tradition, and while I love the challenge of creating such a meal, there's one slight problem. I am not a fan of ghosts."

"You don't have to be part of the ghost hunt. Your main responsibility will be to create the food and the drink that will be the launching board for the investigation. At every location you'll be cooking with the local chef in a working kitchen. A film crew, aka, Ed, Cody, or Mike will follow you as you prepare the meal. You'll then describe the meal in more detail as we sit at the table together—you, me, Giff, and the people who own the historic building—"

"Wait, who's this Giff person?" Bunny was suspicious of the way he had slipped the name in like a sneaky chef adding a leaf of bitter kale to a BLT sandwich. In other words, hoping she wouldn't notice.

"He's the other member of our team who couldn't make it here today."

"And is he a ghost hunter as well?"

Trig surprised her by answering for Brett. "Gifford Mc-Grady is the world-renowned psychic medium on the show. He's also somewhat of a fashion icon as well, which means that he not only has flair, but a busy schedule. The three of you will make quite a team."

What? Bunny thought. *A psychic medium? What in the bloody hell have I gotten myself into?* Although the alarm bells in her head had escalated, she tried to remain calm. "Oh. Right. Of course," she remarked, as if working on a cooking show beside a fashion-forward psychic medium was the norm. Thankfully, Brett continued.

"Did I mention that there will be an extra place set at the table for the spirit or ghost we're trying to connect with?"

Bunny raised her brows. "The spirit chair? It was implied by this Dumb Supper you propose."

"Are you calling the supper dumb?" Ed exchanged a guarded look with Mike.

"The term Dumb Supper indicates that it's a quiet feast, which I am to understand that, since we're hosting a television show, it's not. Am I correct?" The ridiculousness of the notion nearly made her smile. She might have, if she wasn't feeling so ill.

"Yes," Brett remarked. "This supper or feast is the feature

of this show. We sit down to the fabulous meal you're going to make, and then we eat and drink while we discuss the history of the building, the legend of the haunting, and any other things of note. Hopefully, by the end of the meal the spirit will have taken the bait, and then we begin the ghost hunt. Oh, and I almost forgot the show's tagline. *Be careful who you invite to dinner.*"

Trig, she noticed, looked pleased as punch. "What do you think, Bunny? *Food and Spirits* is the first-ever reality food-based ghost-hunting show, and Mealtime Network is extremely excited to carry it."

Bunny was trying her hardest to wrap her head around that one. It might have sounded great to someone who was curious about ghosts, but she wasn't. Not in the least. In fact, ghosts, hauntings, and creepy old buildings were at the top of her list of things to avoid. Curses on Mary Stobart, the old bat. She knew it too, and that's precisely why Bunny was now here—as the star of her own cooking show, only it wasn't all about cooking, now, was it?

"Trig, would you describe this as a cooking show with ghost elements?" she asked, hoping to soothe her raging nerves.

Brett, casting her a sideways glance, offered, "Or, Trig, is this more of a ghost-hunting show with food?" The gauntlet had been thrown, but Trig, like any good producer, knew how to appease his stars.

"Yes. Now, pack your bags. The entire team of *Food and Spirits* has been booked on a flight to London, leaving tomorrow morning. Lucky you, you're all going to Bramsford Manor."

Chapter 4

Good neighbors are a blessing, and Bunny's next-door neighbor, Jane, wasn't merely good, but had also become her dear friend. Having been on the receiving end of more delicious free meals than she could count, Jane had been positively delighted when Bunny had shared her good news about her travel cooking show. However, not being aware that she'd be traveling so soon, Bunny had asked Jane a huge favor. Jane, true to form, had assured her that she'd keep an eye on her condo, take in her mail, and water her plants and container gardens. Regarding the adorable Mr. Wiggles, Ainsley, Jane's ten-year-old daughter, had been thrilled with the prospect of taking care of him for as long as needed.

Mr. Wiggles. It would be hard leaving him for so long, but she knew he'd be in good hands. People often asked her why she had a pet rabbit bouncing around her home. While Bunny admitted that for most people living in apartments or condos, cats made good companions, a rabbit was more her style. As a cook who prided herself on sterile kitchen counters, Bunny felt that litterbox-loving cats couldn't be trusted in that department. Mr. Wiggles also used a litterbox, and he was just as adorable and affectionate as a cat, arguably more so. However, even with all the bounce he possessed, Mr. Wiggles could never reach a kitchen counter.

After dropping him off at Jane's house she kissed his wiggly nose and handed Ainsley Mr. Wiggles's going-away platter, which contained carrot nubs and greens, spinach leaves, kale, blueberries, strawberries, and apple slices to go with his usual hay and pellets. She also gave Ainsley a few extra coconut-fiber chewing balls for him to roll around their house, should he run low on them. With Mr. Wiggles and her condo in good hands, Bunny left for the airport.

As she approached her gate, she saw that hunky Brett Bloom was already there with the rest of the crew. He waved her over the moment he saw her. After a quick greeting, he said, "I'm sorry about the meeting yesterday. We all thought you understood the nature of this show. I hope you're not too upset."

"No, not at you," she told him honestly. "My former boss, Mary Stobart, recommended me for this show. She knew all along that this was a ghost-hunting show, but never mentioned a word about it to me. And my contract is very vague on the *spirit* angle as well. Not one mention of ghost hunting, and that's no accident. Mary, and Jerry Goldstein, talked up the food angle, showed me my new salary, and handed me the contract. It's my fault, really."

"How so?"

She was touched by the look of concern on his face. "We had a disagreement a couple weeks earlier about Halloween," she explained. "Mary wanted me to make ghastly treats for children, and I told her in no uncertain terms that I don't do spooky. I believe this is her little way of getting back at me."

"Look, Bunny, I'm truly sorry about this. Mike, Cody, Ed, and I have all worked together before on *Ghost Guys*, our ghost-hunting show. Although ghost hunting sounds spooky, a lot of what we do is hyped up for the audience. We use a lot of what we term *ghost tech* to try and capture oddities, and we also really play up the lore of a location— you know, the perennial ghost stories? It's a form of entertainment. And yes, it can be spooky. That's the point of it. You're here to add some class to what we do. I understand that this is out of your comfort zone, and we're all sorry about that, but the guys and I are not going to let anything bad happen to you. I promise."

With a guileless smile plastered on her face, she thought, *Dear Brett. Simple Brett. I just want to melt right into your ignorant, heart-melting gaze.* Clearly, the man didn't understand the nature of her problem. It wasn't ghosts in general. It was just one, and she wished to avoid being reminded of it. Spooky places reminded her of it. They made her feel vulnerable. They also made her more aware of her deep-seated personal issues. However, since she had signed the contract and was now on the team, she had vowed to herself to be a professional about it. Therefore, still smiling at her coworker, she said, "Thank you. I appreciate that." Then, thinking it best to get off the subject of ghosts, she said, "Can I ask you a question? I did a little research when I got home and saw that your show had been canceled. Why was that?"

Mike and Cody, hearing the question, came beside Brett. Chin-dimple Ed was too busy playing a game on his phone.

Brett cast a nervous glance around before lowering his voice. "We ran into a bit of bad luck during an investigation at a haunted lighthouse. We were doing a livestream ghost hunt with the owner's friend, who is a popular influencer. During the investigation we all got spooked when an eerie light popped on in the lightroom of the lighthouse. We were all in there when it happened and, unfortunately, we panicked."

"You lost your job because you panicked when a light popped on?" Bunny was horrified by the thought. She hadn't realized what a fickle business ghost hunting was. She was bound to get fired too, if that was the case.

"No." Brett was quick to ease her mind. "However, we don't usually panic like that, but things were a little off that night. Anyhow, we all hightailed it out of the building. Unfortunately, the influencer friend ran smack dab into the body of a woman hanging from a tree. The influencer caught the whole thing on a livestream camera. The woman was dead, of course, and it was soon learned that she had been murdered."

"What? That's bloody awful!" The mere thought caused a rush of blood to Bunny's cheeks.

"Tragic is what it was," Cody confirmed.

"The result of that investigation was that we got canceled," Brett said. "For the first time in years we were out of a job, and all of us really enjoyed what we were doing."

"I'm very sorry about that," Bunny told them, sincerely.

"That's when Brett came up with this new show," Mike piped up. "Well, first he had to wallow in self-pity for a few months. He had to tuck tail and go back home to lick his wounds."

With a shy look at Bunny, Brett said, "Yep, all of that is true. But I'm glad I did. When I was back home, my sister, Whitney, came up with the premise for this show. She was sick of having me hanging around, feeling sorry for myself. The clincher, however, came when I tried to convince my entire family that the B and B they own and run in Wisconsin, is haunted. Whitney didn't like the sound of that. Shortly after that incident, she pulled the idea of the old Celtic tradition out of her hat and told me to start a new show where I could put that to the test. Even though she was just trying to get rid of me, I had to admit that her idea was a good one." He smiled as he said that. His smile faded when the announcement came that they were boarding.

"Where's Giff?" Mike asked.

Brett, looking worried, pulled out his phone. He was just about to make a call when Cody cried, "Look. There he is! Making a grand entrance as usual."

Bunny craned her neck to see what the guys were looking at. Then she spotted him too, a trim, handsome, dark-haired man wearing an explorer's scarf looped around his neck, weaving through a crowd of people as he headed for their gate. The fact that he was wearing blue-mirrored sunglasses might have impaired his vision a measure, but it sure made him look like the reality TV star he was, she thought.

Arriving with a breathless smile, Giff flipped up his glasses. "Hello there. Sorry I'm late. TSA was about to confiscate my crystals, the thieves. I paid good money for them. They help me exploit my psychic gifts." Bunny noted that the way he said this made Brett and the other guys grin. Giff continued. "The large lady with the pointy fingernails was eyeing my rose quartz like a lover. I had to yank it out of her covetous hands. I'll have to sterilize the thing . . . by moonlight, of course." He rolled his eyes as he grinned. Then he noticed Bunny. "*Ohmygod!* It's Bunny MacBride of Bunny's Culinary Corner! Brett, you never told me that Bridget *Bunny* MacBride was part of the show."

"I thought I did," he said. "I distinctly remember calling my sister as soon as we heard the news."

"*Whitney*," Giff breathed in a scandalized manner. "Whitney never bothered to relay the message to me." He looked at Bunny and explained. "I used to work for his sister. Brett assumes that I still do, but I don't. We're just good friends." Giff then held out his hand to Bunny. "Gifford McGrady. Perhaps you've heard of me? I'm the psychic medium on the show. My friends call me Giff."

"Nice to meet you, Giff. Please, call me Bunny."

Introductions aside, the team of *Food & Spirits* boarded the plane.

Chapter 5

"So, what do you know about Bramsford Manor?"

"What? Me? Are you asking me?" Giff cast her a startled look from the passenger seat.

Interesting reaction, Bunny thought, and assumed he was merely still jet-lagged, like she was. After a long and thankfully uneventful flight and a night in a budget hotel, she had climbed out of bed feeling sluggish and slightly disoriented. She really couldn't say if the man sitting next to her was feeling it too, but he was definitely wide-eyed, tense, and a wee jumpy as well. Then again, that could have something to do with the fact that she was driving on the left side of the road through the verdant countryside of Hampshire, where the mysterious manor they were soon to investigate was located. She noticed that Giff flinched a lot at the oncoming traffic, and even crossed his arms over his face a time or two, as if bracing for impact. At first it annoyed her, believing that his sharp inhalation and the tensing of his right leg—as if he was pressing an imaginary brake—was due to her being a woman behind the wheel. She explained to him that she had grown up driving on the left-hand side of the road, hence the reason she was driving the midsize *saloon*, or sedan as the Americans called it, with Giff and Ed as her passengers. Brett was in the van ahead of them with Cody, Mike, and all their gear. However, when she realized that it wasn't her abilities so much as the fact that the car was barreling down the "wrong" side of the road, she thought it best to distract him with conversation. Bunny took a blind corner slightly too fast and looked at Giff. "I thought you, being a medium, would have boned up on the place. After all, you are supposedly going to connect with a lingering spirit there." Bunny glanced in the rearview mirror. Ed was in the back seat with headphones on, editing video he'd taken of their flight and their arrival at Heathrow. He liked to keep tabs on relevant B-roll, he had told her.

Giff offered a slight frown regarding her question. "I am, aren't I. Well, for my process to work, I like to go in blind. I like to psychically feel my way around the place. It's more authentic that way. Ooh, watch that bush!" He pulled his knees up to his chest and grimaced.

With both hands gripping the steering wheel and her eyes on the road, Bunny gave a nod. The bush in question was a thick hedge that wasn't about to move. She then thought to ask, "You said that you used to work for Brett's sister, Whitney. Is she a medium too? Does this morbid passion run in the family?"

"Ah, no. No-no. Whitney's a baker." Giff nervously fondled the large, clear crystal hanging around his neck as he spoke. His "chill" TV-star vibe from the day before seemed to dissipate the closer they got to their destination. She not only found that odd, but unsettling as well.

"You're a baker then?" For some reason this thought delighted her. She had great respect for bakers and thought she might be able to call on him for help in the kitchen if needed.

As she entertained visions of Giff and her working side by side in the manor's kitchen, making beautiful little berry tarts, and totally blocking out any thoughts of the paranormal, Giff shattered her hopes again.

"Baker? Heavens, no! I have barely just mastered the microwave, meaning that I can now heat up my own frozen dinners without destroying them. No, Whitney and I used to work in advertising together." Giff turned to her with a grin. "She got fired over some edgy ad and went home to the family orchard. I spent too much time visiting the family orchard and hanging out with Whitney and her friends. I eventually got fired as well. According to my old boss, I took too many"—he made a pair of air quotes as he added—"'personal days,' 'sick days,' 'mental health days,' and 'holidays.' In other words, I realized that I liked hanging out in Cherry Cove with the Blooms more than I liked working my demanding, thankless job in Chicago."

"Now that I've met Brett Bloom, I imagine that's so. He's very . . . um, very—"

"Attractive?" Giff supplied. "Yep, Brett looks good on camera, even night-vison camera, which is saying a lot. He's got quite a fan base of adoring ladies and even a few gents. He's also totally clueless, which I find adorable."

That made Bunny smile. She had to admit that Giff was quite good-looking as well, and very stylish. He wore slim-fitting dark blue jeans, a thick cream sweater, and the same loosely draped, sky-blue cotton adventurer's scarf around his neck. This morning he'd added a dangly crystal necklace. However, as attractive as he was, she was still trying to puzzle out where his "highly sought-after psychic medium" credentials fit in. Taking a deep breath, she decided on a direct course of action. "When did you learn that you had psychic abilities?"

This question surprised him. He made a noise like he was

choking on something before turning to look at her. With a straight face, he answered, "When I lost my job."

"Wait. How long ago was that? You made it sound like you just recently lost your job."

"Yeah. A couple of months ago. But who's counting?"

"I'm confused." Bunny rounded a corner then looked at him again. "You're the psychic medium on the show. I'm told you're famous. And you just found out that you have abilities a few months ago?"

"Doesn't make much sense, does it?" he admitted. Then, with a resigned look on his face he added, "Look, Bunny, I wasn't going to tell you, but you have a habit of asking a lot of pointed questions. The truth is, Brett and I both lost our jobs around the same time, and we were both hanging out at the Cherry Orchard Inn, the B and B the Bloom family owns. There had been a death at the inn, a murder actually, and Brett believed that the unfortunate victim was still haunting the place. Whitney didn't want to hear it. We then decided to team up and play a joke on her. Brett did his ghost-techy thing, proving his point, while I pretended to contact the spirit and channel her voice. It totally freaked Whit out, it was that good of a performance. I put it behind me and got my résumé together. Then, when Brett got this show at Mealtime Network, the one condition the producers had was that he include a psychic medium on the team as well . . . to give the show more *gravitas*." This last word he emphasized with a dramatic lowering of his voice. "The poor guy was scrambling to find someone when I stepped up and valiantly offered my services."

"You have got to be kidding me?" She took her eyes off the road a moment to look at him and narrowly missed rear-ending a poky caravan that was blocking her way.

"Eyes up!" Giff cried, before adding, "God's honest truth."

Bunny felt a slight flash of anger rise to her cheeks. She

lowered her voice and hiss-whispered, "Are you telling me that you're not really a psychic medium?"

"Whoa." He held up his crystal and thrust it in her direction. "I am a psychic medium. I'm also a fashion icon of the psychic world. Check out my social media pages. What I'm telling you, Bunny dear, is that I'm playing one for the good of the show."

She was so angry that a little growl escaped her. She then reached into the back seat and tapped Ed on the knee. Ed pulled the chunky black headphones from his ears.

"What's up, Bunny?"

"Did you know about Giff?"

Ed looked at Giff, unsure of what to say. "Um . . . that he's gay?"

"About him pretending to be a medium," she clarified.

"Oh, that. Yeah. We needed a medium for the show." He was about to put his earphones back on when she tapped his knee again, this time using enough force to make him flinch.

"Sorry," she apologized. "But don't you think viewers and possibly the owners of the manor house we're about to visit will figure out that he's a fake?"

The two men exchanged a look again before Giff answered her. "Dear Bunny, I hate to be the one to shatter your worldview here, but everyone knows that mediums are fake. It's pure chicanery. Like a magician. The great Houdini himself, who was obsessed by the occult of mediumship, proved it was chicanery. He had to die to do it, of course, but not one professional medium of the day could tell his grieving widow the secret word that would prove he was contacting her from the other side."

"Also," Ed said, leaning over the front seat, "if it'll make you feel better, I'm an editing genius. The audience won't have a clue he's a fake. I'll make him look good. Regarding the manor, usually the people who work in these haunted houses are too polite to contradict a psychic medium."

"True," Giff concurred. "Also, it helps to be vague."

"Do neither of you believe that some people actually have psychic abilities?" Bunny, due to her own experiences, found this highly unsettling. She knew for a fact that some people had the gift. She also found it a little disturbing that she was the only authentic professional on the show. Ghost hunting wasn't even a real occupation. It was a hobby at best. And the psychic medium was a former ad man who needed a job. She, however, was an authentic television chef! Well, sous chef at any rate. But she could certainly cook.

"I'm not saying that I don't believe," Giff offered, noting that she had gone deathly quiet. He also noted her bright red cheeks. "I'm just a skeptic, Bunny." His brown eyes softened like a puppy dog's as he looked at her. "Please, for the sake of the show, keep this conversation between us. Brett needed a job; I needed a job, and you deserve a truly spectacular cooking show."

"I needed a job too," Ed added from the back seat. "Don't forget. We all did."

"See?" He offered a conciliatory grin. "Even if I don't fully believe in what we're about to do at Bramsford Manor, I am fully committed to putting on one heck of a performance. Playing a psychic medium on television sure beats slogging my way through the ad world, although I do have a soft spot for a good jingle."

That, undoubtedly, was true. As for Bunny, she wasn't about to tuck tail and run back to grumpy old Mary Stobart either. That would be defeat, and failure was not an option. No, she deserved this—even if much of the show was farcical. And maybe farcical was better for someone like her, a person who felt great discomfort in old buildings, who avoided the macabre, and who had spent the better part of ten years building an imaginary wall in her mind to block out the one thing that could bring her to her knees. She looked at him once again. "I will keep your secret, Gifford McGrady, if you keep mine."

"Which is?"

"I'm afraid of ghosts."

"Don't be," he said, with a dismissive wave of his hand. "They're not real either. We're just going to pretend they are. You, Bunny, don't have to bother yourself with any of it. Just do what you do best, smile for the camera and cook that beautiful food."

Although he was totally ignorant regarding the subject on which he spoke, she admired his confidence. She wished some of that confidence would brush off on her, but unfortunately, as the green rolling hills fanned out before her, she caught a glimpse of the enormous, three-story structure in the distance. Her stomach clenched painfully at the sight. Like many stoic manor homes of bygone eras, this one was sitting at the top of a gentle hill, its many windows sparkling like jewels in the sun. It had pitched rooflines, crenelations, turrets, wings, and myriad chimneys puffing white smoke into the sky. The enormous structure was flanked by walled gardens and a handful of outbuildings. Yet as stoic as it appeared, Bunny felt the pall of death that clung to it like a barnacle. Bramsford Manor, she mused. Ready or not, here we come.

Chapter 6

❧

"Oddly enough, it was a harmless game of hide-and-seek that turned tragic," Marcus Bean, Bramsford's historian, proclaimed as he stared at his captive audience.

Upon their arrival, and after checking into their rooms (Crivens, Bunny hadn't realized Bramsford was a hotel!), the team had been ushered into the lofty, Georgian-style drawing room where they were being briefed on the manor's ghostly history. Bunny also mused that the owners, Sir Charles Wallingford and his sister, Morgan Wallingford-Green, were certainly not shy when it came to playing up their haunted manor. In fact, she surmised that Bramsford's haunted history was likely responsible for breathing new life into the old place. Rambling manor homes that were passed down through the generations were little more than giant money pits that had lost their usefulness centuries ago. The new owners had to get creative if they didn't wish to turn the historic home over to the National Trust. She knew the trend. In Scotland every castle claimed a haunting, and fools flocked to pay exorbitant prices to stay in their shabby rooms, hoping to be visited in the night by a specter. She shivered at the thought. Her grandma had often remarked on it. Bunny was still trying to wrap her head around the fact that she was sitting in a comfy, darkly upholstered wingback chair while listening to a middle-aged man enthusiastically prattle on about a ghost. She wanted to block him out and focus on the renovated kitchen she was soon to visit, and the show-stopping meal she was soon to prepare, but she had to admit, the man had a compelling manner as he told his tale.

"The young bride, Ann Copeland, a lively girl with a playful spirit, took her vows right here in this room, on Christmas Day in the year 1700," Marcus continued. "Ann's father, Sir John Copeland, was lord of the manor at the time, and a friend to the king. It was quite the event, and every bedroom in the house was filled with guests who had traveled far and wide to celebrate the wedding of Lady Ann Copeland and Sir Henry Wallingford. There was feasting and drinking and much toasting. The day wore into night, and soon it was time for Ann to be taken by her maid to the bridal chamber where she would await her husband. Yet reluctant to leave her party, Ann proposed a game of hide-and-seek instead. She would hide, and Sir Henry and their guests would try to find her. She proposed a prize for the winner, a sum of money. Ann was given a five-minute head start, after which the hunt for the bride began." Here Marcus Bean, a tall, trim man with toffee-colored hair graying at the temples and heavily lidded bright round eyes, dramatically paused to take a sip of his sherry before continuing.

"At first it was all fun and games. However, when the bride hadn't been found in that first hour the guests began to grow nervous. Sir Henry and his guests searched all night, but his new bride was never found. Whispers circulated that young Ann had used the game as a ruse to flee her marriage. It was suspected that she had a lover waiting in the wings to whisk her away, but Sir Henry didn't believe that. Over the years many rumors circulated regarding the young bride. Sir Henry, forlorn and heartbroken, entertained them all in his search to find her. He vowed to turn over any stone to find his Ann. The legend states that poor Sir Henry Wallingford spent his entire life searching for her, but to no avail. She had simply disappeared."

Giff leaned over and whispered, "My money's on the secret lover theory."

Bunny ignored him, admittedly wrapped up in Mr. Bean's tale. The historian continued.

"After fifty years had passed, Sir Henry, now an old man, had gone into one of the attic wings of the house where he discovered a large chest covered with a dusty white sheet. The chest had been obscured by many old pieces of furniture, but there was something about the object that drew his eye. When he removed the white cloth, Sir Henry saw the intricate carvings of mistletoe on the front of the chest. He had no idea where it had come from, or what it might contain. However, when he opened the lid, he got the shock of his life. For there, lying in the bottom of the chest were the skeletal remains of his bride, Ann, still in her wedding gown and with her bridal wreath around her skull. She was also holding the desiccated remains of her bouquet. To Sir Henry's horror he saw that the inside of the lid had been scratched, making him realize that his bride hadn't run away at all, but had hid in the chest and had gotten trapped all along, and no one had ever found her."

"Oh, the poor wee thing," Bunny whispered, as her eyes teared up at the thought of the misguided bride. "She hadn't run off with her lover after all," she said to Giff. "It's a tale of enduring love that tugs at the heartstrings." Although it was just a tale and a legend, Bunny's heart ached for both bride and groom.

"True," Giff whispered back. "Only now she's a ghost.

And rumor has it, she haunts this place. So, any thoughts on what you're planning to make for our spectral bride?"

"*Wheesht*," she hissed at him. "I'm still processing this sorry tale."

Marcus Bean cleared his throat and addressed the team once again. "When I heard about this new ghost reality TV show on Mealtime Network, I immediately reached out to Mr. Bloom, believing that Bramsford would be the perfect setting to launch this project. I then passed it by my gracious employer, Sir Charles Wallingford, who wholeheartedly agreed."

Sir Charles, lord of the manor and a handsome bachelor as well, Bunny noted, stood up from his chair and addressed them. "Indeed, I agreed, and I'm glad that you're here. My older sister, Morgan"—here he gestured to a tall, thin, middle-aged woman who had a regal air about her—"and I grew up here. Both of us have had encounters with myriad ghosts who haunt this place, but the most chilling specter in the manor is the Mistletoe Bride, as she's known. She's named after the chest she was found in, which is now on display in the long gallery. Marcus and I will point it out to you when we take our tour."

Ghosts. Tour. No thank you! Bunny's hand was in the air before she realized it. "Excuse me, Sir Charles. Pardon me, but I'm going to bow out of this generous tour of yours. However, is there someone who might point me in the direction of the kitchen? I'll be making the feast for tomorrow night that will kick off the hunt for this unfortunate bride and I'd like to see what I'm working with."

The handsome bachelor with the smartly cut chestnut-colored hair that was graying at the temples, smiled at her. "But of course, Bunny. May I call you Bunny?" With her heart fluttering a wee bit, she nodded. He then turned to a slim, chic, silver-haired woman in her late thirties, and said, "I'd like to introduce you to Lilly Plum." Lilly stood up from her chair. "Lilly is the head chef at Bramsford Manor. Under Lilly's guidance, Bramsford has gone from a stodgy hotel dining room to a world-class restaurant. Lilly, would you take Bunny on a tour of the kitchen and the dining room?"

"It would be my pleasure," she said. "We've been anxiously awaiting your arrival."

Bunny stood from her chair, adjusted the strap of her leather knife roll higher on her shoulder, and addressed her team. "Good luck, gentlemen. This is where we part ways. Enjoy your tour."

"Whoa! I'm coming with you," Cody said, picking up his camera. "I drew the short straw, Bunny. I'm your cameraman," he teased, following her out of the drawing room.

Sad ghost story aside, Bunny couldn't wait to get out of the oppressive room and into the manor kitchen. After following Lilly through the ornate and stunning dining room, down a long hall and a short set of stone steps, Bunny, with Cody and his camera following behind her, landed in what would have been termed the manor scullery. It was a vast room on the lower level of the manor, and it took Bunny's breath away. The place had been gutted, partially drywalled, and refitted with modern kitchen appliances that had been cleverly fitted into the historic features of the room. Like every professional kitchen, the workstations in the large front section of the kitchen boasted stainless steel countertops, racks of pots and pans, and state-of-the-art ovens with gas burners. However, beyond the workstations and through a doorway was the back of the kitchen. Bunny inhaled at the sight of it, it was so beautiful. There was a large island workspace, racks of pots and pans along the inner wall, and a long granite counter fitted with two huge sinks that sat just below an expanse of beautiful windows. The view outside was spectacular, overlooking manicured gardens in the foreground and a magnificent tree-flanked rolling lawn beyond that. Bunny imagined how lush and vibrant the garden and lawn would look in the summer. However, it was fall and a plethora of colorful leaves now flitted across the grass. Bunny knew that the kitchen had been modernized but she had never imagined that a manor-house kitchen could look like this.

"Think you can work in here?" Lilly questioned with a hint of mischief in her voice.

"It's going to be a dream cooking in this kitchen. I can't wait to get started."

"Good." Lilly looked pleased. "We've reserved this workspace for you, so please make yourself at home. I'll be assisting you, so you can just tell me what else you might need for tomorrow. Also, since this is a working kitchen and we have guests staying at the manor, including you and your team, my staff will be in at two to begin preparations for dinner. They know to keep out of your way."

"Thank you very much. Cody," Bunny said, turning to her cameraman, "are you ready to start recording?" Cody turned on the camera and nodded. "Good. I'm going to introduce Lilly, run through the manor kitchen with her for the camera and then describe the meal I'll be making. Then it's off to the village market where we're going to purchase what we need for our feast."

"Sounds good to me, Bunny. By the way, what are you making for the unfortunate Mistletoe Bride?" Cody had his camera pointed right at her.

"Why, a modernized Christmas feast complete with prime rib roast, Yorkshire pudding, root vegetables, a rustic apple tart with butterscotch sauce, and plenty of wassail to wash it down with."

Cody looked up from the camera screen and flashed her a grin. "Fricken' awesome."

Chapter 7

For the life of her, Bunny couldn't understand why anyone would want to stay in a room stuffed with antiquated furniture in a supposedly haunted manor. The room she'd been given, known as the Fleur-de-Lys suite, was large enough, and boasted a stately canopied bed, Turkish carpet, chaise lounge, an oval dressing mirror, and a porcelain washbasin atop an antique dresser. She had an en suite, so there was no reason for the old washbasin other than a stab at old manor antique décor. After stuffing her ears with cotton to blot out the noise Brett, Giff, Sir Charles, and Marcus Bean were making as they wandered the halls at all hours of the night, she finally fell asleep. When she poked her head into the hallway at two in the morning to complain, they told her that they were filming backstory, and boning up on the history of the manor. Would she like to join them? Absolutely not, she had replied with a polite smile, before shutting the door.

The moment dawn broke, Bunny yanked the cotton out of her ears, threw it in the bin, and sprang out of bed. Yesterday's visit to the outdoor market had been a dream. With Lilly's help the two chefs had perused and discussed the local offerings as Cody filmed them every step of the way. She was positively chuffed at the beautiful, nicely marbled sixteen-pound prime rib roast she had purchased from the local butcher along with three pounds of oxtails that she needed for the au jus. At the outdoor market she had purchased an array of beautiful carrots, parsnips, onions, garlic, and waxy potatoes from various farmstands, along with a half peck of fresh-picked tart apples for her large apple tarts served with warm butterscotch sauce.

With visions of her scrumptious meal dancing in her head, Bunny got dressed, tied on her trainers, and left the oppressive bedroom, heading for the hotel dining room. She was proud of herself for having spent an entire day in the creepy old home without incident. It had boosted her confidence. However, there was no avoiding the long gallery with its impressive collection of dead ancestor portraits and that morbid old chest on display. Although she admitted that the paintings had merit, Bunny was not a fan of the genre.

The moment Bunny hit the bottom of the stairs of the hotel wing, she took a deep breath and fast-walked down the long gallery, aiming for the hotel dining room. To run interference on the creepy feeling that was causing her skin to tingle as if she was too close to an electric charge, she turned her mind to the apple tart she was going to make for dessert. However, the moment she came abreast of the gruesome mistletoe coffin (because that's what the chest had become), she tripped on a wrinkle in the carpet. As she stumbled, nearly falling on the macabre relic, all thoughts of the delicious apple tart evaporated, replaced instantaneously by the sad ghost story of an unfortunate bride. Like a lone wolf under a bright, full moon, Bunny could not resist the allure of the mistletoe chest. The obviously refurbished chest, for it was in good condition for a three-hundred-year-old piece, had been placed against the wall in a prominent spot and lit with strategic track lighting. Above the chest hung a portrait of the tragic young bride, in case anyone needed reminding as to why the chest was there at all. Although old portraits, like old buildings, gave her the heebie-jeebies, Bunny could not help looking into the eyes that stared down at her. She was struck with the notion that the portrait might have been painted years after the unfortunate game of hide-and-seek, well after the legend had been established. That was good marketing. Would young Ann Copeland have looked so melancholy in her bridal portrait? Likely not. However, due to the prickling of her skin and the sinking feeling in the pit of her stomach, Bunny could not deny that there was something positively haunting about the girl. She wanted to run away, but her feet felt like lead, pinning her to the spot.

"Compelling, isn't she? Bet she never thought she'd lead the charge of what not to do on your wedding night, i.e., hide from your groom in a dank old chest that had a habit of locking."

Bunny was relieved to see the teasing smile on Gifford McGrady's face. However, the fact that he was shirtless under the long white robe piqued her interest. He had a Jesus-on-the-mount vibe to him, she thought, noting his baggy white pants and leather thong sandals. He was also wearing a multitude of dangly necklaces. "This portrait is unsettling," Bunny admitted. "Where are you going, dressed like that?"

"To the hotel dining room for a cup of coffee and whatever else they might have. After that, I'm heading into the wilderness to meditate. By wilderness I mean the grove of oak trees at the bottom of the lawn. It helps me connect with the departed."

"I bet it does," Bunny offered with a grin. Secretly she

was glad he had appeared when he had. Giff's comical getup and cavalier attitude had freed her from Ann Copeland's haunting gaze.

He linked his arm with hers and the two continued down the gallery. "Also," Giff confided in a near whisper, "the grove is near the stables. I hear there's a ruggedly handsome stableman who works there. If he's straight, I'll put in a good word for you."

Bunny tossed him a grin. "Gee, thanks. But is it that obvious I'm single?"

"I read your bio. It was implied."

After a quick cup of coffee and a croissant with Giff, Bunny headed to the kitchen. She was excited to get to work. Cody and his camera would be along shortly, but until he arrived, she had plenty to do. She had started her rich au jus the day before by removing the ribs from the roast and adding them to a pot with the oxtails and the aromatics. The ingredients were covered with water and put on a low simmer. The moment she hit the kitchen floor she could smell its wonderfully rich, fragrant aroma.

"Morning, Bunny!" Lilly greeted her with a bright smile. "Your au jus is the talk of the kitchen. I've checked it and it's reducing nicely."

"Why, thank you, Lilly. It smells grand and is just the thing to accompany that succulent meat. Now to get the roast just right."

"You'll have no problem there," Lilly said with confidence. "Before I forget, Callum Digby, the maître d', wanted to talk with you about the table setting for tonight's ghost feast. He asked if you'd meet him in the manor's formal dining room. It's going to be stunning."

"You know, I wasn't too keen on this food-baiting ghost-hunting show, but I have to admit that I quite like it."

"It's all in good fun, Bunny," Lilly assured her. "We may

have a ghost or three that haunt these walls, but that's all part of the Bramsford charm. Now, tell me what you need me to do."

Bunny was grateful for the chaos of the kitchen. After discussing the table setting with Mr. Digby, including instructions for the extra place setting and, per Brett, a white sheet to cover the spirit chair, she was back in the kitchen for a filmed interview with Marcus Bean, Sir Charles Wallingford, and Lilly Plum. The four discussed what a historic Christmas wedding feast might have looked like in Ann Copeland's day, and how the food and cooking methods had evolved since then. After that everyone but Cody left Bunny alone in the kitchen to do her thing. Bunny was used to having cameras in her kitchen and didn't give it much thought as she set about cleaning the vegetables.

She was just about to slice the carrots and parsnips into two-inch-long chunks for roasting, when she unrolled her leather knife roll and saw that one of her precious knives was missing. Certain it had been there the day before, Bunny turned to Lilly, who was working at the island counter, and asked, "I seem to be missing a knife. It's not here. Do you know if anybody's found a knife recently?"

Lilly looked alarmed. "What do you mean a knife has gone missing? It's not in your knife kit?"

Bunny showed her the thick, leather roll. "It's not here. It's my boning knife. I used it yesterday to remove the ribs from the roast. I specifically remember cleaning it and putting it back with the others."

Lilly immediately made an announcement in the kitchen and everyone working at their stations began searching for the missing knife. When the entire kitchen had been scoured, Lilly turned to Bunny. "I'm so sorry. I can't imagine anyone working here would do such a thing. There's no point in taking your knife. We'll keep our eyes peeled. However, I should probably tell you that things do have a habit of disappearing only to turn up later. I wish I had a better explanation for it other than the fact that Bramsford is haunted."

"Umm, not helpful," Bunny said, backing away. She'd never heard of a knife-snatching ghost before but couldn't rule it out. The world, after all, was full of strange happenings. She consoled herself with the fact that it was only her boning knife. With its long, thin, perfectly balanced blade she couldn't imagine why anyone would want it, unless they were deboning a whole chicken. At least it wasn't her trusty chef's knife, her six-inch utility knife, or her paring knife. Pushing all thoughts of her missing knife aside, Bunny turned to the long counter beneath the windows and concentrated on the night's intricate dinner.

The kitchen was her happy place, and Bunny marveled once again at how nice it felt to work in Bramsford's modernized scullery alongside Lilly. It helped that it was a beautiful autumn day. Sunlight streamed through the windows, illuminating the festive punchbowl of wassail Bunny was putting the finishing touches on. Cody, having taken more than enough footage for a cooking montage, and after sampling the wassail, had left with Brett to set up for the Dumb Supper—only, technically, they'd be talking. That was just fine with Bunny. However, when she went to the sink to wash her hands, she happened to look out the window. That was when something on the lawn caught her eye. An odd, surreal feeling washed over her at the same moment, causing her hands to shake. She closed her eyes, thinking it was just her imagination. However, when she opened them again it was still there, sitting prettily on the lawn while nibbling clover. The white rabbit. As if sensing her, its long ears wiggled before turning its head. It looked like it was staring directly at her. "No," Bunny anxiously whispered. "You're not really there. It's just my imagination." But it was there, clear as day.

It was just a rabbit, a wee white rabbit, which on any

green lawn appeared odd. Yet that was only the half of it. She knew that symbolically a white rabbit was good luck. It meant love, tenderness, inner power. That made her laugh, because to her whenever the white rabbit had appeared it meant quite the opposite. It was a reminder of her greatest tragedy. As Bunny stared at the ridiculously harmless rabbit, visions and memories of that day long ago came flooding back—a moment that had changed her world forever. She felt the cold water lapping around her, sucking her under, closing over her, until her lungs burned. It was just a memory, but the ache in her heart was real. Gripping the edge of the sink, Bunny took a series of deep, cleansing breaths, fighting to expunge the vision before turning to Lilly. With a forced smile, she asked, "Do you . . . do you, by chance, see a white rabbit on the lawn?"

With a questioning look, Lilly walked to the sink and looked out the window. A moment later she turned to Bunny. "No. All I see are a flurry of scattered leaves. Why?"

Another glance out the window confirmed Bunny's suspicions. The white rabbit was gone. "It must have been a trick of the light. I thought I saw a white rabbit out there."

"That would be something," Lilly said, brushing off the notion. "We have plenty of wild rabbits here, but I've never seen a white one."

Indeed, because the white rabbit was that rare. It was exactly what she had been afraid of. Running away had helped. So too had shunning all thoughts of the macabre. Yet she had played with fire by coming back to the UK, and it was just as she had feared, likely worse. Bunny could ignore the messenger, the white rabbit, but she could not ignore the visceral sense of doom that had settled into her bones. "Damn you," she said to the imaginary rabbit, and kept chopping.

Chapter 8

Still shaken by her earlier vision of the white rabbit, Bunny took a moment to gather herself together before making her grand entrance in the dining room. She knew that the exquisitely grand dining table with its eerily vacant chair had been set and all twelve candles in the silver candelabra had been lit. Their guests for the night's Spirit Supper (the name they had agreed to call it) were the urbanely handsome Sir Charles Wallingford; his equally stunning sister, Morgan Wallingford-Green; the dogged historian, Marcus Bean; the chic chef (and her new friend), Lilly Plum; and the attentive, mild-mannered hotel manager, Peter Billingsley. Brett and Giff would also be seated while Ed, Cody, and Mike, having already eaten, and with a promise of more food to come, were ready to film their first ever Dumb Supper, or Spirit Supper, as they were now calling it. The thought gave her a cold shiver. However, she could not deny that her bridal Christmas feast had turned out beautifully. If the evening's ghost hunt failed to produce results, it wasn't her fault.

Just as the servers began gathering their respective platters to carry into the grand dining room behind her, Brett poked his head into the kitchen.

"We have two vacant chairs. We're only supposed to have one." He looked panicked. However, when his eyes settled on the platter in Bunny's hands and lingered over the perfectly seasoned and roasted prime rib, she swore that he started drooling a little.

"That's puzzling. Did we count wrong?"

"No. We're missing Marcus Bean, the historian. He's integral to the feast. It's his time to shine, but we can't seem to locate him." As he spoke, the giant roast in her hands grew heavier by the second.

Fearful that he was proposing a delay, which, for the sake of her elaborate dinner, would never do, she offered instead, "It's nine o'clock. You asked that my dinner be ready at nine o'clock, and it is." Perfectly timing a large meal so that every dish was ready at the same moment was the mark of a true professional. "I say we start. If you wish to entice your ghost, there's not a moment to lose. We're at peak aroma. I should think you wouldn't want to lose that impetus on our first *Food and Spirits* dining adventure. When Marcus comes, he can just slip into his chair as if he's been there the whole time. Ed can do his editing thingy. Here, you carry this in." She smiled into his handsome face and thrust the meat platter into his hands. Then she marched into the dining room, trusting that Brett and her servers were behind her.

The food entered the exquisite private dining room to a chorus of oohs and aahs. The sound was like music to Bunny's ears, causing her to bubble with pride. She noted that even the thin, statuesque Morgan Wallingford-Green was grinning with delight.

"Now that's a meal worthy of breaking a diet for," she proclaimed in her cultured English accent. "I'm surprised Bean isn't already here, salivating into his napkin. It's not like him to miss a free meal, especially one as grand as this. Ring him again, Charles."

"What?" Sir Charles forcefully pulled his attention away from the succulent roasted meat to look at his sister. "The old boy still isn't here?" He looked a tad perturbed by this as he pulled out his phone. "Very well, I shall ring him again."

Sir Charles did ring him, but Marcus Bean still wasn't answering his cell phone. It was therefore agreed that his place setting be removed for the opening shot. If he arrived, they would simply put it right back where it should have been, and no one watching would be the wiser. Then the prime rib, Yorkshire pudding, roasted root vegetables, and savory au jus were served along with plenty of wassail. Judging by the slow manner in which the meal was progressing, Bunny doubted her beautiful apple tarts would be eaten at all.

After describing her meal for the cameras yet again, talk of the ghost bride circled the table. Although Marcus still hadn't shown up, Bunny marveled at how much information Brett had absorbed from the historian. Sir Charles and Morgan chimed in as well, sparing no detail about the poor bride they were attempting to entice to the table. Bunny found herself transfixed by Brett's pleasing voice and the way he expertly engaged everyone at the table in conversation. Brett Bloom was a beautiful man, to be sure. Too handsome for his own good, she mused, and cursed her heart for pounding a wee too loudly in her ears as she looked at him.

She didn't have much to add to the conversation. Although the old ghost story had moved her, because it had occurred during a wedding and was utterly tragic, she hadn't paid it much thought since hearing it. Her domain was the kitchen. Her role ended the moment the meal had arrived. It was up to Brett and Giff to carry the show from here. The thought made her smile . . . until Giff opened his mouth to speak.

It all began when Brett pointed to the empty chair—the

spirit chair—and asked Giff if he could feel the Mistletoe Bride's presence at the table yet. All cameras were on Giff as he assured the table that he would try. He then uttered the girl's name, Ann Copeland, called her to the table, and reached for the replica bridal wreath. The moment his fingers came around the delicate headpiece of fresh flowers and greenery, Giff's head dramatically snapped back, his eyes rolled up into his head, and his mouth opened. The sound that came out could only be described as highly disturbing. It was an attention-grabber for sure, Bunny mused; for all eyes at the table were on Giff.

Knowing that he had their undivided attention, Giff then strained at the ends of his vocal range, attempting to sound like a teenage bride, as he said, "*I love games. I do love them, but not this one.*"

Sir Charles leaned over to Bunny and whispered, "My dear, what's he doing?"

"Channeling," she told him, adding an uncommitted, "I think."

"*Why hasn't he come yet? Why hasn't my darling Henry come to find me? It's so dark in here . . . so very dark and cold. I feel trapped.*" Giff, with his dark eyes back to normal, looked heavenward. Breaking through that proverbial glass ceiling, he mimicked, "*Trapped, I say!*"

Morgan couldn't help herself. She giggled.

"Shhh!" hissed Lilly, clearly enjoying the show.

Bunny exchanged a look with Brett. Brett's reply to her questioning gaze was a *just-go-with-it* shrug. Which she did, transfixed, like the rest of them, to Giff's ridiculous one-person performance.

After pausing to quickly gulp down his third cup of wassail, which was undoubtedly fueling the show, he continued babbling on about being trapped, growing anxious, while peppering his monologue with other random thoughts. "*I shouldn't have eaten the pickled fish. It's giving me a stomachache. Why was Mummy talking to Sir Percy behind the curtains in the drawing room? Daddy won't be happy about that. Why did I pick this stupid old chest to hide in? I'm such a big ninny! How was I supposed to know it would lock? It's growing awfully hot and stuffy. HELP ME! I'M IN HERE, YOU NEAR-SIGHTED DIMWITS!"*

Just as Giff's antics were ramping up, a cold, angry breeze blew into the room, quelling the flames on the candles and hitting her square in the face. It caused the fine hairs on the back of her neck to prickle uncomfortably. That was bad enough, yet when Bunny's eyes were drawn to the doorway, her heart clenched painfully. That was because it was there again, her white rabbit. From the way it was looking at her, with those near glowing red eyes and that ridiculous wiggling nose, she understood what she needed to do. That's why when the rabbit turned and began hopping away, Bunny stood up from the table and followed it.

"Where are you going?" Giff asked, breaking his stellar performance to question her.

"Something's wrong," she replied without looking at him. Her focus was on the rabbit. Little else mattered. As she hurried out of the dining room, she was only vaguely aware that the others were following her.

Bunny continued down a short hallway after the white rabbit. She had the feeling that it was leading her somewhere, but where? Why, for that matter? A moment later her curiosity was piqued as the rabbit skirted past a room and headed instead down the long gallery. Not her favorite part of the manor. However, not to be deterred by her own foolish notions, she held her breath and chased after it, passing the case of antique china and silver, passing the family coat of arms, and all the rest of the treasures. After all, she was following a white rabbit—a vision only she could see—

down the dreadful long gallery. She was nearly upon it when it took a sharp left and bounded for the mistletoe chest against the wall. Her heart sank as she watched it wiggle behind the chest where it seemed to vanish. That was when she noticed a stain on the carpet beneath the chest. At first, she thought it was just part of the ornate pattern. Upon closer inspection, she realized it was blood. Seized by both fright and panic, she took a deep breath and heaved open the lid.

And then she screamed.

Chapter 9

The gruesome sight of the body in the mistletoe chest sent waves of prickling shock coursing through her. It was so painful she was about to faint. Just as her knees buckled, she felt a pair of strong arms come around her, preventing her from hitting the floor.

"My God, it's Marcus Bean," Brett cried, holding her tightly. "I think he's dead. Most definitely dead! There's a knife sticking out of his chest!"

Knife? Another wave of panic seized her. The sight of the body had been such a shock that most of her senses had shut down because of it, including her sense of sight. She hadn't noticed a knife. Had she gone blind? No, she realized. Her eyes had reflexively shut against the offending vision. Tightly. As if blocking it out would erase the entire episode. It hadn't, of course, and now Brett was talking about a knife. She had to check . . . just to be sure. It was probably nothing. Just a coincidence. Still in the grip of Brett's strong and surprisingly comforting arms, Bunny chanced another look at the body. She was ready to peel one eye open when Lilly Plum's voice rented the air.

"Bloody hell! That's your missing knife, Bunny!"

Her eyes sprang wide open, and she stared at Lilly's horrified face. That might have been a mistake. Because behind
the look of horror another thought was brewing in the chef's
brown eyes. This one was even more frightening to Bunny
than the first, because Lilly clearly thought she had been the
one responsible for the deed.

"No," Bunny uttered, leaving the comfort of Brett's arms
to stand on her own two feet. "Nope. Can't be." Yet as hard
as she tried to deny it, one look at the body and she could
feel all the blood drain from her face. Sure enough, her boning knife, which had been missing from the manor kitchen
this morning, was now sticking out of Marcus Bean's very
bloody chest. She fervently wished it had remained missing!

"Ghastly!" Morgan uttered as she attempted to shield her
eyes with her hand. Bunny noted that she was still peeking,
but only halfway, as if that would soften the blow. Clearly
Morgan was both horrified and intrigued at the sight. Then,
stating with a lack of empathy that Bunny found rather
common in the upper crust, Morgan added, "We now know
why he skipped the Spirit Supper. Only something this das-
tardly could keep him from a free meal. Is that really your
knife, Ms. MacBride?"

Bunny felt it best to hold her tongue. It wasn't like she
wanted it back or anything, now that it had, quite literally,
taken a life. No matter what your religious upbringing might
be, pulling a knife out of a man's chest, who was, himself, in
a chest, was triple bad luck any way you looked at it.

"How did you know he was in there, Ms. MacBride?"
This question came from Sir Charles. Although he was
clearly upset, Bunny couldn't help noticing a twinkle of suspicion in his eyes as he looked at her.

She crossed her arms and turned her back on the body in
the chest. "I . . . I didn't know."

Just then Giff ambled over to the chest. He was late to the party, likely because he had paused for another mug of wassail. The crystal mug was still in his hand as he peered at the man in the mistletoe chest. He made a face, then launched into act two of his channeling performance. "*Ahh, my heart. It burns, I tell ya. It burns.*" He placed a hand over his heart, pretending he'd been stabbed. His face then contorted in question. "*What's . . . happening to me? Where am I? I see a light. It's so bright, so welcoming. It's beckoning to me but . . . but a girl in a white nightgown is standing in my way. Move aside, darlin' and let me pass.*" At this point he skillfully shifted gears and began channeling the voice of the teenage Mistletoe Bride once again.

"*Don't go, mister. Please don't go. You mustn't leave me here alone in this place with them—*"

"Dude," Mike said, interrupting Giff's ridiculous performance. "The cameras aren't rolling."

"What?" Giff looked confused. "Come again?"

"The cameras aren't rolling. This is real."

"Wait." He sobered dramatically and dropped his act. "Are you telling me that this isn't part of the show?"

"Unfortunately, no," Brett informed him with a chiding look.

That was when Gifford McGrady, grabbing the three dangling crystals around his neck, proceeded to freak out in earnest. Bunny was sorry to think that she preferred his goofy channeling act instead of this total emotional breakdown.

"I'm in the same room as a dead man? There's so much blood! Why is there so much blood? *Ohmygod*, is that a knife sticking out of his chest? That's disgusting! That's horrible! *Ohmygod*, Marcus Bean's been murdered!" He had finally, in his roundabout way, come to the heart of the matter.

"It's Bunny's knife," Morgan added slyly, spilling the tea, so to speak. She was not disappointed. Giff turned to Bunny with a look of abject horror coupled with a sharp intake of breath.

"Nooo! You didn't . . . did you?" She found his bug-eyed look insulting.

"Of course, I didn't!" Bunny snapped. "That knife"—here she reached a hand behind her and shook her finger at the object in question—"was supposed to be in my knife roll. I noticed it missing from the kitchen this morning. I certainly did not expect to see it there!"

"I find that interesting," Sir Charles said in his stuffy English drawl. "You got up and left the dining room in the middle of the Spirit Supper. It was so odd that we all followed as you led us right to this chest. I'm stunned. I'm angered," he added, pointing to the blood pooling on the rich carpet under the chest. "Is this your way of confessing your dark deed?"

Bunny's hand flew over her mouth. "What?" The questioning look on Brett's face frightened her even more. "I . . . I didn't do this. I swear I didn't. Why would I?"

"Then would you mind telling us what on earth drove you to come here and open this lid?" Sir Charles demanded.

What could she say? Clearly, they all thought she was either mad or a murderer. "I . . . thought I saw a rabbit."

Giff inhaled sharply. "A rabbit? In Bramsford Manor? That's crazy talk."

Was it? Because she had purposely left out the fact that the rabbit she'd been following was white. Why had she thought leaving out this one little detail would make a difference?

Then, to Bunny's horror, Lilly tilted her head as she calmly asked, "Would it be that same white rabbit you thought you saw out the kitchen window today?" The pity that oozed from Lilly's eyes nearly undid her.

Dear Lord, what was happening to her? Bunny's heart kicked into an even higher gear as she stared at the chef.

The fact that Bunny didn't say anything spurred Lilly to announce to one and all, "She asked me if I saw a white rabbit. She pointed out the window to the back lawn, but nothing was there. Ms. MacBride was either hallucinating or trying to distract me."

"It was none of those things!" Bunny cried. "I saw a white rabbit!"

The term *white rabbit* circulated on the lips of the dinner guests in a soft murmur. Bunny heard Lilly whisper to Morgan and Sir Charles, "She's a gifted chef, but maybe she snapped under the pressure?"

"I heard that!" Bunny did not take kindly to people challenging her mental health. It was just fine, thank you very much. Then, chancing a look at the man lying in the chest with her knife sticking out of him, she thought again. I'm not *not* mental, she told herself, using a double negative to soften the blow. She had to admit that seeing a vision of a white rabbit is hardly normal. She silently cursed herself once again for signing that damn contract Mary Stobart had dangled under her nose. Then she cursed the white rabbit of doom!

While all this was going on, Peter Billingsley, the calm and collected hotel manager, had wisely called the police. He was now escorting what looked to be the entire village police station into the long gallery.

"Make way," snapped the tall, fit man in the lead with the flaming red hair. The small dinner gathering parted, revealing the gruesome scene. Officer Redhead strode over to the mistletoe chest and crossed his arms as another man came beside him and began snapping pictures. A third officer joined him and took out a small notebook and pen. "My, my," Officer Redhead remarked. "What do we have here?

Does anyone know who this unfortunate fellow is?" As the officer looked around, Sir Charles piped up.

"That's Marcus Bean. He's the manor's historian."

"Write that down," Officer Redhead told his man. "Note the blood pooling on the carpet at the base of the chest, and the splatter marks here." His finger circled the air above the marks in question. Officer Redhead then stood a moment, drinking in his surroundings, until he finally addressed the owner of the manor. "Sir Charles Wallingford, I'm Detective Chief Inspector Styles Standish. And this is now a crime scene. Is there somewhere we might talk while my men process the scene?"

With everyone back in the dining room, DCI Standish was brought up to speed on the Spirit Supper, the night's proposed ghost hunt, the two missing guests at the table (one of them an old ghost, the other likely a new one) and how Bridget "Bunny" MacBride, one of the hosts of this new *Food & Spirits* show, abruptly left her seat in the middle of dinner and led them all to the historic mistletoe chest. Then the ironic twist was revealed, delivered by Sir Charles. "The murder weapon also belongs to Ms. MacBride."

Bunny had known it was coming, yet hearing that final detail from the lips of the handsome and urbane lord of the manor, was akin to that proverbial last nail in the coffin. It was hammered home, and there was no turning back now. Even worse was the look on Brett Bloom's face. Fear, hurt, betrayal, and even a tinge of anger could be detected. She hated to admit how much that look of his tortured her. She wanted to cry out, stating her innocence. After all, her knife had been missing from the kitchen that morning and it was none of her own doing! She was only following the white rabbit to see what it wanted. Yet even she knew how ridiculous all of that sounded.

The tall detective chief inspector strode over to her chair.

Looking down on her like a displeased parent, he said, "It appears, Ms. MacBride, that however we look at this, all fingers keep pointing to you. You led everyone to the chest in the middle of . . . whatever this Spirit Supper is. Then we come to find that a knife you claim to be missing was used as the murder weapon. What was your relationship with Marcus Bean?"

"Relationship? We didn't have a relationship, sir. I've only just met the man."

"Then would you mind telling us how you knew that Marcus Bean would be in the mistletoe chest?"

"I didn't know."

"Then why did you lead everyone straight to it?"

She could tell them, but they would never believe her. The white rabbit, as far as she knew, was a vision that only she could see. Truthfully, she didn't really know what it was, or what it meant, only that it plagued her when her guard was down. The day she had first seen the innocent white rabbit, it was sitting calmly on the bank of the loch she had just been pulled out of. The moment she saw the odd sight, she had a feeling he had died. For reasons she couldn't fully explain, she had always associated her vision of the white rabbit with him. Why then had it led her to a murdered man?

She didn't know the answer to that. Therefore, addressing DCI Standish's question, she shrugged and offered, "A hunch?"

This was obviously not what he wanted to hear. "A hunch? Is that all you have? Because a hunch, as you call it, Ms. MacBride, will not hold up in a court of law. I'm placing you under arrest for the suspected murder of Marcus Bean. The rest of you are not to leave this parish until this matter is resolved."

A rush of hot blood flooded Bunny's cheeks. She was frightened, upset, and mortally embarrassed. How could they believe that she would murder a man she had just met? As she was placed in handcuffs she cast a beseeching look at her team, the men who had placed great faith in her abilities. Their expressions ranged from stunned amazement to extreme displeasure. And then there was Gifford McGrady, the man who had turned spiritual mediumship into a comedy sketch. She doubted that he even believed in ghosts. And yet there was not one ounce of doubt or displeasure in his eyes. With a firm look and a curt nod, he assured her, "I believe you, Bunny. Hang in there. We'll get to the bottom of this."

White rabbit aside, his words were the only glimmer of hope she had to cling to.

Chapter 10

When learning that *Food & Spirits* was essentially a ghost-hunting reality TV show with a food angle, Bunny had bristled. It was a natural reaction, akin to a primal instinct that arose to protect oneself from possible danger. She knew that by putting herself in areas thick with paranormal activity—like haunted old buildings, for example—sensitivities within her would be pried open, sensitivities she preferred remain shut. Tightly shut and forgotten about. Yet as resolved as she had been, Bunny had cracked. All it had taken was one night in haunted old Bramsford Manor, and the ten years she had spent bottling up her emotions and unsettling sensitivities had ended, spewing forth like fine champagne from an uncorked bottle.

Yet now it was worse than even she could have imagined. Not only was she seeing the white rabbit again, but that idiot rabbit had led her to a dead body. She really had no explanation at all as to why her prized boning knife had been found protruding from the chest of the manor's historian. Well, technically, it was only the hilt of the knife that had been sticking out. But to any chef worth a grain of salt, that hilt was recognizable. It was a Henckels S series professional knife, which Bunny was very proud to own. Thinking about the terrible misuse of her knife, DCI Standish asked his question again. They were going around in circles in the interrogation room at the police station.

"Any ideas? Any ideas at all as to how your knife ended up through the heart of Marcus Bean?"

"I wish I had, sir, but here's my answer once again. It was as great a surprise to me as it was to you. I've already mentioned to you several times now that my boning knife had gone missing from my knife roll in the manor's kitchen. Also, I had very little to do with Marcus Bean. I had just met the man and rather liked him."

"Who knew about your missing knife?"

"No offense, DCI Standish, but you could just play back the recording." Here Bunny pointed to the recording device on the table. She then offered a patient smile as she explained for the fifth time, "I've said it four times already, but I'll say it again. Once I discovered it was missing, I broadcasted the offense to the entire kitchen staff. They were helping me look for it. Lilly Plum, the head chef, can verify that for you. She was helping as well." Although the entire interrogation was being taped and observed by those behind the mirrored glass, Bunny watched as DCI Standish scribbled her answer once again in his notepad.

"Let's return to the most interesting part of the evening, shall we? It's the part where you got up in the middle of that remarkable supper you made and strode out of the dining room. It was"—he paused to look at a name in his notebook before continuing—"according to Ed Franco, in the middle of a shoot. You were filming the dinner for your new show. Why would you leave in the middle of that?"

It was the question Bunny feared the most. Like her missing knife, he had already asked this question four times, and each time she had told him the same thing: that she had merely been acting on a hunch. Even she could see how ridiculous that sounded. It was way past midnight, and she was exhausted. She had to tell him something to end this exhausting go-round of questioning. Crossing her arms, she leaned on the table and looked him in the eyes. "How much do you know about me?" This she asked, knowing they had run a thorough background check on her before the interrogation began.

Standish acknowledged the question and decided to humor her. "We know that you were born in Inverary, Scotland, applied for a visa to work in America when you were nineteen, and emigrated to the States shortly thereafter, where you worked in various restaurants in New York City until finally securing a position with the Mealtime Network."

"That's all you know about me?"

"That's largely it, aside from two ticketed moving violations during your teen years in Scotland."

"Fair enough," Bunny said. "Will you allow me to tell you something else?"

Apparently amused by this, DCI Standish nodded.

"When I was five, I wanted a pet rabbit." She watched as his ruddy eyebrows shot up his forehead at this. Bunny pressed on. "My brothers, I have two, teased me about this because we lived on a farm. There was no shortage of wild rabbits on our farm. I don't think my parents were too keen on it either, but I got my pet rabbit eventually. My grandma, Ella MacBride, bought him for me, a cute, wee baby white rabbit. I named him Hopper, because, well, you know . . . he hopped."

"Very nice, Ms. MacBride, but how is this relevant to the murder?"

"Bear with me, sir," she cautioned, and continued. "When

I was eight and Hopper had grown into a beautiful, fluffy white buck, he was still my favorite animal on the farm. I loved him. I was obsessed with him. That's how I got the nickname, Bunny." Noting that this little aside hadn't even elicited so much as a grin, she continued. "Anyhow, one cold winter morning when I was going out to feed Hopper, my father stopped me. He told me that I didn't need to feed him that day. I thought, how kind. He had fed Hopper for me. But he hadn't. That's when he told me the terrible news. Something had torn the rabbit hutch apart in the middle of the night and killed my rabbit. I learned later that it was a neighbor's two German shepherd dogs who were responsible for the murder. Those dogs were getting out at night and terrorizing the local farms. Hopper wasn't the only innocent animal to die. I was eight years old, Detective, and that was the first trauma I had suffered."

"Sorry for your loss, but is this just an attempt to waste my time, Ms. MacBride? Because I am not here to waste time. I'm here to get answers!" His cold, implacable stare irked her.

Bunny wasn't about to answer him. Instead, she raised her voice as she continued with her story. "When I was eighteen my brother Braiden and I were in a regatta on Loch Lomond. It was a chilly October morn, and we were racing a sixteen-foot dinghy that day. We grew up sailing on Loch Fyne, and he had talked me into joining a sailing club on Loch Lomond. The course took us around one of the wee islands to the south of the loch. That wasn't unusual. We were having a great sail that day and were well in the lead. However, we never expected a motorboat to come flying around the other side of the island. A drunk man was driving the boat and he hit us bow-on. It happened so fast that I didn't have time to process what was happening. In fact, I don't remember much about it at all." Bunny paused, because the simple act of recalling the incident was still very painful. After a deep breath she looked at DCI Standish once again. "I think I was supposed to die that day. In fact, I thought I had died. Yet it was only by the grace of God and my brother's hand, I believe, that I didn't. All I remember was awakening on the beach of the island with a violent cough. My lungs had been filled with water, and a man was flushing it out of me with great pressure on my chest, so that I could breathe again. There was much commotion. It was when I started breathing on my own that I turned my head and saw the beach I was lying on. That's when I saw Hopper, my white rabbit again."

DCI Standish sat up higher. "Your dead rabbit? I don't understand." He looked confused. She didn't blame him.

"Well, you and I both know that it couldn't be Hopper. He was murdered years ago by dogs. That's why I was so confused. Also, the fact that a white rabbit was sitting on the rocky beach on an island in the middle of Loch Lomond was very strange indeed. Unsettling, it was. Yet the moment I saw him I knew what it meant. I somehow knew that my brother was dead, my twin brother, before ever being told. To be a twin is a very special thing, Detective Standish. Sure, we were siblings, lifelong best friends too, but we were more than that. Connected in ways that are hard to explain. The only thing we ever really disagreed on was Hopper. My brother didn't like rabbits. I had even caught Braiden and Angus, our older brother, out hunting rabbits once. So, seeing the white rabbit was very odd indeed. I did have the inkling that it was all in my head. Rabbits are gentle, sweet creatures and pose no threat to anyone. Perhaps the rabbit was conjured in my imagination out of kindness, to soften the blow of having nearly drowned. I don't think the others could see him. Only I could see him. It wasn't until three days later that the divers pulled Braiden's body from the loch. It was the second and greatest tragedy of my life so far. My family's too."

Due to the troubled look on his face, Bunny could see that her story had touched him. "Again, I'm sorry for your loss, but I still don't see . . ."

"—I saw the white rabbit again, sir," she added heatedly. "Whether you believe me or not, Detective, I saw the white rabbit tonight sitting in the doorway of the dining room. I don't like it any better than you do, but it appears to me sometimes, and I felt compelled to follow it. That's why I went to the mistletoe chest. The white rabbit led me to it. I saw the blood pooled on the floor and opened the lid. There's the truth for you. It wasn't so much a hunch as it was the specter of my dead white rabbit! Neither, I'll wager, will hold up in a court of law."

DCI Standish sat very still as he stared pensively at her. At last, coming to some conclusion, he said, "You are either a very skilled liar, Ms. MacBride, or we're both in a heap of trouble here. For my part, I hope you're merely a liar, because I don't even know what to make of this. Until we can sort this mess out, you are still our prime suspect. Unfortunately, that means you'll be spending the night in jail."

Bunny wasn't happy to hear that, but she had expected as much. Challenging his intense gaze, she said, "I'd like to make my one phone call now, if you please."

Chapter 11

Brett Bloom was not in a good mood. In fact, the moment the police left, he had stormed out of the grand dining room and headed straight to his hotel room in a cloud of anger and self-pity. It was late. He was exhausted. And yet he was too anxious to sleep. How could this be happening to him again? he bemoaned, pacing the length of his room like a caged tiger. *Food & Spirits* was his baby, his idea, and he had put everything on the line for it, including his reputation. The thought made him ill, nearly as ill as he'd felt when he had looked upon the very dead body of Marcus Bean. He had always considered himself to be a man who didn't shy away from the more macabre side of life, but that gruesome scene in the long gallery had been fire-stamped onto his memory, which he didn't appreciate one bit.

The truth was, he had spent the better part of the day with Marcus. By all accounts, Marcus Bean was an impressive man. Bean was the last person one would expect to turn up dead in the very chest he was attempting to validate. Even he had to acknowledge the irony there, but he couldn't quite turn his mind to that yet. He was that angry. He kept pacing.

Finding that dead body in the middle of an investigation was an uncomfortably familiar feeling. Something similar had happened to them in a small Michigan town called Beacon Harbor last year. That spectacular debacle had resulted in his very successful ghost-hunting show being canceled. And now it was happening again. What were the odds? Also, and quite possibly the clincher of the evening, was learning that sweet, charming Bridget MacBride had lost her knife, and that knife had done the deed. Brett found that little detail next-level disturbing.

And what was it about her anyhow? She clearly wasn't happy with the nature of their show, having some sort of issue with ghosts, old buildings, and spooky things in general. That was understandable enough. Brett knew that not everyone was into his particular brand of adrenaline-inducing adventure. He couldn't help it that he was fascinated with the paranormal—with those strange occurrences that had no rational explanation. It wasn't for everyone, and Bunny had made that perfectly clear from the start. He respected that. He thought he had made it quite clear that she wasn't expected to dive into their post-dinner ghost hunt. He had, however, explained to her that it was necessary for her to join them during the Spirit Supper. To him it had seemed that she had no issues with that request. Why then had she stood up in the middle of it, only to walk out of the dining room and lead them directly to the body of Marcus Bean, who'd been stabbed through the heart with her kitchen knife? He never would have expected that in a million years. He sensed that she was a complicated woman—that she had issues . . . but a killer? He could forgive a lot of things, but not an unthinkable betrayal like that. As his mind spiraled further and further out of control, a sound pulled him back to his senses. It came again, this time accompanied by a voice.

"Knock-knock!" Giff said, opening Brett's door a crack.

He peered inside and held up two bottles of Guinness. "Mind if I come in? I couldn't sleep and knew for a fact that you couldn't either. The pacing gave you away."

Brett crossed the room to formally open the door. "Come in," he said, and took the proffered beer.

Brett sat on the edge of the bed while Giff relaxed in the wingback chair. It was obvious that both men were too troubled to sleep. "You know what this is?" Brett asked before taking another sip of the dark beer.

Giff shrugged, urging his friend to continue.

"I'll tell you what this is, Gifford. This is the final, spectacular, slow-motion train wreck of my career. This show will be canceled before it airs. I'll be out of a job, which means I'll have to get a real job." He looked at Giff with the fear he felt blazing in his bright eyes. "I'm going to have to go back to Wisconsin and work on the family cherry orchard, for cripes sake!"

Giff offered his friend a placid look, although inwardly he was rolling his eyes at this. He was the one hired to bring the drama to the show and here was stoic Brett Bloom—a man who could stare down a malevolent specter without so much as a flinch—having a mental breakdown at the thought of picking cherries.

"Now-now, picking cherries is an honest trade, brother," he said, trying not to crack a smile. "Nothing wrong with that. However, I think you're overreacting a bit. This is just a bump in the road. We weren't broadcasting live. We can just do it again . . . once we spring Bunny from jail."

"What?" Brett's reaction had been so quick and violent that a dribble of Guinness spurted from his lips and rolled down his chin. He wiped it on the sleeve of his sweater as he stared at Gifford McGrady.

"I said, we can just do it again." Giff offered a practical smile.

"No. The part about Bunny."

"Oh, that. I say we spring her from jail. We both know she's innocent."

"Do we?" This shocked Brett. Because, to his way of thinking, he was nearly certain that she wasn't. He tilted his golden head, and asked, "What makes you so sure? She led us right to that chest in the middle of dinner. Her kitchen knife was sticking out of the man!" Brett stared at the other man as he talked, hoping to catch a small flinch or a twist of the lips indicating that he'd been joking. Giff was a joker. He was always saying ridiculous things for a laugh. However, the trim, impeccably dressed man sitting across from him remained serious, prompting him to add, "She told DCI Standish that she had a hunch. A HUNCH! It was like she was trying to confess but couldn't fully commit to the deed."

Giff leaned forward. "Are you kidding me right now? You think that adorable woman with the face of an angel and the soul of an Iron Chef could possibly be involved in murdering Marcus Bean? Have you lost your mind?"

Brooding, while staring through narrowed eyes, Brett grunted. "It's obvious. She's trying to ruin the show."

Giff's eyes flew wide. "Whoa! Put a check on your ego there a minute, buddy. Let's back up and pretend this isn't about you or the show. Also, and most importantly, did you taste that meal? That prime rib melted in my mouth. I have never tasted a Yorkshire pudding so crisp, yet buttery. And those veggies were roasted to perfection. That dining table was as much a feast for the eyes as it was for the senses. In a nutshell, brother, our dear Bunny wasn't mailing it in with that dinner. She brought her A-game. Although she clearly has issues with ghosts, she did all that because she wanted to give you the best odds for conjuring that ghostly bride. In short, Bridget Bunny MacBride is our friend and not a murderer!"

Brett had the decency to think about this for a moment,

realizing that Giff just might have a point. But he didn't have all the answers. Therefore, he challenged, "How do you explain the fact that she stood up in the middle of the Spirit Supper and walked right out of the room?"

After a swig of beer, Giff shrugged. "I think she saw something . . . something that troubled her. She mentioned a white rabbit, remember? Although I have no idea what that was all about. Look, I was in the middle of my act when she walked out. I questioned her about it. I saw the look on her face. Also, need I remind you that we heard her scream? If she knew the body was going to be in that ghastly chest, why would she scream? Also, she nearly fainted from the shock of it."

For the first time all night, Brett took a deep, relaxing breath. The tension in his shoulders began to ease, and his red-brained thoughts began to subside. He drank the last of the beer and set the empty bottle on the night table. "You're right. It doesn't make sense now that you mention it. You and I spent the better part of the day with Marcus while Bunny was in the kitchen. She filmed a short segment with him earlier in the day, but that was it. She wasn't scheduled to see him again until dinner."

Giff stood up from his chair and placed his empty bottle on the table beside Brett's. He then turned to his friend. "Marcus Bean knew more about Bramsford Manor, I'll wager, than any living person, including Sir Charles and his lovely sister. Bean told us that Sir Charles had hired him to dig into the family pedigree, to pore over facts about the manor, and, most importantly, to validate the manor's most famous haunting, the Mistletoe Bride. My understanding is that Bramsford isn't the only stately home in Britain to claim this haunting. Others claim it too. What if Bean found some bit of information that proved otherwise?"

"Like that it didn't happen here?"

Giff was happy to see that Brett was now thinking about the murder a bit more logically. "Precisely. The mistletoe chest is the shining jewel in this drab old manor. It sets Bramsford apart from other drab old manors in the kingdom. If it was proven that the mistletoe chest was a fake and the legend was just a far-flung story, I bet hotel reservations would drop off a cliff—as in there wouldn't be many. Let's face it, seventeenth-century shabby has its charms, but most travelers today want modern luxuries like toilets that flush on the first try, and hot water."

"Good point. I never considered that," Brett admitted with a deeply furrowed brow.

Giff waved his hand nonchalantly in the air. "Understandable. You're phantom-focused. I, on the other hand," he began, holding a hand over his heart, "might have been a little too focused on the lord of the manor. Handsome, wealthy, and utterly snobbish in the best of ways, who could blame me? However, Sir Charles did, after all, hire the historian. He also seemed more troubled by the fact that his chest had been used as a crime scene rather than the murder in question. I found that odd. I also found it odd that he'd been so quick to point the finger at Bunny."

"We were all pretty quick to place the blame on Bunny," Brett confessed and crossed his arms. "You think Sir Charles killed Marcus and is blaming it on her?"

"I think it's a possibility. It makes more sense than blaming Bunny for the dirty deed. Remember, Bunny said that her knife had gone missing from the kitchen that morning. Sir Charles, as the owner, has the run of the manor. He could have easily snuck in there last night, pinched the knife, and used it to murder Bean. Bunny would be a convenient scapegoat. This is all speculation, mind you, but Sir Charles might have a motive, whereas Bunny, as far as we can tell, doesn't."

"My God," Brett said, covering his face with his hands. "I feel like such an idiot." He looked up at Giff. "We have to get her out of there."

"Of course, we do. On *Food and Spirits*, our motto is, leave no man behind . . . even if that man is a pretty lady with obvious ghost issues."

"Actually, our motto is, *be careful who you invite to dinner*," Brett corrected with a slight grin. "In this case, I'd say it holds up. After all, Marcus Bean was invited to dinner, and look what happened to him."

"Ghastly. Thanks for pointing that out, Bloom. However, I'm glad we're finally on the same page. We'll get Bunny out of jail one way or the other."

"They can't keep her too long without any real evidence," Brett offered with a look that was more hopeful than confident. Then another thought struck him. "Cody was with her most of the day, filming her cooking segment. I'm no cook, but even I know that the dinner she made took a heck of a lot of time. With Cody and his camera there, and Bunny up to her elbows in food prep, I'll venture to say that she wouldn't have had the time to sneak away and kill Bean, even if she wanted to."

"See?" Giff leaned forward and pointed a finger at his friend. "You're coming to my way of thinking, brother. Bunny was too busy cooking. A good deal of her time in the kitchen was undoubtedly filmed. The rest can be verified by the kitchen staff and that Plum woman. We're going to spring her out of that jail tomorrow morning, and then the three of us are going to put our heads together and get to the bottom of what is really going on at Bramsford Manor."

Brett nodded. "I agree. Because something very, very wrong is going on here."

Chapter 12

Bunny thought it remarkable that Grandma MacBride had picked up the phone on the first ring at such a late hour. Then again, it was just this quality in Ella MacBride that had prompted Bunny to make her one coveted jail-cell phone call to her gran in the first place, and not a lawyer. Undoubtedly the lawyer would have known how to untangle this legal mess, yet only her grandmother had the ability to untangle the swirl of emotional, mental, and very likely paranormal issues that were plaguing her from the moment she had set foot in Bramsford Manor. Thank heavens for Granny Mac.

"I was havin' a dream about you, dear, and woke up only to hear my phone buzzin' away like an angry hive. You're in trouble, aren't you?" Although Granny Mac's voice was calming as she spoke in her soft, Scottish accent, Bunny was a little unnerved by the certainty in her voice.

"I am, Gran," she had whispered into the phone. "I'm in the village jail of Hartley Wintney, just outside a haunted old manor called Bramsford. They think I murdered a man."

"Crivens! Are they daft? You're not a killer!" Granny Mac's voice rose several decibels at the mere thought of her sweet, happy-go-lucky granddaughter in jail. "I sensed that you were in trouble, dear, but I was under the impression it was of a more harmless nature . . . more of a heightened anxiety driven by the gifts you fail to embrace. I specifically remember there being a white hare, a knife, and a teapot, in my dream, though not necessarily in that order."

At the mention of the white hare or rabbit, Bunny's heart stilled in her chest. "How . . . how do you do that? How do you know about the rabbit and the knife? I'm not sure how the teapot fits in to all this, Gran, but the rabbit and my stolen boning knife landed me here—in jail."

"Ooh, that's very accurate for a wee dream, even if I say so myself." Bunny could just picture her grandmother on the other end of the phone, clutching the neck of her nightgown while wearing an expression that traveled the distance between outright spooked to immensely pleased. Although Grandma MacBride had never shied from her bizarre abilities, they did surprise her from time to time. Her odd dream had obviously done just that. Her gran's voice came over the phone again. "Truthfully, Bridget, it was disjointed and fuddled in the manner dreams are, but the white hare, the knife, and the teapot stood out to me. Then my phone began to buzz, and it all went *POOF*, right out of my head. However, this bit about you being in jail is outright rubbish."

"I wish it was rubbish, Gran, but I'm afraid it's true. I'm in jail, and I've used up my one phone call on you, because . . . because . . ." Tears came to her eyes, and she found that she couldn't finish her sentence. Thankfully, she didn't need to.

"Because it's happening again, isn't it, dear?"

Bunny closed her eyes and shook her head as the word *uncanny* popped into her mind. Her grandmother's gifts were uncanny. "It is," she admitted. "I'll tell you all about it, but not now. Not over the phone, Gran. Can you come get me? Can you get me out of this without telling my parents?"

"I flitter away all the time, like a wee little birdie, I am.

They're used to my comings and goings on the farm. I'll just leave a wee a message for your father. It's a long drive, but if I leave now, I'll get there by teatime. Maybe that's the point of the teapot? Maybe I'm the teapot in my dream?"

"You're like a teapot," Bunny suggested. "Because, like that steeping pot of tea, just the thought of you, Gran, brings me great comfort. Thank you. Love you." With a lighter heart, Bunny ended the call.

The next morning, Bunny was roused out of a deep, dreamless sleep by a guard bearing her breakfast tray. To her surprise, aside from a slight backache due to the subpar mattress, she felt well rested. This, she realized, was because although her jail cell was sparce, drab, chilly, and a bit uncomfortable, it had been pleasantly devoid of ghosts and white rabbits, unlike the grand manor of Bramsford. She thanked the guard for the thoughtful breakfast of toast, jam, and tea—a favorite of hers in any situation—and settled back on her thin mattress, resolved to wait until Granny Mac came to get her. However, just as she took her last sip of the tepid tea, the guard unlocked her door.

"Looks like it's your lucky day, Ms. MacBride."

She cast the guard a puzzled look. Her grandma must have made remarkable time. The mere thought of that capable woman brought a glowing smile to her face as she asked, "Am I free to go?"

"Ahh . . ." The guard stared at her a moment, silently cursing himself for that sarcastic greeting. "Not exactly. DCI Standish wants to see you."

"Lovely," Bunny said, imagining the great tongue-lashing her gran was giving the inspector for keeping her in jail. She then ran her fingers through her tangled mass of curls in an attempt to look presentable, but her fingers got stuck only a quarter of the way down. Not a good sign. Bunny's smile faded as she tried to free her fingers. "Do you happen to have a comb on you that I might borrow? I make it a point to never go out the front door without first taming this mess."

Her request fell on deaf ears. Instead, the guard gestured for her to step out of the jail cell.

Bunny had been expecting to see DCI Standish in the interrogation room. She also half expected to see her grandmother sitting there as well. However, what she hadn't expected to see were her two cohosts from the ghost show, looking grim-faced as they sat beside Cody Jenkins with his video camera and laptop. Unfortunately, Granny Mac was nowhere in sight.

"Have a seat, Ms. MacBride. It appears that these three gentlemen are making a case to prove your innocence regarding the murder of Marcus Bean."

Brett Bloom, with abject concern plastered on his face, jumped up from his seat and pulled out a chair for her. As she sat, he whispered in her ear, "Forgive us for not coming sooner. Are you okay?"

What to say to that? No, she was not okay. Being accused of murder didn't feel good at all. Also, finding a dead body with her missing knife sticking out of it was an image that had been burned on the backs of her eyeballs forever. So, no, she was not okay at all. However, due to Brett's adorably contrite face and the fact that he was here on her behalf, prompted her to lie. "I'm perfectly fine, thank you, although I could use a comb or a brush just now."

He looked at her hair, flinched ever so slightly, and lied to her as well. "You look lovely, as usual." That little fib, coming from his lips, did wonders to bolster her confidence.

Once Bunny was seated, DCI Standish folded his hands, leaned back in his chair, and looked at her in his practiced, intimidating manner. "It appears that you have some loyal friends. These gentlemen have brought an impressive amount of time-stamped raw footage of your movements yesterday to prove that you couldn't have had enough time to find Marcus Bean, bring him to the long gallery on the other side of the manor, stab him with your kitchen knife, and push him into the oak chest on display there. While there is a good amount of evidence here to suggest it would have been a very difficult thing to do—"

"Nay, impossible!" Giff interrupted with a dramatic flair that the chief inspector did not appreciate in the slightest. After a dagger-eyed look, DCI Standish continued.

"Not impossible, but difficult, I'll concede. However, that still doesn't account for the fact that your fingerprints are all over the murder weapon, or the fact that you led everyone to the body."

Bunny fumed. "Of course, my fingerprints are all over that knife! It's my boning knife, for all love! The killer was obviously wearing gloves when they used it."

Cody seized that moment to thrust his laptop in front of DCI Standish once again. "Also, sir, I've just shown you footage from the kitchen where Bunny"—he cleared his throat and corrected—"Ms. MacBride, opened her knife-roll, complaining about how her valuable knife had gone missing from the kitchen that morning. See?" Cody hit a button on the computer and played the scene once again. Although Standish watched the scene with interest, he was unconvinced.

"She could have easily taken it herself, hidden it, and made a point of complaining about it to you for the sake of creating a plausible defense. After all, it is your job to film her in the kitchen, I presume."

Bunny couldn't believe the rubbish she was hearing. "Why would I take my own bloody knife and lie about it? That's mental. Besides, it was missing from my knife-roll the moment I arrived in the kitchen yesterday morning. I have many knives, Inspector. But this person took my boning knife, which has a very sharp blade. It's thinner than my chef's knife, thicker and longer than my utility knife, and perfect for penetrating the tough intercostal muscles between the ribs to get to the heart. Whoever chose that knife knew what they were about."

"It appears that you do too," he added, casting her a look of suspicion.

"It's part of my chef's training," she haughtily defended. "Being familiar with all cuts of meats and how to prepare them."

Seeing that Bunny was digging herself into a bit of a hole, Brett jumped in and changed the subject. "Detective Chief Inspector, all due respect, sir, I have another take on the matter. You see, I believe that whoever murdered Marcus Bean and put him in the mistletoe chest, meant for us to find him during the night's investigation. That historic chest and the ghost story that surrounds it was the reason we came to Bramsford Manor in the first place. Marcus Bean was the person who reached out to me and our producer, after learning that our show was looking for interesting and haunted locations to investigate. We literally just met the man three days ago, when we arrived. He was the historian and knew all the important details about the manor and the haunting that we were interested in. Marcus was our contact. He was also supposed to accompany us last night as we searched for evidence of a haunting. But as you know, we never got the chance. Why would any of us have reason to murder Marcus Bean?"

They all watched anxiously as DCI Standish considered this. At length he took a deep breath and slowly exhaled. "You make a valid point, Mr. Bloom. And I'm inclined to believe you. However, there is one puzzling incident in this terrible crime that is hard to overlook. And that, sir, is the fact that Ms. MacBride hasn't sufficiently explained why she left her seat in the middle of dinner and led your entire party to the chest that contained the dead body." His eyes, sitting beneath the furrowed, ruddy brows, issued Bunny a challenge.

Bunny knew very well that he was trying to make her crack. She found his look insulting. She had laid her heart bare last night and had told him the truth. It wasn't her fault that he didn't believe her. Pushing aside the pain in her heart while summoning all the cheerfulness in her smile, she reminded him, "I explained it to you very well, Chief Inspector. I was simply following the white rabbit."

Chapter 13

It was her mic-drop moment, Bunny mused, having stunned them all in only two words. White rabbit. The interrogation room fell silent, and Bunny was quite finished explaining herself to the detective. She sat amid looks of both puzzlement and concern from her coworkers, and a glimmer of something approaching satisfaction in the detective's eyes, which, Bunny surmised, was due to her conviction in her story. Either that or the detective thought her a total nutter. Whatever the case, Bunny was released from jail. She was still a suspect in the murder of Marcus Bean, as they all were, but they really had nothing concrete to hold her on. The entire team of *Food & Spirits*, along with everybody who lived and worked at the manor, were still under what Bunny considered to be house arrest. They were not allowed to travel beyond the village limits until either their names had been cleared or the murder had been solved.

The moment Bunny took her seat in the van, Giff barraged her with, "Are we back to the white rabbit again? Did you tell Standish about that? He looked irritated. Rabbits aren't attracted to the smell of blood, are they? Why was there a rabbit in the manor in the first place?" He paused to take a breath, then gasped. "*Ohmygod*, tell me you weren't blackout drunk!"

"Wheesht," she hissed at him from the front seat. "I had two sips of wassail the entire night. I promise to tell you everything, but this is not a conversation we're going to have in this van. I'll be happy to tell you all about the white rabbit back at the manor, over a proper pot of tea and a plate of chocolate digestives. Which will have to wait until after I've taken a proper shower. Also, you should know that my grandma is coming to help us sort this all out."

As if stuck by a sharp pin, Giff flinched as his eyes flew wide as saucers. "Your grandma's coming? Let me get this straight. You've been accused of murder, you're mumbling about following a white rabbit, and you called your grandmother? Maybe a lawyer . . . or even a shrink might have been a better choice."

Brett, keeping his innermost thoughts to himself, gripped the steering wheel tighter as he chanced a look at the woman sitting next to him. "I . . . ah . . . think it's a good move, having a grandma around. You'll get no complaints from me."

Cody, still stuck on the mention of food, leaned forward in his seat. "I could use a cup of tea, but you mentioned something about digestives. No offense, but they don't sound very appealing. Do you think you could scrounge up some cookies instead?"

Maybe it was the fact that she'd been accused of murder and had spent the night in a village jail cell. Whatever the case, these men were beginning to grate on her nerves. She craned her neck and stared at the two men in the back seat. "My grandma is a wise woman. And digestives are biscuits, which are basically the same things as cookies, as you call them. I made a batch yesterday while I was waiting for my roast to finish. I like to multitask in the kitchen, thank you very much."

After a hot shower and a change of clothes, Bunny did her best to avoid every member of her team as she stealthily wove her way to the manor kitchen. She was at the large sink, staring out the modern window at the rolling expanse of lawn as she filled a kettle. It was a stunning view, she thought, taking a deep, relaxing breath for the first time all morning. Just as the tenseness in her shoulders began to ease, the sound of a familiar voice knotted them up again.

"You're back!"

Bunny shut the faucet and turned from the sink to greet Lilly Plum. "Hello," she said with a forced smile, keeping her voice light and pleasant. Unfortunately, it did little to erase the deep creases of worry on the older woman's face. That twinkle of suspicion rankled, but Bunny really couldn't blame her. She cursed herself again for being curious and for following that troublesome rabbit. She understood that the sight of Marcus Bean's crumpled and bloodied body in the mistletoe chest was a vison they were all likely to suffer until the end of their days. There was nothing she could do about that now. However, it occurred to Bunny that only she knew for a certainty that she was innocent of murder. It was her burden to prove to the others. Therefore, she offered a sheepish smile and said, "I'm so sorry about all of this, Lilly. I just ran into Peter Billingsley. He told me that all outside reservations have been canceled for the time being, and that only a few guests have been allowed to remain."

"Forgive the bad pun, but since last night Bramsford has turned into a literal ghost town. I've been told that only a handful of my kitchen staff can remain, which is likely all we'll need until this matter of Marcus Bean's murder has been resolved. What a terrible thing to have happened to poor Bean. I rather liked him. He had a curious mind and an endearing way of getting under Sir Charles's skin."

Bunny put the kettle on the stove, and asked, "What do you mean?"

It was clear that Lilly regretted making that remark. She pressed her lips together as she thought about how to reply. After a weighty pause, she asked, "Have you been removed from the suspect list?"

This question caused a dark cloud to descend on Bunny's naturally cheerful demeanor. Poor Lilly obviously believed she was in the kitchen with a killer. Not true. Bunny was as gentle as . . . well, a bunny. Yet the trauma of last night still permeated the air and clung to the walls like strong curry. Again, Bunny forced a smile. "According to DCI Standish, we're all still suspects. Thankfully, the lads brought in all the footage from our shoot yesterday to help clear my name. While I'm technically still on the suspect list, DCI Standish will be hard-pressed to create a viable timeline for when I might have left the kitchen to do the deed. Also, although the murder weapon belonged to me, you were here when I discovered it missing. I didn't know the victim. I didn't have a reason to want him dead. I hope that puts your mind at ease. Because while I'm here at the manor, I'd be happy to help in the kitchen."

"How kind," Lilly remarked, trying not to make it obvious that she was slowly backing away from the celebrity chef. "But there's really no need. We'll be fine. Just fine. I see you're heating a kettle of water." Her wide brown eyes flashed to the industrial stove beneath the copper hood.

Bunny nodded. "I've come in here to make a pot of tea, and to fetch a plate of the chocolate digestives I made yesterday. I put them in the fridge." Bunny was about to traverse the kitchen to the fridge in question when Lilly stopped her.

"Why don't you run along to the hotel dining room, and

I'll have Betsy bring a tea tray out to you. How many cups and saucers will you need?"

"But . . . but . . ." she began to protest, glancing at the kettle on the stove with the longing of an addict. Tea was not only a hot, calming drink, but to Bunny, the simple act of making it was part of the process. Her hands itched to pull it off the stove and pour it into the awaiting teapot, where she'd wrap it up in a cozy and let it steep for five minutes. Yet even she knew that the water was far from boiling. Lilly's stern look stopped her in her tracks. Bunny was no longer welcome in the kitchen. "Five," she finally uttered. "Thank you."

As Bunny walked out of the kitchen, the matter of Marcus Bean's death weighed heavy on her heart, especially now, since the mood in the grand home had shifted from friendly to suspicious. She hadn't been too keen on coming to Bramsford Manor in the first place, due to the nature of their visit. However, she had found a sense of purpose in the kitchen and, if she was being honest, had relished her time preparing the meal in the historic venue. Yesterday as she cooked, she hadn't been part of a team of menu developers in a test kitchen with Mary Stobart breathing down her neck. She had been her own woman; the star of her little corner of the show, and she had turned out a remarkable feast for seven that even a five-star restaurant would have been proud to serve. She had hustled like a demon possessed to pull it off, and yet her heart sang with the joy of angels as she worked. Now, however, thanks to a reckless murder and her utterly ruinous desire to follow the white rabbit of doom, she was as good as banned from that sanctuary. She heaved a pitiful sigh as she shuffled like a prisoner dragging a ball and chain toward the hotel dining room. She felt almost naked without that tray of tea and digestives in her hands. What would the lads make of it, she wondered.

As she came out of the hallway empty-handed, she realized that they were already there, sitting at a round table beneath the wall of historic, mullioned windows. However, to her surprise, Brett, Giff, and Cody were not looking at her, but staring past her to a spot well beyond the dining room. Brimming with curiosity, Bunny turned and saw a sight that instantly elevated her mood.

"Grandma!" she cried, spying the somewhat eccentric-looking woman marching past the French doors of the dining room and continuing down the hall. Grandma Ella MacBride had short, stylish copper hair, and clear blue eyes. She wore a cute pumpkin print tunic over faded bell bottom jeans that Bunny was certain had a forgiving waistband. It was her gran's signature move, as well as wearing at least three dangly gold necklaces and a noisy charm bracelet that often heralded her arrival.

At the sound of her granddaughter's voice, Ella MacBride backtracked and peered through the doors. "Bridget! There you are, my dear. I knew that if I walked around enough, I'd eventually run into you."

"You could have sent me a text," Bunny remarked as she embraced the older woman in a fierce hug. The moment her arms came around her grandmother, Bunny felt a wave of loving energy course through her body that she hadn't felt since leaving Scotland. She suddenly realized just how much she had missed that feeling—that sudden and profound understanding that things were going to be alright no matter how mucked-up they appeared. That feeling was more powerful than a drug, she believed as she ushered Granny Mac inside the dining room to meet the lads.

Chapter 14

"These digestive cookies aren't half bad," Cody remarked, dunking his third chocolate-kissed biscuit into his cup of tea. "I like 'em."

"That is precisely why I made them," Bunny lied with a smile, and poured herself another cup of the delicious English Breakfast tea. She took the liberty of refilling her gran's cup as well before setting down the teapot.

She was chuffed at the warm welcome the lads had given her grandmother. Yet just how well would they take the news that her fun-loving, eccentric gran was spiritually gifted in a way that people found unsettling? Gran was the real thing. Her father, Davie MacBride, felt his mother's gifts to be a blight on the family. As for Bunny's mother, Maggie, she was entertained by them . . . as long as Granny Mac kept her skills in check and didn't enrage the villagers. Heaven forbid, but Scotland couldn't afford to burn another witch at the stake, her mother was fond of remarking. Bunny loved her grandmother, yet regarding the woman's gifts, for the most part she had steered clear of them or had shut them down completely for fear of what she might learn about herself. She liked to have tight control over her emotions and thoughts, but the pressure behind that dam had reached a critical level. When the white rabbit appeared, she knew she was losing the battle.

Bunny watched Granny Mac take a cautious, dainty sip of her tea and knew that the older woman was covertly staring at her three defenseless coworkers over the rim of her cup. It wasn't just curiosity either. The way her gran's cunning, clear blue eyes had narrowed like a cat's told her everything. Granny Mac was trying to get a read on them, in the broadest sense of the word. She then set her cup on its saucer, cleared her throat, and homed in on hunky Brett Bloom. *Dear heavens*, Bunny thought. *Don't do this, Gran!* Yet before she could utter a word, Granny Mac beat her to it. Bunny felt the heat rise to her cheeks so quickly, she feared she was having a menopausal hot flash.

"Brett, is it?" Granny Mac asked coyly. "Your grandfather passed during your formative years. You were quite close. He was a mentor to you, someone you looked up to, wasn't he? Well, he wants you to know—"

Brett had just been about to take a bite of his digestive when Granny Mac started in on him, but he suddenly let go of it instead. Bunny watched the biscuit hit the plate and frowned at the older woman. Brett stuttered, "How . . . how did you know that?"

For one who made a living investigating the paranormal, Bunny felt it disheartening at how frightened Brett looked. Noting that her gran's mouth was about to open again, delivering yet more unsolicited thought-nuggets from beyond, she blurted, "It's a party trick. She read it online."

Brett narrowed his eyes at the older woman. "That's not information I've ever shared. How did you do that?"

"Wait!" Giff exclaimed, jumping to his feet. He pointed a

finger at Granny Mac. "She knew him. She knew your old man. They were probably having an affair. A fine-looking older woman with a killer accent, rocking a Shirley MacLaine vibe, and your handsome, philandering gramps. It's the only explanation here."

"What?" Brett shot a look of extreme displeasure at him. "My grandfather was not a philanderer, Giff! He was an up-standing gentleman of the community, and a God-fearing Christian. He was the best man I ever knew." He shifted his gaze to the older woman. "How did you know about my grandfather?"

"Well, because he's here with us . . . just beyond your left shoulder about there." Granny Mac gestured with a finger to a spot above the shoulder in question.

"Grandma!" Bunny sternly cut in. "Not now. We're not doing this now. A man was murdered here last night, and I've been implicated in that murder. That's why you're here. Not to freak out my team with your . . . your . . . you know, party tricks." Bunny wiggled her hand in the air in frustra-tion, not having the courage to actually state what her grand-mother was.

"Och, that's right, dear," Granny Mac agreed with a smile, as if recalling herself. Bunny implored her with a look that begged the older woman to act like a normal grand-mother. Receiving the message loud and clear, Granny Mac gave a nod and picked up her teacup once again—with her pinky properly extended. After sipping it down to the last drop she returned it to the saucer, then declared, "Well, haven't you all landed in a fine kettle of fish. The last time I talked to my granddaughter she told me she was going to be a cohost on a new travel food show. It wasn't until last night—when she called me from that pokey village police station—that she finally told me the truth about this little show of yours. Sure, Bunny's the expert on food here, but you boys are ghost hunters. I get the very real sense that you're meddling in things that you don't fully understand."

Giff tapped the side of his nose, then pointed that finger at Ella. "Correct again. I'm impressed. Two for two. What gave us away? Am I wearing too many crystals?" He fingered the many dangly necklaces bouncing about his chest.

"No. They look quite fetching on you," she replied sincerely. Then, narrowing her sharp gaze, she offered, "What I am getting at is murder. Also, am I the only one, or does anyone else feel the wonky energy milling about this manor house? It's like a roiling mixture of rotting roses, wet dog, and old linen with the wafting undertones of cigarettes and Old Spice Swagger. Very jarring."

"Wow, that's rather specific," Giff remarked, covertly sniffing his armpit. Not that he'd ever be caught dead using Old Spice Swagger, but he felt compelled to check just in case. Granny Mac continued.

"I understand that you're investigating the untimely death of an unfortunate bride who once lived here. However, might I throw out the notion that there is more than one ghost within these ancient walls?"

Brett eyed her suspiciously. "You said that my grandfather was here too. What was that all about?"

"Ahh . . ." Ella saw Bunny's cautionary look, then offered in a near whisper, "He's not really *here*, dear," she told him, emphasizing the word *here*. "Your grandfather is quite safe on the other side. Perfectly fine. It's just that . . . there's a very bright, protective energy around you at times. Not at all like this"—she waved a hand in the air—"this muddled energy of the earthbound souls who cannot let go of the negative emotions surrounding either their death or their life. It can be a real problem."

"Holy mother . . ." Cody uttered as his head swiveled like a gate in the wind, looking from Giff to Brett to Granny

Mac while trying to make sense of what was happening at their private little tea party. Seeing that the others were just as confounded as he was, he nervously reached for his fourth chocolate digestive instead.

Bunny leaned in, thinking it best to just get it out in the open, since the lads were either being too polite or too obtuse to latch onto the word. "If you haven't figured it out yet, gentlemen, my gran's clairvoyant—a medium, actually."

"Whoa! Like . . . for real?" Giff had the look of a squirrel who'd just discovered that his hard-won nut stash had been pillaged.

"Afraid so," Bunny confirmed, and graced her grandmother with a wan smile. "She has the gift. In Scotland we call such as her a *seer*."

Cody stilled in mid dunk, leaving half his biscuit in the teacup a hair too long, causing it to break off and sink to the bottom. Brett, on the other hand, raked his fingers through his hair.

"I was beginning to get that feeling. Why didn't you tell us about this before?" he asked Bunny.

Ella MacBride watched her granddaughter pale before falling silent at the question. She knew firsthand how difficult it could be to talk about clairvoyance, let alone embrace such a gift. Knowing the conflict that played out in her granddaughter's heart, she reached over and gave Bunny a comforting squeeze on her hand. "It's not her fault," she told Brett. "Clairvoyance is often a taboo subject. People either don't believe in it," she said, looking straight through Giff, "or it falls under the realm of occult." She then looked at her granddaughter with tenderness, adding, "And sometimes when the gift falls on you, you do everything in your power to avoid it or wish it away. Sometimes it's just a burden." Ella gave her a moment to let that sink in before she asked, "Have you told them yet about the white rabbit?"

At the mention of the creature, Brett's back stiffened. "We heard something about it back at the police station. Bunny promised to tell us what it means." This time as he looked at Bunny there was more compassion in his gaze than accusation. Bunny found that encouraging.

"I did promise, didn't I? Well, here's the truth of it." She steeled herself as she looked directly into Brett's eyes. "I once had a twin brother named Braiden. It was his dream to become a chef, not mine. When we were sixteen, our parents helped us open a little farmstand restaurant in one of the buildings on our farm. We baked our own bread and made all kinds of dishes, mostly using the produce we grew and the meat we raised. We only ran it in the summer. It was our summer job, and I was happy there. I loved coming up with new dishes and treats that delighted our customers. I never had any wish to leave Scotland. But that all changed when Braiden died. It was in a sailing accident on the loch, and I was with him. Part of me feels that I was meant to die, not him. In fact, sometimes I believe that I actually know that."

"*Oh, Bunny!*" Giff heaved a sigh as his brown eyes glistened with moisture. His hand clutched the cotton fabric over his heart as he added, "You dear, sweet child. That's not true."

Bunny hated to contradict him, but this was her story to tell. "I believe it is true. You might not understand this, but being twins, we were not only best friends, but we were connected by a bond even stronger than regular siblings share. I thought I was going to drown that day, but by some miracle I didn't. Braiden did. And I knew this because the moment these good Samaritans pulled me from the loch and cleared the water from my lungs, I saw a white rabbit sitting on the beach. We were on a wee island. And while there might be rabbits on that island, I doubted very much they were white. A white rabbit is a rare thing indeed. But there it was, staring at me as I fought to breathe again."

"How . . . how did it get there?" Cody asked. Fortunately, there weren't any more digestives on the plate for him to eat. Bunny felt he might make himself ill from his mindless, nervous eating.

She shook her head. "It wasn't really there, Cody. I was seeing things. It was all in my head." She tapped her head, drumming her point home.

"Why a white rabbit, do you think?" She could tell Brett was trying to process what she was telling them.

"Because the white rabbit I see was my childhood pet. His name was Hopper. Only now I refer to him as the white rabbit of doom. Because whenever Hopper appears, nothing good happens."

"Like death, or murder," Brett said, entertaining the notion. To his credit, he did chase ghosts for a living. "You saw the white rabbit here, in the formal dining room while we were having dinner."

"Yes," she stated with a nod, relieved that they were finally following along. "After my brother died, I was haunted by the white rabbit. I knew that if I was ever going to be free of it, I had to leave Scotland, and so I did. I ran to the US, chasing Braiden's dream, only I had embraced it as my own by then. It seemed to work. The moment I came to America, I knew that I had left the white rabbit behind me. The funny thing is, I love rabbits. I have a pet rabbit at home who's being looked after by my neighbor's daughter. And yet, given all that, I'm still wary of a setback. I spent a good amount of energy avoiding any place or thing that might have a reason to call the rabbit forward again. That's why I was hesitant to come here, and rightly so. Because the moment I began to let my guard down, he popped up again and led me straight to that unsettling old mistletoe chest. Thanks to the ghost rabbit, I'm now suspect number one in Marcus Bean's murder."

Brett, to Bunny's astonishment, was taking this explanation quite well. Cody looked a little green in the gills, but that could be from all the biscuits he had eaten. Giff, however, appeared aghast.

"You're clairvoyant?" he accused her. "You see ghosts? Ohmygod! Ohmygod! I'm supposed to be the medium on the show and you're the one with all the talent. Do you know how useless I feel right now? Pretty darn," he replied in answer to his own question. "I mean . . . if I could cook, I'd swap places with you, Bridget. But I don't cook. I'm so depressed right now I can't even. . . ." With a dramatic exhale he reached for a chocolate digestive. The plate was empty. "Hey, what happened to all the cookies?"

"Relax," Granny Mac said, holding Bunny in a very grandmotherly gaze. "My granddaughter has the gift. She knows it too, but she is hesitant to embrace it, because to do so will come at a price. That's why she called me here. You are the team of *Food and Spirits*. You are here to investigate a haunting, yet now I'm afraid that you will need to solve the murder of Marcus Bean as well. My understanding, after talking with my granddaughter, is that Marcus was investigating a mystery of his own. Gentlemen, gird your loins, for we are about to go where mortal men fear to tread. We need to reach out to the other side to find the answers we're looking for. Bridget, my dear, are you ready to face your demons?"

Chapter 15

Hell no, she wasn't ready to face her demons! The thought was galling, yet not quite as galling as the fact that somebody had stolen one of her favorite knives to do the deed. She had lugged that knife all the way to this bloody manor, and had used it the day before to carefully remove the ribs on the standing rib roast she'd prepared for the spirit feast. It was part of her special recipe—to combine the beef ribs with three pounds of oxtails and other aromatics to create the succulent au jus. Being a guest chef, she knew that there were many sets of knives in that kitchen, but the murderer had taken her knife. What did that mean? For one, it spoke of premeditation. Also, she doubted very much that choosing her knife had been mere happenstance. Somebody had framed her, but why?

She felt the heat of her grandma's penetrating gaze on her and brought her focus on the matter at hand, namely her demons. She flashed an insouciant grin at the men sitting around the table—the men who'd been hanging on her grandmother's every word. Ella MacBride had that effect on people. "Well, now you know why I didn't want to come here in the first place. Old buildings, spooky places, ghosts, they're my kryptonite. My demons, or rather the white rabbit of doom, is now out in the open. Time for me to get slaying." As Bunny said this, she was well aware that the young server, Betsy, was coming to check on them. Betsy, she felt, was her ticket to get back into the kitchen.

"Would you care for another pot of tea?" Betsy asked, focusing her soulful brown eyes on Brett—as if he was the one making all the decisions. Honestly, Bunny couldn't blame the young woman. Brett was far too good-looking for his own good. And Betsy, boasting the dewy smooth skin of a twenty-year-old and perfect white teeth, was very pretty. However, Brett was so caught up in what Granny Mac was telling them, Betsy could have been a supermodel and he wouldn't have noticed. Cody, however, was another matter.

Smiling at the young lady, he offered, "I wouldn't say no to another pot of tea and more cookies. Have you worked here long?"

"I think we're quite done," Bunny remarked, wiping the grin off his face. She then grabbed the teapot and biscuit plate before getting to her feet. With a look to the server, she insisted, "Let me help you with these dishes."

"That won't be necessary, ma'am."

"I'll come too," Cody said, grasping the arms of his chair and getting ready to launch himself out if it.

Bunny held up her hand. "No. Stay," she commanded, smiling inwardly as Cody took the hint. To Betsy, she offered a smile. "I insist, Betsy." Without another word on the matter, Bunny took the dishes and marched off in the direction of the kitchen as Betsy followed in her wake.

The heavenly scent of bangers frying—those delectable, juicy, fat, spicy pork sausages—hit Bunny the moment she entered the sanctuary of the kitchen. Although she'd just enjoyed a spot of tea and biscuits, her stomach growled, none-theless. One of the sous chefs, Rodger, had just put a dozen sausages in a hot pan glistening with golden melted butter. *Good move*, Bunny silently approved, flashing a smile at the man. Fat was essential for good flavor, and the salty butter would combine nicely with the sausage fat as it oozed and sputtered into the pan. The reason the Brits called the sau-sages bangers to begin with was due to the popping sound of the skin as it sizzled and split during cooking. The brown bits remaining in the pan with the fat drippings were also es-sential to make the flavorful onion gravy that the sausages would be served with. Although the sausages were only be-ginning to fry, Bunny knew the kitchen was prepping for the evening's dinner. The star of the evening's menu would be bangers and mash (creamy mashed potatoes) in onion gravy with a side of buttery green peas. It was classic British com-fort food, and Bunny secretly applauded the choice. Because after such a gruesome murder the people deserved comfort food. Amen! She was also sorry to think that she wanted to play her part in the making of the meal. She saw another prep cook removing yet more sausages to be fried, along with a mound of potatoes yet to be peeled.

After depositing the tray and teapot in a bus tray near the industrial dishwasher, Bunny headed to the kitchen office, knowing that Lilly Plum was taking refuge there. Sure enough, the moment Lilly spied her moving about the cook-ing stations, she popped her head out of the office door.

"What are you doing in here?" she asked, attempting to keep her voice free of suspicion. Unfortunately, it wasn't working.

"Thank you for the tea. I wanted a word with you. May we talk?"

Lilly studied her for a moment before ushering her into the tiny office.

As Bunny took her seat, she noticed that Lilly's hands were shaking slightly. *The poor thing is terrified of me*, she thought disparagingly. *However, were I in her shoes—sitting in a small room with a woman suspected of being a murderer—I might feel the same way.* Bunny forced a sympathetic smile. "Lilly, you've shown me nothing but kindness since I arrived, and you have nothing to fear from me. I promise. I'm simply a visiting chef who is now caught up in this terrible crime. While I understand that you feel uncomfortable with me in your kitchen, I just had to come back here and ask you a few questions regarding that poor man. You made a comment a little while ago while I was making tea. You said that Marcus had a curious mind and an endearing way of getting under Sir Charles's skin. What did you mean by that?"

Lilly laced her hands together to stop them from shaking and pressed them tightly to her lap. "I meant nothing by it," she offered with a shake of her chic, silver-haired head. "I hate to speak ill of my generous employer."

"I understand." Bunny was doing her best to lower the tension in the room, but Lilly was wound tighter than a loaded spring. Offering a conspiratorial smile, she confessed, "I used to work for Mary Stobart. And while the opportunity she offered me was invaluable, and I was so very grateful for it, she had her moments. Did Marcus not get along very well with Sir Charles?"

Lilly exhaled as she gave a little wave of her hand. "They got on just fine. The academic and the wealthy patron. It was only that every once in a while Marcus would stumble on some arcane piece of information that would contradict Sir Charles's favorite family narratives regarding his predecessors."

"Can you give an example?"

Lilly thought a moment. "Sir Charles is very fond of his

family history, especially when it comes to the world wars," she said. "He used to brag about how his great-grandfather, Winston Wallingford, was a war hero in the First World War. He has a fine collection of war memorabilia in his private wing that he's very proud of. Unfortunately, not long after hiring Marcus Bean, Marcus brought him the news that his great-grandfather had never served in the war, but instead had served the British interest in India by overseeing one of the British railroad companies there. It was a lucrative position, and while the family made out like bandits, the fighting on the Continent continued. Young Winston Wallingford, envious of the war heroes returning home to fanfares and accolades around the same time he was returning home from his service in India with his moneybags, paid some young officer for both his uniform and his tales of heroism. Old Winston kept the charade going until his dying breath. Sir Charles was crushed by that bit of information, but he handled it quite well in the end, eventually having a good laugh over it."

"That had to be hurtful," Bunny offered, wondering how well she would have handled such news. However, it was old news and hardly relevant in the great scheme of things. Learning that one's ancestor had been more concerned with amassing wealth than doing his duty for King and country, might shake up the family tree a bit, but was it a reason for murder? Bunny wasn't sure. However, being a fond tabloid reader, she knew that if ego and pride were aligned with the same purpose, anything was possible. Did Sir Charles have a big enough ego? Was his pride worn like a coat of armor, or a mere gossamer shell? She would have to find out.

"I believe it was hurtful at first," Lilly continued, "but it sure brought the old boy down a peg, if you know what I mean. Although he's quite a laid-back chap, Sir Charles is very aware of his station and wealth. Although, to be honest, ancestral wealth is getting harder and harder to hang on to these days. Hence the reason Bramsford Manor is now open to the public."

"Do you think it's possible that Marcus might have stumbled onto something else that might have angered Sir Charles?"

Lilly leaned forward in her chair. "What are you suggesting? Are you suggesting that Sir Charles had something to do with Marcus's murder?"

"Look, I'm just trying to get to the bottom of things here. I don't like it any better than you do, but Sir Charles hired the man."

"If he didn't like him, he could have terminated his employment at any time," Lilly heatedly argued. "What reason would he have had to murder Marcus?"

That was the question. Maybe Marcus had stumbled onto something else . . . something far more damaging than a lying, avaricious great-grandfather. Sir Charles might have had a motive to want his historian silenced, but now was not the time to press the issue. Lilly was visibly upset, causing Bunny to wonder if she had any romantic ties to the handsome aristocrat. It wasn't out of the question. That was something she'd need to look into as well. Instead, she thought it best to steer the conversation in another direction, lest she get kicked out of the kitchen again.

"What about access to the kitchen? Do you lock up at night?"

"You're thinking about your missing knife, aren't you?"

Bunny nodded.

"I told you that things sometimes go missing around here. An oven mitt, a wooden spoon, an egg timer, things of that nature. One of the staff will complain that they put an item away, only to find it missing. It happens in other parts of the manor as well. Most times it's a simple case of a misplaced item. The item is found elsewhere, due to the fact that some-one had moved it and forgot about it. However, other times it's not so simply explained away as that. A small item will disappear for a time. Then, quite out of the blue, it will reap-pear again, right in the place where it was last seen, only no one claims to have touched it. Those incidents are harder to explain. We generally blame them on paranormal activity."

"While that is unsettling, a missing oven mitt has never been used in a murder, I'll wager. My knife was. Who has ac-cess to the kitchen besides the staff?"

Lilly grimaced. "I do lock up at night, mainly so that guests don't come poking around in the fridge or attempt to make a midnight snack. Both have happened in the past. However, Sir Charles, Morgan, Callum Digby, and Peter Billingsley all have keys."

Bunny made a mental note of it before firing off her next question. "How well did you know Marcus?"

Lilly flushed at the question, causing Bunny to wonder just how close their relationship might have been. Lilly cleared her throat and said nonchalantly, "I knew him about as well as anyone else around here. Marcus was a good man but a bit of a flirt. He was bright, intelligent, passionate about his work . . ." And not bad-looking, Bunny mused, watching Lilly squirm a wee bit as she spoke. Then, how-ever, another thought blazed in the woman's eyes. "The ghost hunt," she suddenly remarked. Her dark eyes, still touched with a dose of suspicion, held to Bunny's. "I know you're claiming to be innocent of murder, and maybe you are, but I think Marcus's murder had something to do with this ghost hunt of yours."

"Hey, I'm just the chef on the show," Bunny told her, bristling a bit at the accusation. "I leave all that ghost busi-ness to the lads."

Lilly noted this before continuing. "We all knew that

Marcus especially loved to delve into Bramsford's haunted history. There is something quite wistful about the ghost story of Ann Copeland, and yet it's so hauntingly sad in the same breath. I've seen her, you know."

That gave Bunny the shivers. She shook her head, mumbling, "No. Do tell?" She was only being polite. She really hoped Lilly wouldn't tell. Yet Lilly, like every other person who's ever heard a bump in the night, was compelled to share the tale.

"It was out on the elevated patio," she stated, staring off at some spot on the spine of an old cookbook. "They say the Fleur-de-Lys room is the most haunted in the manor. That was Ann's room . . ."

Bunny's eyes bugged outward at this. Holy shizzle! That was her room! Was she serious? Did they seriously put her in the most haunted room in the haunted mansion? No wonder the rabbit had plagued her. And yet, as she inwardly melted down, Bunny forced a serene smile as Lilly continued.

". . . But that poor, weeping bride is seen in many places, including standing by the mistletoe chest. It's a wonder couples want to tie the knot in this place, given Bramsford's unlucky history. But they do, all the while the Mistletoe Bride keeps weeping over her misfortune. When she confronts you," Lilly continued, shifting her gaze back to Bunny, "they say some can feel her pain and sorrow. Most break down in tears without ever really knowing why. Marcus never did. However, the ghost of Ann Copeland held a particular fascination for him. I think he wanted to help her."

"Help her? She's dead."

Lilly nodded. "I specifically remember Marcus telling me about your new show, and how he wanted to reach out to your producer and extend an invite to come investigate here. I know he was a big fan of Brett Bloom's from his days on *Ghost Guys*. I think he believed Brett and the team might not only contact Ann's ghost but be able to help her in some way. When he received the news that *Food and Spirits* had accepted his offer and was going to film its pilot episode here, we couldn't believe our good fortune. We were all genuinely excited. International exposure would do wonders for business. We all want Bramsford Manor to be successful. Our jobs depend on it."

"You said that Marcus liked to dig up dirt on people, particularly Sir Charles," Bunny reminded her. "Yet Sir Charles could have fired him at any time. However, he could have stumbled upon something else, some other little tidbit of information about somebody else that they didn't want revealed?" As Bunny asked this, Rodger poked his head inside the office. "Did you ever hear anything regarding this?"

"Sorry to bother you, Chef," Rodger apologized, stepping into the room, "but I've used the last of the potatoes. You'll have to order more." He then turned to Bunny and said, "There was a rumor."

"What rumor?" Bunny asked, intrigued. Lilly also held her assistant in a curious look.

"The one about Bean's secret reveal during the ghost investigation," Rodger clarified with a conspiratorial grin.

Bunny's jaw dropped, recognizing that this wee tidbit of information could potentially be a huge lead. She looked at Lilly to see if she'd heard this rumor too.

Lilly wiggled her eyebrows in answer. "I did hear something about that, but it was just a rumor."

"Where did you hear this rumor?" she asked them both. "Do you have any idea what this reveal of his could have been about?"

Lilly looked at Rodger, then shook her head. "I have no idea. The thing about Marcus was that he was always very secretive about his research until he had all his ducks in a row. Once he was certain that his research was sound, only then would he share his discoveries. He was very professional in that way."

"He must have discovered something important," Bunny surmised.

"It's only a rumor," she cautioned, casting an impatient look at Rodger. "He never said a word about it to me."

"But both of you had heard this rumor," Bunny reminded them. "You must have heard it from someone." Bunny covertly crossed her fingers on both hands, hoping one of them would spill the beans. Kitchen gossip could be so proprietary!

Lilly shrugged. "I heard it from Rodger," she admitted, looking at the sous chef, who was lingering a bit too long in the kitchen office for her taste.

Rodger shrugged. "Betsy Copperfield. I overheard her mentioning it to one of our other servers the other day. I even asked Betsy about it. She claimed she didn't know what it was, only that it was bound to be a bombshell. Those are her words, not mine. Naturally, I came into the office and mentioned it to Lilly."

"Naturally," Bunny agreed with a conspiratorial grin.

"We couldn't imagine what it was," Lilly admitted. "And I didn't really care. It was typical Marcus Bean."

"Well, we will never know now, will we?" Rodger gave a sorry shake of his head and left the office, heading back to his station in the kitchen.

To Bunny, a secret reveal during a ghost hunt had all the makings of a reason for murder. She forced her excitement down and offered instead a sincere thank-you to the chef.

She then added, "As you know, we are all going to be here for a while. I might as well make myself useful and check out this rumor. And speaking of being useful, do you need any help with tonight's meal? Bangers and mash is a specialty of mine."

"I imagine so. But we're only cooking for a small party of guests tonight, and you, Bunny, are one of those guests.

Thank you for the offer." Lilly ended their little chat with a stiff smile.

Foiled again, Bunny mused, casting a wistful glance out the office window. She then thanked Lilly and left the woman in peace. Although she might not be allowed to slip into the kitchen and cook with the staff, Bunny also knew that she was no longer entirely banned from being in the place she felt most comfortable. The mere thought lightened her heart a measure.

Yet the real meat of the meeting had been the mention of this supposed rumor. Was Marcus Bean planning a surprise reveal in front of the cameras during a ghost hunt? What did it mean? And was there any truth to it? Even if it was just a wild-goose chase, Bunny was going to do her best to track that lead down, wherever it might take her.

Chapter 16

✥

"There you are."

Bunny had just left the kitchen with her sights set on finding Betsy when the familiar voice stopped her. She hadn't anticipated seeing Brett there, and attempted to cover her surprise with a quick, "Hello. Fancy seeing you here." She glanced around his broad shoulders, noting that the dining room was empty. "Where's my grandmother?"

"They've taken their séance off to the drawing room, where Mike and Ed have joined them. The guys were in town raiding a fish and chip shop. Are you hungry? They've brought back an entire sack of fried food."

"Sounds lovely," she began, noting that Brett seemed adorably contrite. She was sorry to think it was a good look on him. "However, I'm going to have to pass on the offer." Then remembering the remark about her gran, she asked, "She's not really holding a séance in there, is she?"

Brett's chuckle was deep and melodic as he denied the séance comment. However, he did admit, "She's got them spellbound, Giff particularly, and is answering their most probing questions regarding the afterlife. She's very fascinating. She told me that my grandfather was proud of me."

With eyes narrowed, Bunny remarked, "Did she, now. And is that something you wanted to hear?"

She could tell he found her question intriguing. "I didn't ask for it, no. But to your point, it made me happy to hear it. Is it, in fact, just a party trick?"

Answering the probing question in his eyes, she offered, "Sometimes I think it is. My gran is very good at reading people. She's quite observant and sometimes uses tiny things revealed in one's personality or what a person is wearing to spark a conversation. Taking a leap like that, telling you about a deceased grandfather when you've just met, takes you off guard and makes her the center of attention."

Brett shook his head in dismay. "You said she was clairvoyant, and now you're telling me she's a mentalist?"

"I said she sometimes does that. I think her aim in taking you off guard is that it allows her to make a connection. When she makes a connection, she can see things. Heck, I've seen her walk up to strangers in Tesco and tell them personal things—while they're selecting produce—that make them burst into tears. It can be embarrassing. I think she enjoys it."

"But she is the real thing, and that's why you called her," he said, just to be clear. Bunny nodded. Brett then motioned for her to walk with him out to the stately patio that overlooked the gardens and rolling lawn.

Although there was a chill in the air, Bunny found the view to be as breathtaking as it had been from the kitchen windows, only the patio sat an entire story higher and had two sets of sweeping stairs that emanated from an oval outcropping. The stairs led to a lower patio in the garden. Flanking the picturesque garden on both sides were high brick walls with rustic archways leading to yet more natural delights. On one side Bunny could see a grove of fruit trees, while on the other was a maze created out of manicured hedges, with a lovely marble bench in the center of it. Bunny imagined what a spectacular wedding venue the manor must be. Then, because she couldn't help it, she had the audacity to visualize herself as a bride, dressed in a pure and flowing gown of white while holding a spectacular bouquet of roses. Her groom—here she cast a covert glance at the man walking beside her—would be a sun-kissed, blond-headed man. Yes, she silently mused. Definitely a tall, strapping man with clear blue eyes. Her groom would be waiting in the lower garden, watching as she descended the curved staircase with her gown billowing in the breeze behind her. She was shocked at how clear this fantasy was in her mind, yet just as she was about to take her imagined groom's hand, her vision changed to something terrifying and soul-crushing. Her lovely hand with its firm young flesh and capable fingers had turned skeletal. It was now just a jumble of white phalanges atop metacarpals atop carpals reaching out to thin air. An ear-splitting cry ripped through her brain before the wailing began. It was haunting. It was soul-hacking. It was the ghost bride of Bramsford Manor. That was all Bunny knew before her knees gave out from under her.

"Whoa!" Brett cried, grabbing her before she hit the hard surface of the upper patio.

His loud cry and firm grasp had pulled her back, vanquishing the images that had taken over in her head. "Are you okay?" he asked. His face was pinched with concern.

No, she was not okay. She was terrified—terrified of what was happening to her. She had very probably just connected with the ghostly bride who haunted the manor, getting a glimpse of the horrific trauma that plagued her poor earthbound soul. It was too much for her. It was just as she feared. That dang white rabbit was a harbinger of horrors.

And yet, looking into the achingly handsome face that hovered above her, the ghostly images and wailing had been thrust out of her head. In fact, she was feeling much better now. However, what do you say to a man who has absolutely no idea what to make of you? *Nothing truthful*, she thought, and so she lied. "I tripped. I'm so embarrassed. Thank you for catching me." She forced a smile, certain that her face was as white as the bleached bones of the skeletal hand she had seen.

"No problem," Brett said, brushing the incident off as fast as she had. "Though you should probably watch your step. These flagstones aren't even close to being smooth."

Welcoming the heat back to her face, she agreed and followed him to the oval outcropping, where he leaned against the impressively thick railing.

"I brought you out here because I owe you an apology," he told her in a soft and personal tone. "I didn't know . . ." he began. "What I mean is . . . you never said . . ." He was struggling to find the words, and Bunny was certain she had never seen anyone so disarming in her life. She stared at him, knowing her cheeks glowed like embers in the night. She really couldn't help it. She really didn't care. Finally, like that wee baby bird flapping with all its might to leave the nest, Brett blurted, "I'm sorry for your loss."

"What d'ye mean?" Taken off guard, first by a romantic vision, then by a ghostly vision, and then more inklings of romance, her Scottish accent had flared up.

"Your brother . . . in that accident. I can't even imagine what that must have been like for you."

At the mention of Braiden, her heart sank again, and this time it ached. "You are referring to my story about my brother and the white rabbit," she said, feeling the embers of her cheeks fade in the cold light of day. Really, what had she been expecting? Flattery? A kiss? She mentally flagellated herself as Brett continued.

"I didn't understand your reluctance to join this show. I

didn't know it was so personal or had such a profound impact on you."

"You couldn't have known," she consoled. "It's not something I've ever shared before, or even admitted to."

Brett gave a little nod at this as he took a deep breath of the crisp fall air. "My apology isn't over," he cautioned. "I'm ashamed to admit this, but when you led us straight to the mistletoe chest and threw open the lid, I . . . I didn't know what to think. Your shock at discovering Marcus Bean was real, and yet a part of me felt that you were responsible for his murder."

Up to this point, Bunny had been moved by his words, wooed even. But that all changed. "You what?" she cried, glaring at him. "You thought I did that to that poor man? You think I'm capable of murder? *Ohmygod!*" she exclaimed, borrowing the expression from Giff.

Brett tried to take a step backward but realized he was already pressed against the railing. He had no choice. He had to stand his ground. "It . . . was your knife," he reasoned, yet to no avail.

"Well, *mister man*, I was just as shocked as you to see it used like that," she told him sternly, using her mother's favorite high-handed manner of addressing a male, her husband included. "It was stolen from the kitchen. I thought I explained that to you."

"Well, yes. I know that now. I'm . . . I'm trying to apologize here." He looked flustered. He was wringing his hands.

"This is how you apologize? You accuse first, then make nice?"

This time she noticed that he was the one turning red, and not from embarrassment. Brett gritted his teeth and doubled down. "Why shouldn't I think you did it? You've given me little reason to trust you. You don't like ghosts, or the people who investigate them. You don't want to be here. You've made that perfectly clear since day one. You're moody. You think you're better than us because you were on a popular food show with a famous host while our show had a more . . . targeted audience." He took a breath and, against his better judgment, continued. "You hide out in the kitchen all the time. And when I saw that body in the chest, it brought back bad memories of a previous investigation!" This he admitted a tad too loudly.

"*I'm moody?*" For some reason that criticism, in a sea of many, struck a nerve with her. "For your information, *mister man*, I'm bubbly. Bubbly, do y'hear? I'm also cheerful and fun to be around. And for your information, I know why you lost your last job! No need to bang on about that old news."

"Bubbly? Here's a news flash for you, you're not sounding very bubbly to me, *Bunny*." Brett, conscious on some level that he was acting like a bratty thirteen-year-old, instantly regretted saying that. However, he had flung it at her with all the gusto of a bored chimpanzee.

"Maybe that's because I'm scared, Brett," she fired back. "And I don't feel very *bubbly* when I'm scared."

Her bold admittance of fear brought him back to his senses like a hard slap in the face. He instantly felt ashamed and cradled his head in his hands. Why had he let her get under his skin like that? He had no good answer. Mustering the courage to look at her again, he said, "Christ. I know that. I know that, Bunny. That's why I wanted to apologize to you in the first place. When I realized that Bean had been murdered, I was filled with near debilitating self-pity, thinking that you were trying to sabotage the show."

Her anger flared again, but Bunny consciously schooled it, choosing instead to be honest. "But . . . I would never do that. Like it or not, this is my show too, Brett. And Giff's. And the lads'. I truly want us to succeed. I may not embrace the ghost angle of this production, but I love my role here. I shine in the kitchen."

This made him smile. "You certainly do. I never said it, but that meal you made for us was sublime. It was beyond perfect. I have no idea why our first Spirit Supper went off the rails, but it did. I am so sorry. Every time I stumble upon a great thing or embark on something that's important to me, I seem to screw it up—like this apology, for example. I also want to say that while I might have doubted you, Giff never did. He reminded me that you couldn't have murdered Marcus Bean because you were in the kitchen most of the day cooking that meal. Cody caught most of it on camera."

"That's true," she admitted. "But also, I'm not a murderer." The point was driven home, and Brett had the decency to acknowledge it.

"Deep down I always knew that, but what I didn't understand was why you had led us to the mistletoe chest in the first place."

"Then you met my grandmother," she offered knowingly.

Brett nodded. "Then I met your grandmother. I also had to remind myself that I've spent my adult life as a paranormal investigator, and that you have just presented me with what might be the most real piece of evidence of an afterlife that I've ever come across. I'm fascinated by this white rabbit you see. Your grandmother believes you're clairvoyant as well."

She looked at him, and stated with honesty, "That's what I'm afraid of. I don't want to be weird like that or like her. I want to be normal. I'm a chef. I want to cook, not converse with ghosts."

"We want you to cook too, but I think that you also need to be true to yourself, regarding this gift you might have. If you really are clairvoyant, then, as Giff loudly declared, that makes you the only one among us with any real talent. I know how to use ghost tech. Giff's mediumship is all an act, but he is entertaining. If you are the real deal, Bunny, I promise that your secret will be safe with us. We will not exploit it, but we might call on you to help us from time to time, like, for instance, now."

"You're talking about the murdered man, Marcus Bean?" With a grim set to his lips, Brett nodded. "You want me to find his murderer?"

Brett shrugged. "It's a big ask, but we cannot leave until we do. He had a traumatic death. It's reasonable to assume that he still might be here."

Dear heavens, she thought, *he actually wants me to contact the ghost of Marcus Bean.* That was crazy talk, but she didn't want to go down that road with him again. Instead, she graced him with a smile. "Let's table that for now. I have a better idea. You see, I was told, while in the kitchen just now, that there's a rumor Marcus was planning to make some big reveal on camera during your investigation last night. No one seems to know what this big reveal was, but it just might be the reason he was murdered. I happen to have the name of the person that sous chef Rodger overheard talking about it in the kitchen."

"What? You have a lead? You're already investigating the murder?"

Bunny nodded. "I accept your apology, Brett Bloom. Please accept mine. But you should know that I can go from bubbly to angry in a heartbeat when provoked. Now, are you with me?"

"I am," he said, then made a sweeping gesture with his hand. "Lead the way."

Chapter 17

Bramsford was a large manor, and finding one young woman who was on her afternoon break from the kitchen, while avoiding her grandmother and the rest of the guys in the process, was more challenging than Bunny had thought. However, after a visit to the maître d's office, which was in a hallway outside the kitchen, Callum Digby gave Bunny and Brett a little hint as to where Betsy might be found.

"On beautiful days like today, I'd look in the apple orchard if I were you. I know the servers like to take their lunches out there or spend time in one of the gardens during their breaks. To get there, go out the rear exit to the patio, go down the stairs, and walk through the archway in the right-hand wall. That leads to the orchard." Bunny thanked him, yet just before she and Brett were about to leave his office, Callum cast them a look of mild suspicion. "What do you want with Betsy? Did she do something wrong? Was her service not up to par?"

"Oh no-no." Bunny was quick to defend the girl. "Everything was fine. We just wanted a word with her."

Callum, in his fifties, with salt-and-pepper hair and blue eyes bordering on gray, carried the weight of his profession in his prim and precise movements. He lifted his chin and asked, "This wouldn't be about the murder of Marcus Bean, would it?"

"Actually, it is," Brett told him plainly. "Being a server, we wanted to see if she might have overheard something."

Callum closed the reservation book on his desk with a snap, having canceled most of them for the evening as required, and pursed his thin lips. "Even if she did overhear something Bean said, she's not allowed to repeat it. I don't tolerate eavesdropping servers."

While Bunny fumed at this, Brett changed the subject. "Did Marcus come here often?"

"Often?" Callum sneered. "Nearly every day, every day he worked here. That man was always skulking around the place, snooping through all the old books and papers. Sir Charles said that all Marcus's meals, until dinner service started, were on the house. Can you imagine? On the days he was here, you could count on Bean showing up for breakfast, lunch, and tea."

"That's very generous of Sir Charles," Bunny remarked. "I imagine that other servers might have overheard something as well."

Callum shook his head. "Could have. We have a few here, but Marcus made it a point to sit in Betsy's section. They got on very well together."

"Were they . . . you know?" Brett raised an eyebrow to relay his meaning to the maître d'.

Catching his meaning, Callum frowned and shook his head. "Heavens, no. At least I hope not. Bean was close to my age. He could have been her father."

Seeing that Brett was about to counter the argument with

an observation of his own, Bunny jumped in with a loud, "Thank you for your time," ending the conversation. Callum, while polite enough, took his job as restaurant manager very seriously, as one would expect in an establishment like Bramsford Manor. It was his job to oversee the dining rooms, the waitstaff, as well as the head chef, Lilly, and to ensure that every guest enjoyed their visit to the fullest. However, Bunny found him a wee overly managerial for her taste. She had no wish to prolong the visit and pulled Brett out of the office with her.

"Hey, maybe he knows something about the murder," Brett protested.

"He might," she agreed, heading for the patio once again. "However, he's just told us something important. Marcus made it a point to sit in Betsy's section. Why would that be?"

To her annoyance, Brett grinned. "He was a guy. The obvious reason is because she's cute."

Bunny paused in her step to cast him a chiding look. Secretly she wanted to snarl at him, but thankfully refrained. Men could be so blunt sometimes about their hungers! Instead, she offered, "Fair enough. But to my point, he just gave credence to what Rodger said about Betsy. He said that he overheard Betsy talking to another server about some big reveal during the night's investigation. If Betsy knew Marcus well, he might have told her about it."

"You think that she knows what this secret reveal was about?"

"If Bean took most of his meals in the dining room in her section, that speaks of friendship, or familiarity at best."

"Or, to my point, infatuation," Brett added with a pointed look. "You forget, we spent an entire day with the dude. I wouldn't put infatuation with a hot waitress beyond him."

Hot waitress? He thought her hot? Why did that silly

statement make her cheeks feel like they were on fire? Bloody men! Again, she forced a smile. "Great. Noted. Either way we need to talk with the young lady before she heads back to work."

As the two proceeded down the sweeping patio steps, this time Bunny was too miffed about the hot waitress comment to be accosted by feelings and visions of the ghost bride. Then, once in the garden, they headed for the correct archway in the ancient wall. The moment Bunny passed beneath the crumbling stone, she felt she had entered another world, a quieter world filled with sunlight, birdsong, and the gentle rustling of leaves. Since the apples were ripe and many had already fallen, it not only smelled like a cider mill, but there was a slight buzzing sound as well. That came from the bees. As Brett and Bunny gingerly walked along the many rows of fruit trees, careful not to provoke the buzzing insects, they searched for Betsy. Since the trees were thick with both leaves and fruit, it wasn't an easy task. In fact, they both assumed they had missed her until they were on their way back. That's when they finally spotted the pretty waitress sitting against a west-facing wall. Her tear-streaked face glistened in the afternoon sun. The moment she heard their footsteps, her eyes flew open, spotting them. She instantly stiffened and wiped her cheeks with the backs of her hands.

Bunny gingerly approached. "We're so sorry to have disturbed you," she said softly. "We were told that you might be here, taking your lunch."

"What do you want with me?" The girl looked startled by this. "Is something wrong?" Her soulful brown eyes skipped past Bunny and latched onto Brett. The moment they did, Betsy ran a hand over her hair and sat up a little higher. Then, to Bunny's further dismay, the girl smiled.

Brett took a step closer and smiled back. "Nothing's wrong, Betsy," he assured her before gracefully squatting, putting him at eye level with the young woman. "We'd just like a word with you regarding Marcus Bean."

Hearing the name of the dead man, the girl's face pulled into a look of fright. *Och, we've struck a nerve*, Bunny thought. *There's definitely a connection here, but what exactly is it? Heaven forbid, but could Brett be correct?* Deciding to strike while the proverbial iron was hot, she asked, "We've heard that Marcus Bean was very fond of you and only sat in your section in the dining room. Is that correct?"

"What . . . what is this?" Betsy pushed her back against the high garden wall and scrambled to her feet. "Why are you asking me about this?"

"Because he was murdered," Bunny stated plainly, pinning the girl with her large, unblinking green eyes.

Betsy didn't like that one bit. "I know that!" she snapped at them. "It's so sad! It's so terrible!" Then, filling with either sadness or remorse (Bunny couldn't determine which), Betsy added, "He was such a kind man."

"Exactly how kind was he?" she pressed.

"It is sad," Brett cut in, casting Bunny a cautionary look— one she took to mean *retract the claws*. He continued. "We're all saddened by his death, and that's why Ms. MacBride and I are here. We've been told that you might have overheard something Marcus said, something about a secret big reveal he might have been planning during our ghost hunt. We think it might be important. We'd like you to walk us through that moment if you can."

"Where did you hear that?" The girl looked suspicious.

Bunny, thinking how nice it would be to be invited back into the kitchen, wanted to protect her source. She simply said, "Someone overheard you talking with another server. By the way, how many people did you mention this to?"

Bunny could sense that she'd gotten under the girl's skin. It was only because Brett had gotten under hers. She inwardly chided herself for letting that happen. However, if she was ever to get to the truth regarding the murder of Marcus Bean, she was going to have to appear trustworthy. That shouldn't be hard for a friendly, sweet-natured person like her, should it? For heaven's sake, that was her brand! Bunny then cast a covert glance at hunky Brett before shifting her gaze to the youthful waitress—wholesome, round-cheeked complexion and all. She then revealed her most trustworthy, television smile. "Let me rephrase that, m'dear. If you did happen to overhear something interesting, and you happened to mention this interesting tidbit, who might you have mentioned it to?"

Betsy seemed more at ease under this kinder smile and paused to think. With a carefree shrug, she offered, "I told my mate, Lewis."

"When you say mate, does that mean you're dating?" Brett asked. Betsy blushed.

"Friend. Lewis is my friend. He works with me."

"Let's back up a minute," Brett said. "Explain how you overheard this information in the first place?"

"Marcus and I were friends of a sort," she told him. "He liked to sit in my section and talk with me. Sometimes he'd tell me things about Bramsford's history. He was really into history. Other times we'd talk about news or the movies we'd just seen."

"Did you ever see a movie together?" Bunny inquired, trying her hardest to appear merely friendly and not accusatory. Obviously, it was a hard nuance to capture.

"What are you insinuating?" Betsy snapped at her. "Marcus was in his late forties. I'm twenty-one. That's gross!" She glared at Bunny before bringing her attention back to Brett.

"You wanted to know how I overheard him talking about this big reveal?" Brett nodded. "Mr. Bean was taking his three o'clock tea as usual. He also had the London *Times* with him, which was also his habit. I brought him his usual turkey sandwich and biscuits and was just about to pour his tea when I asked him about the ghost hunt that he couldn't stop talking about. He told me a little bit about what you guys do and what you had planned to do at Bramsford. I thought it was pretty cool. I'm not a fan of ghosts but I have a healthy respect for them. Marcus was really excited about your visit. Then his phone rang. I don't know who was on the other end, but it seemed important, so I topped off his tea and set the pot on the table. I was just about to walk away when I heard him say that he had stumbled upon something big, something groundbreaking that he wasn't going to mention to anyone until the cameras were rolling. It was going to be a bombshell."

"Whoa," Bunny breathed. "And you didn't hear anything else?"

"Nope. I wasn't even supposed to hear that much, I'm sure. And I certainly didn't want to ask him about it either. Digby would have my job for that. But . . . but I thought it was interesting." At the thought, moisture began to form in Betsy's eyes. "We're not supposed to eavesdrop, and I'm certain that I shouldn't have said anything about it either. I didn't think there was any harm in telling a friend. Lewis was fond of Marcus as well. Marcus was always kind to us. Always." Her bottom lip began to quiver. "He had a secret, and . . . and I think it got him killed. I . . . might be partly to blame. I didn't mean for anyone to hear us talking, but Rodger did. He's a good man, and always jokes with us. We were standing in the kitchen when I told Lewis, and Rodger walked in with a tray of pork chops. He raised his eyebrows at us and went on cooking. I should have known. Once one person knows, word gets around."

Bunny could see that the thought was distressing to the

young woman and was likely the reason she'd been crying in the first place when they found her. She had misjudged Betsy and was feeling guilty about it. Besides, as she well knew, grief from loss was the hardest emotion to come to terms with. Bunny was about to console her when Brett beat her to it.

"Betsy, you can't blame yourself for what happened to Marcus Bean. However, if it was groundbreaking information that was going to be revealed during our ghost hunt, I'd love to know what it was."

"That's what's eating me up, Brett! I knew it was big news. A secret reveal is exciting. That's why I might have mentioned it to Morgan as well, to see if she knew what it was about. If I would have known it would get him killed, I would have kept my big mouth shut!" She then burst into a fit of tears. Bunny was ashamed to think that she was happy to learn that Betsy Copperfield ugly-cried. It was so unsettling that the stoic Brett Bloom slowly backed into the apple grove.

It's okay," Bunny assured the girl. "It's not your fault, Betsy. But I am curious. Why Morgan?"

Betsy hiccoughed and tried to catch her breath. "Because . . . she and Marcus were friends too. But I don't think she knew about Marcus's big reveal."

"Thank you for talking with us," Bunny told the girl, sincerely. "You've been a great help, and I'm truly sorry for your loss."

"Tha . . . thank you, Ms. MacBride. Bu . . . but how did I help when I might have gotten him killed?" Bless her, she looked confused.

Offering her kindest smile, Bunny explained, "Because you didn't know what Marcus Bean had stumbled across. The person who murdered him did. The fact that Rodger overheard you talking about it was a lucky stroke for us. We might not know what the information was, who knew about it, or who had the most to lose by it, but it gives us a possible motive."

Betsy sniffled and wiped her tears away again. "What can you do about it now?"

"Find the information he'd stumbled upon in the first place. If it was found once, it can be found again."

Chapter 18

"I'm sorry, but crying unsettles me," Brett explained the moment Bunny caught up with him in the orchard. Truthfully, he hadn't gone far, but he also hadn't been willing to return and face the tears. "It makes me feel helpless," he explained, marching posthaste along the rows of apple trees toward the ancient archway. "Especially when a girl is crying. It makes me feel as if I've done something wrong."

"Do you have a habit of making girls cry?" With his fine looks Bunny imagined he left a wake of tears wherever he went.

He looked at her, offering, "I made my mom cry when I told her that I was going to hunt ghosts for a living. She cried over that one for a couple of days. That was hard to deal with."

"I'm sorry," she said, running a little to catch up with his long strides.

"When I was younger, I made my sister cry all the time, but that was for fun. I don't mind her tears . . . unless they're *real*," he clarified.

"And what about girlfriends?" Bunny probed as they walked under the archway, landing in the garden once again. "Do you make them cry as well?"

Brett stopped walking and looked at her. "I don't mean to. But now that I think about it, every relationship I've had usually ends in tears. Of course, that comes after the door slamming and the insults." He looked at his feet a moment before glancing up at her through thick, dark eyelashes. "I'm probably not the easiest guy to understand."

It was delivered with such sincerity that her heart skipped a beat. She covered it gracefully with a wave of her hand. "Oh posh! I find all men in general to be confounding. You're in good company, Brett Bloom." That made him grin. "Now, regarding tears, I'm not a fan either, but I can handle them. For instance, in Betsy's case they were incredibly productive. While the poor girl suffered loss and a real feeling of guilt, she has just confirmed for us that Marcus Bean stumbled on an explosive bit of information that might possibly have gotten him killed. I can't think of any other reason to stab him in the heart with a stolen knife, can you?"

With hands on hips and eyebrows furrowed at her, he said, "Unfortunately, I can. We just discussed it. Remember? Insults, slamming doors, followed by bouts of hideous crying? Love, Bunny. Love can drive people to madness."

"Are you saying that there are two possible motives for murder here?"

"At least," he replied. "And the reason I brought up love in the first place is because I don't believe her. I don't believe that Betsy and Marcus were merely friends. She's lying about their relationship, but I can't say with certainty why that is, just yet."

"You think they were lovers? You think they were embroiled in a tawdry winter-spring romance? She said the notion was gross." As she offered this, she could see that he was battling a grin. Why did that irk her?

Brett shrugged. "I can't say. I just don't believe her."

Bunny placed her hands on her hips as well. "What, are you an expert on women's body language now?"

"Obviously not or I wouldn't make them cry so often. All I'm saying is that I have a hunch, and you of all people should respect that."

She hadn't expected him to go for the jugular, but he had. "Touché, Bloom."

They found the rest of their party ensconced in Bramsford's stunning, wood paneled, historic library, a room that immediately captured Bunny's imagination. She had briefly seen this room when they had first arrived, but hadn't given it much thought, due to the fact that she was in a haunted manor and had a stellar meal to prepare. Also, for the life of her, she couldn't remember where it was located. It was as far from the kitchen as one could get, being tucked away at the end of the west wing of the manor. Thankfully, Brett had a much deeper knowledge of the house than she had. It was Peter Billingsley who told them to check the library in the first place. The moment Bunny entered the two-story room with a spiral staircase and three arched windows that spanned both stories, she felt like Belle from Disney's *Beauty and the Beast*. And just like Belle, she pondered the fact that this stunning library, filled to the gills with old books from every era, might just make up for the fact that this castle also housed a beast along with a handful of ghosts. Then, just as that thought worked its way through her imagination, she turned around and saw an image that jarred her back to reality.

"Grandma! What are you doing sitting on the floor like that . . . and with Giff?"

It was so odd she did a double take. Sure enough, Ella MacBride was sitting cross-legged on the worn yet beautiful Turkish carpet opposite Giff, who was sitting in the same pose. Their knees were touching, and Ella was murmuring to him while tapping his forehead with her finger.

"Hello, luv." Granny Mac opened her eyes and smiled beatifically at her granddaughter. "Giff was very upset at the possibility that you might be a medium, so I thought I'd try to help him open up his own third eye and give it a go."

"It's true," came a voice from over the middle seating area. Illuminated from the light of the third arched window, Bunny could see Mike Miller, who looked to be reading a very old book on witches. Ed was also reading a book, while Cody appeared to be waking from a nap.

"Your grandma thinks Giff is a sensitive," Ed remarked with a wink.

"He's sensitive, alright," Mike added. "Had a bit of a meltdown after you two left us."

"Hey," Giff snapped at him, "I'm working here. It takes great concentration to open one's third eye. Bunny," he continued, shifting his focus to her, "your grandma is a gem. Not only has she assured me that love is on the horizon, but she also believes that I have hidden talent that needs to be coaxed out of me. We're in the process of coaxing, aren't we, Ella?"

"We're trying to meditate and tap into the fourth dimension," she clarified.

Ed closed his book. "Whatever talent Giff has is so deep down there that it's either going to take a miracle, or a handsy ghost encounter to spook it out of him."

Even Giff laughed at this. "That may be, but I have to earn my keep somehow, now that Bunny can both cook and connect to spirits."

"Look," Bunny addressed him, "I'm happy for you, Giff.

I hope it works. As for me, I don't know what I have, and I certainly can't control it. I prefer the kitchen to ghostly white rabbits. Rest assured, I'm not about to usurp your place on the show. You were doing just fine up until we found that body."

"I'm working with you next, dear," Granny Mac informed her. "For whatever reason, you were led to discover a body in a historic chest that once housed a spirit who still lingers here. There are so many layers to this mystery that we need to peel them back one at a time to fully understand what's going on here and why. Don't go anywhere."

Bunny exchanged a look with Brett, before continuing. "About that body. Brett and I have been poking around in the world of the living, asking important questions. We think we know why Marcus Bean was murdered."

Bunny had everyone's attention, including Giff's. "What have you discovered?"

"It's been confirmed that Marcus Bean uncovered some piece of explosive evidence that he was planning to reveal to the cameras during the ghost hunt. Obviously, someone found out before he had the chance."

"Who do you think it was?" Giff asked.

"It could be anyone in the manor," Brett informed them. "While there might be other motives regarding Bean's murder, we feel that this particular motive might be the strongest. The only trouble is we don't know what information Bean stumbled upon, or who would want him silenced."

"There are two main things to consider regarding this murder," Bunny told them. "The first is that the murderer took my boning knife from the kitchen, either when it was closed or when no one was looking. The second thing to consider is that it was Betsy Copperfield, the server, who overheard Marcus Bean on the phone discussing this big discovery he was going to reveal during the ghost hunt. Regarding my knife, five people have keys to the kitchen: Lilly Plum; Sir Charles; his sister, Morgan; Callum Digby; and Peter Billingsley. Any one of them could have snuck in there after hours to steal it from my knife kit. Regarding this rumor about Marcus's big reveal, Betsy told two people, Morgan and a server named Lewis. Betsy and Lewis were overheard in the kitchen by a sous chef named Rodger, who immediately told Lilly. Betsy feels that Lilly, a known lover of gossip, might have spread the news even wider."

"Well, there are your suspects," Cody said. "It has to be either Lilly, Morgan, Rodger, this Lewis person, or, and I hate to add her to this list, but I feel I have to, Betsy. All of them were told about Marcus's big reveal, and all of them had access to the kitchen."

"Well done, Veronica Mars," Giff said, golf-clapping for him. "Pointing out the obvious connection. However, if television detectives taught me anything it's that it's never that simple."

"I think Giff is correct," Brett offered. "Bunny has already questioned Lilly. And both of us talked with Betsy. However, think about the historian and his job. If there was some piece of information uncovered that could be damaging to the history of Bramsford Manor, who has the most to lose?"

Giff raised his hand pretending he was in class. "Ooh! Ooh! I know this. It's Sir Charles Wallingford, or his sister, Morgan. But mostly Sir Charles. I'll tell you what. Since my third eye has been exercised by a true professional, I volunteer to throw myself on my sword—to boldly walk into the viper's nest. In other words, I volunteer to interrogate the man."

"I thought you might," Brett said with a wry grin. "That's very noble of you, but Bunny and I are going with you."

"I think that's wise," Granny Mac said. Bunny noted that

the woman's carefree demeanor had shifted, and that her gran was now looking into that *other place* as she spoke. "There is evil lurking within these walls, and it's not on the other side. It's here, with the living. It's shifty. It's sly. It's clever. And it is also capable of great harm. You three must stay together, as we will stay together," she said, gesturing to the three men lounging in the comfy library chairs. "There is safety in numbers."

Brett stared at the older woman and asked, "Who is capable of great evil? Who is responsible for Marcus Bean's murder? Do you have a name?"

Granny Mac shook her head. "That I cannot tell you. However, we might be able to glean some answers we seek from those on the other side."

Chapter 19

"Do you think she can really do it? Probe for answers on the other side?" Giff looked intrigued. It was then Bunny recalled that he had never encountered a spirit before. If he had she was certain the look on his face would be more pensive and fearful, like the look on Brett's face.

"I doubt it," she told him as they marched down the echoing hallway toward the long gallery. "It's not that easy. If it was, every psychic would be doing it."

"But she has the second sight," Giff protested.

"That may be," Bunny admitted. "But we're investigating a murder. I doubt that the lingering spirits haunting this manor give a fig for what occurred here last night. Doubt they were even paying attention."

"She's right," Brett said, casting Bunny a nod. "Not the part about them paying attention, but we really don't know what type of haunting we're dealing with to begin with. It could be a residual haunting, or an intelligent one."

Giff stopped walking and stared at him. "What? Are you telling me there's more than one type of ghost?" He looked gobsmacked by the notion. Brett looked merely serious.

"Yes. Did you not read the source material I sent you? Have you even watched an episode of *Ghost Guys*?" The answer was clear on Giff's face. Apparently, he had not done either of those things.

"Forgive me for being too busy researching mediumship and creating a viable social media presence to read that packet you sent me. We're here to connect with ghosts. I assumed they were all the same."

"There are residual hauntings, intelligent hauntings, poltergeist activity, demonic activity, and shadow-people stuff, which no one really knows much about, only that they're creepy. What I believe we have here is either a residual haunting, which is basically negative energy that is so strong it gets imprinted on the atmosphere where it then replays repeatedly, like a clip of a movie; or it could be an intelligent haunting, where the spirit can interact with the living. However, ghosts, to my knowledge, aren't informants."

"What if Bean is still here, like Granny Mac is suggesting?" Giff argued.

"She might be able to contact him, but even if she can, how do we know the information is correct? It also must be proven in a court of law."

"Good point," Bunny said, smiling up at him. They continued walking and soon realized that the man they were looking for wasn't tucked away in his private wing at the other end of the manor but standing in the long gallery arguing with DCI Standish.

"Good afternoon, DCI Standish," Bunny said, walking up to the man who had taken her into custody the night before for murder. She met his curious gaze with a smile. She then shifted her attention to the man standing next to him, Sir Charles, and he looked fraught with worry.

"I wish it was a good afternoon," Sir Charles told them, watching as a team of forensic investigators, dressed head to toe in white protective gear, photographed and collected yet more evidence in the historic mistletoe chest. "Careful with that!" he cried as a woman accidentally bumped the open lid, causing it to slam shut with authority. Sir Charles flinched, as did Giff. The people in white were getting ready to roll the chest back on its side to better examine the bloodstained wood on the bottom as well as the soiled tile floor beneath it. "I do so hate it when strangers fiddle with a piece of our history," he admitted to Bunny, who was now standing beside him. The aristocrat, as if watching a beloved child endure a bout of rough handling from a school bully, rounded on the chief inspector. "What do you think you're doing, handling my relic like that? That, dear sir, is a three-hundred-year-old antique!"

"That may be, but it's still the crime scene," DCI Standish remarked coolly.

Sir Charles, nervously wringing his hands as he watched the chest get put through its paces, offered another possibility. "Couldn't the crime scene be elsewhere . . . perhaps a scuffle in one of the hotel rooms? It could have gotten heated; Bean could have been stabbed in the chest, and the murderer could have transported the body in a bag or something, due to the blood. I will concede that the chest makes a rather ironic resting place."

DCI Standish held the aristocrat in an ice-hard look. "That's not how it happened," he said. "Bean's body was never transported. He was led right here to this chest," the cop explained, staring at Bunny as he did so. "Since the lid on the chest was closed, there's a strong possibility that he was asked to lift it. Being the manor's historian, he would have had permission to do so." He glanced at Sir Charles for confirmation. Sir Charles nodded, and Standish continued. "Let's say this person was a guest, one with a particular interest in the old mistletoe chest. Perhaps a ghost hunter newly invited to investigate—"

"Whoa there, Inspector," Brett interrupted. "That's conjecture. That never happened, and we know that for a fact because all of us from *Food and Spirits* were busy. We've explained that to you already and have provided evidence. However, there is a very strong possibility that we were meant to find Marcus Bean during our investigation."

"Well, one of your team members blew the surprise and discovered him a bit early."

Bunny, ruffled by his pointed look, offered, "In my defense, sir, it would have been far worse had the body been discovered after midnight with cameras rolling. It would have been caught on tape, and you would have been pulled from your warm bed."

"Maybe," he replied, staring at her through narrowed eyes. He then shifted his focus. "Regarding the scene of the crime, once Bean opened the lid and turned to face whoever had convinced him to show them the chest, we believe he was then immediately impaled with Ms. MacBride's kitchen knife."

"My *stolen* kitchen knife," she corrected then shuddered at the thought.

"Right," he acknowledged with impatience before continuing. "The poor bloke likely didn't realize what hit him until it was too late. There's a blood splatter that hit the front of the chest and a few drops on the floor, around the right front leg." DCI Standish pointed a thick finger at the small, stout leg in question. "Most of the blood was absorbed by Bean's clothing and, of course, the wood at the bottom of the chest."

"My poor relic," Sir Charles uttered, and placed a hand on his forehead. He removed his hand and stated, "I'm calling the antique restorers the moment your people are finished, Inspector. I still cannot believe some heathen would debase my relic like that."

Clearly the detective chief inspector didn't know what to say to that. Instead, he looked at the three young people gawking at the forensic inspectors and asked, "Why are you three here?"

"Because, DCI Standish, you told us that we couldn't leave the manor." Bunny, embracing her passive-aggressive side, smiled at him.

"You know that's not what I mean."

She did, but she was hardly going to tell the detective chief inspector that she, Brett, and Giff were trying to find the murderer, and next on their suspect list was the man they were standing next to, bemoaning the misuse of his historic chest.

Brett, however, had no such qualms. "Actually, sir, we were on our way to speak with Sir Charles." The man in question cast him a thoughtful look. DCI Standish looked merely suspicious.

"Why? What's this about? I hope you're not playing detective. That's my job. You three are still suspects."

"We do want to investigate, Inspector," Brett admitted. "Only our investigation looks a tad different from yours."

"What he means," Giff chimed in with a twinkle in his eyes, "is that our investigation focuses on the other side — the dearly departed, not the boring old living. What do they know? And thanks to the psychopath who despoiled the family chest, we just might have another disgruntled spirit on our hands." Here Giff paused and closed his eyes. He then held up his hands and pressed his thumb and middle finger together mimicking Granny Mac. Then, for effect, he mumbled a chant, opened his eyes with a start, and declared, "Yep. It's just as I thought. Bean's still here and he's ready to talk."

Bunny rolled her eyes at him before whispering, "We explained to you that's not how it works."

"What do you know?" he fired back in a like whisper. "You're still stuck on ghost rabbits." And just as he stated that, Bunny's heart clenched painfully in her chest. That was because at that very moment she caught the unsettling scent of cigarettes comingling with a manly, soapy scent. A spicy, soapy scent. *I'll be darned*, she thought. *Is that Old Spice Swagger I'm smelling?* Granny Mac had smelled it too. That's when Bunny knew, beyond the shadow of a doubt, that the spirit of Marcus Bean was lingering just beyond in the fourth dimension. After casting a pointed look at Giff, entertaining a flash of a thought that he just might have sensed it as well, she inwardly cringed. Then she drew in a sharp breath. Hopper, aka the white rabbit of doom, was peeking at her from behind the chest and through a pair of white-covered legs, as if mocking her. The fact that he wiggled his adorable pink nose at her drove that thought home. He was mocking her. She narrowed her eyes at him, and he vanished.

"I don't see why they can't continue their ghost hunt," she heard Sir Charles say.

"We're in the middle of a murder investigation here. Do you really feel that's necessary?" There was mild irritation in the detective's voice as he said this.

"Bean brought them here for that purpose. We told them they could. I say, why not?"

"Not tonight," Standish grumbled. "We're still working here."

"Very well, tomorrow night then."

Bunny got the feeling that Sir Charles's sudden championing of their ghost hunt had more to do with the way the police were treating his antique chest than fulfilling a promise.

Sensing that Standish was about to argue this, Bunny broke in. "Might we continue this conversation in your office, sir? All this talk of murder and bodies has put me on edge."

"Yes. Yes, my dear. Grand suggestion. Truth be told, I find I don't have the stomach to watch another degradation of my family heirloom."

"What a sorry turn of events," Sir Charles said as he poured a measure of pricey amber liquid into four awaiting glasses. He replaced the crystal decanter on the cart and handed out the glasses. Bunny realized the moment she took a good sniff of it that it was fine Scotch whiskey, the good stuff, single barrel, finely aged, and with a peaty richness only found in the Highlands. In one sip she was back in her home country, sitting around her father's hearth, watching him sip the same good whiskey while he talked about his cattle. Granny Mac had been fond of a nip of whiskey as well, while her mother preferred wine. Truth be told, Bunny preferred wine too, but there was nothing like a shot of good Scotch whiskey served neat.

The study Sir Charles had brought them to in his private wing was a stunning display of baronial wealth, from the rich oak paneling to the imported burgundy carpet and every handsome piece of heavy furniture so perfectly displayed. As Bunny scanned the walls, filled with pictures, framed documents, a family crest, and a display of historic swords and shields, she was reminded of the story Lilly had told her in the kitchen. She had said that Marcus had a knack for getting under his employer's skin, particularly when it came to shedding new light on a piece of family history. For instance, Charles's ancestor, Sir Winston Wallingford, had never fought in World War I, and yet his picture still hung on the wall, costumed in the uniform of a hero. The things money could buy, she mused. Was Sir Winston's picture still there as a reminder of one man's folly and deception, or did it remain because the fiction was better than the truth? Bunny didn't know, but she had to admit, Sir Winston Wallingford cut a handsome figure in a uniform.

"So, you three are still bent on continuing with this ghost hunt of yours?" He tilted his handsome head as he looked at them.

"We'd like to," Brett told him plainly. "We feel that we might still be able to salvage our show while we wait for things here to clear up regarding the murder."

"You really wish to confront the Mistletoe Bride?"

Brett nodded.

"Many have," Sir Charles continued, "and the experience is not said to be very pleasant. Some merely see her. Some only hear her pitiful moans. However, there are some who encounter her and experience a disturbing sense of dread and sorrow. It's so strong it can affect them for days."

"Sounds pleasant," Giff remarked mockingly. "I can't wait."

Sir Charles waved a hand nonchalantly. "Not to worry. Most just get a good fright. As for me, I've seen her a few times now, and every time I do it makes me believe that Bramsford Manor is the rightful owner of the mistletoe chest and the legend. It's what I've been trying to prove for years now. Otherwise, we merely have an old chest, a white lady, and a handful of random ghosts."

"Are you telling us that we can conduct our investigation tomorrow night?" Bunny thought Brett looked adorably hopeful.

"I say, why not. What do we have to lose now? We've already lost a good man and a piece of the family history." Sir Charles lifted his glass in the air and proposed a toast. "To Marcus Bean, a good man and a passionate historian." Everyone took a sip before Sir Charles settled back in his lush leather chair.

"How long have you known Marcus?" Brett asked, posing the question to seem merely curious and not probing.

Sir Charles shrugged. "At least ten years. He studied history at Oxford, became a professor, and taught at the University of Reading, just north of here. That's where I met him. Bean was passionate about history, especially local history. I formally employed him as the manor's historian over five years ago, particularly to brush up on our family history and to verify, if he could, our claim to the Mistletoe Bride legend. As I've mentioned, Bramsford Manor isn't the only grand home in the realm to claim the privilege. The trouble is many palaces, manors, and houses in the UK report hauntings by white ladies and forlorn brides. It's easy to combine a local haunting with a legend like ours."

"I agree," Brett said, hanging on Sir Charles's every word. "I've investigated many white ladies here in the UK. Every old tower has one."

"Indeed." Sir Charles smiled. "However, Bramsford is the only manor I'm aware of that has a historic chest from the correct period. Sure, others have come up with a chest as well. Most are marketing ploys. Bean had investigated many of them and had equally discredited them. Most old chests, he told me, were from the nineteenth century. Ours, however, has been authenticated as being the correct style and age for the legend. It's from the late seventeenth century, which fits the timeline of our tragic story. It also has the intricate carving of mistletoe on the front of it, giving rise to the name of the haunting. Take all that, combine it with our tragic white lady and the fact that our family has been linked to the legend for centuries, and it gives credit to our claim."

"And that claim is important, why?" Bunny probed, wanting Sir Charles to explain it to them again.

"Because, Ms. MacBride, as I might have stated before,

that old chest and the legend of the Mistletoe Bride is very good for business. Travelers not only love a good bit of history, but a haunting as well."

"That's very savvy of you," Giff offered with a cheeky grin. "But I have another question. Was Bean ever able to prove, beyond the shadow of a doubt, that the legend was true and that it happened here?"

"He was working on it," Sir Charles told them with a maudlin expression in his eyes. "It was his passion. And the worst part is, I believe he was very close to proving it."

"Do you have proof of that?" Brett questioned.

"Not hard proof, unfortunately. However, about a week ago he told me that he had found something remarkable that could not only prove our claim to the legend but would also shed new light on the historic tragedy that was said to have occurred here."

Bunny inhaled sharply. Did Marcus Bean tell Sir Charles of his big reveal? Could Sir Charles have been on the other end of the phone conversation that Betsy Copperfield had overheard? Bursting with curiosity, she asked, "He told you that he had found something important? Did he tell you what it was?" The fact that Sir Charles shook his head dashed her hopes.

"Said he couldn't tell me yet but would reveal this important piece of information when the timing was right."

For instance, during the filming of the ghost hunt, Bunny thought, studying Sir Charles. Thanks to Betsy Copperfield, she now believed that's exactly what Bean had meant to do, only someone stopped him before he could do it. She wasn't fully convinced of Sir Charles's ignorance. Denial was a powerful ploy and often hard to disprove. Unfortunately, Brett was having a hard time believing this as well, only it showed on his pinched and puzzled face.

"And you didn't press him on that? That didn't bother you?"

"If you're asking whether I killed Marcus Bean, Mr. Bloom, my answer is no. I did not kill my friend. Why would I? He worked for me. He was on my side . . . well, most of the time, at any rate. Most importantly, I believe he had actually found a piece of information that connected Bramsford Manor with the Mistletoe Bride legend."

"Did he specifically tell you that?" Bunny asked.

"He strongly hinted at it."

"Do you think he told anybody else about it?" Giff asked.

"Why would he if he wouldn't tell me? Bean, being a dogged historian, had a dramatic flair about him. He liked to reveal his findings in a grand manner. Sometimes it was annoying and other times it was entertaining. I believe that to him a little theatric flair gave credence to all those long hours spent in the trenches, so to speak. It wouldn't be like him to drop such an important morsel of knowledge willy-nilly. He liked to hint at it first and talk it up a bit before delivering his punch. I admired his style."

Unless that important morsel of knowledge didn't benefit Sir Charles as much as it might have benefited another, Bunny thought. Otherwise, why the surprise? Why keep his employer in the dark? She looked at the man in question. Even if he did know what Bean had uncovered, he wasn't about to tell them now. Therefore, Bunny struck out on another tack. "Sir Charles, whatever it was that Mr. Bean had uncovered, we think it might be the reason he was murdered." There. Her theory was out in the open. She then felt compelled to add, "We also believe he was going to make this big reveal during our investigation."

Sir Charles's lips twitched upward, not forming a complete smile, but an echo of one. "That sounds about right, the fool. He was very excited to have you here."

"Sir," Brett said, holding Sir Charles in a concerned gaze. "The fact that he was murdered in that historic chest indicates to us that somebody learned the nature of this information, and they didn't like it. We also believe the murderer chose the mistletoe chest as the site of the crime out of either spite or irony. That old chest, after all, was the focus of his studies."

"This is true, and it's a tragedy," he proclaimed. "The murder is bad enough, but using the mistletoe chest as a bloody coffin goes beyond the pale!"

"Do you have any idea who might have wanted Marcus dead or out of the way?"

Sir Charles finished the last swig of his whiskey and studied his empty glass a moment before answering. "I haven't a clue, Mr. Bloom." Silence fell and he took a deep breath before continuing. "The truth is, I'm not certain Bean was murdered due to his profession or what he might have uncovered. You only saw the professional side of Marcus Bean, and that was only for the space of a day or two. Sure, Marcus was a bang-up historian, but he wasn't a saint. He knew how to dig up information on people, information best left buried. He also had an eye for the ladies, even the married ones."

Bunny had heard as much before, but it got her thinking. If Marcus had uncovered an unsavory bit of information on someone at the manor, he could have been blackmailing them. Otherwise, what was the point of prying into people's private lives? Giggles? Gossip? It didn't sound right. This person, who might have had something to hide, would have known Marcus's role at the manor and could have even staged the murder to appear that it was somehow connected to the Mistletoe Bride legend. That way it would shed suspicion on Sir Charles, and even on them, the team of *Food &*

Spirits. It would be an easy deception to pull off, and a clever one. Bunny made a mental note of it.

Then there was also the suggestion that Marcus Bean was a player. Maybe he had dallied with the wrong woman or had broken some poor lady's heart. The old quote, *Heaven has no rage like love to hatred turned, nor hell a fury like a woman scorned*, sprang to her mind, reminding her that the playwright William Congreve knew all too well that love could be a dangerous, deadly game. Also, she considered the fact that Brett didn't believe Marcus Bean and Betsy Copperfield were merely "work" friends. For one, Betsy had been very distraught. She also claimed to have overheard Bean talking about this mysterious big reveal. What did it all mean? As possibilities and theories swirled in Bunny's mind, there was something about the look on Sir Charles's face that stopped her in mid-thought. Maybe it wasn't so much a look, she mused, than a premonition. She took the last sip of her whiskey and set down the glass.

"You know who Marcus Bean was having an affair with, don't you?" This was met with a forcibly blank look. Bunny wasn't buying it. "You should tell us who it was, Sir Charles. As it stands, Marcus Bean's murder doesn't look good for you or for us. If we can find another suspect, it might help to clear your name and ours."

"Whoa there. I thought you three were merely here to investigate the dead, not the living."

"We are," Giff assured him with a cheeky nod. "We're prepared to launch a full paranormal investigation tomorrow night. There's a rich tapestry of departed souls in this place, and we will get answers. Speaking of answers, the young bride—Ann's her name, I believe?—she's calling to me now. She's here, in this room, and she's crying." He closed his eyes. Bunny could tell he was about to launch into a bout of paranormal folly when Brett, thankfully, stopped him.

"Save your gift for later, buddy," he told him, placing a hand on Giff's arm. Giff peeled one eye open and stared.

"Right. Don't wish to waste them. We've talked about this, but in my defense, when the voices come . . ."

Bunny, seizing her opportunity, took the reins of the conversation again. "What's her name? All we need is a name."

Sir Charles huffed and stood from his chair. "That, I'm afraid, is the problem. Her name is Morgan. My sister."

Chapter 20

"I honestly didn't see that coming," Brett admitted as they left Sir Charles's vast apartments. "His married sister was having an affair with his historian friend, and he knew about it. There's a very good chance that Mr. Green, Morgan's husband, knew about it too. Maybe we should talk with him."

"We know nothing about him, or where he lives," Bunny reminded them. "But he would have a motive if what Sir Charles was telling us is true."

"I say we go straight to the horse's mouth with this one," Giff added. "In other words, we need to pay the lovely Morgan Wallingford-Green a visit. Let's see if we can get her to talk."

"Let's put her at the top of our list for tomorrow," Bunny offered with a sigh. "Right now, I'm not only starving, but I'm tired as well. I didn't get much sleep last night, if you can imagine." This was true. It had been a series of long days followed by a night in a small jail cell and interrogation. Odd as it seemed, Bunny was looking forward to a long, dreamless

sleep in the giant bed in her room, even if that room was ru-
mored to be the most haunted in the manor. Granny Mac
was here now, and she'd be staying there with her. If any
restless spirit felt inclined to visit in the wee hours, Granny
Mac would set it straight.

"Bunny's right," Brett said. "We should all get a good
night's sleep, especially since we'll be conducting our investigation tomorrow night. We'll let the fellas know the good
news at dinner."

After a short rest in the large four-poster bed, Bunny got
dressed for dinner. She was still tired but found that she was
looking forward to being a guest in the hotel's renowned
dining room rather than working in the kitchen behind the
scenes. Being a chef, Bunny had a vast appreciation for food
and loved experiencing not only long-established restaurants
but other highly rated or trendy food establishments as well,
including offbeat cafés, food trucks, and diners. Often local
diners were the most satisfying places of all. She felt it was a
necessary part of the job, to sample the extraordinary dishes
created by others and to keep up with the local trends.
Whenever she'd taste an interesting combination of spices or
sample a creatively prepared dish, it would kick her brain
into high gear, causing her to think of other ways to use the
spice or to think of different ingredients that might either
enhance or work better with the dish. Often, as in the case of
good ingredients, simplicity was the best measure. Other
times, clever ingredients and a progression of complicated
steps could create a masterpiece. Certainly, there were many
times Bunny suffered diner's remorse—the very real regret
at having ordered a subpar dish that she herself had made
many times over and many times better—but that was just
one of the pitfalls of being a good cook. Tonight, with a lim-
ited menu at the hotel that included bangers and mash—one
of her favorite comfort foods—she knew she wasn't going to

be disappointed. In fact, just thinking about it made her mouth water.

After staring at the handful of nice dresses she'd thought to pack for just such an occasion, she happily traded in her jeans and sweatshirt for a vintage cocktail dress in emerald green. It matched her eyes and set off her bright ginger curls to perfection. Diamond stud earrings, a delicate gold necklace, and a pair of two-inch black heels completed the transformation. She knew she had chosen the right dress the moment she walked into the dining room. It occurred to her, as she looked at the confused faces of her dinner guests, that the lads had never seen her in anything other than comfortable clothing and an apron. Her gran was the exception at the table.

"Sorry I'm late," she apologized.

"No. No problem at all. You look . . ." Brett swallowed, then added, "beautiful." He then stood and pulled out her chair. This simple yet chivalrous act, she noticed, caused her grandmother to smile.

"I agree." Giff, smiling, nodded his approval. "Our Bunny sure cleans up well. Nice of you to join us. Since there's only one thing on the menu tonight, we took the liberty of ordering for you."

"Why, thank you very much."

"Ella ordered your booze," he jauntily added, raising his thumb like a hitchhiker and thrusting it at Granny Mac, who was sitting next to him.

"Just wine. A full-bodied red our server suggested. Said it would pair nicely with pork sausage. Imagine that?" Granny Mac grinned at the notion.

"Server?" Bunny was stuck on that one word. She then scanned the dining room for the first time. Only half the tables were occupied, and she recognized most of the people dining. There were the three couples that had opted to stay at the hotel and another couple who were on holiday with two older children. DCI Standish was also in attendance, dining with a woman Bunny believed to be his wife, or perhaps a girlfriend. There was another couple with them, the other man she recognized from the police station as well. She glossed over a few of the other tables until her eyes settled on a table in the far corner of the large room.

Sir Charles was sitting at the head of the table with his sister, and three other guests. The middle-aged man, Bunny surmised, had to be Morgan's husband. Either that or another lover. The bleached blond woman, pretty in a manufactured way, was laughing at something Sir Charles said, while the other young lady, with the same color hair as Morgan, sat with her back facing them. Bunny's gaze continued moving through the room until she spied Betsy Copperfield heading toward them. However, the moment she caught Betsy's eye, the girl stopped abruptly, turned, and disappeared back into the kitchen. Just then a thickly built young man with light brown hair and a pleasant smile on his face took her place, appearing from the swinging door with a tray full of drinks.

"I take it Betsy is not our server tonight?"

"Pretty Betsy?" Cody remarked. "Nope. I think you two scared her away. No worries, though. We have young Lewis instead. He was a fan of *Ghost Guys*. Go figure. Lewis, my man!" Cody greeted the server as he approached the table with a grin.

Lewis? Bunny mused, studying the young man. So, this was the Lewis Betsy was talking to in the kitchen when Rodger had overheard them. He was a tad awkward, a tad clumsy, and a tad overzealous in his movements, but he was also undeniably charming.

"The *Ghost Guys*!" he said with a grin. "And girl. Chef, I mean. Sorry, miss. I . . . um, have your wine." After offering

Bunny an apologetic grin, he looked at his tray and carefully selected the glass of red wine. Bunny watched as he gingerly placed it on the table before her.

"Thank you," she said. "Tell me, Lewis, did you know Marcus Bean very well?"

As she asked the question, the young man, about to wrangle the tall gin and tonic on his tray, fumbled and knocked it instead. For a split second it looked as if he was about to lose the entire tray, until he miraculously got a hold of it once again. He breathed a sigh of relief and set the drink before Cody. Once his tray was empty, he looked at Bunny and replied, "Ah, yeah. I mean, not well. But he used to come here all the time for tea and lunch. He liked a good gin and tonic on occasion too. It's gutting, what happened to him. Dying like that in the old chest." As Lewis spoke, his chin began to quiver, and his eyes grew moist at the thought. He cleared his throat before adding, "He was a really good man." Lewis folded the empty tray under his arm, bent his head, and with a deflated demeanor, informed them that their dinners would be up shortly.

"Way to go, Bunny," Cody chided. "Scaring away the only other server in the dining room. If you keep this up, we'll be serving ourselves. I like Lewis. He's a good kid."

"He appears to be," she admitted. "However, Lewis was the young man Betsy was heard talking to in the kitchen about Marcus's big reveal."

"They're friends, dear," Ella reminded her granddaughter before taking a sip of her wine. "They both work here, and they both knew Marcus Bean. You told us that Betsy admitted to not knowing what this big reveal was about, so neither would Lewis. Not everyone's a suspect."

"Sorry," she apologized to the table. "This murder business is getting under my skin."

They were enjoying their drinks and making small talk

when Granny Mac said, "Brett has told me the good news. I hear Sir Charles is allowing you to conduct your investigation tomorrow night. In light of all that's happened, I say that's good news."

Bunny, for her part, was not overly excited. "The murder has put a damper on things, but we don't want the series to fail. We also learned something else today." Bunny chanced a glance at the table in the corner. Sir Charles caught her eye, and she had no choice but to wiggle her fingers at him in greeting. As the blond woman whispered something in his ear, he grinned and waved back at her.

"What was that?" Granny Mac leaned in and caught the man waving at her granddaughter. "Is it Sir Charles? He's smiling at you, and that woman hanging on his arm is half his age, for shame. Do you think he had a reason to murder his historian?"

"It's certainly a possibility," Brett said, setting down his glass of dark beer. "Only we need to figure out what exactly it was that Bean stumbled across. However, Sir Charles told us something else interesting."

"That's what I'm trying to tell you, Gran. He told us"— Bunny lowered her voice before sharing her news with the table—"his sister, Morgan, was having an affair with Marcus Bean."

"What?" Ed blurted, momentarily forgetting his cider. His dark Italian gaze shot across the room at the speed of light, homing in on the table in question. "Damn," he uttered in appreciation. "The randy rascal."

"Shhh," Giff hiss-whispered. "She's right over there, with her husband, the cuckold."

"We don't know that!" Bunny admonished, fighting to keep her voice down. Men! What was wrong with them? Unfortunately, at that moment another man, DCI Standish to be exact, was staring straight at her. Again, Bunny smiled and wiggled her fingers at him. She noted with a ripple of satisfaction that the woman seated next to the detective was frowning at her. That was the power of a great-fitting dress!

"You'll need to talk with Morgan in private," Granny Mac said with a pointed look. "See if she'll give you a straight answer. Matters of the heart can turn deadly. I don't mind telling you that I'm sensing a storm of internal conflict from their table, only I can't put a finger on just who it's coming from."

"Morgan Wallingford-Green is first on our list tomorrow, Ella," Giff informed her.

As the bangers and mash arrived, they continued to talk in muffled tones about the murder of Marcus Bean. The meal was simple yet divine. Bunny was thoroughly enjoying it, yet she couldn't shake the thought that Betsy, the server, knew something that she wasn't telling them. The young lady was doing a good job of avoiding them as well. As for Sir Charles, Bunny found it interesting that he admitted to learning about the grand discovery Bean had stumbled across, only he swore that he didn't know the nature of it. None of them claimed they did, yet many had known about the big reveal. Sir Charles had also hinted at the possibility that Marcus might have been blackmailing somebody, while also admitting that he knew that the man was having an affair with his married sister. What a tangled web it was swiftly becoming.

Giff stabbed his fork into the last delicious morsel of sausage on his plate. As he savored this last bite, he suddenly held up his empty fork and blurted in what looked to be an ah-ha moment, "Alex Bimsby!"

"Come again?" Mike looked at Brett for support. Brett was at a loss as well.

"Grimsby," Giff clarified, once he had swallowed his mouthful. "Alex Grimsby. I almost forgot. Yesterday morning, after wandering the manor with Brett and Marcus, getting an earful about history and the unfortunate ghost bride, I went out to the oak grove to meditate in the fall sunshine. It's how I hone my abilities as a medium."

"Save it for the camera, bro!" Frank heckled with a grin.

"Right. Tough crowd. Anyhow, as I was saying, I was in the oak grove, preparing for the night's investigation. The oak grove, my dears, is conveniently located near the stables. That's where Alex Grimsby, the ruggedly handsome stableman works. While I was quote-unquote meditating"—here he inserted a pair of air quotes as he spoke—"and working up my nerve to approach Mr. Grimsby, Morgan returned from a ride. She was all windblown as she handed her sweaty horse to Grimsby and stalked off in the direction of the manor. Shortly after she left, Bean showed up and wanted a word with Grimsby. Of course, I was all ears. I strained to listen to what they were saying, but the leaves overhead were rustling so loudly in the breeze, I only caught snatches of the conversation. However, the conversation soon turned heated, and they took it inside the stable office. I'm not sure what they were talking about, but I think we should follow up on that as well."

"An argument in the stables between Bean and this Grimsby fellow? You bet we'll follow up on that. Good work, Giff," Brett added sincerely. "Looks like we have our day cut out for us. Everyone should get a good night's sleep tonight. We'll meet back here at eight tomorrow morning for breakfast."

"Sounds good to me," Bunny said. She then turned her attention to her grandma.

"Are your bags still in the hotel office, Gran?" she asked the older woman.

"Why no, dear, they're in my room."

"Your room? I thought you were staying with me. I have

plenty of room in mine." Why did this thought make her
sweat. She could feel tiny beads of perspiration forming on
her brow. She lifted the heavy fall of her hair to cool her
neck. It wasn't working.

"The hotel is nearly empty. And I thought . . ." Here Ella
MacBride covertly shifted her gaze to Brett then back to her
granddaughter, and whispered close to Bunny's ear, "I just
assumed, being a lovely young woman in the company of so
many handsome men, that you'd like your privacy." The
mere notion set fire to Bunny's fair cheeks. Where did she
get that idea, and why, dear heavens, had she voiced it? Utterly inappropriate yet typical for Granny Mac, she thought.

"*Grrran*," she admonished in a like whisper. "This is a
business trip! And . . . we don't really know one another
very well yet."

"Crivens!" Granny Mac replied with a wily look as she
leaned back in her chair. "Also, I thought that you might be
tired, after your night in the village jail. You've only got the
one bed, as do I. One large, spacious bed. At least we'll get a
good night's sleep, m' dear."

She looked at her grandmother, hoping she was correct.
In fact, at that very moment, Bunny couldn't think of anything she'd like more than a blissful night's sleep in the big,
canopied bed. For her sake, she prayed that all the rumors
regarding her haunted hotel room were just barmy rumors.

Chapter 21

Why was she so nervous to retire to the Fleur-de-Lys suite? It was ridiculous. Bunny had spent a perfectly good night in there two days ago, snuggled beneath the quilts on the big old bed with hardly a care in the world. Sure, she had stuffed her ears with cotton to blot out the noise Brett, Giff, and Marcus Bean were making as they stomped through the hallways in the wee hours, filming backstory and chasing down ghostly legends. Boys will be boys, she supposed. Yet as far as she knew, they had come up empty-handed regarding ghosts. Which was just fine by her. And there were none in her room now, she told herself, as she quickly pulled a flannel nightgown from the closet, being careful not to look in the dark corners. Flannel, she mused, was the perfect choice for chilly autumn nights, especially ones spent in drafty old manor homes.

Bunny took the nightgown with her as she stepped into the spacious en suite and continued with her nighttime ritual. Once her face had been washed and moisturized, and her teeth and hair had been brushed until both glistened, she then took off her dress and slipped into the nightgown. She turned off the bathroom light, the bedroom lights, and dashed straight for the covers on the tall, canopied bed with only her reading light to guide her. That's when she made the mistake of glancing in the long oval mirror in the corner of the room. The image of a woman in a long white gown, staring at her with hauntingly sad eyes, was enough to freeze the blood in her veins.

Just two giant steps from the bed, Bunny stopped in mid-stride. Her heart pounded in her chest as her focus was drawn to the mirror, like the helpless needle of a compass to true north. *Dammit*, she thought. *Don't look!* But she couldn't help herself. She looked.

Her eyes widened in the darkness, of their own accord. The light was scant. The mirror was set at an angle. And the image that first struck her, hitting all the way to the marrow of her bones, had somehow morphed into something far less frightening. That must have been it, she thought, clearly staring at herself in the full-length mirror, although her heart still beat erratically in her chest. She had to admit that the long flannel nightgown in pale pink with lace trim on the neck and the cuffs of the sleeves looked very old-fashioned. And dour. Utterly dour. Also, if she was being honest, a bit sad in a frumpy-old-maid sort of way. Oh, if her grand-mother could see her now! Seeing her granddaughter, push-ing thirty, in a buttoned-up flannel nighty with a pouf of frizzy red hair nearly obscuring her pale face, and frightened of her own reflection, Granny Mac wouldn't have even bothered to make a comment about sharing her big bed with a former Ghost Guy. This very unsexy thought was enough to lift the corners of her stunned lips, turning them into something resembling a smile.

"It's just me," she boldly announced to the mirror, owning the look in an effort to settle her nerves. "Bridget MacBride, super-sexy flannel jammies model who is not afraid of her own reflection, thank you very much. Good night!" She turned from the mirror and leapt onto the bed, aiming for the pillows. Just as she landed the bed creaked, and a soft pitiful moan echoed in the room.

Did that come from me? she thought, knowing perfectly well that it hadn't. She closed her eyes tightly and convinced herself that it wasn't a moan at all. It was just the wind. The wind, she reminded herself as she scrambled to get under the covers before stuffing cotton in her ears. She then cast a longing look at the cookbook sitting on the bedside table, turned out the book light, and buried her head, ostrich style, in a pile of pillows.

Bunny slept. In fact, she'd been so tired that the moment her wild imagination settled, and her thoughts turned to the gentler pursuit of cooking, she fell into a blissfully dreamless sleep. It wasn't until much later that the dang white rabbit hopped into her room.

Although Bunny recognized Hopper immediately—that adorable fluffy white rabbit—his presence in the opulent bedchamber puzzled her. How did he get into the manor in the first place? How had he gotten up the many flights of stairs? How had he known which room she was in? And, most importantly, what was he doing sitting like that at the edge of her bed, wiggling his pink nose at her as if he had something to say? *Silly rabbit*, she thought, until he spoke.

"Dinna be frightened," he said, in a distinctly male voice. "It's just me."

"Hopper?" she uttered. "Oh, Hopper, it's so good to see you again! I didn't know you could talk." For some reason, call it Doctor Doolittle envy, she was delighted that her rabbit talked and that she could understand him. It was, in a word, empowering. "I have so much to tell you. But first, how are you doing?"

"I'm not Hopper," the rabbit told her in no uncertain terms, sucking the wind from her sails. "Hopper's dead, so not fine. Besides, rabbits can't talk."

"Don't be silly. You're clearly a rabbit and I can hear you. You don't have to hide your voice from me."

The rabbit tilted its head at her and thumped its hind foot on the quilt in disapproval. "I'm not really a rabbit and I'm not really here. But I do need you to open your eyes. Please, Bunny, open them."

That was all the rabbit said. After delivering his odd message, he slowly faded from the foot of her bed, and for some reason Bunny was overcome by a debilitating sadness. That's when she opened her eyes.

The sight of the woman standing before the dark window, made Bunny suck in a gasping breath, as if her lungs had been deprived of oxygen for several minutes. Maybe they had. She really didn't know, but what she did know was that the talking rabbit had only been a dream. Disappointment shot through her at the thought. The dream was fading, and she knew it was about to disappear forever. That was the cruel nature of dreams. The woman, dressed head to toe in white and staring out the window, wasn't a dream at all. Bunny was awake, sitting up in bed, and staring at the ghost of a bride.

The woman was weeping. Not only could Bunny hear her, but the woman's emotions were so overwhelming that Bunny realized she was weeping too. Great big tears welled in her eyes and rolled down her sleepy cheeks. And she resented the hell out of it.

This is exactly what she was running from. This is what she was trying to avoid at all costs. And now here she was, sleeping in the bedchamber of a haunted manor and staring at the ghost of a poor young woman who had hidden a little too well from her groom on her wedding night. Well, to hell with that! Angry, yet aching with a real feeling of loss that was not her own, Bunny addressed the woman. Unfortunately, she really didn't know what to say to a ghost.

"Umm, I see you," she said, projecting her voice across the room. "I see you clear as day." If she thought the ghost would be happy about this, she was wrong. The ghostly bride ignored her and continued weeping. Bunny tried again. "I also see that you're very sad. Thank you for sharing your pain." Why had she said that? Stupid. "I don't blame you for being sad," she added, wiping the tears off her own cheeks. "I'd be sad too, in your situation, but could you move along? Please? I'm trying to sleep here." Unfortunately, this plea fell on deaf ears.

"Dammit," Bunny uttered under her breath. She gave a thought to trying to close her mind to the paranormal, as Granny Mac had once taught her to do, and turn her back, banishing every specter from her presence. However, the truth of the matter was, she hadn't the strength. Ever since setting foot in Bramsford Manor her defenses had weakened. The white rabbit had come back, a man had been murdered, and now she was seeing a ghost, one she believed to be young Ann Copeland, the girl who had tragically disappeared on her wedding night, only to be found fifty years later by her grieving husband, who had stumbled upon an old chest. It was the saddest story Bunny had ever heard. Feeling the pain of it, she had no choice. Using Granny Mac's own words, Bunny knew she had to face her demons. She had to face those otherworldly voices that plagued her. In fact, on some level she knew that this spectral visit was important. Maybe, just maybe, she could learn something important from this ghost.

Angry that her eyes were still shedding tears caused by this specter, Bunny gingerly got out of bed. Lord, how she hated the swirl of emotions coursing through her body, knowing that only one of them was truly her own. Unfortunately, that was anger. A feeling she was becoming way too familiar with lately. She felt that the fear prickling her skin and seizing her gut might have been hers as well, but she couldn't be certain. She took a deep breath, fighting to recall any tidbits of mediumship her Gran might have imparted to her. Unfortunately, her mind drew a blank. She decided to go for broke and just be direct.

"Ann," she said, taking a step toward the weeping bride. "I am so sorry. Can you tell me what happened?" She took another step when the ghost turned from the window and looked right through her.

She doesn't even know I'm here, Bunny realized, feeling her heart pounding against her ribs with fear and anger so palpable, she thought it might explode. It wasn't a pleasant feeling. It was a mind game, steeling herself against this ghostly tide of roiling teenage emotion. Because as the girl looked right through her, Bunny realized that Ann Copeland had been very young when she died. The pity of that realization washed through her, and Bunny felt truly sorry. The ghost bride was also, if Bunny was reading the girl's emotions correctly, very scared, very sad, and utterly heartbroken. They were all emotions Bunny could identify with. She had once been a teenager too and had suffered loss, even heartbreak, but her loss had been tempered by the passing of time. This poor soul still suffered, and Bunny began to realize that the young ghostly bride was still emotionally stuck in that terrible day. She likely didn't even realize she was a ghost. It was a sad, sobering thought, and Bunny knew she had to do something. For the sake of the ghost and her own mental health she had to try. Yet as hard as she tried, she could not connect to this agitated spirit. Her years of running from and blocking out her abilities had rendered her useless. Now, standing in a room mere feet from a soul tormented with excruciating anguish, Bunny wished she hadn't run from her greatest fears, but instead had faced them. Had she done so, she might be able to help this poor soul now. But no, she'd been a selfish coward, and now she was paying the price.

"Tell me how I can help you!" Bunny cried, losing both her patience and control. "What can I do to make it stop?"

Suddenly, as if startled, the ghost faced the bedroom door. For the space of a second the fear and sorrow turned to white hot anger. As Bunny fought to make sense of what was happening, the ghostly bride fled in the opposite direction, heading for a wall where she vaporized the moment she touched it.

The ghost of Ann Copeland was gone, and Bridget Bunny MacBride crumbled to the floor in a blubbering mess of tears and sobs.

Chapter 22

There's nothing like a good cry before going to sleep, and that's exactly what Bunny did. She was so overcome by a flood of emotions that at one point she didn't even know why she was crying. Her own fear, her own uselessness, and the ghost's sad story were all part of it, but there were other reasons too. The loss of her brother, the way she missed her family, and the fact that she didn't yet have a man of her own to hold on cold nights such as this, all vied for expression as well. It wasn't pretty. Once she had cried all the tears that were in her, Bunny, exhausted from her emotional encounter with the manor's most famous ghost (and now she fully embraced the story) climbed back under the covers and didn't move until her alarm went off the next morning. Even if other ghosts had visited her in the night, she remained none the wiser. Her one encounter with the ghost bride of Bramsford Manor had been enough for a lifetime.

The next morning as Bunny stood under the fall of hot water in the shower while wearing an ice-cold washcloth over her eyes to help ease the puffiness, a pestering thought struck her. Anger. She clearly remembered a strong feeling of anger emanating from the weeping ghost. Sure, Bunny had been angry enough at the ghostly intrusion, yet in comparison to the emotions of the specter, hers felt more like a minor annoyance. And that got her thinking. Maybe the ghost of Ann Copeland was trying to tell her something after all.

"Morning, Gran," she said, taking a seat next to her grandmother in the hotel dining room. She'd been the last one to the table, thanks to the unsettling encounter of the night before and the hefty amount of concealer she'd needed to hide the bags under her eyes. The under-eye bags were from all the crying. She still didn't fully understand why she had felt the emotions of the ghost bride so keenly. That was a question for her grandmother. The moment her rear landed in the chair she offered a smile to the lads. They were all staring at her, or, more correctly, at her puffy red eyes. Brett was especially unnerved. For a man who recoiled at the sight of women's tears, and he had seen many a lady cry, he knew the signs well. She didn't like the way he looked at her. Fortunately, she had just the thing to shock him out of his silent revulsion.

"So, get this, lads. Last night the ghost of Ann Copeland paid me a visit in my room."

"What?" Giff cried. "The Mistletoe Bride was in your bedroom last night and . . . you saw her?" The mere thought made him turn a few shades whiter.

"No way," Brett breathed, shifting his focus to her words instead of her swollen eyes. Honestly, she felt that the excitement brewing within him was a little insulting. *Men*, she thought with exasperation, and not for the first time. Oh, how she wished that he wasn't so hot!

Cody, Ed, and Mike were just as intrigued. As for her grandmother, Bunny got the distinct impression that she wasn't surprised at all.

"It's true," Bunny continued. "I was sound asleep when

all of a sudden, I woke up and saw this ghostly figure of a woman standing in my bedroom. She was staring out the window, the one that overlooks the garden." Technically speaking, the talking white rabbit had woken her up, but she thought it best to leave out that little detail. It had only been a dream, and she really didn't remember anything about it, only that the rabbit had talked to her. At that moment, Lewis came over to take her order. Bunny glanced around the dining room, noting that there were only two other tables in the spacious room that were occupied. Betsy was nowhere to be seen.

"What can I get you this morning, Ms. MacBride?" Lewis politely asked.

"Tea, a croissant, and two eggs scrambled, please." She then smiled at him and asked, "Lewis, is it just you this morning, or is Betsy here?"

"Just me, ma'am, but that's not unusual. It's Betsy's morning off."

Bunny thanked him and continued with her story. The entire table was staring at her, urging her on with their eyes. "Sorry about that. Now, back to the ghost bride. That's who it was. It was her pitiful weeping that woke me."

"She was weeping?" Brett asked. "You actually heard her?"

"It was hard not to, it was so loud. It's frightening, waking up like that to find a ghost in my room."

"What did she look like?" Giff was cradling his coffee between his hands while leaning on his elbows.

"It was hard to tell at first," she admitted, "but when she turned to face me, I was struck by how young she was. I'd place her to be sixteen or seventeen."

Giff took a sip of his coffee. "That sounds about right, according to Bean's story. They married 'em young back in the day. I wonder how old the groom was. Maybe he was an old coot, and that's why she hid from him in the first place?"

"He's got a point," Mike offered. "Maybe that's why she was crying—because she didn't want to marry him?"

Lewis arrived with her tea, and not a moment too soon. Tea, coffee, she needed some form of caffeine to set her right. After stirring in a measure of milk, she took a sip and remarked, "That's an interesting theory. I can't speak for the age of the groom, but the ghost that confronted me last night was not only young, but extremely heartbroken."

"How did you know she was heartbroken, dear?" Granny Mac asked, looking intently at her.

"I think it was the way she was crying. Also, and here's the weird part, I could feel it. I could feel her emotions. All of them, even the ugly ones."

"That's sick," Cody remarked, utterly intrigued. "You could actually feel what she was feeling? I heard that the Mistletoe Bride has that effect on some people."

"I'm one of them," she admitted. "She was crying, and I realized that I was crying too, but there was no reason for my tears. I could feel them rolling down my cheeks. It was, if you must know, highly disturbing."

"And awesome," Brett remarked. "Bunny, this is huge! You made contact with the legendary Mistletoe Bride. That's what we came here to do."

"She not only made contact, bro, she was swimming in MB's residual emotions. That's next-level special," Cody added. He flashed Bunny a grin and a thumbs-up for good measure.

Unfortunately, Bunny wasn't nearly as enthused with her encounter as they all were. Quite frankly, the whole incident had been next-level disturbing. And, dwelling on disturbing, she wasn't too keen on the way her grandmother was staring at her with her penetrating sea-ice gaze.

"What did she tell you?" Granny Mac asked, narrowing her eyes. "Did MB, as Cody calls her, have a message for you?"

Bunny thought for a moment then shook her head. "She didn't talk, if that's what you're asking. The truth was, I tried to communicate with her, but I don't even know if she knew I was there. All I could do was feel her emotions. I really don't know how else to explain it."

"It's called clairsentient, dear." Granny Mac picked up her teacup and took a thoughtful sip before returning it to the saucer. "It's quite remarkable. I knew you had the gift, but I wasn't certain what form it would take."

"What do you mean what form it would take?" Bunny snapped, staring back at her grandmother. "This isn't Harry Potter. I'm not a witch. I don't have a wand . . . or a familiar, and I don't have a specialty. In fact, for your information, ghosts freak me out. I don't want *the gift*, as you call it."

"Umm, may I remind you that you see a white rabbit?" Giff offered unhelpfully.

"What are you insinuating?" Bunny's voice was peppered with annoyance, and she didn't care.

"Just pointing out your familiar."

Yet before she could fling properly aimed eye-daggers at him, her grandmother's slightly admonishing *tisk-tisk* caught her attention instead. "You're a chef, not a witch, but you are clairvoyant. And clairsentient, which means that you have the ability to feel a ghost touch you, or to feel its emotions. It's time to stop running from it, Bridget." Her grandmother only used her Christian name when she was being formal or stern. "You best learn to control it, or you'll be absorbing every unwanted emotion in this old place."

The trouble was, she knew that her grandmother was correct. She had to face this demon, but in the cold light of day, she had to admit the thought terrified her. Power-pouting over this truth, she picked up her tea and sipped it down.

The moment she finished she felt a firm yet warm hand on her arm. It was Brett.

"I'm sorry," he told her softly. "I know how scary this must be for you. Truthfully, I regret pulling you into all of this—this highly unorthodox show. But we're in the thick of it now, Bunny. All of our careers are on the line and all of us are still suspects in Marcus Bean's murder. What I'm trying to say is that you're not alone. We're all here with you. We're a team. And we're not going to let anything happen to you. You have made contact with the Mistletoe Bride. That's huge. That's why we're here. Although this ghost-hunting stuff is far out of your wheelhouse, your grandmother is here to help you. She has the unique ability to teach you more about your gift. In fact, I believe that's why you brought her here in the first place." Bunny gave a sheepish nod, admitting this was true. "For whatever reason," Brett continued, "this old, haunted manor has awakened this gift within you, and I, for one, can't help but think it's for a good reason. Maybe the Mistletoe Bride can help us understand why Bean was murdered."

"I think you might be right," she finally admitted. "I told you that I could feel her emotions. Sorrow, fear, pain, and loss, they were all there. But there was something else that struck me as odd."

"What was that?" Granny Mac leaned in with interest.

"Anger. White, hot, burning anger. For the love of me, I cannot figure out why that young ghost bride would be filled with such anger."

"Maybe we can figure that out during your investigation tonight," Granny Mac told them. "I have a plan."

Chapter 23

After breakfast Granny Mac set off with the lads to discuss strategies for the evening's investigation. It was to be filmed as planned, only now they had a better idea of what they were up against, and where the specter in question might be found, namely in Bunny's hotel suite. They all agreed that it was imperative they make contact. Not only would it make for sensational television, but they also might learn something important regarding the dealings in Bramsford Manor. Bunny begrudgingly agreed to play her part. She really had no choice. As Granny Mac pointed out, she had a special connection to this ghost. It was necessary that she learn how to control her abilities lest they overwhelm her like they had last night.

Bunny pushed all unsavory thoughts of ghosts and hunts from her mind and instead embraced the problem at hand, namely Morgan Wallingford-Green. Sir Charles had told them yesterday that his sister had been having an affair with Marcus. Last night at supper, she had seen Morgan with her husband and daughter sitting at Sir Charles's table. If she was having an affair with the historian, she couldn't imagine her husband would be pleased. Maybe he didn't know. Knowing that Brett and Giff would return shortly to join her in questioning Morgan, Bunny decided to make the most of her time by paying a visit to the kitchen. Restaurant kitchens were often hotbeds of gossip. Also, Bunny was itching to bury her hands in some good, sticky dough. To her way of thinking, there was no better way to work out one's demons than to get busy in the kitchen.

"Good morning," Bunny called cheerfully to the two cooks working on breakfast orders as she made her way to the back of the kitchen. She assumed Lilly was taking a break in her office. However, spying Rodger, Bunny paused to say hello. The sous chef was working at another counter, slicing an enormous pile of yellow onions. On the stove behind him a stockpot simmered beside a Dutch oven. Due to the onions and the smell of the rich beef broth, Bunny deduced, "French onion soup?"

Rodger looked up at her, tears streaming down his face, and nodded. "I'm just about to sauté the onions."

"Thank goodness for that. It's a painful job, slicing so many. Short of wearing ski goggles in the kitchen, there's not much one can do about the tears." Bunny's heart went out to him. Whether slicing onions or channeling the emotions of a ghost, profusely watering eyes were importunate at any time of the day.

"Ski goggles?" Rodger remarked, his face expressing mild regret. "I never thought of that."

"It's not a tool one usually has in the kitchen. I tried it once during my spot on *Mary Stobart's Memorable Meals*. It didn't go over very well. Mary saw it and told me that I looked like an idiot, slicing onions with flaming orange ski goggles on. Maybe I should have worn white goggles instead. Whatever the case, it worked." They shared a grin over this antic. "You can also soak them in cold water, but the benefits won't last in a pile this big. My pro tip: try not to get too attached to the onion, and certainly don't name them." She made the man crying over a pile of onions, laugh. She laughed too. "Will it just be the soup then?" she finally asked him. Although French onion soup was rich enough, topped with a slice of toasted French bread, Gruyère cheese, and broiled to a bubbly golden-brown perfection, she felt it a bit underwhelming for the likes of the manor's kitchen.

"Served with a ploughman's lunch on account of the low number of guests," Rodger informed her.

That sounded better. Although both dishes had humble origins—onion soup being an affordable staple of eighteenth-century French peasants, and the ploughman's lunch a quick, hearty, cold meal packed for England's hardworking ploughmen—both had been elevated into epicurean wonders. French onion soup in a rich beef broth and topped with melted cheese was divine. As for the ploughman's lunch, Bunny regarded it as the precursor for today's obsession with charcuterie boards. A typical ploughman's lunch was protein heavy, with sliced cold meats, wedges of local cheeses, hard boiled eggs, meat pies, and sausage rolls. Even a good Scotch egg made an appearance on occasion. And no ploughman's lunch could be complete without delicious, homemade crusty breads, and a whole host of other garden delights, fruits, chutneys, and spreads. It was a simple meal that dazzled the tastebuds. "It sounds positively delicious," Bunny remarked. She bid him a good day and continued to the back of the kitchen, aiming for the long counter beneath the wall of windows where she had cooked her elegant, ghost-baiting meal.

The moment Bunny stood at the sink and began washing her hands, Lilly poked her head out of her office. She pulled her cell phone away from her ear, and asked, "What brings you into the kitchen this morning?" Bunny noted that she still appeared slightly guarded toward her.

"I'm stuck here for a few days and thought I'd whip up a batch of scones for tea later today. That won't be a problem, will it?" Bunny presented the chef with her brightest smile.

"We'll chat later. The guest chef is back in my kitchen," Lilly told the person on the other end of her phone and ended the call. She grabbed an extra apron and stepped out of her small office. "Here," she said, handing it to Bunny. "I don't have a problem with that. Must keep busy somehow, I suppose."

Bunny thanked her and began gathering her ingredients.

"Anything special you need?" Lilly pulled out a mixing bowl and a baking tray for her.

"No. I'm just making basic scones. I assume you have jam and clotted cream?" Lilly nodded. "Excellent," she proclaimed, then slyly confided to the chef, "After the fright I had in my bedroom last night, I need this. A quick batch of scones should ease my nerves enough to carry on."

She had Lilly's attention. "What do you mean by fright in your bedroom?"

"The Mistletoe Bride paid me a visit last night. I don't mind telling you that I didn't like the experience at all."

"You saw her, or just heard her?"

"Both, actually," Bunny remarked while carefully measuring out the self-rising flour. Next, she added the baking powder, sugar, and a pinch of salt.

"What did she look like?" Lilly was intrigued.

"You told me that you saw her once," Bunny reminded her. "Out on the patio."

"I did. I was wondering how she appeared to you."

"Dressed in a ghostly white gown," she stated. "She appeared young, distraught, sad. Now that I'm thinking about it, she really did look like the young woman in that creepy old portrait hanging on the wall beside the mistletoe chest. What did she look like to you?"

Lilly shrugged. "She was more of a glowing white haze, nothing specific."

"How did you know it was her?"

"I . . . I just assumed. That and the hair on the back of my neck stood on end. It was very spooky."

Bunny gave the flour mixture a quick stir, then nodded. "I bet it was. The thing is, I not only saw her, I heard her as well. I also felt her emotions. She is so sad."

Lilly stared out the window a moment before shifting her attention to Bunny again. "I have heard weeping as well, once when I was alone in the dining room. Also, as I told you before, things tend to go missing from the kitchen."

Bunny had just dumped the cold butter cubes into the flour mixture and was in the process of rubbing it between her fingertips when she stilled. "I think the weeping you heard was her, but you and I both know that it wasn't a ghost who took my knife, if that's what you're insinuating."

"Regarding your knife, I agree. I've talked with DCI Standish. He said you had a sound alibi. I'm sorry for doubting you." Lilly offered a weak smile as she handed Bunny the pitcher of milk.

Bunny made a well in the flour mixture, then swiftly filled it with a measure of milk. She added a dash of vanilla and a squeeze of lemon, before thrusting in both hands for a good kneading. The dough was sticky, clinging to her fingers like thick paste as she worked the dough. Once satisfied, she then plucked a handful of flour from the container and gently tossed it across the cutting board. The sticky dough went next, but not without some effort. Bunny coaxed it out of the bowl, added another dusting of flour, and gently began shaping the gooey lump into an inch-thick rectangle. Keeping her focus on her scones, she said, "There are several people with access to this kitchen, Sir Charles and his sister among them. Both had strong connections to Marcus Bean." Bunny lifted her eyes until they met Lilly's. "I think one of them took my knife," she boldly stated.

Lilly, clearly flustered, took a step back. "Not Sir Charles!" she averred. "In spite of what you might think, that man is generous and kind to a fault."

"What about Morgan? I heard she was having an affair with Marcus Bean." Bunny watched Lilly's eyes closely for a reaction to this. She wasn't disappointed.

"Who told you about that?" she demanded, handing Bunny a biscuit cutter.

"Sir Charles. He told us about it yesterday. So, it is true?"

Lilly forcibly blew out her breath. "Aye, it's true enough. They had an affair, but it ended well before Marcus's death."

"Are you certain?"

"Yes," Lilly stated almost defiantly. "Morgan is beautiful, but troubled, and mightily fickle as well. She's like a caged lioness, a feline who knows her remarkable potential, but is helpless to do much about it. So, she does whatever she pleases to pass the time."

"You make it sound like she's trapped here." Bunny rolled her eyes, taking in the magnificent kitchen, and thought that she wouldn't mind being trapped here at all . . . as long as it wasn't haunted.

"As the older of the two, she shares the financial burden with her brother," Lilly stated. "Her husband wanted an heiress; Emma, her daughter, wants a doting mother; and Morgan wants . . . Well, I'm not exactly certain what she wants, but you get my point. Marcus Bean was a convenient escape."

"Is that all it was, you think?" Bunny quirked her lips to the side, considering this. "Perhaps she's just trying to find herself?" she offered. After all, she had felt much the same way after Braiden died. She'd been young, and at a crossroads, and needed more than her home and family could offer. She couldn't imagine what it might have felt like if she had stayed. A caged lioness, Bunny mused. When backed into a corner, the lioness became lethal. Bunny transferred her scones to the baking sheet, then cracked an egg for the egg wash. She picked up a whisk, and asked, "Is Morgan still married?"

"Technically yes, but she and Percival are living apart at the moment. I would say poor Percival, but he knew what she was when he married her."

"He had dinner with her last night, didn't he?" Bunny brushed the tops of her plump, round scones with the beaten egg as she talked.

"They're still friendly, mostly for the sake of Emma, their daughter."

"I never thought to ask, but does Morgan live here too . . . in the manor? I don't see her around here as much as I do Sir Charles."

"Charles loves the company. He's also quite proud of the manor and its history. Morgan would have preferred the manor remain private, but they don't have the money for that. She's friendly enough with the guests and does a good job coordinating large events and the daily activities, but once she's done, she prefers her privacy. Her apartments are located at the very end of the east wing." Lilly pointed over her shoulder to the side wall, indicating which way was east. "Just out here. Sir Charles's apartments are located at the head of that wing. Morgan occupies the larger part of the wing, all the way to the end. But you cannot access them from inside the manor. You must go outside and around to her front door. She also has a door that opens onto the courtyard."

"Would she be there now?"

Lilly glanced at her watch. "She usually takes a morning ride before work. Riding is her one true passion. She tried to make it Emma's passion as well, but her daughter rebelled. She's a footballer. Loves the sport. Anyhow, after her ride, Morgan always heads to her wing to freshen up before work. And I forgot to mention, if it's gossip you're after, there is some speculation that Alex Grimsby is her next conquest, although no one seems to know if Morgan has *sealed the deal* yet."

"You are a font of knowledge, Lilly." Bunny grinned, then handed Lilly her tray of unbaked scones. "Being a chef, I love a good bit of gossip as well. Would you mind baking these for me?"

"Not at all. Why?"

"I just remembered something." Bunny took off her apron and headed for the door.

"I hope you're not meddling, Bridget MacBride. DCI Standish won't be pleased!"

Chapter 24

Meddling. Bunny didn't consider it meddling when one's reputation was on the line, not to mention the fact that she and the lads were essentially trapped at the manor until DCI Standish deemed them cleared, and Lord only knew how long that could take. For instance, the moment she left the kitchen, Bunny saw the detective chief inspector sitting at a dining room table. The man had three Danishes on his plate and a steaming pot of tea before him. Eating Danish with his eyes glued to his smartphone, he didn't strike Bunny as a man racking his brain to find the killer. She couldn't resist the temptation to annoy him a little.

"Morning, Chief Inspector." She'd deliberately left off the detective part, feeling that he wasn't living up to his name at the moment.

"Ms. MacBride." He nodded and took another bite out of his first raspberry Danish. Bunny stood, watching.

He was ready to take another bite when he stopped and looked at her. "Is there something I can help you with?"

"Have you found out who stole my knife yet?" she kindly inquired.

"We're working on it," he grumbled. Bunny saw that as an opportunity to take a seat.

"Intriguing," she whispered. "So, what's your angle?"

"Angle?" His bushy red eyebrows furrowed in consternation.

"What theory are you working on regarding my knife and the death of Mr. Bean?"

Standish held her in a scrutinizing gaze before taking a sip of his tea. On some level he knew that she wasn't going to leave without an answer. He returned the cup to its saucer and sat back in his chair. The riveting news article on his phone was just going to have to wait. "Why should I tell you? May I remind you that you're still a suspect."

"Crivens," she exclaimed, waving her hand. "I was just low-hanging fruit to be plucked first. I discovered the body and my missing knife. Suspicious, I'll agree, but we've already been over this. You know I didn't murder that poor man. But someone here did. You're still conducting interviews and collecting evidence, which tells me that you're still trying to put the pieces of this troubling puzzle together. You obviously are developing a theory. I'd like to know what it is."

A soft chuckle escaped his lips. "Of course, you would. You have an inquisitive mind and an active imagination. You're part of a television show. Some might argue that discovering a body during your *investigation* would make for sensational television."

Bunny held him in a look of extreme disapproval. "We're not murderers, and this body, as you call it, just might get us cancelled before we air our first episode. In a nutshell, not a good motive for team *Food and Spirits*. I'm going to throw out another name, Morgan Wallingford-Green. I know you've talked with her. She obviously knew Marcus, and she was having an affair with him."

"An affair?" Bunny was pleased to see she had his attention. "How do you know this?"

"Gossip, and Sir Charles. He told us yesterday. Whatever angle you're working on, maybe you should add *jealous husband* or *sordid love triangle* to it. Have you spoken to Percival Green yet?"

Standish stared at her a moment before speaking. "I thought I told you not to get involved in this."

"I'm not involved," she lied, "but I do hear things. Also, the sooner you find the killer, the sooner I can leave here. I think we both want that." This tidbit of truth elicited a smile from him.

"We're conducting more interviews today. I'll add him to the list."

"Good. Another thing, have you stumbled upon any, um . . . sensational information that Marcus might have uncovered?"

"Interesting you said that. We've searched his office for clues, but we think someone might have gotten there first."

"Don't look at me! I didn't know the man even had an office in the manor." Here she looked at him to see if his expression might confirm that Marcus's office was, in fact, located in the manor and not one of the outbuildings. Standish's face gave nothing away. Bunny smiled. "Where in the manor is this office?"

"You really don't know?"

"Why would I know, Detective? I spend most of my time with my team, or in the kitchen."

"On the fourth floor," he said, offering the location like a challenge. "In the attic. It's definitely haunted up there."

"Funny," she said in a humorless tone. "I won't be going up there." However, the moment the words left her mouth, a little voice in her head told her that she would be. She ignored the voice, and the shiver that traveled up her spine, and squared to the detective once again. "Do you think this is about Marcus Bean stumbling upon some damning piece of information that someone didn't want revealed?"

Standish shoved the rest of the Danish into his mouth and chewed while holding her in his hawkish gaze. Bunny stared back, praying he wouldn't choke on the obnoxious bite he'd just taken. "That's a fair guess," he said when he could, and leaned on his forearms. "We think Bean was blackmailing somebody."

Bunny inhaled sharply. The thought had crossed her mind as well, but hearing it from his own lips gave it more gravitas. "Who?" she whispered. "Do you have evidence?"

"Sorry, Ms. MacBride, but that's all I'm going to tell you. Also, your friends are here." DCI Standish pointed over her shoulder to the open French doors. Bunny turned in time to see Giff and Brett standing there. She waved at them and stood.

"Thank you," she told him. "If we find out anything of importance during our stay, I'll let you know."

"Don't stick your nose where it doesn't belong," he snapped, but it was too late. Bunny was already out the door.

"Lilly also knew that Morgan was having an affair with Marcus," she told the men the moment she met them in the large hallway off the hotel's dining room.

"Interesting," Giff remarked with a grin. "But what were you doing in the kitchen? I thought you were banned from there."

"Lilly's warming up to me again," she told them breezily. "I was killing time, making scones, and getting the scoop on Morgan Wallingford-Green."

"Scones?" Brett remarked, stuck on that one little word. "Sounds delicious, but we've only been gone a few minutes."

"It was a half hour," she corrected. "Plenty of time to

make scones and fish for information." She pulled them with her as she crossed the grand hotel lobby and out the massive front entrance. They were heading down the wide front steps when Bunny said, "And get this. Standish told me that they believe Marcus Bean was blackmailing somebody. Also, he has an office in the manor. It's on the fourth floor."

Brett stopped on the second to the last step and looked at her. "Really? He told you all that?" He looked impressed. "Wait. Where are we going?"

"Morgan's apartments. According to Lilly, they're at the end of the east wing. Her front door is somewhere down there." Bunny pointed to a hedgerow in front of another ancient wall that formed a border of sorts, and to the little gravel access road that ran between the hedgerow and the east wing of the manor. "Gentlemen, care for a walk?"

Morgan's front door was easy to spot. Not only had it been painted the most pleasing color of pale mint green, but it was also flanked by flowerpots overflowing with colorful fall mums. The door and the frame were both arched, and the thick vine that clung to the salmon-colored brick, hosted leaves in shades of red and yellow. It was the most charming entryway Bunny had seen in a long while. It made her think of home and the cozy Scottish farmhouse she'd grown up in. As Bunny reached for the knocker, she imagined how beautiful the door must look when surrounded by summer blossoms. In a manor home the size of Bramsford, this little door, tucked away at the far end of the east wing, seemed like a little slice of heaven, a cozy cottage tacked on to a grand five-star hotel. No wonder Morgan preferred her privacy.

"Yes?" Morgan said, opening her door with a look of question comingled with a touch of suspicion. Bunny noticed that the handsome middle-aged woman was still dressed in her jodhpurs and riding boots, with the tang of horse sweat clinging about her. She looked exhausted yet content, like one does after a good run. "Are you three lost, or is there a reason you're knocking on my door?"

Noting that she was staring right at Brett, Bunny gave him a little nudge and urged him to step forward. "We're very sorry to bother you," he told her. "It's just that, um, we are conducting our investigation tonight . . . in the manor, and we'd like to ask you a few questions, since you are a co-owner of the estate."

She narrowed her eyes at him. "If Charles told you it was fine, then you don't need my permission."

"He did," Brett informed her. "We'd like to ask you about any paranormal encounters you might have experienced over the years."

She pursed her lips, thinking. "There are too many to count. Come in," she told them graciously. "I can't believe you're going through with it, in light of the recent tragedy. But maybe that's the point." She cast a look at Brett as she led them down a long hallway. "If I know my brother and his obsession with family history and ghosts, he's likely hoping that you're going to make contact with the recently departed, and figure out who killed him."

They followed Morgan into her living room. Unlike her brother's manly, baronial tastes, Morgan's taste was equally grand, but with a lighter, more feminine touch. The walls were painted that same shade of pleasing mint green, the woodwork and window trim had been painted white, and a lovely area rug covered the wood floors in shades of burgundy, white, and light green. Sunlight streamed in from the tall window in the center of the wall, overlooking the courtyard garden with the oak grove in the distance. Bunny found it breathtaking.

"Have a seat," she told them, indicating the comfy chairs covered in floral chintz. "Please forgive me," she said, taking a seat as well. She crossed her long legs and waved a hand. "I've just come from my morning ride and was about to change. Now, what would you like to know?"

They listened intently as Morgan told them about a few of her encounters with the Mistletoe Bride, the ghost of a maid that frequented her apartments, a dark, shadowy entity on the second floor, and the specter of a man in eighteenth-century clothing she'd seen wandering the garden.

"I grew up here," she told them. "It's just part of the framework of this old house. But it still gives me the shivers whenever a door slams, or I see a figure out of the corner of my eye, or I feel something isn't quite right."

"I bet," Brett said, soaking in all the details. He then shifted gears, and asked, "As you know, Marcus Bean brought us here to investigate the Mistletoe Bride haunting. He was very knowledgeable regarding the legend. We were wondering how well you knew Marcus." Brett leaned in and gave Morgan his winning smile. Morgan smiled back.

"Very well," she stated. "He was like one of the family."

"Did he tell you recently about something that he might have stumbled upon? The reason I ask is that we've heard that he was planning on making some big reveal during our investigation."

Bunny watched Morgan closely as Brett talked. At the mention of the *big reveal* her eyes widened, and her body stiffened.

"Marcus shared all his findings with us, in his own time. I'm not familiar with this big reveal you mention."

Bunny wasn't convinced. "We think the reason he was murdered was because he stumbled upon something big and told the wrong person about it."

"He might have," she said, an aristocratic smile plastered on her lips. "It's an interesting theory, but I think you best leave the real investigation to the police."

"We're helping the police," Giff lied. "From the one angle they can't tap into. The paranormal angle. Tonight, I'm going to contact Bean. He's still lingering within these four walls. I sense he has an axe to grind before he heads into the light. He's likely going to spill everything. Any last messages you'd like to pass along?"

As Giff talked, Bunny watched Morgan closely, searching for any signs of surprise, regret, or loathing. Unfortunately, the woman had perfected her blank-eyed stare. It was impressive. Then, however, the facade broke, and she laughed.

"I hope you do," she challenged. "How Bean would love the irony if he were here. He's now part of the history of this place, for better or worse."

"I also heard that you and Marcus were having an affair."

Morgan stopped smiling and turned her attention to Bunny. "I should have known. You've been talking with Lilly."

"She mentioned it, yes. I'm not accusing you, but I can't help wondering what your husband thought of Marcus Bean."

"Not much, actually." Morgan stood from her chair and walked to the window. Looking across the vast garden, she said, "Our marriage was in trouble way before my little fling with the family historian. I love my daughter. I'd do anything for her, but staying married to her father is very difficult. Percival is selfish, arrogant, and has never been what you'd call faithful. When he finally did figure out that I was having an affair, he took his revenge in the form of a cute little Mercedes Roadster and a girlfriend half his age. The truth is, Marcus cared about our family history with passion. He cared about us. History has never been my thing. However, I found Marcus's passion for uncovering little tidbits and sniffing out stories to be highly erotic. He was lonely and I was bored. Not a match made in heaven, but it was nice.

Now, I'm afraid I must ask you to leave. I'm needed at the manor, and I must get ready."

"Just one more question," Bunny said, standing from her chair. "You knew Marcus well. Maybe he confided in you. Was he having an affair with Betsy Copperfield?"

Morgan's eyes narrowed as she frowned. "I highly doubt it. Marcus liked the ladies, but unlike Percival, he preferred them wise, intelligent, confident, and closer to his own age."

Chapter 25

"What do you think? Do you believe her?" They were sitting on the wide front steps of the manor, taking a break while contemplating their recent visit with Morgan Wallingford-Green. It was a glorious September day, and Bunny half dreaded the thought of returning inside.

Brett shrugged. "I don't know. It's possible that Bean could have told her about his discovery. They were close. But again, until we figure out the nature of this earth-shattering find, we can't know if it was damaging to Morgan or not."

"What if he was blackmailing her?" Giff cast a sideways glance at Brett.

"It is a possibility," Bunny agreed, having told them that the cops were working that angle. "You could ask Marcus tonight . . . when you make contact with him during the investigation."

"Hey, I just might," he said, countering her sarcastic remark. "And if I can, I might be able to crack this case wide open."

"Buddy"—gentle concern touched Brett's voice as he

spoke—"it doesn't work that way. And you don't exactly have the skills to do it, either. Have you even seen a ghost?"

"Not yet," Giff admitted and ran a hand carelessly though his styled dark hair before leaning back on his elbows. He lifted his face to the midmorning sun, adding, "I'm working on it, thanks to Granny Mac. Either way, you know what we have to do now. Bunny's just stalling." He opened one eye to look at her.

"I'm not stalling. I'm just taking a break. Besides, Marcus's office is up on the fourth floor. I wouldn't even know how to get there."

"We do." Bret smiled. "Bean took us up there briefly on our tour. As you can imagine, the attic in this place is not only huge, but also broken up into many different sections, each with a different point of access. I honestly have no idea where his office would be up there, but we need to find it. Chances are, it's going to be locked, and Standish is here with his boys."

"They're conducting interviews in the drawing room again," Bunny informed them with a pointed look. "They'll be too occupied going around in circles with the staff and guests to notice us."

"We should've asked Morgan if she had a key." Giff looked at Brett. "I bet she has one."

"Sir Charles probably has one as well," he agreed.

Bunny sat up, recalling what DCI Standish had told her. "Standish said the office looked like it had been searched before they got there. If there was something important, it's safe to bet it's already gone." The thought was slightly depressing. "It stands to reason that the murderer would have access to Marcus's office key, which points us once again to Sir Charles or his sister."

"Not necessarily," Giff said. "Peter Billingsley has the master key. Everyone knows that, just as they know where he keeps it. In the top left-hand drawer of his desk. I'll go see if he'll lend it to us." He delivered a wink before jumping to his feet and heading up the steps, taking them two at a time.

Fifteen minutes later, Bunny found herself traipsing with the lads through a series of hallways in the main part of the building and up three flights of stairs, until Peter Billingsley brought them to the end of a hallway. Apparently, under the circumstances, he refused to give the master key to Giff, but he had no problem escorting them to the attic office in question. Bunny stood in the narrow hallway marveling at the many valuable paintings that lined both walls. However, what she couldn't understand was why Billingsley had brought them to a dead end.

"You've taken a wrong turn," Brett offered good-naturedly. "Understandable in this place. Shall we head back that way?" He pointed down the hallway in the direction they'd just come from.

"Not a wrong turn," Billingsley told them, focusing on a large eighteenth-century painting hung above the decorative wainscoting. The painting, Bunny noted, depicted a rather beautiful scene of rolling countryside dotted by riders and hounds on the hunt.

"An art lesson, perhaps?" Giff offered. "Doing a little bait and switch on us, Billingsley?"

Peter grinned. "It would be so easy, but no. Bear with me." He then gripped the side of the hefty, gilded frame and pulled. The large painting, complete with the wainscoting below it, swung open, revealing a hidden staircase rising to the next level.

"Whoa!" Giff exclaimed. "That's totally cool. A hidden passageway. Bean never showed us that."

"He had it installed himself when they allowed him to build his office in the attic. Before that there was a door here. He felt the hidden passageway added a touch of whimsy." Flipping the lights on, Peter added, "Please follow me."

The attic was essentially just another story of the great

manor but with exposed beams, aging wood floors, and varying ceiling heights due to the sloping rooflines. Bean's office, a room specially constructed for that purpose, was conveniently located at the top of the landing. Peering down the narrow hallway, between a sloping roofline and the outer wall of the office, Bunny could see a long worktable sitting in what looked to be a larger, open space. The table was empty, but beside it was an astonishing collection of relics from bygone eras. She could only see a small part of the attic, but she knew that, just like a rabbit warren, the attic continued in several directions and levels.

"This is remarkable," she told Peter.

"If you ask me, it's the perfect lair for a historian like Bean. He liked it up here, rest his soul." As he spoke, Peter removed a large key ring from his pocket, found the right key, and unlocked the door. "I hope you find what you're looking for. Remember, be careful not to touch anything, and do not remove anything either. Technically, this office is still part of the crime scene. You are free to take pictures. That's all. Also, remember to lock the door when you leave."

Like most residential bathroom and bedroom doors, he showed them the button to press that would lock the door when they closed it. Brett tried to hide his surprise. Even Bunny knew it was the easiest kind of lock to pick, challenging the theory that one needed to have a key to unlock Bean's office. All one really needed was a long needle or a piece of metal wire thin enough to go through the tiny hole in the opposite door handle. Sheesh!

"Will do," Brett told him. Then, as if he couldn't help himself, he asked, "Who else has a key to this office?"

"Marcus, the owners of the manor, and me," Billingsley offered. Yet even as he said this, his expression relayed what they were all thinking. It hardly mattered with such a common doorknob. He then offered, likely from embarrassment, "Yesterday, when I escorted the police to this office, the door was unlocked, and a key was found in the left-hand drawer of the desk. Bean had little reason to lock this door, given its location. However, if he did hide something of importance up here—something that might have gotten him killed—it is very likely it's gone by now. At least the police think so. Maybe three pairs of fresh eyes will find differently."

"We hope so," Brett told him. They thanked Billingsley, assured him they would lock the door when they left, and got to work.

Bean's desk was a mess, covered with scattered papers, notes, old books, pictures, pens, a half-filled coffee mug, two double-A batteries, crumbs, earphones from a cell phone, and many old coffee stains. For the life of her, Bunny couldn't figure out if the desk had been rifled through or Bean was just a slob. Likely a little of both. Yet aside from the messy desk and the disheveled room in general, the paramount thing that struck Bunny the moment Peter Billingsley left was the smell. She had detected it before in another part of the manor, as had Granny Mac. But here it was strong, nearly knocking her back as she entered the room. "Is it just me, or are you lads smelling a heavy fug of cigarette smoke bathed in Old Spice Swagger?"

"I'm getting a hint of cigarette smoke," Brett said, picking up a hefty ashtray that contained two butts and a lot of ash. "Bean obviously smoked up a storm in here. It's a smell that lingers and permeates the walls."

Giff nodded in agreement.

"What about Old Spice Swagger?"

"Not smelling that," he said, snapping a picture of the disheveled desk. He looked at Bunny, adding, "Although, to be honest, I'm not sure what that smells like." He flipped through a couple of ancient-looking books and kept taking pictures.

Giff began opening desk drawers. "Bingo!" he cried at length, holding up a red deodorant stick. Sure enough, it had the words OLD SPICE SWAGGER written across it. "Is this what you're smelling?"

Bunny pulled off the cap and took a sniff. "Yep. That's it. It's Marcus Bean's calling card. Lads, I think he's in here with us."

"No way." Excitement blazed in Brett's eyes. "Where?" he asked, his head swiveling like a weathervane in a storm. Giff, on the other hand, looked much like Bunny felt: totally freaked out.

"I'm not sure, but there's a very strong smell in here. I can't see him if that's what you're asking."

As Bunny spoke, Brett held up his smartphone and began taking pictures of the room, aiming in the dark corners, hoping, no doubt, to catch a ghostly image.

Giff, steeling his nerves, spoke to the room at large. "Marcus, are you here with us? We're in your office. We're hunting for clues." His brown eyes shot to Bunny's in question. He mouthed, *Can you hear him?*

"No, I can't *hear him*," she snapped. "I can only smell him, and it's not overly appealing."

"Great. That doesn't help much." Just as Giff spoke, the door slammed shut behind them, causing him to not only scream, but jump so high he hit his head on the low ceiling. "Ouch!" he cried, rubbing his head. "What the hell was that?" He said it so fast it came out as one word. His face blanched, and he looked ready to bolt.

"Shhhh!" Brett warned, keeping his cool. Bunny noticed that he was now recording the unfolding drama on his phone.

"It's Marcus," she told them. The hair prickling on the

back of her neck confirmed it. As Giff backed up to the wall, Brett aimed his phone at her and nodded slowly, encouraging her to engage with the ghost of Marcus Bean.

Fighting all her instincts to run, Bunny held her ground instead, and swallowed. "Marcus, we're trying to find the person who murdered you. We believe that you stumbled on some piece of information that got you killed. We're looking for a clue. We're hoping you might help us."

When Bunny stopped talking the room became deathly still. No one moved. No one breathed. Nothing stirred, yet the smell of cigarettes and Old Spice Swagger remained. If anything, it was getting stronger. *I don't have the gift*, she thought. *Maybe I'm just an emotional wreck? Maybe I dreamed up the whole ghost bride incident last night? Maybe it's all because I have a massive crush on my coworker and don't know how to handle it? Oh no!* She cringed inwardly, suddenly hit with the urge to cry. She didn't know where it was coming from, but her eyes burned with unshed tears. *Don't cry, MacBride*, she mentally rallied. *He hates it when you cry!* But she couldn't help it. Amidst an off-putting swirl of aftershave and stale cigarettes, she felt an overwhelming sense of sorrow, regret, and failure. Complete failure. Heart-wrenching failure that was so overpowering she felt both sad and sick at the same time.

"Turn away," she warned Brett and his iPhone as the floodgates opened. Ashamed, she bent her head to the floor as tears coursed unchecked from her eyes. She tried to stop them by pressing her fingertips to her eyes. Her efforts proved unsuccessful, so she was left with no choice but to wipe them away, employing the sleeve of her shirt to do so. That's when she noticed something on the floor just beyond the toe of her shoe. It was a picture. Bunny plucked it up and quickly dried the teardrops that had landed on it.

The moment she took hold of the picture she was able to

regain her composure. Marcus Bean was smiling in the picture. He was dressed in full British hunting attire—from a dapper tweed jacket to a pair of tan breeks and tall black boots. A rifle was slung over one shoulder while in his other hand he held a brace of quail. Standing next to Marcus was a man Bunny didn't recognize. A handsome man also dressed for the hunt. While Marcus grinned for the camera, the man next to him was focused on the historian instead, his expression unreadable.

"What in the world?" Bunny breathed, studying the picture.

"That's Marcus Bean," Giff said, appearing beside her. He pointed to the man next to Marcus and grinned. "And that man right there is Alex Grimsby, stableman extraordinaire. Totally hot, right?"

"This is a clue!" she told him in no uncertain terms. "I think Marcus is trying to tell us something."

"She's right," Brett said, standing on her other side. He was still recording. "I don't think that picture was on the desk. Where did it come from?"

"It could have been on the floor all along. But it doesn't matter. I felt him." Bunny placed a fist on her chest. "Right here. I was overcome by sorrow and regret. But mostly failure. A real sense of failure. So odd. It's gone now, thank heavens, along with that pungent scent."

"Failure?" Brett questioned. "I bet it's because Bean failed in his mission. He failed to make his big reveal." He turned to Bunny. "I think you're right. He wants us to help him."

"Help him?" Clearly Giff thought they were both crazy. "I just got the stuffing scared out of me in this creep-tastic office, and now you're telling me Captain O. S. Swagger is summoning us for help?"

"Yes," Bunny and Brett replied at the same time.

"May I remind you that you were the one who wanted to

contact him and solve this mystery." Brett cast him a hard stare.

"I admit that I found the idea appealing. But I don't care for his style. It's spooky, and he made Bunny cry."

"Buckle up, bro. This is just the beginning. It's going to get much worse before it gets better."

"On the bright side," Bunny began, feeling much the same as Giff, "it looks like it's time for a visit to the stables."

Chapter 26

After enjoying the delicious ploughman's lunch with Granny Mac and the crew, including a side of rich, savory French onion soup, Bunny, Brett, and Giff were ready to have a word with Alex Grimsby. During lunch, they had brought everyone up to speed, including the real possibility that the picture found in Bean's office could be just that, a random picture. Yet Bunny didn't think so, and neither did Granny Mac. Hopefully, they'd be able to figure that out once they spoke with Mr. Grimsby.

Bunny was also pleased to see that Betsy was back at work. With a dose of professional politeness, she had tended to their table, even smiling a little at Brett. Under the circumstances, Bunny found that encouraging, yet she still wanted to know just what Betsy's relationship had been with Marcus Bean. Morgan had assured them that Betsy was too young for Marcus regarding a sexual relationship. Even if that was true, Bunny still couldn't shake the feeling that Betsy and Marcus had been close, far closer than was normal for a young dining room server and the manor historian.

Betsy had shed tears over him, knew about his big reveal, and possibly had known the nature of Bean's discovery as well, but wouldn't admit to it. In Bunny's mind, she was definitely one to watch.

Before leaving, Bunny told Granny Mac about the scones she had made earlier, and promised they'd make it back for afternoon tea. With their sights set on the stables, the stars of *Food & Spirits* exited through the French doors at the back of the dining room and crossed the wide expanse of patio. As they headed for the two sweeping sets of stairs, they were awarded a breathtaking view of the garden and rolling lawn. It was one of those perfect autumn days, blessed with sunshine and a cool breeze. Brett and Giff, with their long-legged stride, practically ran down the right-hand staircase to the garden. Bunny happily followed but stopped suddenly on the third step. That's when she was hit by a vision of a young bride. She sucked in her breath. It was like bad déjà vu. She knew that Bramsford Manor was a popular wedding venue. She also assumed that many joyful brides had descended these very steps to join their grooms in the garden below. However, the feeling that washed over her filled her with a sense of destitution—a feeling like being stranded on a desert island without hope. Bunny knew in that instant that the ghost of Ann Copeland haunted these stairs as well as her bedroom. But why? Surely Ann's wedding to Sir Henry Wallingford had occurred in a chapel . . . or somewhere inside the manor, having taken place in December? Why was she out here on these steps? As Bunny posed the question in her mind, she was instantly hit with an overwhelming feeling of jealousy. Burning jealousy!

"Crivens!" Bunny blurted, fighting it for all she was worth. "Not now, Ann. I'm not doing this now!" Yet just as she spoke, she felt her knees weakening as the overwhelming emotion tingled down her legs and seeped into her bones.

Although the wailing sadness of last night had been bad enough, this jealousy nonsense was far worse. "Lord," she uttered to the heavens, grabbing hold of the thick railing to keep her balance, "please, help me!" As Bunny prayed, she closed her eyes, waiting for the emotion to pass. Then, as fast as it had overtaken her, the barbs of jealousy vanished. Her eyes flew open, only to see the white rabbit, Hopper, waiting for her at the bottom of the steps.

"What?" she breathed, having no idea what in the world was going on. The white rabbit of doom had a habit of showing up at the most importunate times. Determined to get to the bottom of it, she glared at the rabbit and ordered, "Stay!" She then ran down the stairs with the notion of grabbing him. But the rabbit, with his long ears, didn't listen. Instead, he bounded into the garden and disappeared behind a bush. Bunny followed the rabbit, but he was nowhere to be found.

"Bridget!" Giff called to her. He and Brett were way out on the open lawn, halfway to the stables. "Are you coming?"

With her heart beating wildly in her chest, Bunny nodded and ran after them.

The handsome brick and timber Bramsford stables, topped with an overhanging slate roof, were fitting for such a grand manor. As Bunny entered the brick courtyard with the lads, several curious equine heads poked out of their stalls to greet them, ears forward and eyes bright. They were gorgeous creatures. Just seeing them induced a pang of homesickness. She'd grown up with horses, but none as beautiful as these. While Giff and Brett headed for the archway that appeared to tunnel through the building, leading, no doubt, to a paddock or two and the office in question, Bunny couldn't help herself from walking to a softly whinnying black horse to say hello. From the nameplate on the stall, she gathered that his name was Zeus. She reached up to stroke his sleek neck, and said, "Well, mister, aren't you gorgeous."

"Thank you." The reply, in a strong West Country accent, shocked her. Confused, she stared at the horse. That's when the distinctly male voice added, "Most women aren't usually that direct, but I like it."

She turned in the direction of the voice, and blushed. It was the man they'd come to see, poking his handsome head out of the next stall. He was grinning at her. The picture hadn't done him justice at all. Likely because the man had been looking at Marcus Bean and not at the camera. His sun-kissed brunette locks, a beard so closely trimmed it resembled long stubble, white teeth, and smiling light brown eyes, set Bunny's cheeks on fire. Holy shizzle! She had to get him to stop smiling at her or she feared she'd run away.

"I meant . . . him," Bunny clarified, tapping her finger on Zeus's nose. Zeus went in for a nibble, and Bunny swiftly removed her hand.

"I'm crushed, but I understand. One cannot compete with a stud like Zeus. Literally a stud. Right, Ginger?" Ginger, the horse he was visiting, threw her head back in a gesture that resembled a nod.

"A stud, eh?" Bunny remarked, getting his joke. "You must be Alex Grimsby."

"I am. And you are the celebrity chef with the ghost hunters. Bridget MacBride, I presume?" He was correct, and that fact made her blush even more.

"How do you know that? I've never seen you at the big house. If I had, I'd remember."

Alex crossed his arms and rested them on the lower stall door. "I only go there when I have to, which isn't often. My office is here, and I have a cozy little cottage out back. Come through the breezeway and I'll show you." Without waiting for her to agree, he disappeared. Talk about presumptuous!

It wasn't presumptuous at all, Bunny realized the moment Alex Grimsby appeared in the middle of the breezeway, greeting her and the lads. He explained that he had spotted them on their way to the stables and had figured they were coming to talk with him. He then gave them a brief tour of the impressive building before escorting them to his office, located at the far end of the stables.

"Please." He offered them a seat and took his own behind a stout desk. It was a rustic office, with serviceable leather chairs, a rough-and-tumble loveseat beneath a built-in bookshelf, and a couple of deer heads gracing the walls. It resembled a hunting lodge more than an office, Bunny mused. Alex crossed his arms, leaned back in his chair, and said, "I was wondering when you'd get around to paying me a visit. I've already talked with DCI Standish, but I've heard that you three are asking questions in the big house as well. I respect that. Maybe you can get to the bottom of this mess. After all, Marcus brought you here for a reason, although I doubt this was part of the plan."

Bunny looked at the men on either side of her, then back at Alex Grimsby. "I doubt it was. Who told you that we've been asking questions?"

"Charles," he said. "Comes here daily to check on the horses and to keep tabs on things here. His sister does too, but for other reasons."

Giff's eyes twinkled. "You, perhaps?"

"Lord, no. I have a strict policy to never dip my pen in the company ink, so to speak. Also, I don't get involved with married women. Wish Bean had the same sense. You know he was having an affair with Morgan?"

Brett nodded. "We were told. Morgan confirmed it for us. We were wondering if her husband was the jealous type, or perhaps there were lingering bad feelings between Morgan and Bean."

Alex shook his head. "Percival Green is an idiot and a snob. I do think he is jealous of Morgan, but I'm not sure his petty, self-serving nature would drive him to murder Marcus Bean. If he was going to harm Bean, he would have done it long ago, when he had found out about the affair. Trouble was, he was having one too. Regarding Morgan, once the affair had ended, she and Bean seemed friendly enough."

"What about you?" Brett asked. He leaned in and placed the picture they had found in the historian's office on the desk. "We found this picture on the floor of Bean's office. What was your relationship with Marcus Bean?"

Grimsby picked up the picture and studied it. He looked at Brett. "You were in his office in the big house? Did you find anything in there?"

"Not much," Brett told him. "It's part of the crime scene. Truthfully, we don't even know what it is we're looking for. We're still trying to find a motive. We were wondering if you could help us."

Alex looked at the picture again before putting it back on the table. "We were mates," he said. "Marcus was a good friend of mine, the only real friend I had here. Like Charles, he came out here whenever he needed a break from the big house and his work. If it helps, he was very excited to bring you here. History was his profession, but there was something about that morbid old Mistletoe Bride legend that really lit his fire. I think he thought that if you are the real thing and you did make contact with the ghost, it would help validate what he was working on."

"Do you know what that was?" Bunny asked.

Alex Grimsby closed his eyes and pinched the bridge of his nose, as if troubled about something. "No. Not really. The ghost, I think. Bean could bang on about that all day if I let him, but I didn't. Can't stand that stuff. Not a fan of ghosts and that sort of thing."

"Me either. Is that why you stay out here?" Bunny asked.

"It's part of the reason. I find the big house too fancy for my tastes. The food is good. I eat an occasional meal there, but heading to the local pub at the village for a pint is more to my taste."

"Mine too," Giff piped up. Bunny ignored him and pointed to the picture on the desk.

"What's going on in this picture?"

With a melancholy expression, Grimsby offered, "We were hunting quail. Marcus is . . . was an enthusiastic sportsman, but the man was a terrible shot. Those birds are mine. I let him hold them for the camera."

"Who took the picture?" Giff was unable to pull his eyes from the handsome man.

"Charles took it. The three of us often hunted together."

"You hunt here?" Brett found that interesting.

Grimsby nodded. "Bird hunting mostly. While weddings are the bread and butter of the manor, we do book several weekends each year during the proper season. I take the parties out. It's part of my job. I manage the stables and do general land management for the Wallingford family. For instance, the horses kept here are not for our guests. The hotel guests are welcome to come out and tour the stables, but those are Wallingford horses. It's Morgan's passion. She's bidding to host an equestrian event on the property. We'll see how that goes."

"Very nice," Giff offered. "Now back to Bean. Two days ago, I was meditating in the woods over there and heard you two arguing. That was the day he was murdered. I don't mean to be a party pooper, but would you mind telling us what that was about?"

Grimsby pursed his lips. "Arguing? We were in a heated discussion, mate. Pheasant season is about to begin, and I was simply waxing lyrical on the virtues of using mid-century shotguns instead of the modern ones. Marcus liked the newer guns with fancy sights because he felt they gave him an advantage. He needed all the help he could get, rest his soul. I was simply taking the piss out of him. Told him it was mid-century guns and that he'd better hit the range and practice, or he'd come home empty-handed."

Coming to some conclusion, Brett crossed his arms and leaned on the desk. "I'm going to be honest with you. The police think Bean was blackmailing somebody and that got him killed. We believe otherwise."

"I won't deny that he had a knack for digging up dirt on people," Grimsby offered. "Only I think that was a byproduct of his job. He found out things about the Wallingford family mostly. I never thought it was malicious, but he did enjoy new discoveries. What's your theory?"

Bunny took the lead on this one, holding Grimsby in the heat of her gaze. She had the distinct feeling that he knew something and needed more prodding before he'd reveal what it was. "It's along similar lines," she stated. "We believe Marcus Bean stumbled on something big regarding the Mistletoe Bride legend. We also learned that he was going to reveal this discovery on camera during Brett and Giff's paranormal investigation the night he was murdered. We think somebody found out, took my knife from the kitchen to frame me, and murdered him before he could make his big reveal. Whoever did that, also went to his office and possibly stole important information, but we can't be sure. We don't know what he discovered, but we'd like to find out."

She watched as Alex's handsome face blanched. "That's a good theory," he whispered, and gestured with his eyes to the far upper right corner of the room. "Don't look," he whispered again. "It's a security camera." In a louder voice, he said, "A pleasure meetin' you three. Let me give you a ride back to the big house. I'll take you in the RTV, the rugged terrain vehicle," he clarified with a wink.

The moment they got in the doorless vehicle, Alex turned

to the back seat and said, "Lads, join me for dinner and a pint tonight in the village. We can talk freely there. I'll be at the White Hart."

"We're conducting our investigation tonight," Brett told him, much to Giff's chagrin.

"What time?" Alex pulled out of the stables and aimed for a gravel road. It was the same gravel road that took them past Morgan's front door.

"Midnight."

Alex grinned. "No problem there . . . unless you're having a grand time and forget all about your previous engagements, which has been known to happen at the White Hart."

Bunny cast a sardonic look at the attractive man sitting next to her. "You're talking to Brett Bloom. No pub in the world could keep him from a promising ghost hunt. However, Giff? He's another matter."

Chapter 27

❧

"Gran, can ghosts be jealous?"

"Jealous? Explain," Granny Mac said, looking across the table at her granddaughter.

After their trip to the stables, they met Mike, Ed, Cody, and Granny Mac in the drawing room on the main floor. Granny Mac had made sure that the scones Bunny had made and Lilly had baked were brought there along with strawberry jam, clotted cream, and three pots of tea. The plate of scones now sat in the center of the coffee table, nearly empty. All the gentlemen had left to prepare for the evening's investigation. Brett and Giff, having been invited to a village pub by Alex Grimsby, were going to head out before dinner in the white sedan. It was everyone's hope that they'd learn something important that would bring them closer to discovering why the historian had been murdered. As for Bunny, she was perfectly happy to stay behind. After all, she had a plate of food to whip up to entice the ghost bride to the table. Not only did they need more footage of the Spirit Supper, but the team wanted to put the theory to the test once again.

Bunny and Granny Mac were now alone in the drawing room. Knowing that she was expected to play a part in tonight's investigation, Bunny had plenty of questions that only her grandmother could answer. She grasped her teacup with both hands and explained.

"Today when I was walking down the back steps of the upper patio, I felt the Mistletoe Bride. For whatever reason, she haunts those steps as well as my bedroom. It's not the first time I've run into her there either. The same thing happened to me yesterday when Brett and I went to talk with Betsy." She shook her head, recalling the incident. "No, it wasn't quite the same thing. Yesterday I saw the image of a happy bride turn into a skeleton. It was clear as day in my mind, and it quite undid me. It was the first time I felt that debilitating sorrow. Today, however, she hit me on the third step, only this time I felt desolation and jealousy. Burning jealousy. I know that many brides get married here. I've imagined them walking down those sweeping steps into the garden where they meet their awaiting grooms. I'm not sure that's even true, but even if it was, Ann Copeland couldn't have gotten married in the Bramsford gardens. She got married in December. It would have been far too cold. So, I think she's jealous of all the brides who get married here."

Granny Mac pursed her red-painted lips as she considered this. "It could be, but I've never heard of that happening—a ghost being actively jealous of the living. It would be highly unusual. In my experience, those souls who depart this world and linger, are stuck in *their* present, not ours. If you felt jealousy on those steps, it must be coming from the ghost bride's own experience."

Bunny set her empty cup back in its saucer. "But that doesn't make any sense. Last night, when she came into my room, I felt her sorrow and her fear. It was terrible."

"I'm sorry you had to go through that, dear. But I also thought you said that you felt anger as well?"

"I did, and I can only imagine why. If I got stuck in that moldy old mistletoe chest and my groom never found me, I'd run the gamut of all those emotions too. It's heart-wrenching just thinking about it." Bunny's eyes nearly teared up at the thought. "As far as jealousy is concerned, I'm not sure how that fits in with what we know."

"Indeed." Granny Mac nodded. "That's why this jealousy you experienced is so interesting." A troubled look crossed the older woman's face, causing her to place both elbows on the table and lean toward Bunny. "I'm going to be honest. Ghosts and hauntings aren't my forte. I feel a wee bitty out of my element here."

"Come again?" Bunny couldn't believe what she was hearing. "But . . . you're a medium, Gran! You have the second sight!"

"My gift, and I believe yours too, is connecting with the spirit world, meaning departed loved ones who cross over into the light right away. It's the natural order of a soul's journey, crossing from this world into the next when it's time. That was how I knew Brett's grandfather was around him. I felt his spiritual essence. Spirits can communicate with loved ones and sensitives like us with what I like to term, divine spiritual energy."

"Okay. I sort of understand that, but what about ghosts?" Bunny was feeling very confused. Also, if she was being honest, she felt a little disheartened as well. If she was supposed to be able to connect with the spirit world, and spirits weren't ghosts, according to her gran, then why could she connect to the ghost of Ann Copeland?

"You are young, Bridget," Granny Mac told her gently. "You are just now willing to embrace your gifts and there is a lot to learn about that. Most of your learning will be through experiencing those entities that attempt to contact you. I'm just relaying my experiences. Now ghosts, specters, and apparitions, on the other hand, manifest in human energy, which is earthly and heavy, unlike spiritual energy, which is bright, profound, and uplifting. There is usually a dark feeling attached to ghosts—a coldness, prickling senses, shivers running down the spine, that sort of thing. Some have even learned how to manipulate objects in our time, or even touch us, but that is rare."

Bunny was trying her hardest to follow this. "So, when I get that troubling, foreboding feeling I'm sensing a ghost, not a spirit?"

"It's a good chance you are. Here's how you can tell the difference. Spirits know they've moved on, yet it is the strong bond of love that connects them to the living. They often show up in times of need, acting as spiritual guides whispering to our unconscious. It's quite common for a departed loved one to send messages to those they love, but not everyone knows how to recognize them. Spirits, when I see them, appear bright or just visible in a hazy light. Sometimes I see sparkles in the air. Very seldom is there a dark feeling associated with such a spirit.

"Ghosts, on the other hand, don't know they're dead. They've either turned from the light, ignored it, or they've missed it altogether. Ghosts are stuck in a cycle of reliving their powerful emotions, experiencing their traumas over and over again. It's quite awful."

"Oh, Gran! What can be done?" Bunny's heart ached for the ghost bride.

"Sir Charles isn't going to like my suggestion, but if we can find a way, my dear, we need to bring her to the light and end this."

"Cross her over?" Bunny never considered this. "We can do that?"

"I need to read up on it, but I think we can. It will take both our efforts. Which brings me to my point. You have the ability to feel the emotions that Ann Copeland felt in her darkest hour. She's connecting to you for a reason. I believe, although I could be wrong here, but I think she knows that you can help her. If you were feeling jealousy while encountering her on the patio steps, it is likely another emotion that binds her here."

Thinking about all Granny Mac had said, Bunny eventually nodded. "I think so too. But why?"

"We obviously don't know the whole story yet. Hopefully, tonight we'll get some answers."

Chapter 28

"Here we are," Brett said, pulling into a parking space at the side of the White Hart. The building, a traditional English pub in the Tudor style, had appeared before them, rising like an oasis in the desert, at the last bend in the road. From the many cars parked along the roadside and in the parking lot, it looked to be a popular watering hole for the locals. As he got out of the car, Brett was happy to see that the old pub, and he imagined it was very old, had been lovingly maintained. His eyes were then drawn to the hand-painted sign above the door that depicted a majestic white deer with a broad rack of antlers standing in a glen. It wasn't only beautiful, but necessary, denoting the business within. Unlike the grand manor of Bramsford, there was something cozy and inviting about the historic building, aside from the promise of a mug of ale and warm food. It was a sense of community, Brett thought. A feeling of fellowship, and history. Definitely history, because a building this old was undoubtedly haunted.

"What a place," Giff remarked, breaking Brett's silent musings as they made their way to the front door. "I have to hand it to the Brits; they have the best pubs in the world. This old place looks like it's right out of a travel guide. No wonder Grimsby hangs out here. It's not nearly as oppressive and stuffy as the big house, as he likes to call it. I hope the food's good as well because I'm starving."

"Me too. But we have a long night ahead of us, so pace yourself."

"Urgh," Giff groaned, and rolled his eyes. "Thanks for reminding me. We're hunting ghosts. I didn't realize how much I was going to regret this new career choice, but I do."

"You'll get used to it." Brett tossed him a pointed grin before soaking in the ambiance of the pub. The White Hart had not disappointed him. Filled with happy customers, he admired the exposed dark beams, the authentic fixtures, the antique tables, and the warmth from the fire in the large hearth. He was just getting his bearings when he heard their names being called. Across the room Alex Grimsby waved to them. He was sitting in a high-backed wooden booth with a pretty woman beside him.

"Gentlemen, I'm glad you could make it. This is Gwen, my girlfriend." After the introductions were made, and Brett and Giff were seated, Grimsby continued. "As I indicated to you earlier, there is little privacy at the stables, and this matter of Marcus's murder is far too important to take any chances. Now, before we begin, what are you lads drinking? Also, if you're hungry, I recommend the cottage pie."

After their orders had been placed, pleasant small talk circulated the table until three mugs of ale appeared along with an English rose gin martini for Gwen. Giff graced her with one of his disarming grins, privately disappointed that Grimsby had a lovely girlfriend. After taking a long sip from his mug, he set it down and looked at the man across from him. "This is a good call, asking us here. I can tell you how happy Brett and I are to have escaped the manor for a while. But I must ask, why is there a camera in your office?"

"Security," Grimsby told them plainly. "There are cameras in several locations at the stables, mostly so that I can monitor the horses from home."

"Those Wallingford horses are worth a lot of money," Gwen supplied, with a pointed nod. "That Morgan Wallingford-Green cares more for those horses than she does that poor daughter of hers."

"That's not exactly true, Gwen," Grimsby chided. "Morgan is passionate about those animals, but she loves her daughter. They're going through a difficult time. Riding is Morgan's diversion. Now, back to those security cameras," he said, bringing his attention back to the matter at hand. "The stables are also monitored at the manor by Peter Billingsley. He's Charlie's right-hand man."

"Is he, now?" Giff lifted a brow in question. "I didn't know that."

"He's not a bad chap, but he keeps tabs on things. It's his job. For instance, he'll have seen that you were in the stable office talking with me, and no doubt he'll have told Sir Charles of your visit."

Brett lowered his voice. "Do you think Sir Charles had a hand in Bean's murder?"

Grimsby was about to take a swig of his ale when a troubled look crossed his face. Losing his appetite, he set down his mug and shook his head. "I don't know what to think. That's why I brought you two here. I hope Miss MacBride doesn't mind. But if she left the manor in your company, whoever is behind this would take notice. After all, it's no secret that the three of you have been poking around, asking questions. I thought it best that just you two meet with me here. There's nothing overly suspicious about two men stepping out for a pint."

Brett agreed.

Grimsby continued. "Good. As I told you earlier, Marcus was my friend. What I didn't tell you was that he did confide a secret to me, one that I haven't told anyone, even the police."

"That's what has me so nervous," Gwen told them. "If Marcus was murdered because of something he found out about the Wallingfords, what's to stop the murderer from going after anyone else who knows about this secret?"

That got Brett's attention. "Do you think this is about Marcus stumbling on a damaging secret?"

Alex Grimsby nodded. "I think it very well might be. But here's the rub. I don't know what damaging evidence he found. He never told me. However, four months ago he came to my house with a startling find. You already know that Bean was obsessed with the legend of the Mistletoe Bride. He was trying not only to learn more about the poor couple at the center of the sad tale, but he was also trying to prove that it had indeed occurred at Bramsford Manor."

"So we've heard," Brett told him. "Was he successful?"

"I think so," Grimsby admitted. However, before he could continue his story, their server arrived with their dinners. The entire table fell unnaturally silent as the woman handed out steaming plates of cottage pie, a basket of homemade rolls, and another round of drinks. The moment she left, Grimsby continued his story while they ate.

"Marcus had an office in the attic of the manor. He used to tell me that they never threw anything out over there, that it all went into the attic where it was largely forgotten, just like the chest that poor bride was supposedly found in. Anyhow, while rummaging through another ancient chest, he found a locket."

"A locket?" Giff blurted in mid-chew. He quickly swallowed, and said, "What was so special about this locket?"

An odd smile sat on Grimsby's face. "It was a very special find, according to Bean. The locket, he told me, had been found with other articles supposedly belonging to Sir Henry Wallingford, Ann Copeland's unfortunate groom. Marcus was certain he had stumbled upon a key piece of the mystery."

"Had he given it to her before she disappeared? How did he know it belonged to Ann?" Brett, having already eaten half his cottage pie, was enthralled by this story. He set down his fork and studied Alex Grimsby.

"What made it so special was the fact it contained a lock of hair—a lock of golden-blond hair encased in glass with the initials ACW carved on the silver casing."

"Ann Copeland Wallingford," Brett said, recognizing the initials of the Mistletoe Bride's true name. He added, "Wallingford, because Ann had married Sir Henry before she played her last game of hide-and-seek?"

"Correct. Yet because the initials ACW were on the locket, Marcus believed that Sir Henry had the locket made after he had made his gruesome discovery about his missing bride. Remember, the legend states that she was found in a chest fifty years later by her groom, still in her wedding gown and with her bridal wreath on her head."

"It's still a heart-wrenching tale every time I hear it." Gwen sighed, placing a hand over her heart. The men all agreed.

"What did Marcus do about this new discovery?" Brett asked. "I have to be honest. I've never heard that a locket with the bride's hair in it had been found."

"That's because Marcus never told Charles or Morgan about it, as he was supposed to do. He didn't want to tell them because he wanted to run DNA tests on the hair. He had discovered an actual biological piece of this poor bride, and he was determined to get every ounce of information from it that he could. That required him to open the antique locket to get at the hair, most of which would be destroyed in the process of extracting DNA. He didn't want to tell anyone about it for fear they would deny him access to it.

He knows that Charles loves his antiques and family history more than the truth. He'd want to display the piece next to the chest."

"I imagine he would. So"—Giff leaned forward, staring into the dreamy brown eyes of Alex Grimsby—"Bean stole an artifact from the attic and ran some tests on it. Do you know what he learned?"

"No," Grimsby said. "He never told me. But he did tell me that he had made a very significant discovery that was going to change the way history regarded the tale of the Mistletoe Bride."

Brett inwardly groaned. They had learned of an important artifact, but to what end? They were still no closer to learning what Bean had discovered about the DNA or its significance. Addressing Grimsby, he asked, "Did Bean happen to tell you that he was going to announce this great discovery during our ghost investigation?"

"He did. He called me on the phone one afternoon, he was so keyed up about it. Said he was going to rock the manor with his findings."

"You must have been the person on the other end of the phone call Betsy told us about. She overheard Bean telling someone about a big reveal while serving his tea. We," Brett said, indicating Giff, "believe this is why Bean was murdered." Grimsby nodded in agreement. "Do you know if he told anyone about his discovery? Anyone at all?"

"He must have, but it wasn't me."

With the wheels of his mind spinning over this new revelation, Brett finished his meal and drained his second mug of ale. He then asked another question. "You knew Marcus better than anyone. What was his relationship to Betsy Copperfield?"

Grimsby shrugged. "He got her the job in the hotel restaurant. I think Betsy was one of his students from the university. She's a very responsible young lady and a real asset to the hotel staff."

"What?" Giff nearly choked on his beer. "She was his student? That would indicate that Bean taught school!"

"Of course, he did," Grimsby said, casting them both a look of disappointment. "He was a professor of history at the university in Reading. He split his time between Bramsford Manor and the university. He only taught a few classes, just enough to keep his standing there."

"That explains it," Brett said, mentally berating himself. "I knew they had a connection, but I couldn't figure out what it was. Was there a reason Bean got Betsy a job at the manor?"

Grimsby shrugged. "It's hard to find good employees these days. A recommendation from Bean went a long way with Charles and Morgan. Bean also got Lewis his job at the restaurant as well, although Lewis was never one of Bean's students." Here Grimsby paused before adding, "I shouldn't tell you this, but there's little point in keeping this secret now Bean is gone. Lewis is Sir Charles's biological son, although neither one of them knows it yet. It was another one of Bean's genetic discoveries. He liked to meddle, and not always with the best intentions either. He only told me about it because he was so chuffed with himself for having figured it out."

"Lewis? That likable young man? How long has Lewis been working at the hotel?"

"He started this summer. Bean found him on one of those popular genetic testing sites. He told me that Lewis recently learned that the man he thought was his father wasn't his biological father and took a test to see if his real father could be found."

"Ohmygod!" Giff exclaimed. "That's diabolical. Bean knew who the kid's father was and didn't tell him? Instead, he offers him a lowly job at the castle like a male Cinderella. What a d-bag!"

"A right wanker, he was, rest his soul." Grimsby shook his head just thinking about it. "Lewis is a good kid," he added. "I advised Bean against revealing this 'love child of Sir Charles's unless Lewis's mother agreed to it first. As far as I know, Bean was working on that, but not as hard as he was working on his other big surprise."

"I hate to say it," Brett began, "but Bean obviously took a huge risk uncovering so much troubling family history that it's going to be difficult sorting out just what discovery he made that got him killed. Are you certain Sir Charles didn't know about Lewis?"

Grimsby shrugged and shook his head.

"He might have told somebody else about it, like for instance, the lovely and possibly jealous Morgan?" Giff offered. "How would she take the fact that her very single brother has an heir?"

"Not well," Gwen added spitefully. She was obviously miffed at the fact that Morgan Wallingford-Green flirted shamelessly with her man every chance she got.

Brett flashed a look at Giff. "Looks like we're going to have to do more digging ourselves if we're going to figure this one out."

"Indeed," Grimsby said. "That's also what I wanted to talk to you about. I suggest you pay a visit to his office at the university tomorrow. I've phoned a colleague of his there, a man named James Bellemy. He'll assist you in any way he can."

Brett thanked him, looked at the time, and took out money to cover their bill.

"Lads, this one's on me," Grimsby said, handing them back their cash. "Good luck."

Chapter 29

"Glad you gentlemen could make it," Mike teased as Brett and Giff walked into the historic dining room, dressed and ready to begin recording the investigation. The beautiful dining room table had been set in the exact same way as it had during their first run, when they had tried to contact the ill-fated Mistletoe Bride. However, instead of the lofty, roast prime rib feast cooked to entice the ghost to the table, Bunny had improvised, using leftovers instead. Although the cameras would be recording, this Spirit Feast was meant to spark their second attempt at a ghost hunt. Everyone was praying that this time they would be successful.

"How was your dinner with Alex Grimsby?" Bunny asked them, looking up from the plate of food she had placed before the spirit chair.

"Good," Brett remarked, coming beside her. He took one look at the expertly crafted meal and smiled. "Really good. I have a lot to tell you." Looking around to make sure no one was listening, he whispered, "Marcus Bean did stumble upon something very interesting. According to Alex Grimsby,

Bean found a preserved lock of hair presumed to be from the Mistletoe Bride."

"What?" she whispered back, her face mirroring his excitement. "That's huge. Do you know what Bean found out regarding this lock of old hair?"

Brett shook his head. "That's just it. No one knows, but we have the name of a man who can help us. Also, possibility number two, Bean uncovered another bombshell about the Wallingford family. Sir Charles fathered a son twenty years ago. He never told Sir Charles about this finding. He kept his employer in the dark, and the kid too. However, somebody else might have found out."

Again, Bunny looked truly stunned. Forgetting all about her beautiful plate of food, she uttered, "A son?"

"Hi, Ms. MacBride. I'm ready for the investigation. Where do you want me?" Bunny and Brett both turned to find Lewis standing across the table from them.

Brett blanched while Bunny smiled at the young man. "You're joining us for the investigation tonight?"

Lewis nodded vigorously, causing his longish, backswept bangs to flop over his eyes. He brushed them back and grinned.

"That's grand, although you're a braver person than I am, Lewis. Brett will be sitting at the head of the table, I'm sitting to his right, and Giff will be to his left. You'll sit next to me, and Sir Charles will sit next to Giff. He should be along any minute."

The moment Lewis took his seat, Brett pulled Bunny out of earshot and whispered, "They're joining us? Whose idea was that?"

"We wanted Sir Charles and Morgan to join us, since Marcus Bean is unable to. Sir Charles is excited to participate, but Morgan declined. She offered to swap places with Lewis. Apparently, the young man has a ghoulish side to him. I think it's a great idea. He's genuinely excited about this, where Morgan was not. Is there a problem?" Bunny asked him.

Yes, there was. To Brett's way of thinking, Morgan might have put father and son together tonight for a reason. Did she mean one of them harm? Was this simply a little joke purely for her enjoyment? Or perhaps Morgan, like her brother, was as ignorant of Lewis's true identity? Either way, Brett was going to be on high alert during the investigation. Giff too, judging from the way he greeted the boy. However, looking at Bunny, Brett told her, "No problem at all. By the way, that looks delicious."

Bunny tried not to blush as she looked into Brett's bright eyes. "Thanks," she said. "I simply rummaged through the kitchen refrigerator and threw it together. Not fancy, but delicious all the same. It's leftover bangers and mash served in a Yorkshire pudding crust and covered with onion gravy. Hearty pub fare. I've also added a piece of hotel wedding cake for dessert to further entice the ghost bride. Lilly pulled that from the freezer, thinking it would be a nice touch."

Brett agreed. Looking at Sir Charles, who had just walked into the dining room, then at Lewis, who was beaming with excitement as he talked softly with Mike, he mumbled grimly, "Be careful who you invite to dinner."

Everyone took their seat at the table. "Ready?" Cody asked, peering at them from behind his camera. "We're going to start where we left off the other night. Sir Charles, Lewis, if at any point either one of you feels uncomfortable to proceed, just let us know and we can escort you to safer quarters." Sir Charles gave a curt nod. Lewis, who had a goofy smile plastered on his lips, thrust his thumb in the air.

Cody continued, this time directing his attention to Bunny. "Bunny, you'll be coming along as well tonight."

"Don't remind me," she told him with a palpable lack of enthusiasm.

"Also, if you happen to see any more white rabbits, let us know immediately." This was partly said in jest, and yet everyone on the team knew what a serious harbinger Bunny's dreaded white rabbit of doom was.

"White rabbit?" Lewis questioned in wide-eyed intrigue. "Is that some sorta code word?"

Bunny, dreading the thought, nodded. "It's code for *ghosts*," she lied.

"Giff, do you have your earpiece in?"

Giff, sharply dressed yet looking slightly pale, gave Cody a nod.

"Good. Ella will remain off camera, but if she contacts one of the entities that haunts this manor, she is going to relay the message to you. You just say what she says. Brett will interpret the messages, ask questions, and run the ghost tech with Mike, who will also be filming as needed. Ed is in the library in the west wing, monitoring the feed. Any questions?"

"What if . . . she contacts me first?" Bunny asked, casting a look of fear at her grandmother. Ella MacBride was sitting in a chair in the corner of the dining room behind one of the stationary cameras. Unlike Bunny, whose stomach was in a knot, the older woman looked calm and serene.

"You'll know if she does," Granny Mac said. "If you begin to sense her, let me know immediately. I have a feeling it's going to be another wild night."

It was a real possibility that Granny Mac knew just how prophetic her words were going to be, for the moment the cameras were turned on, the air inside the dining room seemed to crackle with electricity. Bunny could feel it. Her nerves were pulled taut as guitar strings, and every hair on her body prickled uncomfortably.

"Ann Copeland, we've heard your story," Brett said to the empty chair.

Near the plate of elevated pub food sat an EVP meter, (electronic voice phenomena). This piece of ghost tech Brett often referred to as a spirit box. It worked by scanning different radio frequencies to catch and record disembodied voices. *Pretty creepy*, Bunny thought. In his hand he held what he referred to as a *ghost meter*, or an EMF (electromagnetic field meter) which he pointed at the chair. Supposedly, it measured changes in the electromagnetic field. According to Brett, ghosts were thought to be made up of energy and therefore would set off the meter if any were nearby. Again, creepy. However, it dawned on Bunny, as Brett monitored his ghost tech, that she didn't need any of it to connect with a ghost.

Brett continued. "We know you are still here, at Bramsford Manor. We invite you to join us tonight at the table for a wedding feast. We know how sad you are. For generations, many have felt your sadness and have heard your moaning. We want to know how we can help you."

To everyone's surprise, a rogue wind blew into the room, fluttering the flames on the candles in the candelabra.

"Whoa," Giff said, looking directly into Cody's camera. "I just felt a cold chill. I think she's here . . ."

Just then a high-pitched electrical beep pierced the silence, startling everyone. Brett looked at his EMF meter and turned it to the camera. "Dude, look at this. It's going off. Someone is most definitely here with us."

He had no sooner spoken when another, stronger rogue wind blew through the room, snuffing out every candle and plunging them into relative darkness.

"Ohmygod!" Giff screamed, jumping off his chair in the darkness. The chair tilted and he caught it just before it hit the floor. "What just happened?"

"Bussin'," Lewis cried, his eyes glued to the empty ghost chair.

"Bussin'?" Sir Charles questioned in his proper English accent, staring at the young man. "What on earth does *bussin'* mean?"

Lewis turned to him and thrust up two thumbs. "Awesome. Really awesome!" he clarified.

Brett, momentarily distracted by their banter, addressed the elephant in the room, namely the ghost bride. "Ann, are you here with us? Was that you who blew out the candles? We want to know what happened on your wedding night."

"*Murder,*" a deep voice said, coming through the spirit box. "*Murder.*" Everyone felt a chill at the word.

"Whoa! Did you hear that? It said *murder*," Brett reiterated, adrenaline pumping through his veins. "Were you murdered?" he asked and stared at the spirit box.

"No," Bunny said. She looked at Brett and shook her head. He didn't understand what she meant. "It's not her. She's not here. I smell cigarettes and Old Spice Swagger." She shot a questioning look at Granny Mac, still sitting peacefully in the corner.

"Marcus Bean is here," Ella MacBride concurred. Unfortunately, it went straight into Giff's ear.

"Marcus Bean is here!" he cried, looking wildly at Brett. "He's here! The recently murdered historian. What the virtual F!"

"Calm down," Brett told him, placing a hand on his friend's shoulder. "We can edit that out later. Get ahold of yourself, buddy. You're a world famous medium and fashion icon, remember?"

"He's angry, I think," Bunny whispered, feeling it in the air. "Maybe frustrated as well. I'm not sure." She noticed that Sir Charles looked truly frightened, while the young man sitting across from him, leaned in, wanting to hear more. Twenty-year-olds, she thought, ghouls to the core!

Giff, pulling himself together, took that as his cue. With eyes wide with fear, he looked directly into Cody's camera, repeating, "He's angry. I can feel it. He blew out the candles. He wanted to get our attention because . . . because he was murdered!" He was now just improvising, and yet it was a far better performance than the one from the other night. Cody, looking at him from behind the main camera, made a circling gesture with his finger, urging Giff to continue. This new Gifford McGrady medium act was pure gold!

That's when Brett cut in.

"Dude, the EMF meter is going crazy. Like, it's off the charts crazy." He turned it to the camera again to show the needle flipping past the red zone.

Giff, taking inspiration from Brett, turned to the empty chair. "Marcus Bean, who murdered you? You can tell us. Just say it into the spirit box." Giff stared at the box, hoping for an answer. His emotions were teetering on a knife edge between abject fear and burning anticipation.

The voice box crackled and hummed with static. Suddenly the same deep voice came over the spirit box stating, "Chest."

"You were stabbed in the chest?" Brett asked. "Or you were in the chest?"

Then another word floated on the air, but it was lost, drowned out by a horrendous crash that shook the dining room. The noise had come from down the hall, breaking their concentration. Sir Charles jumped from his chair and ran to the source of the noise. Everyone else followed as he ran to the long gallery.

Not again, Bunny thought. *Not again.*

"Bloody hell!" Sir Charles cried, staring at the destruction on the floor. "The china cabinet! Bramsford's historic china and crystal that were on display have been destroyed. What the devil is going on here, Bloom?" His fists were balled at his sides while he heaved with both fright and anger. Close to tears, Sir Charles then fell to his knees where he picked up a shard of fine bone china, etched with a delicate blue design and rimmed with gold. It was heartbreaking to imagine. Everyone stared at the historic display cabinet, not sure what to do next.

While Granny Mac knelt beside Sir Charles, who sat on the floor surrounded by shards of the family china, Brett sidled over to Bunny and Giff, and whispered, "This is not the work of a ghost."

"No, duh," Bunny shot back in whisper. "That china cabinet is heavy. Too heavy for swirling air."

"Bridget's correct," Granny Mac offered. "Ghosts are residual energy and human emotion. Pushing that over would take herculean effort."

"Right," Bunny said, looking at her grandmother. "Also, the ghost of Marcus Bean was still in the dining room. I smelled him."

Giff flashed her a horrified look. "Lordy, what a curse that must be for you."

"The spirit box," Brett broke in. "I heard another word after *chest*, but it was drowned out by the china cabinet crashing. This was no accident," he said, feeling a pang of compassion for the aristocrat on the floor surrounded by his shattered heirlooms. The others were consoling him. "This was a diversion."

As this thought sank in, Brett, Bunny, and Giff ran down the great hall, aiming for the dining room again. However, once they arrived, their worst fears were realized. All the stationary cameras that had been recording the Spirit Supper had been knocked to the floor. They were still on, but the room was dark. Yet even in the darkness they could see that the spirit box was missing.

"The murderer!" Bunny cried. "Whoever killed Marcus must have been listening in. They stole the spirit box! But who?"

Before either Brett or Giff could reply to that statement, Ed cut in over Brett's walkie-talkie.

"Whoa! What just happened in there? I heard a loud crash and all the cameras got pushed over. Everything went dark. I've been trying to reach you!"

"There was an accident. A china cabinet got pushed over in the long gallery," Brett told him.

"Pushed over. That's some dark energy, bro. Was anyone hurt?"

"No."

"Good. Then you had better get up to the second floor. The motion sensor cameras are going off outside the Fleur-de-Lys room. We caught an image of a woman in white. I think the Mistletoe Bride is here."

Chapter 30

Sir Charles was in no state to continue the investigation. However, with news of paranormal activity on the second floor, the team was anxious to get up there. But first they had to make sure that Sir Charles and Lewis were protected. Because whoever it was that had murdered Marcus Bean would do anything, including gross vandalism of private property, to make sure their identity remained anonymous. Granny Mac, who loved, collected, admired, and appreciated fine china as well, turned to Sir Charles.

"This wanton destruction of your family heirlooms is unacceptable. You do realize that someone here did this?"

He looked at her, his troubled gaze unwavering as he nodded. "I've lived here all my life, and while I have seen a ghost from time to time, nothing like this has ever occurred. Bean's murderer is here, in this manor house. I can't believe it." He shook his head before flashing an apologetic look at Bunny. "It was so much easier when I believed that you were responsible, Ms. MacBride, leading us all to my beloved and debauched mistletoe chest like that. But all of you were in the dining room with me tonight. I now know for a fact that it couldn't have been any of you."

Bunny felt like rolling her eyes at him, but under the circumstances, she refrained. "Honestly, sir, we'd only just met the man. And we needed his help to conduct our investigation. Why would we want him dead?"

"You make a good point, my dear." He then looked to the young server standing next to him and held up his hand. "Be a good lad and help me up." Lewis did as he was told. Bunny felt a little sad that the boy's high spirits had been dampened by this recent calamity.

"Sir," he said, "I think we should call the police. Whoever did this is still here."

"Right. Right, my boy. I'll phone DCI Standish right now."

"Sir Charles," Brett cut in—just as the man pulled his phone from his pants pocket. "Will you allow us to continue? Right after this china cabinet fell over, we were alerted that there is activity on the second floor. We think it's the Mistletoe Bride. We think she may be able to help us understand why Marcus Bean was murdered in the first place."

"But . . . but the murderer is here, Bloom! I don't think it's safe."

"With all due respect, sir, the murderer has been here all along. Call the police, but I think that you and Lewis should wait in the library with Ed until DCI Standish and his men arrive. We have cameras set up in hot zones, along with the feeds from Cody and Mike's cameras. You'll be able to monitor our investigation from there. If you could give us a little bit of a head start on our investigation before you make the call, I'd appreciate it. We work best in a controlled environment, meaning that if there's anyone else walking around in this part of the manor, we'd pick it up on our recorders. Will this work for you?" He looked hopefully at Sir Charles and

Lewis, who, when standing next to the older man, had an uncanny resemblance to him. It tugged on his heartstrings, and Brett wondered again at a man who could track down a biological child and keep the secret from both child and parent. If this had been Marcus Bean's big reveal, then it was a troubling one indeed. Lewis could be in grave danger. They needed to get to the bottom of this, and soon.

Sir Charles took one last look at his toppled china cabinet and nodded his agreement. "Let the ghost hunt commence."

Once Sir Charles and Lewis had been brought into the library, Brett knew they wouldn't have long until the police arrived. So much bustling activity on the main floor over the china cabinet incident would not only pollute their audio, but it would change the wonky energy that everyone had felt since their investigation began. The energy would still be wonky, he mused, but in a different way. Now, after making contact with the ghost . . . or spirit of Marcus Bean, his senses had been ignited in the ectoplasmic soup of the paranormal.

Reaching the landing on the second-floor hallway, Bunny groaned. "What in the world is going on up here? It's so creepy. I feel a bit sick." She looked at Granny Mac for confirmation on this.

"You're right," Giff agreed, staring down the dark hallway that had an eerie glow to it. "*Toto,*" he whispered to the team, "*I've a feeling we're not in Kansas anymore.*"

Brett stared at him a minute before turning on his handheld thermal imaging camera. "Alright," he said, looking at Giff. "You and I are going down to the end of that hallway. That's where the camera caught the image of a woman. Bunny and Ella, are you ready to go into the Fleur-de-Lys room?"

Bunny shook her head no, at the same time Granny Mac

answered, "We are. It's not quite ground zero, but the ghost in question is very active in there."

"That's my hotel room, Gran!" Bunny reminded her, feeling ill at the thought of another encounter with the sad ghost bride.

"It is," she said with a no-nonsense lift of her head. "Have you ever heard the old saying, *There is no such thing as an accident*? I believe that you were put in that room, dear, for a reason."

Bunny cast her a deer-in-the-headlights look. "I don't like that saying at all. That implies I was meant to get that ridiculously haunted room." Just as she said this, however, she caught something small and white out of the corner of her eye. *No*, she thought, yet turned toward it anyhow, as if she couldn't stop herself. There, sitting near the door to the Fleur-de-Lys room was Hopper, her white rabbit of doom. It wasn't a good omen, she thought. He was looking at her in a manner that suggested he wanted her attention. Well, he had it, she thought. Why not? As if this place couldn't get any creepier! Then, with a wiggle of his nose, he turned to the closed, solid oak door and hopped right through it, vanishing completely. She turned to Granny Mac, certain that she had seen him too.

"Did you just see that?" she whispered, staring at the older, wiser woman.

"I saw nothing," she said, pulling her gaze back to her granddaughter. "Now, come along, Bridget. We've got work to do."

Brett and Giff, with Cody and Mike filming, made their way to the end of the hallway, which was a mere three doors down from the Fleur-de-Lys room where Bunny and Granny Mac would be. While Bunny was connecting with the Mistletoe Bride, Granny Mac was going to attempt to communicate with her. She would be wearing a microphone so that whatever she said would go straight into Giff's ear, making him appear to channel the conversation for the cameras. It was an elaborate scheme, and one they hoped would work. The team was still in the hallway when a door slammed behind them, making everyone but Granny Mac jump. They spun around. Giff screamed.

"Ohmygod! Ohmygod! What was that? Did you see that?"

Brett nodded. Motioning to Mike, he ran down the hallway to the door that had slammed shut. He opened it and gasped. For a split second he saw a dark, shadowy image of a woman in black clothing. He felt a jolt of terror as she faced him, her average features morphing into something from a horror movie. Then she laughed and vanished.

"Did you hear that?" Giff said to Cody's camera. "I heard a laugh."

"Me too," Cody acknowledged. "It sounded demonic."

With a look of extreme distaste, Giff cried, "Why did you have to say that?"

"I don't like this one bit. This is not what I signed up for," Bunny told them in no uncertain terms.

"I don't know who that was, but it wasn't the Mistletoe Bride." Brett looked shaken, but not defeated. "Fellas, we're going to stay in here. Ladies, proceed as planned. Giff, take a deep breath, brother. It's about to get real."

Once in the Fleur-de-Lys room, Bunny was relieved to see that there was no sign of Hopper. She then sat on the edge of the bed while Granny Mac sat in a chair in the corner of the room. Although the lights were off, the curtains on the large window were open, allowing the light from the full moon to trickle in. The soft glow of moonlight helped ease her nerves and was more than enough for them to see what they were doing.

"Alright, dear, close your eyes, clear your mind, and ask the ghost of Ann Copeland to come into the room."

Bunny grimaced and massaged her face with her hands. "Urgh, I can't believe I'm doing this. This goes against my better judgment, you understand." If she thought she was going to get any pity from her grandmother, she was mistaken. Instead, the woman made a circling gesture in the air, urging Bunny to get on with it. Her gran was right. It was best to get it over with. She then took a deep breath, closed her eyes, and said to the room at large, "Ann, I know you're here. I saw you last night. Please come and visit me again." After a moment of complete silence, Bunny opened one eye and looked at her grandmother in the corner. She shrugged and was about to close her eye again when a cold wind fluttered the curtains.

"Look in the mirror," Granny Mac whispered with urgency.

Fear seized Bunny, but she did as she was told. Stifling a gasp, she saw the hazy white image of the Mistletoe Bride staring back at her. "Nope!" she said, shutting her eyes again, fighting to obliterate the image. However, before she knew what was happening, a debilitating sense of sadness engulfed her. "Crivens!" she cried, feeling her heart breaking as the telltale sting of unshed tears burned her eyes. "Gran, she's here!" She was, just like the night before, appearing in the room while staring out the window.

That was when Granny Mac got to work. Knowing that Giff was on the other end of her microphone, she described what the Mistletoe Bride looked like, and then began asking the distraught apparition questions.

"Why are you crying?" she asked then relayed the ghostly reply to both Bunny and Giff, through his earpiece. Bunny looked on, amazed, from the bed.

Trapped.

"Where are you?"

A dark place.

"How did you get there?"

Hiding.

"Bridget, can you hear her too?"

Bunny nodded, tears streaming down her face. "She's so sad, Gran. And so scared."

Granny Mac nodded before continuing. "Who are you hiding from?" she softly asked the white lady.

My husband.

"Does he frighten you?"

No.

"Why are you hiding?"

A game.

"What is the purpose of this game?"

Find me.

"Are you hiding in a chest?"

Yes.

"Did you climb into the chest?"

Yes. Please. Find me.

"Gran," Bunny whispered. "The sadness is gone. She's angry now. Really angry!"

Granny Mac nodded and pressed on, sensing the change of mood in the room. "Ann, why are you angry?"

Tricked.

At this bombshell, Bunny and Granny Mac exchanged a look in the dark room. *Tricked?* Bunny mouthed. The mere thought sent shivers down her spine.

"You were tricked into getting into the chest?" Granny Mac asked.

"Fear," Bunny whispered. "She's afraid now."

Granny Mac nodded. "I feel it too. Ann," she addressed the ghost again, "did someone trick you into getting into the mistletoe chest?"

Betrayed.

"Who, Ann? Who betrayed you?"

The ghost turned, looking directly at Bunny.

Waiting. Still waiting. Find me.

After these heart-wrenching words, the ghostly bride of Ann Copeland started to fade into a white mist.

"Who betrayed you?" Bunny cried as fat tears rolled down her cheeks. But it was too late, she was gone, the ghost of Ann Copeland was gone, leaving only a swirling mist where she had been. Bunny was certain they'd never know who betrayed the poor bride until a disembodied voice floated a name on the air.

Jean.

Chapter 31

It was a chilling encounter, by anyone's standards. The moment the mist completely dissipated from the room, the door burst open, revealing Giff, doubled over while trying to catch his breath. Brett, Cody, and Mike were right behind him.

"We got it, all of it," Giff said, tapping his ear. "Only it was wild. There was definitely something uber spooky in the room Brett made us go into. However, I channeled your conversation with the Mistletoe Bride instead. It was pure bone-chilling gold! The back of my neck feels like it's been impaled by porcupine quills, the prickling was so intense."

"Sorry, Giff. As I said before, Ann Copeland is not the only ghost who haunts this manor," Granny Mac replied. "Do you have any idea what you encountered in there?"

"A shadowy woman," Brett said. "I saw her only for a split second. Her clothes were dark, as if she was in mourning. But she laughed. Super creepy. Whoa!" he pulled up, looking at Bunny. She was still sitting on the bed, but now her pretty face was red and puffy. Brett narrowed his eyes as he studied her. "Have you been crying again?"

"Of course, I've been crying, you bampot! That poor woman was tricked into hiding in that chest! She died in there! I think she's still waiting for her husband to come and find her. It's so heartbreaking!" The mere thought sent another wave of tears brimming in her eyes and spilling down her cheeks.

"Sweetheart," Giff said, sitting beside her on the bed. As he put his arm around her to comfort her, he shot Brett a dagger-eyed glare. Then his attention was back on Bunny again. "It is truly one of the saddest things I've ever heard. Before we came to this manor, it was just a legend, a ghost story. But she chose to show herself to you, Bunny, and now we know the legend is true. Thanks to you and your brave decision to face your proverbial demons, we also know something that I don't believe anyone else does. According to what I heard in my earpiece a moment ago, that poor girl was tricked into hiding in that chest. That contradicts the legend."

"Oh no," Brett uttered as a thought occurred to him. An epiphany blazed behind his eyes. "Ann Copeland was murdered."

It was a sobering thought, and one that induced another bout of tears for Bunny. "I'm sorry," she said, looking at her handsome coworker. "But I can't help it! Because I think you might be right. That poor young bride was murdered!"

"Murdered," Cody repeated. He looked at Granny Mac. "Back in the dining room, when you told us that the ghost of Marcus Bean was there, we caught a word. *Murder.* We all assumed he was referring to himself, but what if he was trying to tell us about the Mistletoe Bride?"

Granny Mac nodded, thinking. "You make a good point. It could have been that, but we won't know for sure. You were using an EVP detector. They're not too reliable. Another word came thought the spirit box, as you call it, right after that, but it was drowned out by the china cabinet crashing."

That fact sparked another idea in Brett's mind. He pulled out his walkie-talkie and pressed the button. "Ed, how's it going in there?"

"Excellent. You guys were great. That was amazing. Super chilling. Is it a wrap?"

"Yes. We're coming downstairs now."

"Good. Sir Charles has just phoned the police. They should be here any minute."

"Great. I have a favor to ask you. The recording of the spirit box session in the dining room, can you upload it into the editing software and see if you can isolate the word that came through the box the moment the china cabinet crashed?"

There was crackling on the other end and Ed considered this. Finally, he told them, "I'll isolate the audio file and try to subdue the background noises. It should work, but keep your fingers crossed just in case."

"Excellent. See you in a couple of minutes."

Bunny dried her eyes and addressed Brett the moment he put the walkie-talkie back in his pocket. "Do you think Marcus Bean figured this out—that Ann Copeland was possibly murdered and not trapped in the chest as everyone for three hundred years has believed?"

"Thanks to you and Granny Mac, we just might have figured out what Bean's big reveal was about. If Ann Copeland had been tricked into hiding in the mistletoe chest on her wedding night, and that chest had then been locked and hidden so that no one would find her, that, in my book, is murder. That's huge. That changes everything."

Bunny thanked Giff, whose arm was still around her, and stood from the bed. She looked at Brett, and said, "Does it though? Although incredibly sad, how does stumbling upon evidence of a three-hundred-year-old murder affect anything here, in our time? That's assuming Marcus Bean even did stumble upon something pointing to murder."

"Or, it could be Lewis," Giff offered. That got everyone's attention.

"Lewis? That nice young man? You think he's a murderer?" Bunny looked horrified.

Giff's grin, when it appeared, was as wide as the Cheshire cat's. "That's right. We forgot to tell you. Actually, we didn't have time to tell you, but while we were at the pub with Alex Grimsby, he told us something interesting. Apparently, old Bean got ahold of some DNA and was poking around on those ancestry sites. We were told he liked that sort of stuff. Well, after a little typing, a little searching, *botta-bing botta-boom, voilà*! It turns out that our favorite playboy aristocrat fathered a love child twenty years ago. That child is Lewis."

Jaws dropped. Eyes sprang wide in disbelief. Bunny didn't know how to process this. That's when Giff added, "The rub is, neither Sir Charles nor the young man has any idea. But old Bean thought it would be great fun to get the young man a job working on the grand estate his daddy owns. Positively mercenary, isn't it?"

The walkie-talkie in Brett's pocket was crackling. He pulled it out and Ed's voice came over loud and clear.

"Hey, guys, you probably didn't realize this, but your mics are still hot. Also, you might want to get down here, pronto."

Chapter 32

"Oh no!" Giff cried, looking at Bret. "This isn't going to be good."

It wasn't. The moment they arrived in the library they realized the gravity of what their "hot mic" situation had done. Giff had spilled the beans, so to speak, and both father and son had been listening intently to the conversation.

They entered the library only to find Lewis doubled over in his chair with his face in his hands, quietly sobbing. Sir Charles, on the other hand, simply stared at the young man in stunned disbelief. He was so still Bunny thought that he had gone catatonic.

"We . . . didn't realize . . ." Brett stammered.

"I imagine not. Is it true?" Sir Charles asked.

Brett nodded. "We just learned this information tonight from Alex Grimsby. Marcus had told him about it some time ago. Alex mentioned to us that neither one of you knew about this . . . relationship. When we realized that Lewis was going to be joining us with the investigation tonight"—here Lewis looked up at Brett. Brett offered the young man a wan smile and continued—"our goal was to make sure that both of you were safe. We don't know who the murderer is or why exactly Marcus was murdered, but this is very explosive information." Brett cautiously gestured between the aristocrat and the young man, who was now drying his eyes with the sleeve of his sweatshirt.

Lewis turned to Sir Charles. "You . . . you're my biological father?"

Sir Charles shrugged. "It's news to me too. What did you say your mother's maiden name was?"

"I never said," Lewis replied. Then, urged on by the aristocrat's pointed gaze, he offered, "Whinny Fable."

"Oh my," Sir Charles uttered. He was visibly stunned by this, leading Bunny to realize that Sir Charles definitely knew who she was.

"You knew my mum?"

Charles nodded. "I did," he said in an almost dreamlike state. "I met her many years ago when I was at Oxford."

"My mum never went to university," Lewis proudly informed him.

"She wasn't a student," he gently replied. "Your mother sang at a local pub. She was very beautiful. We dated for over a year. I was a bit of an arse back then. When I thought it was getting too serious, I broke it off with dear Whinny. How old did you say you are?"

"Twenty-one." Lewis was staring intently at the man.

"Dear heavens." A troubled look crossed his face as he uttered this. Bunny surmised that Sir Charles had calculated the boy's age and realized something he had never even thought of before. The woman he'd broken up with all those years ago had been pregnant. The poor woman. Sir Charles then asked, "How well did you know Marcus Bean?"

Lewis was just about to answer when DCI Standish and one of his officers stomped into the library with authority.

As they took one look at the situation before them, Bunny felt they suffered a bout of regret for their chosen occupation.

"We came as soon as we could. What . . . what's going on here?" Standish asked, staring at Lewis. "Have you been crying, lad?"

"I just found out I have a dad," Lewis bluntly replied and pointed his finger at Sir Charles.

"No bloody way." Standish was gobsmacked. He turned to Sir Charles. "Is this true?"

Sir Charles shrugged. "It's quite plausible."

"I thought you said this was about your china cabinet? It's in ruins down the hallway." He pointed a finger in the general direction.

"There's that too," he informed the officer. "And troubling ghosts. However, thanks to a hot mic situation, we've just learned about Bean's other surprise. Do you suppose this was the information he was going to reveal during your investigation?" He looked at Brett as he asked this.

Brett momentarily closed his eyes as if pained. "I hope not."

At a loss as to what was going on in the manor, DCI Standish thankfully took control of the situation. Sir Charles summed up the matter and Lewis continued explaining how he came to be at Bramsford while Standish and his assisting officer took notes.

"It all started when my mum got divorced from my dad last year," Lewis explained. "Only it turns out that he wasn't really my dad, now, was he? Imagine my surprise. All my life the man was my father until he wasn't. That's when I decided to take one of those home DNA tests. I was hoping it might tell me who my real father was."

"But I've never taken one of those," Sir Charles replied, looking puzzled. Then, thinking, he uttered, "Damn you,

Bean." He looked at DCI Standish, and said, "He was very into that sort of thing, genetics. I did give him a sample."

"What was your relationship with Marcus Bean?" Standish asked Lewis.

"I met Professor Bean while working at the Mr. Cod in Reading, near the university. It's a rubbish, fast-food fish and chip place, and I hated working there. But I don't come from a rich family. I needed a job to pay my expenses at the university. I knew Professor Bean was from Oxford and worked in the history department at Reading, because I had met him before. He was super nice, and funny when he came in. He had a habit of asking me lots of questions. One time he asked me how I liked working at Mr. Cod. I told him the truth. It was shite. He then told me that he could get me a job that was far nicer, paid better, and that the owner gave out scholarships regularly to his student employees. Wait," he said, suddenly looking at Sir Charles. "Is that true?" Sir Charles closed his eyes and slowly shook his head. The poor young man looked even more dejected than before, if possible. "That was a lie as well? What a bloody wanker!"

"Agreed," Sir Charles said.

More like a joker, Bunny thought. Because once Lewis's true identity was publicly acknowledged, he was likely to not only get a hefty scholarship, but an inheritance as well. Percival Green, whose daughter, Emma, was currently the sole inheritor of Bramsford Manor, wouldn't be happy about that—a working-class boy getting a piece of the pie! Neither would Morgan, for that matter. It got the wheels in Bunny's mind spinning.

"I'll tell you the truth, Lewis," Sir Charles said. "I don't hate the idea of having a son. However, would you agree to another DNA test, just to be certain?"

The young man agreed. It was also agreed to keep this new revelation a secret until it could be confirmed. It was another angle for DCI Standish to investigate. Then the poor man had to tackle Sir Charles's toppled china cabinet. It was a very long night.

By the time Bunny climbed into bed in her haunted bedchamber, dawn was brimming on the horizon. She really hadn't wanted to ever visit the ill-fated room again after spending the creepiest and saddest night of her life in there, but she was so exhausted that she felt the gates of hell could open in her closet and the devil himself could come trotting out in one of her dresses, and she'd be none the wiser. In fact, in many ways coming face-to-face with the devil in a red dress would be preferable to facing another evening like she'd had in Bramsford Manor.

Encountering the ill-fated Mistletoe Bride with her gran, and conversing with the distraught spirit, had drained her both physically and mentally. If a ghost could be trusted to tell the truth, then they had learned a terrible secret. There was a possibility that the poor young bride had been purposely locked in the mistletoe chest on her wedding night and left to die. It was the most savage thing Bunny had ever heard of. However, there was a lot of digging to be done in order to prove it. There was also the possibility that they never would be able to prove it, given that the incident had happened over three hundred years ago. Still, there was something about the discovery of possible foul play that had gotten under Bunny's skin. She couldn't quite wrap her head around all the details just yet, but she truly believed this was the secret that had gotten the historian, Marcus Bean, murdered.

Yet there was also another possibility, one that was equally as shocking and far easier to prove. Sir Charles had sired a son and never knew it. Likewise, his biological son, Lewis, had been none the wiser either, until Giff spilled the beans while they were listening in. Urgh, it had been an awkward scene!

Regarding the toppled china cabinet incident, it was assumed that the murderer, afraid of being outed by a ghost speaking through some ghost tech thingy called a spirit box, had pushed it over to create a diversion. That same person, or perhaps someone working with them, then snuck back into the dining room, knocked over the stationary cameras without being seen, and stole the creepy spirit box from the table. To Brett's great disappointment, the spirit box was still missing. Standish had called in the crime scene unit to inspect the china cabinet and to lift any fingerprints if possible. Bunny could see that Standish was desperate to find any clue that might lead them to the person responsible for the destruction. And while toppling an antique china cabinet wasn't exactly the mark of a murderer, the person responsible, once found, would logically move to the top of Standish's suspect list. Thankfully, due to Sir Charles's statement, Bunny and the lads were knocked down a few pegs on that same list. Really, they should have been taken off completely, but Standish was a hard man to convince. That likely had something to do with the fact that they had no clue who had toppled the chest and destroyed the manor's historic china and crystal.

Once calmed down, Lewis didn't hate the possibility that Sir Charles might be his biological father. Likewise, Sir Charles seemed to genuinely like the young man. However, DCI Standish had pointed out that if someone other than Marcus Bean found out about Sir Charles's secret love child and wanted to keep it a secret, it might be cause for murder. In light of this recent discovery, and the fact that Lewis's life might also be in danger, it was agreed that the young man wouldn't say a word of this to anyone at the manor and would take a paid leave of absence until the murderer was brought to justice.

Then there was the paranormal investigation and the possibility of a historic murder and coverup. Bunny was leaning toward this theory, but there were still more questions than answers. If Ann Copeland had been tricked on her wedding night by some woman named Jean, what ramifications would that have to a person living today?

While DCI Standish and his man were investigating the toppled china cabinet, Ed, back in the library, was able to use the camera recording of the Spirit Supper to isolate the audio recording of the spirit box in the dining room. Although the spirit box had been stolen, the digital recording was intact. There was a lot of background noise from the cabinet crashing. Once that was pulled out, Ed had been able to isolate a garbled word coming from the spirit box that sounded like Ann, or *an*, before the cameras were pushed to the floor and the box was taken. Was the ghost of Marcus Bean revealing his discovery about the Mistletoe Bride? Or was he telling them the name of his murderer? Bunny considered what she was listening to and realized it could have been the end of the name Morgan. Brett agreed, putting the Wallingford-Greens at the top of their suspect list. However, there was still Betsy Copperfield, Lilly Plum, Peter Billingsley, and Callum Digby to consider as well. There was also sous chef Rodger. After all, Rodger had been the first person to mention Bean's big reveal, having overheard the conversation between Betsy and Lewis. If Bean had been intending to spring such a surprise on Sir Charles, it would stand to reason that he might have had information on the others, making his death about blackmail and not a ghost story.

Bunny's alarm went off at noon, startling her from a dead sleep. Her brain was still fuddled as her eyes sprang wide, and she found herself staring at the light blue canopy above her. She stayed like that for a minute, not daring to glance at the creepy mirror in the corner, where twice she had seen the hazy image of a bride in the glass. Then she remembered why she had set her alarm. She was driving to the university in Reading today with Brett and Giff to meet one of Marcus's colleagues there.

As she took a shower and got dressed, she offered up a little prayer that this person they were to meet would help them make sense of what was going on. Some of the historian's machinations were beginning to come to light, and they weren't pleasant. Another unpleasant thought was that Marcus Bean was still at the manor, in the form of a ghost; or, more correctly, a spirit. Bunny felt that if he became too much of a nuisance, an exorcist might be in order.

She fast-walked down the long gallery, keeping her eyes pointed forward so that she wouldn't have to see the dreadful mistletoe chest, still cordoned off with the blue and white police tape. What had occurred inside that chest was too terrible to even think about. At the end of the long gallery, where the china cabinet should have been on display, was now an empty space on the wall. All that beautiful, antique china and crystal were now just a memory. Poor Sir Charles. It was another tragic thought. Thankfully, once Bunny reached the main lobby, she spotted Brett and Giff waiting for her.

"Well, well, if it isn't Sleeping Beauty," Giff remarked with playful sarcasm. "I hope you slept well."

"Just a wee heads-up, lads, I'm tired and cranky."

Brett handed her a large to-go cup of coffee and something wrapped in tinfoil. "We thought so. Lilly made us egg sandwiches, and I got you the coffee. It was a rough night. By the way, you did amazingly, Bunny."

The compliment made her blush. "It was way, way out of my comfort zone, Bloom, but thank you. The university, on the other hand, should be a piece of cake . . . unless it's haunted too."

"Lord, I hope not." Giff shook his perfectly styled hair in distaste. "You were visited by a sad bride, while I'm sure the entity in the room we were in was a succubus." The darkly quizzical look on his face was amusing.

"Not a succubus," Brett informed him, heading for the door. "When you come across a succubus, you'll know it, bro. I'll explain it to you later."

Giff and Bunny exchanged a look before breaking out in a bout of unprofessional giggles.

"Are you two coming?" Brett was slightly annoyed. "We have an appointment with Professor Bellemy in thirty minutes and, speaking from personal experience, I know that professors don't like to be kept waiting."

Chapter 33

After driving to the University of Reading, finding the correct building, and flagging down a student willing to point them in the right direction, Brett, Bunny, and Giff finally found themselves on the third floor of the history building, standing before the door to Professor Bellemy's office. Brett knocked. A moment later a voice on the other side bid them to enter.

"Professor Bellemy?"

The man who answered that name appeared to be in his midforties, with a head of thick chestnut-colored hair, intelligent brown eyes beneath bushy eyebrows, and an engaging smile. Trim, energetic, and welcoming, he pushed away from his computer and sprang up from his chair like a jack-in-the-box. Bunny took an instant liking to him.

"Welcome to the history department."

"Thank you for meeting with us on such short notice."

"My pleasure," he told Brett. Shifting his attention to Bunny, he said, "You must be Bridget MacBride, the celeb foodie. I've watched you on YouTube. Love cooking, but

I'm awful at it. And Mr. Bloom, I've seen you on that spooky ghost show of yours. Marcus loved that stuff. No offense, but I am not a believer. It makes for good telly, though." He turned to Giff with a hopeful expression that slowly melted into a puzzled frown. "I'm afraid, my good man, that I don't know who you are."

Giff admired his frankness and extended his hand. "Gifford McGrady. Former ad man turned psychic medium. But don't worry," he added, noting the surprised look on the professor's face, "I can't really read your mind. I just play a medium on the telly."

Professor Bellemy laughed at that. "See, I knew it was all malarky, but you're the first man I've met brave enough to admit it. And even if you could read my mind, I'm afraid it would take more than a psychic medium to make sense of the jumble of data, facts, and utter rubbish in here." The professor tapped the side of his head to make his point. "A student the other day used a charming term to describe it. They were studying for a test. He called it infobesity. Too much information to make sense of. God love these youngsters!"

After chuckling over the funny term, the professor grew serious.

"I understand that you are here to talk about Marcus Bean. His death came as quite a shock to everyone. So sorry about it all. He was a good man, a respected professor, and his students were quite fond of him. I've already talked to the police. Not much information here regarding what happened over at Bramsford."

"What did they ask you?" Bunny was curious to know.

"Background information mostly, Bean's schedule, what he was like, did he have any enemies, that sort of thing. They took his computer, but I'm not sure what they were looking for."

"We hadn't realized Bean was a professor here," Giff remarked. "Is that usual—a professor of history tinkering around with old artifacts at a local manor house?"

Professor Bellemy nodded. "Um, it is. He was only a visiting professor here, having worked most of his career at Oxford. His specialty is English history—artifacts and antiquities, but he also had a passion for genealogy. He only taught one or two classes a semester. His employment here was mostly to do with his research at Bramsford Manor. It gave him access to professional databases, the latest technology, archives, and that sort of thing."

"We only knew him for a short while," Brett explained. "I was impressed with his knowledge of Bramsford Manor. In fact, Marcus Bean was the one who reached out to us and brought us there to conduct a paranormal investigation."

Professor Bellemy let out a soft, ironic chuckle. "Unlike me, he bought into ghost stories. Loved local legend and lore. He told me about your new show and why he wanted to bring you to Bramsford. He was trying to create a little buzz with your new paranormal show, and drum up a little drama in the process, I'll wager." A melancholy smile crossed the professor's face. "The poor sod. Working tirelessly all these years. He wanted his fifteen minutes of fame, as we all do. A historian's job is essentially to research historical documents and other sources, analyze what you've found, interpret it, then write about your findings with the hope of bringing new insight to an established belief, or making a new discovery altogether. At the core of every historian is the dream of discovering a holy grail—that one elusive piece of the puzzle that changes everything or turns conventional thought on its head. Marcus was always searching for his holy grail." He paused in his narrative and reached for the bottle of water on his desk. After taking a sip, he exclaimed, "Where are my manners?" and crossed the room to the mini fridge under a long counter on the back wall. After handing everyone a bottle of cold water, he continued.

"A month ago, Marcus and I were at lunch when he told me that he believed he'd found his holy grail. He wouldn't say what it was, but I could see that he was very excited by some discovery he'd made. I think it had something to do with validating that ghost story at Bramsford Manor, you know, that Mistletoe Bride nonsense."

It wasn't nonsense, Bunny thought, but didn't have the nerve to tell him. Some people were lucky enough to be unaffected by the paranormal or chose not to believe in anything beyond the human experience of three-dimensional existence. How Bunny had wished to be among them, but that dream had ended for her at Bramsford Manor. That dang white rabbit had made sure of it. That was why she was here now and not safely ensconced in a kitchen somewhere doing what she did best. Cook. There was really no point in shattering the professor's worldview regarding ghosts and hauntings. She rather envied him.

The professor continued. "I don't know what he stumbled across," he said, staring at his half-empty water bottle.

"What about blackmail?" Giff asked. "The police seem to think that Bean might have been blackmailing someone at the manor. After all, he had access to databases, was fond of genealogy, and had been hired to dig into the Wallingford family ancestry."

The professor looked surprised. "I never thought of that. Like most of us, he kept his private research private. But who knows?" He shrugged.

"We recently learned that Bean located a student here through a DNA database. He learned that the student was the biological child of the man who employed him at the manor. However, neither one of them knew about it until last night."

"Oh dear. That doesn't sound good at all. And you think that is why he was murdered?"

"Honestly, Professor, we don't really know what to think," Bunny told him. "But is there any way we can take a look around his office?"

The professor nodded. "I can unlock his office for you. I can even do one better. There is a grad student here who worked with Bean, assisting him with research and ordering materials from various archival sources. I'll call him now and see if he can assist you." He pulled out his phone and dialed a number. While he was waiting for the grad student to answer, he said, "I assume that if you do find anything of interest in Bean's office that you will share your findings with the police?"

"You have our word, Professor," Brett assured him.

Chapter 34

꧁꧂

"Professor Bean located an original source he was interested in looking at," the grad student, Eddie Roberts, told them as they followed him down the hallway to another office. Eddie was a short young man with black glasses and freckles, his dark red hair pulled into a thick bun at the back of his head. They found him polite and eager to help. Eddie paused before a door, put the key into the lock, and opened it. "He was really excited to get his hands on it," he continued, flipping on the light. "It's an old diary. No one's read it in ages, maybe never. You see, it was the diary of an ordinary sailor in the British Navy who was born and raised not far from Bramsford Manor. That's what got his attention. He was always looking for historic documents from the local area, mostly to see if any of them mentioned anything about the legend of the Mistletoe Bride. A paragraph, a line, even mentioning the big house got him interested. He didn't know what was going to be in it before he read it, but that's how research goes. One must sift through a lot of information to get to the gems."

"Do you think Bean found a gem in this diary?" Giff asked.

Eddie wasn't ready to divulge any secrets just yet, not without finishing his story. He cast Giff an owlish glance through his rimmed glasses and continued. "The professor had the highest credentials. He was able to put the old diary on reserve and borrow it. I drove all the way to the National Archives in London to pick it up for him. It was so cool. It was waiting for me when I got there, all sealed in a padded case and everything. I had to fill out five forms, show my ID, and give my word that only Professor Bean would open it."

"That sounds very important," Bunny said, looking impressed.

"Did you mention this old diary to the police?" Brett asked, taking in the number of old books on the bookshelves in Bean's office.

"I told them that Professor Bean had recently acquired it, but they weren't interested in it. It's an old diary from a sailor in the British navy. I told them that it belongs to the National Archives and assured them that nobody, as far as I knew, was trying to steal it."

"Back to this gem you mentioned. Bean found one, didn't he?" Giff hit him with his most disarming grin. The grad student couldn't help himself; he mirrored Giff's grin and nodded.

"Three-quarters of the way through this diary is a never-before-heard account of Ann Copeland, the young woman who lived in Bramsford Manor and had played an unfortunate game of hide-and-seek on her wedding night. Professor Bean was obsessed with that story."

"And was never seen again . . . until fifty years later. Yes," Giff said, rolling his eyes. "We know all about the tragic young lady, and Bean's obsession with the ghost story. What makes this account so interesting?"

Eddie, with a poker face a professional gambler would admire, offered, "I think you should read it for yourselves. Only you can determine if you think it's relevant to the professor's murder." He took out another key and unlocked a cabinet beneath a long counter. Eddie then removed a case and set it on the counter before them. "Also, I must ask all of you to thoroughly wash and dry your hands before touching this diary."

Bunny was amazed at what they were reading. The old diary, bound in soft brown leather, was relatively unremarkable. The pages were yellowed, the dates on each entry were old, and Robert Ludlow, the owner of the diary, wrote beautiful, uniform cursive. He was a rather literate man for the age and his profession. Robert Ludlow started the diary when he was a young man of twenty and served as an officer in the British navy in the 1760s. According to Eddie, his career was unremarkable. What was remarkable was the officer's detailed account of daily life on the sea, and his many experiences in the navy.

As they flipped through the pages, Bunny looked up at the grad student. "This is all very nice, Eddie, but I don't understand how anything in here that might have happened in the seventeen-sixties is relevant to what happened at Bramsford Manor in the early seventeen hundreds. That's when Ann Copeland's wedding supposedly took place."

"Well, you're not at the right part yet. Let me help you." Eddie carefully turned the old pages until he came to a date in November of 1768. "Start here," he told them.

As Bunny, Brett, and Giff read the passage, they soon realized that Robert Ludlow had traveled to a village outside of Portsmouth where his beloved grandmother was on her deathbed. He was a devoted and loving grandson. However, the moment Bunny's eyes landed on Granny Ludlow's

Christian name, her body erupted in tingles. Written in the beautiful handwriting was the name Jean. Seeing it there, in the old diary, gave Bunny a start. It was the last word uttered in the room by the ghostly bride. Could it be? Jean was the name of Ann's betrayer, or so Bunny imagined until she read on.

> *Granny was on her deathbed when the priest arrived. We were all very sad that she had come to the end of her life, for she was a good woman, and mother was crying. Father Chesterton was about to read the last rites over Granny Jean when she stopped him in a voice barely above a whisper. "I have carried with me a terrible secret all these years," she tells him. "I cannot meet my maker with this heavy burden on my chest." We were stunned. My mother stopped crying, and the priest pulled up a chair, being given this short reprieve. Granny Jean then uttered the name of a woman we all recognize, but not for any good. Ann Copeland. This name is a mystery to us. We believe Granny Jean has gone daft. Ann Copeland is the name of a white lady, who haunts a place called Bramsford Manor. Her story is tragic, and we all cannot fathom why Granny has uttered this cursed name. With her next precious breath she says, "I had the privilege to serve that young gentlewoman up at the big house at Bramsford Manor when I was just a girl . . ."*

According to the diary, Jean had been Ann's personal maid, which was a position of honor. Before Ann's Christmas wedding to Sir Henry Wallingford in December of the year 1700, which was the biggest event of the season, a gentlewoman, who was a guest at the wedding, pulled Jean aside. This gentlewoman offered Jean a large sum of money if she would suggest to lady Ann that she propose a jolly game of hide-and-seek before retiring with her new husband on her wedding night. Ann would get a five-minute head start to hide. If one of the guests should find the bride before the groom, they would get a small sum of money. Ann was to put up the money, betting on her groom to find her. Jean agreed, knowing that Ann would be delighted with the suggestion.

But the woman wasn't finished. She then told Jean to take Ann to a chest in the attic wing on the fourth floor. The chest in question had a carving of mistletoe on the front. The gentlewoman had discovered the chest while exploring every nook and cranny of the manor house and thought it would make the perfect place to hide. Jean was to put the new bride inside the chest, close the lid until the latch clicked, and then cover it with the white sheet that would be near the chest. When Jean protested, the gentlewoman assured her it would be fine. She simply wanted to be the one to find the bride and win the game, drawing admiration from the bride, the groom, and all the other guests. Then she told Jean that once Ann was safely hidden in the chest, she must take her money and leave Bramsford Manor immediately. The gentlewoman didn't trust her. She told Jean that she was afraid that if she was still in the manor when the guests began the game, Jean would tell the groom where his bride was hidden. If she left immediately after hiding her lady in the chest, the gentlewoman would know that no cheating would occur. Jean didn't like the sound of that, but she'd been given more money than she had ever seen in her life to execute the lady's wishes. She had been young, foolish, and agreed to the deception, never thinking it would turn deadly.

It wasn't until months after the wedding that Jean finally learned the truth of what she had done. Rumors circulated in the countryside, stating that young Ann Wallingford had tricked her groom on her wedding night by running off with her lover and her maid. She was never seen or heard from again. Her grieving groom, Henry Wallingford, became heir to the manor upon marrying Ann. But he didn't believe the rumors about Ann. He knew she loved him. For two years he searched for her until finely marrying a woman named Catherine Villers. Catherine Villers was the gentlewoman who had tricked both Jean and Ann on that terrible Christmas Day.

Jean had kept this terrible secret to herself, knowing that if she returned and told the truth about what happened, she'd be blamed for Ann's death. After all, she was the one who had put her in that chest, telling Ann to hide and be quiet until her groom found her. It wasn't until fifty years after the unfortunate wedding that Sir Henry Wallingford found Ann's body in the mistletoe chest. The lid of the chest had locked the moment it closed, and Ann had been trapped inside. Jean stated that Sir Henry's second wife had already died by the time Henry found Ann's remains. But she had always suspected that once Ann's body had been found, Sir Henry knew the truth of what had happened.

With this weight off her chest, Robert Ludlow's grandmother passed peacefully that night. It had been agreed by every witness in the room that the tragic tale would be buried with Granny Jean. Thankfully, Ludlow had kept the passage in his private diary.

"Dear heavens," Bunny gasped, after reading the diary. She looked at Brett and Giff and silently cursed her eyes for betraying her. Tears were coming, and this time they were truly her own and not some ghost's. She could feel them, and there was nothing she could do about it but try to wipe them away as they came. "Ann Copeland-Wallingford was murdered, but not by Jean, her maid. She never knew. She never knew the truth of what happened on that terrible night. Oh, lads, I'm just gutted by this!"

"It's alright," Brett whispered as his arms came around her, pulling her to his chest. "It's alright, Bunny. What a terrible thing to have happened to a young, happy bride on her wedding day. I know it's three hundred years too late, but we need to make this right."

Chapter 35

"That poor young bride!" Bunny declared after processing her initial grief. They were sitting in chairs in Bean's office, trying to make sense of what they had just read—had learned about poor Ann Copeland-Wallingford all those years ago. "Lies, deceit, a jealous rival, and a payoff, it reads like a Greek tragedy, but it really happened. It's a wonder Marcus ever stumbled upon Robert Ludlow's diary. Lads, my gut is telling me that this information is what got Marcus murdered."

"I want to think you're right," Brett agreed. "But what is the connection? How does this new piece of the puzzle equate to murder?"

"It changes the narrative," Bunny offered. "The current Mistletoe legend states that the young bride proposed the game of hide-and-seek herself, got a five-minute head start, then hid so well they never found her until fifty years later. This deathbed admission points to premeditated murder—by the woman who ended up marrying Sir Henry Wallingford, Charles and Morgan's ancestor!"

"It is horrible," Brett agreed. "It also might be embarrassing for the current Wallingfords if this dark twist in the ghostly legend ever came to light, but we have to ask ourselves, could this really be grounds for murder?"

Giff, still wrapped in his thoughts, offered, "The only thing I'm asking myself at the moment is how that Catherine Villers witch, who basically murdered a teenager, could live in a house knowing that the rotting corpse of her rival was in the attic. Urgh!" He shivered with disgust. "Maximum creepsville! No doubt in my mind she's the succubus we encountered last night!"

"Again, not a succubus," Brett corrected, "just a very dark entity. But I agree. It could have been her. Yet just a few rooms down on the same floor, Bunny and Granny Mac were connecting with the ghost of Ann Copeland, who has historically haunted the Fleur-de-Lys room for ages."

"And the patio steps," Bunny added.

Brett concurred and continued. "Giff, you were channeling that conversation while we were in the room with something very different. Ann the Mistletoe Bride perished in a traumatic way, that's why her ghost still haunts the manor. Let's say the dark entity is the ghost of Catherine Villers. Why would she still remain? Did she die in a traumatic way as well, or is it her evil deed that binds her to Bramsford Manor?"

"Evil deed," Giff assured him with a nod. "She had a maniacal laugh. I know she's not *technically* a succubus, Brett, but that ghost-witch sucked all the joy from the room while Granny Mac was saying words in my ear like, *trapped. A game. Find me.* It was hellish. Do you think the joy-sucker in our room was enjoying it? *Joy-sucking apparition,*" he mused, thinking, no doubt, about his advertising days. "Is that a thing? We could make it a thing."

Eddie, after carefully returning the diary to the locked

cabinet, had been sitting on the edge of the counter taking it all in. However, his skeptical, academic gaze landed on Brett. "Am I hearing this correctly?" he asked. "Because it sounds an awful lot like you three ghost hunters are discussing the ghosts of these . . . these people from long ago— from the old Mistletoe Bride legend—like you've actually met them?"

"I'm a chef, not a ghost hunter," Bunny swiftly corrected.

"And I'm not really a medium, I just play one on the *telly*." Giff stressed the British term in an effort to seem more relatable.

Brett, the true professional of the bunch, looked Eddie in the eyes and nodded. "Yep. We've encountered them at Bramsford several times now, as well as the lingering spirit of Marcus Bean."

"What? Impossible!" Eddie's eyes nervously roved between them. "You think that Professor Bean is there too?" He shook his head so hard that his eyeglasses nearly flew off his head. He pushed them back up the bridge of his nose and stated very matter-of-factly, "Ghosts aren't real."

"Not all have experienced them," Brett conceded. "However, the phenomenon of ghosts, hauntings, and paranormal dealings are very real to those who've encounter them, Eddie."

"Probably because they've gone mental. There's always a logical explanation for these things." Eddie's hackles were up as he defended his stance on the paranormal.

Bunny felt a flutter of pity for the man because she could relate. Now, however, she knew better. "Eddie," she addressed the academic, "Marcus Bean isn't really there. We all know he's dead. As you know, his body was found in the old mistletoe chest he was so fascinated with. Yet he died under traumatic circumstances. It's hard for me to even explain this, but at times I know his spirit is still there. I believe he's trying to tell us something about his murderer."

"Whoa! I thought you said you were a chef?"

"I am," she calmly assured him. "But I'm also realizing that I do have the ability to sense ghosts and even connect with them on occasion. Does that make sense?"

"None at all!" he cried, looking frazzled.

She steeled herself and decided to just be direct with him. "I smell him. Old Spice Swagger deodorant, stale cigarettes, and a lingering maleness that's hard to pinpoint. It's a rather distinct scent. It hits me when I least expect it, but I know the moment it does that your beloved professor is nearby."

Eddie, listening to this, massaged his hairless chin as he stared at her. "Ah, yeah, he did smell like that." He cleared his throat and sat straighter. "Let's say, for the sake of this argument, that Professor Bean is still there, and that you have talked to these notable ghosts and joy-suckers. Have you learned anything important?"

"Today we have," Brett said. "Before coming here, we thought that only one murder had occurred at Bramsford Manor. Now, thanks to Robert Ludlow's dying grand-mother, we know that two murders have taken place there. The first murderer we now have a name for, the lady Catherine Villers—"

"The joy-sucker," Giff proudly proclaimed, coining the term.

"The name of the other murderer, unfortunately, still remains a mystery." Brett pursed his lips at the thought.

"There's a connection here we're missing," Bunny stated. She then looked at Brett. "Last night we learned about the young man Lewis, who works at the manor, and his connection to the Wallingford family. That was shocking enough, especially the fact that neither Lewis nor Sir Charles had been made aware of the connection. This fact alone speaks volumes of the weird power dynamic between Marcus Bean and his employer. What was he meaning to do with the information that the young man was Sir Charles's biological son? Clearly Charles never asked him to look for the boy. Clearly Lewis never asked him to look for his father. The whole situation seems very cruel to me. It had the dynamic of blackmail, but clearly, he wasn't blackmailing Sir Charles, because Sir Charles had no idea the boy even existed until we said so . . ." She thought it best to stop talking. No need to bring up that horrible scene from last night again.

"Blackmail," Brett said, his bright eyes glistening with inspiration. "That's it. He wasn't blackmailing Charles. So, who was he blackmailing? Marcus Bean was digging through history, digging through the past of Bramsford Manor and everyone who lived there. Thanks to the diary of Robert Ludlow, Bean found his holy grail. So, here's what we know. The Mistletoe Bride was really murdered by the soon-to-be second wife of Henry Wallingford. That's salacious. Then we have the fact that Sir Charles has a love child who works in the manor. Also salacious. But I don't see how they're connected."

"What about the hair in the locket?" Giff offered. "Where does that fit in?"

"That's right!" Bunny's eyes blazed at the thought. "Brett told me about that last night, but in lieu of all that has happened since then, I forgot about it."

"That old hair sample in the locket," Eddie said, recalling the item in question. "The professor had me take it to the DNA lab for genetic testing. It was an old sample, but we got great results. Poor Professor Bean. He might have loved his local history, but he was really passionate about genealogy."

"Did he learn anything important about that sample?" Bunny prodded. "Anything that might be related to his murder?"

Eddie grew very quiet, thinking. "Umm, maybe," he finally said, looking a little pale. "Professor Bean was committed to enhancing the DNA ancestry database. The test was offered to students interested in genealogy. Really, anybody who wanted one could take one. But sometimes that wasn't enough. Sometimes he took the liberty of collecting samples himself, like . . . from the people living and working at Bramsford Manor without them knowing."

"That's not legal," Giff blurted.

Eddie ignored him. "He wanted to fill in the gaps on the Wallingford family tree. However, the old hair sample was from Ann Copeland. She obviously never had any children. Why this is important is because Bramsford Manor belonged to the Copeland family. Yet after Ann's father died three years later, the estate passed to Sir Henry Wallingford."

"He married Ann," Bunny reasoned. "I assume she was the only child and heir."

"The marriage was never consummated," Giff added. "Remember, she was locked in the chest before all the marital fun could begin. So, was Henry really her legal husband?"

Bunny thought about that. "We all know that English common law back in the day regarding inheritance embraces primogeniture, which essentially states that property should pass to the eldest son, and so on, to keep the family name tied to the estate," she explained.

"We don't *all* know that," Brett corrected. Bunny shrugged and continued.

"Yet the law of primogeniture can be overwritten by an entail, but that would have to be written before the owner of the estate died. Ann's father could have made her his heir, which wasn't too unusual if a father only had daughters. Let's say that Ann is his heir. She gets married, disappears right after the wedding, and both father and groom are heartbroken. If no one contests the marriage, then Henry would inherit."

Eddie nodded. "That's all well and good. But Professor

Bean found out that Ann had a younger brother by the name of Cecil. We don't know what happened to him. He just vanishes from the picture. Why this is important is because, according to the professor, Cecil lived long enough to pass on his genetic code."

"And Marcus Bean found a living direct descendent of the Copeland family!" Bunny exclaimed, as pieces of the puzzle began to fall into place in her head. Eddie nodded. Then, realizing the magnitude of what Bean had done, Bunny covered her mouth with her hand and uttered, "He did it! Marcus solved a three-hundred-year-old mystery that no one knew was a mystery until that diary surfaced. Bramsford Manor belonged to the Copeland family. However, after Ann's death it shifted into the hands of the Wallingfords, likely through illegal means."

"The joy-sucker!" Giff cried. "Caught red-handed three hundred years too late. Now what?"

"I suppose if criminal activity can be proven then this modern descendant can make a claim to the estate," offered Eddie.

"Who is it, Eddie?"

The grad student shrugged. "I don't know. The professor never told me. But I do know that it was all compiled in a folder the professor kept in his office at Bramsford Manor."

Chapter 36

"Welcome back," Peter Billingsley greeted them the moment they entered the manor. "Where have you three been?"

Giff lowered his blue mirrored sunglasses and peered at Peter. "Working for the cops now, Billingsley? Or did you miss us?" There was no way he was going to tell the manager about their trip to the university.

"None of those things, Mr. McGrady," Peter assured them. "I'm merely curious. It's a beautiful day. I hope you enjoyed yourselves." He leaned across the front desk and lowered his voice. "I also heard you had quite the paranormal investigation last night. Sir Charles is still mourning the loss of the family china."

"I bet he is. But that's just the half of it," Giff said, pausing before the desk while Bunny and Brett continued walking. "Last night, up on the second floor of the guest wing, we encountered a full-bodied, floating joy-sucker. It was terrifying."

Peter's eyes went wide as he sucked in his breath. "That was upstairs . . . in this manor? I don't even know what that is, but it does sound terrifying."

Giff gave him a thumbs-up as he fast-walked to catch up with Brett and Bunny, who were heading for the Fleur-de-Lys room. After leaving the university, they had called a team meeting to discuss what they had learned. Since Granny Mac had Bunny's extra key, it was a relief to find everyone already there, waiting with beverages in hand while nibbling on an assortment of cheese and crackers that sat on the antique dresser.

"You're not going to believe this," Bunny said, taking the proffered wineglass from her grandmother's hand. She took a sip, sat on the bed next to Granny Mac, and looked at the gentlemen across from them. Brett and Giff were sharing the chaise lounge, Ed was in the wingback chair, and Mike and Cody were on folding chairs brought to the room for this meeting. "Marcus Bean found evidence that Ann Copeland was murdered."

Granny Mac's eyes grew wide in surprise. "By Jean?"

"No," Bunny corrected. "Jean was the name of her maid. A young woman who worked for her until the night of her wedding. Ann was led to believe the person who betrayed her was Jean. But the true mastermind behind the terrible deed was a woman named Catherine Villers, the second wife of Henry Wallingford. It was all in an old diary written by a former sailor named Robert Ludlow."

Bunny, Brett, and Giff then explained to everyone what they had learned while visiting the university.

"Marcus Bean was a busy, busy man," Granny Mac remarked. "No wonder he's still about . . . in spirit form, that is," she clarified for the lads. "He not only uncovered the murder of that poor bride, but a missing heir in the form of Ann's younger brother, Cecil, an inheritance that was likely fraudulent, and the name of a woman suspected to be behind it all. And now you're telling us that there might possibly be a living descendant of the Copeland family working here? If this is true and Marcus Bean had proof of it, then this person might have a legitimate claim on Bramsford Manor. I can't imagine that the current Wallingford family would be too happy about that."

"We don't know if this mysterious person is physically here at the manor or not," Brett clarified, "only that the documents naming the person in question were kept in Bean's attic office—the one that had been broken into before the police could get to it."

"No wonder. It contained damning evidence," Cody offered before taking a sip of his craft beer, one appropriately called, Adnams Ghost Ship.

"What are we supposed to do now?" Mike asked. "We're at another dead end. We don't have any idea who this possible relative is. Wait. What about Lewis? How does he fit into all of this?"

"Likely just a random find while Bean was playing around on the ancestry DNA databases," Brett offered. "Think of it. If he's Charles's son, that makes Lewis a Wallingford descendant, not a Copeland. Although both seemed blindsided by the revelation."

"Unless Lewis's mother is the Copeland descendent?" Giff offered hopefully. "Our Lewis could be the link that ties this diabolically dysfunctional family together again. What a beautiful thought."

"Not likely," Bunny said, crushing Giff's hopes. "It's somebody different, but it doesn't even matter who it is at this point. Our murderer found out. That same person stole my boning knife, stabbed Marcus, concealed him in the legendary chest at the center of this mystery, then broke into his office and took the file containing the evidence, silencing both the messenger and the message while framing me for murder."

"You're not a murderer, dear," Granny Mac said right before refilling Bunny's wineglass. "However, maybe we should compile a list of suspects."

"I already have one," Bunny said, hopping off the bed and reaching for the pink, hardbound notebook on the bedside table. "This is my recipe journal," she explained to the inquiring looks. "I write down new recipes I'm working on, meal ideas, exceptional meals I've eaten, that sort of thing. And now suspects." She flipped open the book to her suspect page.

"Well, let's hear what you've got," Ed prodded.

Bunny looked at the names, including the ones she had already crossed off the list. "The first thing I did was write down everyone's name who had a key to the kitchen. That's because my boning knife was in there, and somebody stole it from my knife kit. I'm assuming that the murderer stole my knife after the kitchen was locked up for the night. We learned that five people have a key, Lilly Plum, Callum Digby, Peter Billingsley, Sir Charles Wallingford, and his sister, Morgan. Then I wrote down the names of the gossips, meaning the people Betsy told about Marcus's big reveal. Remember, Betsy claimed that she didn't know what Marcus's secret was, only that she had overheard him telling someone over the phone about it."

"Right," Brett interjected. "We now know that Bean was talking to Alex Grimsby, his one true confidant at the manor. Grimsby knew about this secret, and the fact that Bean had an office at the university. However, he claims that he didn't know what sensational information Bean had stumbled upon either."

"I don't have Alex on my list," Bunny remarked, looking at the gang. "Do you think I should add him?"

"I think Alex Grimsby has been on the level with us," Giff remarked. "I know I overheard him and Bean arguing the day Bean was murdered, but he clarified that for us. He seems like an honest man. Put him on the list, but at the very bottom," he suggested.

They all agreed, and Bunny added his name. "Okay, my list of gossips includes Betsy Copperfield, Lewis, Rodger, Lilly Plum, and I'm sure most of the other kitchen staff, because kitchens are hotbeds of gossip. Then there's Callum-Digby because, as the maître d', he's directly in the hub of kitchen gossip. Next on the list is Peter Billingsley, because he told us he heard about the big reveal, as did Morgan Wallingford-Green."

"Alex Grimsby should be on the gossip list too," Brett said, toying with a slice of cheese he was about to eat. "He was on the other end of the conversation that Betsy overheard." Bunny agreed and made a note of the connection.

"There are a few names that keep floating around on the list," Bunny remarked. "However, now that we know a member of the Wallingford family has the most to lose from the information we uncovered at the university, the list narrows. Substantially. I think we can all agree that Sir Charles comes off the list. He was with us last night during our investigation. And let's just say that he seemed clueless about everything, including the fact that his biological son was sitting across the table from him."

"Morgan wasn't there last night," Brett pointed out, stating what everyone was thinking. "She traded places with Lewis. It could be that Lewis was simply more excited about confronting ghosts than Morgan, or she got wind that Lewis's biological father was her aimless brother and wanted to thrust them together . . . after, of course, learning about the threat to her livelihood."

"She could have been the one listening in while we were in the dining room," Bunny speculated. "She's fit for a woman in her forties and could have easily toppled the china cabinet in the long gallery. She would know, better than anyone, what effect that would have on her brother. That might have enabled her to sneak back into the dining room, topple the cameras and take the ghost box. It's still missing, isn't it?"

"Ahhh, no, we found that," Mike told them. "I forgot to tell you. While you three were at the university, Cody, Ed, and I went looking for it. I found it in the industrial trash bin outside. It had been smashed to pieces and thrown in there with the rest of the garbage."

"Did you retrieve it?" Brett asked.

Mike shook his head. "I didn't feel there was a point. It was covered in stinky trash, so I left it in there."

"Even if there are fingerprints still on that thing that don't belong to one of you lads, it would take a while to process them." Bunny looked at her list again and made a note. Looking up once again, she stated, "At this point, most fingers are pointing to Morgan. She might even be working with her estranged husband, because they have the most to lose. As we've learned, Ann Copeland was murdered before she could consummate her marriage. The estate should have naturally stayed in the Copeland family, but it didn't. If this can be proven it might make things difficult for the Wallingford family. Another thing to consider is that Morgan, in the midst of a midlife crisis, was having an affair with Marcus Bean. Her husband, Percival, is greedy and a philanderer. However, they have a daughter, Emma, who stands to inherit the entire estate, until Lewis was discovered by Marcus. Marcus could have told Morgan everything. They were, after all, friends."

Granny Mac nodded, then offered, "Here is what I think we should do. We have been confronted with a lot of information regarding this matter. A deadly secret has been uncovered and the ghosts trapped within these walls are tormented. There is still much work to be done regarding these spirits. As for this murder, it's best that we leave it to the police from here. Tomorrow, you three"—she gestured to Bunny, Brett, and Giff—"should take all you've learned, including your suspicions about Morgan and all you have learned from that old diary, to DCI Standish. Let him deal with this. We have more than enough information to confront the dark entity lurking here. Once the power is taken away from that entity it can be banished from the manor, allowing us to move the ghosts of Ann Copeland and Marcus Bean into the light."

"We . . . we can do that?" Giff asked, looking both hopeful and terrified. Banishing ghosts was good, but he wasn't certain he could survive another encounter with the creepy, cackling joy-sucker.

"No," Brett said. "Not us. Granny Mac can do this. I don't have the gift, but I have seen it done before by a medium. I was hoping you were that person," he told the older woman. He then addressed his team. "If all goes well, tomorrow we'll be cleared by the police. Once that happens, we should prepare for our final investigation tomorrow night."

Bunny pursed her lips. "That means I have to spend two more nights in this haunted room, doesn't it?"

"It'll only be haunted for one more night, my dear," Granny Mac said, patting her leg. "If all goes well."

A bubble of sarcastic mirth erupted from Giff. "Sure, confronting a joy-sucker and shooing a weeping ghost bride into the light along with a late, meddling historian. What can go wrong with that plan?"

A lot, Bunny thought, and nearly spilled her wine.

Chapter 37

❧

One more haunted night at Bramsford Manor, Bunny mused as she climbed beneath the sheets on the large, antique bed. Thankfully, she was dead tired. She doubted that even if the ghost bride blew into the room in the middle of the night in a ball of tears, that she'd awaken. She was that tired. Yet, just in case, she'd covered the creepy mirror in the corner with a blanket, and she stuffed her ears so full of cotton that all she could hear was the beating of her own heart. Not ideal, but it had worked before, and she hoped it would work again. Tomorrow promised to be another unsettling day at the manor, but the end was in sight. All she had to do was focus on that.

Also, focusing on recipes and meal preparation was another tried-and-true strategy Bunny often used to relax. The moment her head hit the pillow she thought of the lovely dinner Lilly Plum and her staff had prepared. The main course had been a delicious fish pie, one of her favorite traditional dishes, which was essentially like a shepherd's pie, only with cod, shrimp, peas, and pearl onions cooked in a cream sauce then topped with mashed potatoes and baked. It had been served with honey-glazed baby carrots and a green salad with a light lemon and oil dressing. For dessert Lilly had served a St. Clement's pie, which was similar to the American key lime pie, but with the juice of lemons and tart oranges instead of key lime. The citrusy pie paired nicely with the fish pie, although Bunny inwardly bristled at serving two pie dishes at the same meal. She felt it was a culinary faux pas, given all the delicious dishes and desserts one could choose. Well, that was just her. She'd kept her mouth shut and enjoyed the meal.

As Bunny pondered pies, both sweet and savory, she drifted off into a dreamless sleep. However, not even the cotton in her ears could prevent her from feeling the sudden and startling pressure on her feet—as if something or someone had pounced on them. The annoyance pulled her to the surface of consciousness. Unwilling to open her eyes, she gave a hard kick and rolled under the sheets to the other side of the bed. Yet whatever demon was in her room had found them again. And again. And again. Bunny was highly annoyed.

Her eyes flew open, and she spied the glowing white rabbit of doom sitting on her legs. "Get off me, Hopper. I'm trying to sleep!"

Seeing that she was awake, the rabbit hopped off the bed, bounded across the room and right through the solid wood of the door, where he vanished.

"Good riddance," she called after him and rolled over, taking the blankets with her. She closed her eyes and willed herself back to sleep, yet the moment she relaxed, he was back at it, sitting on her legs again. That dang rabbit was tenacious. Bunny sat up this time and yanked the cotton out of her ears.

"What are you doing? I don't understand you. What's this all about?" Yet if she thought he was actually going to say something profound to her, she was wrong. The rabbit stayed where he was, his glowing red eyes staring at her.

"You want something from me, don't you?"

The rabbit wiggled his nose.

"You want me to follow you?"

Hopper's ears perked up and twitched forward.

"Alright," she relented, swinging her legs off the mattress. She was already wide-awake and doubted he'd let her sleep until she followed him. The moment her feet landed on the little braided rug, she stood and wrapped a robe around her. She then picked up her phone and shoved it in her pocket. "I'll follow you, but then you must leave me alone. Got it?" The moment she spoke she mentally berated herself. Was she really trying to reason with a ghost rabbit? It blew her mind just how far down she had fallen in that proverbial paranormal rabbit hole since coming to Bramsford Manor. Against her better judgment she followed him anyway.

As she followed Hopper, a niggling feeling of doom settled around her and she feared he was taking her to another body. When Hopper turned the corner and bounded across the threshold of the long gallery, she was certain. The hair on the back of her neck prickled. "No more dead bodies," she hiss-whispered at the glowing white animal who continued down the long hallway seemingly without a care. "I'm done with this. Seriously, Hopper!" she said, chasing after him. "I just want to get out of here."

Halfway down the long gallery, the rabbit stopped. It was like bad déjà vu, Bunny thought, because she knew that Hopper was focused on the space the mistletoe chest had occupied before being removed the other day by the antique restoration company. Plagued by thoughts of bodies, she tentatively came beside the rabbit. She forcibly exhaled when she noticed that the space was still empty. The mistletoe chest was gone. The only thing that remained was the creepy old portrait of the unfortunate bride who had been locked inside it and left to rot.

It was the picture that drew her eyes this time. She pulled

her smart phone from the pocket of her robe, turned on the flashlight app, and foolishly asked, "This is what you brought me to see?" Yet when she glanced at the floor beside her, she realized the rabbit had gone. "You bring me all the way down here—to this creepy gallery—and now you disappear? I didn't realize that you were such a fickle rabbit, Hopper." She took a quick look around, realizing that she was all alone. Then she pointed her light at the painting and took a closer look. That's when Bunny suddenly and sharply inhaled.

"Dear heavens, am I seeing this correctly?" she whispered to thin air. She took a step closer, apologized to the old painting, and covered the lovely dark blond hair of Ann Copeland with a hand in order to get a better look at the face staring back at her. The young face was oval in shape, with a milk and honey complexion. The mouth was small and heart-shaped while the nose was straight, a tad too long, yet with a cute little rounded tip at the end. Ann's cheekbones were high and round and tinged with a rosy glow. Yet it was the eyes staring back at her that seemed familiar. Round, heavy-lidded, and deceptively guileless with just a hint of mischief in them. Bunny was certain she had seen eyes like these before. She marveled at how the portrait had been painted over three hundred years ago, and yet, due to the power of genetics, a familiar, atavistic trait had endured. The eyes. The Copeland eyes. In that moment Bunny believed she had unlocked the last piece of the mystery. Thanks to that pesky white rabbit, she believed she could identify the Copeland ancestor, the true heir of Bramsford Manor.

Chapter 38

"Whoa! Someone looks like they had a rough night," Giff remarked with a grin the moment Bunny took a seat at the table. She'd been the last person to arrive, and she did look slightly disheveled. "Don't tell us. You had a ghostly visitor again?"

Bunny paused to pour herself a mug of tea, took a long, much-needed sip, and leaned back in her chair. "Kind of. Not really. Not the weeping ghost bride at any rate."

"Who, dear?" Granny Mac asked, looking intrigued.

Giff covered his mouth with a hand. "Noooo! Not the murderous joy-sucker!"

"Hopper," she bluntly told them.

"The ghost rabbit?" Brett leaned forward, wanting more details. "When? Last night? Why? What did he want?"

Bunny shook her head and gave a little shrug. "Crazy as this sounds, I think he wanted to help us. I think I know who this long-lost Copeland descendant is, but I need to verify that before I say anything. I could be wrong. However, I made a call to the university this morning and asked Professor Bellemy to confirm something for me."

"What?" Brett asked.

"I'll let you know in a moment." She knew this answer would only spike their curiosity, but she needed to be certain. Instead, she advised, "Don't go to the police just yet, not without this last piece of the puzzle in place."

"You know who the murderer is?" Brett asked.

"I have my suspicions. But this isn't about that." Spying her person of interest walking into the dining room with a tray loaded with breakfast orders, Bunny downed her mug of tea. She then waited until Betsy served out the plates to a table of guests then excused herself. "I'll be back soon."

Bunny headed off after Betsy before the girl could disappear back into the kitchen. "Betsy, I need a word with you." She blocked the girl's look of suspicion with a friendly smile. "It'll only take a moment." Betsy nodded and they both stepped out onto the patio.

"What's this about, Ms. MacBride?"

"I was trying to figure out what exactly your connection to Marcus Bean was. At first, we thought that maybe you and Marcus were having an affair—"

"What? Gross!" she cried, flashing eye daggers at Bunny.

Bunny held up her hand. "I know. We were wrong. Then it was suggested that you were his student at the university. That's what Marcus told Alex Grimsby. But that's not correct either."

"Why do you say that?" she asked defensively.

"Because I checked. There is no record of a Betsy Copperfield attending the university. Then I had Professor Bellemy check under a different name, Betsy Copeland. Again, not a university student. However, when he put the Copeland surname in a genealogy database, he came up with something interesting. Marcus Bean's mother's maiden name was Copeland. Marcus had a sister, Anna Bean, who married a man named Erik Copperfield. They had a daughter named Betsy."

"Alright!" she hissed-whispered. "He was my uncle. I knew about his obsession with this place. So did my mum. It was just a hobby. He loved the Mistletoe Bride ghost story. He loved the history of this old place. Just being in this grand manor enlivened him. I think that may have been enough . . . until my father died of cancer a few years ago. Uncle Marcus might have been a confirmed bachelor, but he loved my mum. We were worried about money, and Uncle Marcus told Mum that if he could prove Bramsford Manor had been stolen from the Copeland family right under their noses over three hundred years ago, that our money problems could be over. It was a tall order. But there was this old family legend—which is more of a curse, really—but it has been passed down through the Copeland family for generations. It's not the Mistletoe Bride legend, but one from around that same time. It speaks of the true heir of Bramsford Manor, Cecil Copeland, the ghost bride's younger brother. Apparently, he'd been poisoned around the same time his father, Sir John Copeland, lay dying. Everyone believed the boy had died too, but he hadn't. His near lifeless body had been smuggled out of the house by a loyal servant and put into the care of a wisewoman. The woman nursed him back to health but warned that he must never return to the manor. He'd been given the gift of life, but a great evil resided at Bramsford Manor, and no Copeland would ever be safe within its walls again."

"That is quite a legend," Bunny remarked. "I'm beginning to believe it might be true. So, your uncle got you a job here knowing what this legend stated?"

"The legend that the Copeland family would always be in danger at the manor was from a long time ago. Uncle Marcus didn't believe it, at least not any longer. Remember, he worked at Bramsford Manor for years and was able to delve into its history without a problem." Betsy then pursed her lips and fell quiet. "Maybe he grew too comfortable," she offered. "Maybe the curse is real." Bunny could see that the thought wasn't sitting too well with the young woman. "Anyhow," Betsy continued, "he got me a job at Bramsford because he wanted me to understand what it was like here . . . how grand it was."

"Does anyone else here know that you and Marcus were related?" Betsy shook her head. "But you were overheard telling Lewis that Marcus was going to make a big reveal. Many people knew about that."

Her composure began to crumble under the weight of that truth. Her eyes filled with tears as she admitted, "It's true, but I never said what it was. But . . . it obviously got him killed. This is all my fault. I was just so sick of everyone who worked here lording it over me all the time, like I'm some type of peasant. But I am not. I'm a Copeland. My family . . . my ancestors built this place."

"You know what this big reveal is though, don't you?"

She dropped her head and nodded. After a deep breath she looked Bunny in the eyes once again. "Ann Copeland's disappearance on her wedding night wasn't an accident. She was murdered. However, I swear I never told anyone else about that."

"That would mean Marcus must have told somebody here," Bunny said softly, as much to herself as to the girl. She suddenly looked at the young server. "Somebody here knows that he was planning to challenge the Wallingford claim to Bramsford Manor. Betsy, I know you're in the middle of your shift, but I don't think this place is safe for you any longer."

"But . . . but I can't just leave. I still have tables to serve and we're short-staffed."

"You're a Copeland. Remember? Your family built this place. You're entitled to walk out," Bunny cajoled before becoming serious again. "Also, I need you to come with me to the police station. It's time we hand this matter over to the authorities."

Betsy nodded, took off her apron, and let it fall on the patio as she followed Bunny back into the dining room.

"Gentlemen, Grandma," Bunny announced to the table. Everyone, she noted, had finished their breakfast. "This is Besty Copperfield, Marcus Bean's niece, and the other Copeland descendant. The primary one being Marcus himself."

Giff stared at Bunny and made a gesture where his curled fingers sprang off his forehead like a mini explosion. "Mind blown!" he declared. "So, Marcus was the secret Copeland descendant all along?"

"Of course," Brett said, having a latent epiphany. "That's why he was obsessed with this place—with the history here. It was personal for him. And you, Besty," he added, shifting his gaze to the girl, "it's personal for you as well." He looked back at Bunny. "Does she know who the murderer is?"

"The short answer is, it's a Wallingford," Bunny told the table. "We know it's not Sir Charles, so it must be Morgan or her husband. Betsy's going to give her notice to Lilly in the kitchen and then I'm taking her to the police station with me."

"I'm coming with you," Granny Mac said, excusing herself from the table.

"Cody, Mike, Ed," Brett said, "you guys can start packing. Meanwhile, Giff and I will see if we can locate Sir Charles and his sister. I want to know if Sir Charles knew about Bean being a descendant of the Copeland family. And if we're really lucky, maybe we can get Morgan to confess."

Chapter 39

"That went rather well," Granny Mac said as they drove back to the manor. "I believe DCI Standish was shocked that you and the lads had learned so much about Marcus Bean, including his motives for announcing his big reveal to the cameras during the paranormal investigation. Clearly, Marcus had suspected that he might be in danger, that's why he wanted his reveal recorded—so it could go on the inter-webs and become, as they say, viral."

Bunny smiled at her hip grandmother's attempt at under-standing technology. "Standish sent a man to the university to retrieve that diary, while he was going to drive Betsy home. He was amazed that we had found out about that old diary."

"I think he likes you."

Bunny turned her head so fast to look at her grandma she almost gave herself whiplash. "Ridiculous. And yuck. Also, he's married. One of my cardinal rules, Gran, is that married men are off the table."

"I forgot he was married. Likely because he gives off that

wolf-on-the-prowl vibe. Very alpha male. If I were twenty years younger, I'd take him out for a drink." Bunny couldn't help herself from grinning at her outrageous grandmother.

"Listen to yourself. It's precisely that behavior—that and your woo-woo psychic medium stuff—that my father, your son, has issues with."

"Davie takes after his father, God rest his soul. Donald MacBride was a stolid, salt-of-the-earth man. Yet a girl's got to have a little fun sometimes, too. Your grandfather wasn't bothered by my psychic abilities. He was rather fond of them. Truth be told, he still is."

Bunny's eyes snapped on her grandmother again. "You . . . can still talk to him?"

Granny Mac nodded. "If you love someone, they never really leave you, Bunny. Love is the strongest bond in the universe. You have a lot yet to learn about your abilities, my dear."

Wasn't that the truth, Bunny mused, as she turned down the long tree-lined driveway that led to Bramsford Manor.

Once they arrived, Granny Mac announced that she was going to her room to clear her mind, balance her chakras, raise her vibration, and meditate. Now that they knew all but one secret (the identity of Marcus Bean's murderer) she felt she'd best be mentally prepared for the last remaining task ahead, something she liked to call *spiritual house-cleaning*.

"Enjoy," Bunny remarked with an ironic grin. "I'm going to wash up, check in with the lads, then head to the kitchen. It really is quite beautiful. One of the best I've ever had the pleasure to cook in. I need to pack my kit and thank Lilly for allowing me to be a guest chef in her kitchen. See you at dinner."

* * *

By the time Bunny entered the hotel kitchen, all the lights were still on, yet it was empty. It was that quiet yet fleeting transition period between meals. It had been a disruptive few days at the manor, and it would take some time to get Bramsford's kitchen back on track, serving its five-star meals to the public once again. Truthfully, Bunny was grateful for the peace and quiet. There was something restorative about the lull in the heart of a bustling kitchen. In many ways it was akin to a runner's high, that draining of tension after a long, frantic bout of nonstop activity in a hot environment. It ended after the last meal was served and everyone settled in to clean their stations. A cup of tea or coffee could be enjoyed. Although she hadn't served a meal, Bunny was itching for a cuppa now as she walked into the immaculate kitchen. She stood at the sink and stared out the large picture window, soaking in the stunning expanse of lawn edged by an old-growth forest. It was late afternoon, and the sun had already dipped beneath the tree line. It would be a beautiful sunset, she mused. However, the sudden buzzing of her phone interrupted her whimsical thoughts. Bunny pulled it out of the back pocket of her jeans and looked at it. The call was from Brett.

"Hello there, mister man," she playfully answered.

"Where are you?"

Bunny was taken aback by Brett's abrupt tone. "I'm in the kitchen, staring out the window. Where are you?"

"At the stables with Grimsby and Sir Charles."

"Oooh, that sounds fun," she teased. "How's Sir Charles doing today? Was he aware that Marcus Bean was a descendant of the noble house of Copeland?"

"No. He had no idea. Neither did Grimsby. But that's not why I'm calling. Morgan is missing. Charles hasn't seen her since yesterday, and no one can find her. After discussing all we've learned, including the fact that she had swapped places last night with Lewis, Charles's biological son, which he's still trying to process, we've come to the conclusion that she's the murderer. We believe she might be hiding somewhere in the manor. You and Granny Mac need to get out of there now."

The hair on the back of Bunny's neck stood on end at Brett's warning. The air around her suddenly changed, as if it had been charged with crackling energy. Bunny believed she could feel evil approaching. Not wishing to alarm him, she offered brightly, "Will do," and ended the call. The moment she did, all the lights in the kitchen went out. Although there was still ample light streaming through the window, Bunny froze. She knew exactly where Morgan Wallingford-Green was. Right behind her. Her heart pounded with fright.

A voice in her head told her to duck. She did and felt the blade of a knife sail over her head with such force it stuck blade-down in the cutting board in front of her. Bunny's heart sank at the sight of it. It was her prized chef's knife. The sight of it there . . . the misuse of her precious knife angered her. A hand was about to reach for the knife handle again when Bunny suddenly grabbed the wrist and turned to face her attacker. She inhaled sharply, realizing her mistake. Morgan hadn't tried to kill her. Lilly had.

"It was very clever of you to use my boning knife," Bunny said, fighting to remain calm. "You knew I wouldn't be needing it."

"Not clever, just practical," Lilly corrected, smiling unsteadily. "I wanted to use your chef's knife, given its size and heft, but I knew you'd miss it. You needed it for all that chop-chop-chopping. And using my own was out of the question. You know how much a good professional knife can cost these days."

"You tried to frame me. Was that your plan all along?"

"Not really. Call it a sudden flash of genius. You were here, you're popular, and quite frankly, you're just a little too good in the kitchen for my taste. I needed to cut you down to size." At that, Lilly grabbed another knife off the back counter and waved it at Bunny. The woman had snapped. Bunny took a step backward, but there was nowhere to go. Her backside was pressed up against the granite countertop.

"Why kill Marcus Bean?" she asked Lilly. "What was he to you? Surely, you're not a Wallingford. Was he blackmailing you?"

That seemed to anger Lilly. The woman lunged at her again with this new knife. Bunny jumped on the counter and rolled to the side, avoiding Lilly's knife while grabbing a cast-iron frying pan as she did so. She gripped the handle and held it like a shield before her.

"Why do you make these stupid assumptions?" Lilly snapped. "*Surely you can't be a Wallingford,*" she mocked.

"You are?" Bunny couldn't have been more surprised by this . . . until Lilly's angry knife aimed for her heart.

She grunted as she held up the cast-iron pan to deflect the blow. "What's wrong with you?" she cried, getting very tired of this woman. "Put your knife down. Explain yourself!" If Bunny thought that was going to work, she was wrong. Bunny deflected another angry blow, then offered, "Alright, let's say that you are a Wallingford. Why kill Marcus?"

"I am a Wallingford!" Lilly cried. The woman was definitely unhinged. "I'm a cousin of Charlie and Morgan's. Marcus knew that. He also knew that I had a criminal past. He dug it all up for fun. He didn't mean anything by it. He loved my food. No, he was more like a rambunctious hound following the pull of his nose. He could no longer help himself from rootling around in the garbage of people's past than a hungry dog can resist a dung heap. He'd dig up a piece of juicy gossip and bring it right to you with an expectant smile. Even though he knew I had a past, he didn't care. And I found him irresistible. We were having a torrid affair."

"You and Marcus?" Bunny nearly choked. She had never considered this. She slowly backed away until she came against the walk-in refrigerator. "But . . . why did you kill him?"

Lilly stilled. Her dark eyes seemed to grow even darker as she tightened her grip on the knife. "Because he told me his secret. He knew that I was a cousin, but then he had the hubris to tell me what he planned to do. As if it was some great coup! The nerve of him! I couldn't let him do it."

Certain that Lilly was going to try to impale her again, she blurted, "Why? Were you afraid of losing your job? Doubtful that you would. Lilly, you're a top-notch chef."

"I'm pleased that you think so, *Bridget MacBride*." She let out a cackle of laughter and rolled her eyes before launching another vicious attack. It took all Bunny could do to block the blade with the heavy frying pan. Her arms were burning with exhaustion. She blocked another swipe and kicked Lilly in the shin, allowing her to move away from the door to the walk-in.

"It's that snotty little Betsy Copperfield," Lilly explained, as much to herself as to Bunny. "Marcus lied to me. He told me she was his student. He always brought me good employees from the university, like that darling, sweet boy, Lewis. But there was something about Betsy that ruffled my feathers. She was always chit-chatting with Marcus, always lingering around his table when he took his tea. When I finally confronted him about it, he told me the truth. She was his niece, and not a student. Why didn't he just say so, I asked. But then he told me his secret. Betsy was a Copeland too, and the thought of her and him possibly getting their hands on this grand place made me sick. Charlie is a good man. Morgan has her moments, but they're family. It was

Charles who hired me when the chips were down and gave me a second chance." Bunny had relaxed her grip on the frying pan, causing Lilly to strike again. Bunny ducked and covered.

"Look at me!" Lilly cried. Bunny peered over the pan. "I run this kitchen! I won't let anything happen to Charles or to me. I didn't want to hurt Marcus, but there was no deterring the man. So, I had to kill him. I had to bury his secret for good! Once his secret was buried and his proof destroyed, Betsy's dream of getting her hands on this place would die with him. And it did. She's helpless to do anything about it now."

"Did she know that you killed her uncle?" Bunny couldn't believe what she was hearing.

"No. Because I've been playing her. I'm on to her game. She didn't know about her uncle and me, and she didn't know that I knew who she really was. The one thing history has taught us Wallingfords is that the Copeland family are easily fooled. If Betsy puts a toe out of line, I simply invite her to play a little game of hide-and-seek. See"—Lilly pointed to her noggin—"clever."

"Not clever," Bunny snarled. "Heartless!"

"Easy!" Lilly averred. "Those Copelands are fools to the core. Luring Marcus to the old mistletoe chest was like waving candy in front of a baby. He never saw it coming. That was because he was so excited about your ghost hunt and making his big reveal. No one would possibly think that the old mistletoe chest would ever hold a body again. I thought it was a clever twist. Also, you were easy to frame. It is, as they say, the perfect crime." Lilly smiled. Bunny felt sick.

"What about Sir Charles and Morgan. Did they know about any of this?"

"Love Charles to bits and pieces, but he's an underachieving dilettante. He was just so delighted with every morsel Marcus brought him that it never occurred to him that Marcus had ulterior motives. Morgan, on the other hand, is the clever one. She's had her flings with Marcus over the years, but they were just good friends. I believe that she knew what Marcus was up to and she didn't care. She hates this place. She wants out. She might have even been helping him. However, she was truly shaken by his death. While you and your ghost-hunting boys were running around the manor, trying to find Marcus's killer, Morgan was putting two and two together. Like I said, she's the clever one. She had the nerve to confront me yesterday morning. That was her biggest mistake. Morgan is self-obsessed. Always trying to find herself. The poor dear is no match for a mastermind like me. I had to stop her, for the good of the Wallingfords."

Bunny's heart dropped to the pit of her stomach at this. "What have you done with her?"

"I buried my first husband," Lilly bragged, advancing on her. "Poisoned him with a gourmet meal of beef Wellington spread with a toxic mushroom paté then wrapped in puff pastry. It was his favorite meal. He couldn't resist. Made the mistake of stabbing my second husband, but that was in self-defense."

"Why are you telling me this?" Bunny cried, just as Lilly rounded on her again with the knife. Bunny shielded her body, but the iron pan was getting heavy. "Did you stab Morgan?"

"No. Nothing that obvious. Like that unfortunate bride who still haunts this manor, I simply locked her away. It's tradition. I'm sorry, but I have to kill you now." Lilly then picked up another knife. Brandishing two knives like a crazed Edward Scissorhands, she advanced on Bunny with redoubled fury. Bunny's hopes sank, and she braced herself for impact, certain that she was about to meet her end in her dream kitchen. She covered her eyes and prayed.

Lilly let out a mad battle cry and took a step forward. That's when Bunny heard a loud, knee-weakening crack. At the sound her eyes flew open, and she watched Lilly sway a little before falling flat on her face on the floor.

"What an annoying woman," Granny Mac said, standing over the unconscious chef. She was still holding the large frying pan with a two-handed grip. Bunny kicked the knives away from Lilly's hands then ran to her grandma, giving the older woman a big hug.

"How . . . how did you know?"

"I had a very strong premonition that you needed me."

Chapter 40

As the police hauled Lilly Plum away, after she had confessed to the murder of Marcus Bean, she still wouldn't reveal what she had done with Morgan. The woman had snapped, and her last parting cackle as they dragged her from the kitchen had been, "A curse on you all. You will never find her alive!"

"She better be alive," DCI Standish warned very softly. "Or I'll make sure that the only food you eat from this day to your last is served out by the prison cafeteria." To Bunny it was an unthinkable fate.

Charles was visibly shaken. He looked at Standish. "What's your plan? That's my sister! We've got to find her!"

"It appears to be an all-hands-on-deck situation," Standish remarked. "Call the staff. Have them meet us in the hotel lobby."

Sir Charles pulled out his phone and began making calls. In less than fifteen minutes, all the staff had gathered in the hotel lobby, including Lewis, Betsy, and Morgan's estranged husband, Percival, and their daughter, Emma. The direness of the situation hadn't been lost on Percival. Bunny thought he looked worried sick for a philandering husband. Emma was in tears, wringing her hands. DCI Standish handed out walkie-talkies to each team.

"Callum and I will search every hotel room," Peter Billingsley said, holding up the master key.

"We'll search the outbuildings," Alex Grimsby said, signaling for Lewis and Betsy to assist him.

"This is a huge place." Giff looked overwhelmed as he spoke. "She could be anywhere. It could take us days."

"We need to look everywhere," Charles said. "Leave no stone unturned. Let's spread out and start on the first floor."

As each team began the search, Bunny looked at her grandmother, and whispered, "Gran, can you get a read on her? Can you narrow the search any?" Bunny was desperate.

Grandma Mac nodded and motioned for Bunny to follow her to the drawing room. Once there she looked at her granddaughter. "I'm a medium," she stated. "Aside from family and those I have a personal, loving bond with, it's easier for me to key in to the departed." Granny Mac then took a seat in one of the wingback chairs and closed her eyes. Bunny nervously watched her until she opened them again. "Morgan is still alive," she declared. "I'm getting nothing from her. However, the spirit of Marcus Bean still lingers here."

"He and Morgan were very close. I bet Morgan knew his secret. I bet she knew he was a Copeland descendant, and that he was going to announce the fact the Mistletoe Bride had been murdered."

Granny Mac nodded. "I figured that there must be a reason why his spirit is still lingering here. If we want to get to Morgan quickly, he might be able to help us. He might still have a strong connection to her. I'm going to summon him." She then closed her eyes again and leaned back in the chair.

A moment later Bunny smelled his calling card, a fug of Old Spice Swagger and stale cigarettes.

"He's here."

"He is," she said, focusing her light blue eyes on Bunny. "And he knows what to do. Ready? Let's follow him."

A handful of people were milling about the main floor. The kitchen had been searched, and now they were looking under tables, opening cabinets, peering in closets, when Bunny and Granny Mac came out of the drawing room. Giff and Brett stopped what they were doing and looked at them.

"Marcus Bean," Bunny said to their curious gazes and gestured for them to follow.

"What about him?" Giff asked, holding them both in a skeptical gaze as he marched beside them.

"He's here," Bunny whispered. "We're following his scent—"

"This way," Granny Mac said, taking a sharp turn toward the stairway. "He's going up here."

"Wait." Brett was trying to wrap his head around what was happening. "You can do that?—He can do that?"

"When one is desperate, one will try anything," Granny Mac told him and marched up the stairs. They had reached the third floor. Granny Mac turned the corner and walked down a long hallway, coming to a stop at the end of it. She stared at the large painting depicting riders on the hunt. "This is quite lovely, but I'm not sure why he brought us here." She turned to Bunny. "I think he went through this painting." Bunny wasn't used to seeing her wise grandmother looking puzzled.

Recognizing where they were, Brett grinned. "He did go though there. This is the way to his office at the top of the stairs." Brett opened the painting, revealing the hidden staircase.

"Morgan has to be in a chest," Bunny told them as they raced up the steps to the attic. "Lilly mentioned hide-and-seek to me in the kitchen," she huffed, reaching the historian's office and the long hallway that opened to the attic. "She stabbed Marcus and pushed him in the mistletoe chest. It's her calling card."

"You have a point," Brett agreed, and the five of them began searching the attic for a chest large enough to hide a body.

While they rummaged through all the old artifacts strewn about the attic, Granny Mac steadily continued past them, as if in a trance.

"Here," she finally called out to them. "Marcus is saying that she's here."

Everyone stopped what they were doing and gathered around the spot Granny Mac indicated. The ceiling above sloped to the right, leaving a three-foot wall beside them, and a solid oak plank wall in front of them. Aside from a stack of covered portraits that leaned against the sloping roofline, the space was empty. There wasn't any sign of a chest. Stumped, Bunny put her hands on her hips and bent over, taking a deep breath. Her hopes were dashed. She covertly looked up through her lashes at her grandmother, believing that the woman had made a mistake. However, she could still smell the telltale scent of Marcus Bean lingering about them. Maybe the spirit of Marcus was the problem. Maybe ghosts made unreliable guides. Yet just as she was beginning to doubt her grandmother's abilities, she heard a click. The wall in front of them slowly creaked open, revealing a hidden room.

"I'll be damned," Brett uttered as he bent his head and walked into the hidden room. "It's here! A chest!"

Morgan Wallingford-Green had been brought into the attic by Lilly, the chef having held a gun to her back. The psychotic chef had then bound, gagged, and locked her in a chest where she was left to rot in a secret room in the attic, just like young Ann Copeland had three hundred years ago on her wedding night. Sir Charles had declared it a miracle that his sister had been found in time—that she'd been found at all. It was a sobering thought. Even Percival had been overwhelmed by the notion of losing his wife. When Bunny had announced the rescue over the walkie-talkies, Percival had raced up the attic stairs ahead of everyone and had embraced Morgan so hard she had coughed and sputtered to catch her breath. Then she embraced him back, tears streaming down her face, and clung to him as if her life depended on it. It was such an intimate and touching scene, Bunny had to look away.

No one had known about the secret room in the attic. No one, Bunny mused, except for Marcus Bean. The old Bunny would have scrambled to find a rational explanation for the hidden door suddenly creaking open like it had. The wind. Loose hinges. Gravity. However, having sensed his presence, there was no doubt in Bunny's mind that his spirit, having lingered at Bramsford Manor after his sudden and violent death, had helped them find Morgan.

While Brett and Giff had been helping her out of the chest, and freeing her from her bonds, Granny Mac had leaned close to Bunny and whispered in her ear, "He's gone. His spirit has crossed over. He's at peace in the light with his maker, God rest his soul."

She had never admired her grandmother more than in that moment. They had saved Morgan, and the soul of Marcus Bean had left the building. Maybe being a medium wasn't so bad after all, she thought. However, Bunny's joy was short-lived. Her grandmother then reminded her, "We're not done yet. There's still the matter of the dark female presence, and the Mistletoe Bride. It's going to be another all-hands-on-deck situation, I'm afraid."

Chapter 41

After the harrowing rescue of Morgan Wallingford-Green, all the staff had been sent home for the rest of the day. They had endured enough at Bramsford Manor. Morgan, having spent over twenty-four hours locked in a wooden chest in the attic, had had plenty of time to reconsider the direction her life had taken, and what really mattered to her.

"All I could think about was you, Emma, not being there for you, or to watch you grow into the incredible woman I know you're going to be one day. And you, Percival"—she shifted her teary-eyed gaze to her husband—"I've made a mess of our marriage."

"You didn't do that alone, my dear. You had plenty of help from me."

"And you, Charles, my dear little brother. I learned you had a son. I want to be part of that journey as well, wherever it leads you. I was always thinking of myself and how I wanted to escape this dreadful old place and this dreadful life. Then I almost died here, locked in that chest like that poor girl long ago. For all those hours all I could think about was all of you, the happiness I've had here, and the bitter irony of such a fate for me. I vowed to change my ways if I was ever lucky enough to be found."

Morgan, Percival, and Emma had left the manor as well, taking a much-needed family holiday. That left Sir Charles, the team of *Food & Spirits*, and oddly enough, Betsy and Lewis. Sir Charles and Morgan had graciously welcomed both young people into the family.

"The pizza should be arriving any minute," Sir Charles announced, walking into the dining room where two of the tables had been pushed together. Bunny had disappeared into the kitchen to toss together a quick garden salad. Betsy and Lewis gathered drinks and set them on the table. "This is so much fun!" Charles announced with childlike glee. "We're having a pizza party at the manor. We haven't done this sort of thing since I was a boy."

"We have your permission for tonight, correct?" Brett asked again. "You're okay with Ella and our team moving the ghosts along?"

Charles took a seat at the table and rubbed his chin. "I am," he said at length. "If it can be done. People like the idea of staying in a haunted manor, but even if the ghosts are no longer around, we still have a very chilling legend to tell here. What a messed-up family history we have," he said to Betsy and Lewis, then laughed.

As they ate pizza and salad, Ella told them her plan. "The dark entity on the second floor, who we believe to be the vengeful ghost of Catherine Villers, is holding the other ghosts here hostage, including Ann Copeland's ghost. Because she was a murderer in life, her energy is very dark, very low, and it's going to be resistive. I'd like Giff to assist me."

"What?" he blurted, nearly spilling his soda. "You want me to assist you with that joy-sucker?"

"She likes you," Granny Mac told him. "Wear every crystal you've got, my lad. You're coming with me to the second floor."

"I'm coming too, with my camera," Cody told them.

"I'm in," Lewis said, brimming with excitement.

What was wrong with the young man? Bunny thought.

"I mean, this is it, right?" he continued. "We're banishing the ghosts from Bramsford. This is going to be legendary."

Betsy rolled her eyes at him.

"Excellent," Granny Mac told them. "The rest of you will be with Bridget on the upper patio out there. From what you've told me, dear, for whatever reason, I believe that's the place the spirit of Ann Copeland wants to be. The dark entity is keeping her in the Fleur-de-Lys room. Once that ghost is banished and the energy is cleared, I believe she's going to appear here. Clearing the joy-sucker, as Giff has so aptly termed it, might be enough. However, just to make sure, I want all of you to stand in a circle near the stairs, join hands, and fill your hearts with love. Pure love. Can you do that?"

Brett caught Bunny's eye and nodded. She blushed as everyone else nodded too. Ed, stepping aside from the love circle, announced that he was going to film them.

"Is everyone in place?" Cody announced over the walkie-talkie.

"Everyone on the patio is ready," Bunny replied, looking at her team. Brett was on her right, Sir Charles on her left. Mike and Betsy completed the circle.

"I'm not," Giff said, his voice crackling over the static. "I'm terrified. I'm underqualified for this. I write jingles and ads. What am I doing here? I am virtually a big marshmallow with a shiny, attractive exterior. That joy-sucker is coming for me."

"I'll edit all that out, boss," Cody told them. "Gotta keep the myth alive somehow."

"Copy that." Brett grinned at Bunny. "He still looks good on night vision, right?"

"Fashionable as ever."

"I'll protect him!" Lewis announced over his walkie-talkie. "I've got his back. And if he should become possessed, my mum knows this priest from Reading who does exorcisms."

"Not helpful, kid." Giff was definitely on edge.

"That kid of mine's got spunk," Sir Charles remarked to the circle with a grin.

"He's a dunderhead," Betsy declared with dripping attitude. "But kinda cool too, for a Wallingford."

"You guys ready down there?" Cody's voice came over the walkie-talkie. "Hold hands. The joy-sucker is in the building. Ella is engaging."

What followed then was ten stressful minutes of hand holding, channeling love and joy, and waiting. Then something miraculous happened.

"She's here," Bunny alerted them, feeling the familiar sadness washing over her. She opened her eyes and saw the ghostly bride standing on the garden steps in the darkness. She looked at Brett and knew that he could see her too. They all could. "She's still sad," she told them, and gripped Brett's hand tighter. He squeezed back, speechless. "Love. Feel it in your hearts. Think of something, someone that you love. Now!" It was a command.

They must have all felt love, because in that moment the sadness left Bunny completely. And that's when she saw him standing below in the garden. A ghostly image of a gentleman. She didn't need anyone to tell her who he was. The love she felt radiating through her from the ghost of Ann Copeland was enough. It was her groom, Sir Henry Wallingford, as he appeared on his wedding day three hundred years ago. Filling with awe and speechless wonder, they all watched as the ghost bride swept down the steps and took Henry's hand in the garden. The moment she did, they gently faded into the night. A memory. An echo from a time long ago. And Bunny was certain she had never witnessed anything so remarkable in her life. At least that's what she thought.

Later that night, after everyone had a chance to rehash what had happened and tell their side of the story, Bunny felt that the air inside the manor had shifted—had become lighter, brighter, less oppressive.

Giff had survived the joy-sucker.

Thanks to Granny Mac the evil entity had been cleared away.

Sir Charles, having witnessed the long-awaited reunion of the ghost bride and groom, realized that he now had an even better story to attach to the manor. What had been the sad legend of a couple on their tragic wedding night three-hundred years ago had been given a happily-ever-after ending in the afterlife. Doubtful anyone would believe him, but it was a pretty great story.

As for Brett, he hadn't said much. But he had held Bunny's hand. He had held it tightly and hadn't let go until it had become almost awkward. Bunny hadn't even blushed. Like her, he was likely still trying to process what they had witnessed.

The first episode filming of *Food & Spirits* was a wrap. Brett, Giff, and Bunny, standing in the original dining room, had one last shot to make. With three champagne glasses filled with bubbling champagne, they toasted the camera and recited their tagline. "Be careful who you invite to dinner." Wasn't that the truth!

Their time at Bramsford Manor had come to an end. And what a time it had been. Even though Bunny hadn't loved every minute of it—actually most of it had been pretty terrible—she realized how much she had missed her grandmother. How much she loved and admired the woman. She had even grown fond of her team on *Food & Spirits* and was warming to her role as chef on a ghost show. The medium part she was still grappling with. However, it was reason enough to celebrate.

After imbibing a few drinks in celebration, Bunny walked into the Fleur-de-Lys room for the last time, feeling confident that she'd finally get a good night's sleep. She then flicked on the lights and saw the white rabbit sitting on her bed. Her dreams of a peaceful night's sleep faded.

Slightly tipsy, she sat on a chair and addressed him. "All the ghosts have gone. Why are you still here, Hopper? What are you?"

With one more wiggle of his nose, the image of the rabbit started to shimmer. The soft, white fur became translucent, then it started to flutter. A white butterfly arose, then another, and another until the rabbit slowly faded and white wings circled the air, rising to the ceiling. That's when she saw him, standing in the center of the kaleidoscope of fluttering wings. Her brother. Her twin. Braiden.

"You," she uttered, tearing up at the sight of him. She wiped her tears away as fast as they came, trying to get a good look at him. He looked exactly as he had before the accident—young, handsome, grinning, only now there was a shimmering brightness to him that she found comforting. "That was you all along? I've spent ten years running from the ghost of a white rabbit and it was you?" She could hardly believe her eyes. They were filling with tears as her heart was bursting with a pure and profound love. Yet all she could think to say was, "You idiot!"

He smiled again, and then he was gone, fading into the ether, just like the butterflies.

Author's Note

The Legend of the Mistletoe Bough Bride

When I was tinkering with the notion of writing a novel series that would focus on both ghosts and food (a very unusual notion indeed!), I was confident about the food angle I'd be tackling. However, ghosts were another matter. I don't have much experience with ghosts at all, thank goodness. But I did know, loving a good ghost story as much as the next person, that at the heart of every legendary haunting is a pretty good story. I set out to find a good story to shape my mystery around and knew that I wanted to write about a white lady. For those who don't know, a white lady is a ghostly apparition that is usually seen in a flowing white garment. Legends of white ladies are commonly associated with tragedies, particularly accidental death, murder, betrayal by a husband or fiancé, or unrequited love. I had heard such a story about a white lady from an Irishman who told me that when he was a boy, he used to ride his bike past a haunted Irish castle on his way to school. He had seen the white lady more than a few times. Apparently, she had been murdered on her wedding day in the 1600s. According to this gentleman, she still haunts the crumbling castle. It was ghoulishly tragic!

I was searching for this very story when I came upon another that stopped me in my tracks. It was a tale known as *The Legend of the Mistletoe Bough*. In other searches it came up as *The Mistletoe Bride*. The moment I read about this poor girl who'd gotten locked in a chest on her wedding night while playing an innocent game of hide-and-seek and wasn't discovered until fifty years later by her faithful groom, I knew I had found what I'd been looking for. The story of this white lady was the most heart-wrenching tragic tale I had ever stumbled across, and I couldn't stop thinking about it. It was the starting point for *A Fatal Feast at Bramsford Manor*. I'm far from the only person compelled to write about this haunting legend, although I might be the only person who's turned it into a food-baiting, ghost-hunting, murder mystery.

Oddly enough, *The Legend of the Mistletoe Bough* is widely known in Britain, and many stately homes claim it as their own. While I was researching this ghost story, it appeared that a stately home called Bramshill House had the strongest claim, in my opinion. Supposedly, they even display the mistletoe chest the unfortunate bride had hidden in. Bramshill House, in Hampshire, England, is also reported to be one of the most haunted homes in Britain, having no less than fourteen ghosts that have been seen there. My story, *A Fatal Feast at Bramsford Manor*, is entirely a work of fiction spun around *The Legend of the Mistletoe Bough*. I hope you have enjoyed it. If you would like more information about this tragic ghost story, you can learn more by following the links listed below.

https://en.wikipedia.org/wiki/Legend_of_the_Mistletoe_Bough

https://burialsandbeyond.com/2019/12/21/the-bramshill-house-bride-or-the-legend-of-the-mistletoe-bough/

Bunny's Culinary Corner

Recipes & tips to entertain your family & friends.
(And ghosts, if that's what you're into.)

Harvest Pork Chop Bake

Prep time: 15 minutes. Bake time: 60 minutes
Serves 4

Ingredients:

4 boneless pork chops, between ¾ and 1 inch thick.
1 large yellow onion, thinly sliced
2 tart apples, peeled and sliced (I use Pink Lady or Granny
    Smith)
2 tablespoons butter
1 tablespoon fresh rosemary or 1 teaspoon dried
Coarse salt for seasoning
2 whole acorn squash (1 to 1¼ pounds each); trim stems, cut in
    half crosswise and remove seeds*
3 tablespoons brown sugar
4 tablespoons butter
½ teaspoon ground cinnamon
½ teaspoon coarse salt
¼ cup of Danish blue cheese, crumbled

Bunny's pro tip: If the ends of the squash are pointed, trim the
point so that the squash will sit flat when ready for the final
bake.

Directions:

Preheat oven to 375°. Place the prepared squash halves in a
roasting pan or large baking dish, cut side down. Add ½ inch of
water to the baking dish and bake for 35 minutes, or until almost
tender when pierced with a sharp knife. Larger halves may take
longer.

While the squash is baking, prepare the pork chops.

In a large frying pan on medium heat, add 1 tablespoon of
butter. Once the butter has melted add the sliced onions and ap-

ples. Sauté until tender and slightly caramelized, about 10 minutes. For the first 5 minutes I cover the pan with a lid to soften the apples and onions. Once done, place in a bowl and set aside. Add the other tablespoon of butter to the pan. Once melted add the pork chops. Sprinkle pork chops with salt and fresh rosemary. Cook 5 minutes on each side until nice and brown and the internal temperature reaches 145 degrees. Turn off heat and add the apples and onions. Cover with a lid and set aside.

In a small saucepan heat the 4 tablespoons of butter over medium heat until butter starts to bubble. Lower heat and continue to cook, stirring occasionally, until all the foam has cooked off and a nice brown liquid remains, about 5 minutes. Remove from heat and stir in the brown sugar, cinnamon, and coarse salt until well blended. This mixture will be coarse.

Once acorn squash has been cooked, remove from oven. Using a baking sheet, place the squash halves cut side up and liberally brush with the brown butter sauce, letting it drip into the wells of the squash. Return to oven and bake 10 minutes longer until the squash is tender and glazed. Remove from oven.

Once pork chops have cooled, choose one at a time and slice the pork chop into bite-sized pieces. Place one whole pork chop inside the well of one of the squashes. Top with a scoop of the apple/onion mixture. Next, place a heaping tablespoon of crumbled blue cheese on top of the apple/onion mixture. Repeat this process for the remaining three pork chops. Return to the oven for 5–8 minutes, just until the cheese has softened. Remove from oven and serve immediately.

Cornbread Muffins with Honey Butter

Prep time: 15 minutes. Cook time: 12–15 minutes.
Makes 12–14 regular-size muffins.

Ingredients:
For the muffins:
1½ cups fine cornmeal
1½ cups all-purpose flour
1 cup granulated sugar
½ cup butter (1 stick) softened
2 eggs
1 tablespoon baking soda
½ teaspoon salt
1½ cups whole milk

For the honey butter:
1 cup (2 sticks) unsalted butter, softened
⅓ cup honey
3 tablespoons pure maple syrup
½ teaspoon sea salt (or less)

Directions:
Preheat oven to 350°. Combine cornmeal, flour, baking soda
and salt in a bowl and set aside. In the bowl of an electric mixer,
cream butter and sugar until light and fluffy. Add the eggs and
continue beating until well blended. With the mixer on slow, add
half the dry ingredients and half the milk. Continue until the batter is combined.

Grease and lightly flour muffin cups.* Fill each muffin cup
three-quarters full, leaving room to expand. Bake 12–15 minutes or until muffins are done. Remove from oven and let cool.
Muffins are best served warm and slathered with honey butter.
Leftovers can be stored in a zip-lock bag and refrigerated.

Make the honey butter: In the bowl of an electric mixer, beat softened butter until it's light and fluffy, about 3 minutes. Drizzle in the honey and the maple syrup. Add the sea salt. Whip the mixture for five more minutes until nice and fluffy. Put in an airtight container and refrigerate leftovers.

Bunny's pro tip: To save time you can make this cornbread in a 9 x 13 pan, or a 9-inch round cast-iron frying pan. Both work great. Make sure to grease the pans. Butter works best on cast iron. If using a 9 x 13 baking pan, flour it as well. Bake for 45 minutes.

Pumpkin Spice Cupcakes

Prep time: 15 minutes. Cook time: 20 minutes.
Makes 2 dozen cupcakes

Ingredients:
For the cupcakes:
2 cups all-purpose flour
1 teaspoon baking powder
1 teaspoon baking soda
2 teaspoons pumpkin pie spice
1 teaspoon ground cinnamon
½ teaspoon salt
1 (15-ounce) can pumpkin
1 cup granulated sugar
1 cup firmly packed brown sugar
½ cup butter, melted and cooled
½ cup vegetable oil
4 large eggs

For the frosting:
1 (8-ounce) package cream cheese, softened
½ cup butter, softened
3½–4 cups confectioner's sugar
1 teaspoon vanilla extract

Directions:
Preheat oven to 350°. Line 24 muffin cups* with paper liners.

In a large bowl, whisk together flour, baking powder, baking soda, pumpkin pie spice, cinnamon, and salt. In another bowl, whisk together pumpkin, sugars, butter, vegetable oil, and eggs until well blended. Make a well in the flour mixture and add the pumpkin mixture, gently blending the batter together by hand or with an electric mixer until smooth and free of lumps.

Fill each muffin cup three-quarters full, leaving room to expand. Place in oven and bake 20 minutes or until a wooden toothpick inserted into the center of the cupcake comes out clean. Remove from pan, and place on a wire rack until completely cooled.

To prepare the frosting, in the bowl of an electric mixer, beat cream cheese and butter together. Add the vanilla and beat again. Gradually add the confectioner's sugar and beat until smooth. Insert a large star tip into a pastry bag and fill with frosting. Pipe frosting onto each cupcake in a pretty swirl pattern.

Bunny's Pro Tip: If you're running short of time you can make this cake in a 9 x 13 pan instead. Pour batter into the greased and floured pan and bake in the oven for 25–30 minutes, or until a toothpick inserted into the center comes out clean. Cool completely and frost with the cream cheese frosting.

Bunny's Chocolate Digestive Biscuits

Prep time: 10 minutes. Rest time: 30 minutes.
Cook time 12–15 minutes.
Makes 18 cookies.

Ingredients:

⅔ cup old-fashioned oatmeal
1 cup all-purpose flour
¾ cup confectioner's sugar
1 teaspoon baking powder
½ teaspoon sea salt
½ cup (1 stick) cold butter, cut into small cubes
¼ cup cold buttermilk
1 cup milk chocolate or dark chocolate, chopped

Directions:

To make oat flour, place the ⅔ cup of oatmeal in a food processor with a metal chopping blade. Grind the oatmeal until it resembles coarse flour.

In a large bowl, combine the all-purpose flour, ground oats, baking powder, salt, and sugar and mix with a spoon* until well blended. Using a pastry blender (or your fingers), cut in cold butter until mixture resembles coarse sand. Stir in cold buttermilk and form dough into a ball. Cover with plastic wrap and place in the refrigerator for 30 minutes.

Preheat oven to 350°. On a floured surface, roll out dough until it's just under ¼ inch thick. Using a fork, prick the dough all over. This will prevent the cookies from buckling as they bake. Using a 2½ inch biscuit cutter (or the rim of a glass), cut out cookies and place them on a parchment-lined baking sheet, spacing them 1 inch apart. Bake for 15 minutes or until golden brown on top. Remove to a cooling rack.

In a microwave-safe bowl, melt the chocolate, heating it for

30 seconds at a time. Stir well between each heating until chocolate is velvety smooth. You can either dip the bottom of the cookies into the chocolate or dollop a spoonful on the bottom of each cookie. Using a knife, smooth the chocolate, making sure it covers the entire bottom of the cookie. Place cookies chocolate side up on cooling rack. Allow the chocolate to cool completely before serving.

Bunny's Pro Tip: I prefer to make this cookie dough by hand, as my mum taught me. However, if you have a food processor and are making the oat flour, by all means, make the dough in the food processor. Using a metal chopping blade, blend all dry ingredients together before adding the cold butter. Add the butter and blend again until the dough resembles coarse sand, then add the buttermilk for the final blend. Easy-peasy!

Winter Wassail

Prep time: 5 minutes. Cook time: 30 minutes. Serves 10

Ingredients:
8 cups of apple cider
2 cups hard apple cider (for nonalcoholic use orange juice instead)
½ cup brandy (for nonalcoholic wassail, omit the brandy)
1 tart apple, washed
1 orange, washed and sliced into thin circles
8 whole cloves (or ½ teaspoon ground cloves)
2 cinnamon sticks
1 tablespoon fresh ginger, peeled and sliced
1 teaspoon ground nutmeg
1 teaspoon ground cardamom

Directions:
Pour both hard and soft ciders into a large pot and stir in the brandy. Poke whole cloves into the apple and add it to the pot. Add the rest of the spices and give a gentle stir. Add the orange slices and gently warm the wassail over medium heat until it begins to steam. Turn the heat to low, cover the pot and allow it to mull for 30 minutes. Using a fine mesh strainer, strain before serving. Garnish with a thin slice of apple or a cinnamon stick.

Hearty Bangers and Mash in Yorkshire Pudding

Prep time: 1 hour. Serves 4–6

Ingredients:
For the bangers:
8 sausages (bratwurst works best in the US)
1 tablespoon butter for pan
2 yellow onions, sliced
1 clove garlic
2 sage leaves
1 cup beef broth
¼ cup marsala wine
1 teaspoon Dijon mustard or coarse grain mustard
1 teaspoon sea salt
½ teaspoon ground pepper
2½ to 3 pounds potatoes, peeled and cubed*
¼ cup butter (4 tablespoons)
¼ cup milk or more
Salt and pepper to taste

For the Yorkshire pudding:
4 large eggs
1¼ cups all-purpose flour
½ teaspoon coarse salt
4 tablespoons melted butter plus six additional teaspoons of
   melted butter for each pop-over cup

Bunny's Pro Tip: Need a timesaver? Instead of making
mashed potatoes, buy your favorite premade mashed potatoes
from the store. Heat according to package.

Directions:
   Make the Yorkshire pudding batter. In a blender, add the eggs,
flour, salt, and 4 tablespoons of melted butter and blend well

until batter is smooth and lump-free. Place in refrigerator for 30 minutes.

Heat oven to 425°. Once batter has rested, using a large muffin tin or popover pan, add 1 teaspoon of melted butter to each cup and place in oven, watching carefully. You want to get the butter very hot, almost smoking. Take the pan out of the oven and fill each cup ¾ full with the Yorkshire pudding batter. Bake 15–20 minutes or until golden brown.

Meanwhile, place potatoes in a pot of salted water and bring to a boil. Boil for 10 minutes, or until the potatoes are soft. Drain the pot and add ¼ cup butter and ¼ cup whole milk. Using a masher, mash the potatoes. Salt and pepper to taste and hand whisk the potatoes until smooth. Keep warm.

Place a large pan over medium heat for one to two minutes. Once the pan is hot, add 1 tablespoon of butter. Once the butter has melted add the sausages and cook until done, turning them so each side gets nice and brown. Remove to a plate and keep warm.

Keeping the pan on low heat, add 1 tablespoon of butter. Once melted add the onions and the clove of garlic and cook until soft, about 5 minutes. Add the beef broth, marsala wine, and the sage leaves. Turn up the heat and bring to a boil, making sure the alcohol cooks off. Lower the heat and stir in the mustard and salt and pepper. Cook for 5 more minutes.

To serve: Turn out the crisp Yorkshire puddings from their pan. Place one pudding on each plate, and fill each Yorkshire pudding with a generous serving of mashed potatoes, top it with sliced sausages and cover the entire thing with onion gravy. This is pub food at its finest. Enjoy!

Rustic Apple Tart with Butterscotch Sauce

Prep time: 20 minutes. Cook time: 45 minutes. Serves 6–8

Ingredients:
For the tart:
1 (14 oz.) package refrigerated piecrusts, room temperature
2 pounds peeled, cored, and thinly sliced tart or sweet-tart
   apples
2 tablespoons granulated sugar
1 teaspoon cinnamon
$\frac{1}{4}$ teaspoon nutmeg
$\frac{1}{4}$ teaspoon allspice
$\frac{3}{4}$ teaspoon cornstarch
1 egg, beaten with 1 tablespoon water
2 teaspoons turbinado sugar or coarse sanding sugar

For the sauce:
$\frac{1}{2}$ cup butter
$\frac{2}{3}$ cup firmly packed brown sugar
$\frac{1}{2}$ cup heavy whipping cream
1 teaspoon coarse sea salt
1 teaspoon vanilla extract

Directions:
Preheat oven to 400°. On a floured surface stack both pie crusts and roll them into a 14-inch circle. Fit crust into a 10-inch fluted tart pan with removable bottom. A pie pan can also be used. Let extra crust extend over sides of pan.

Gently arrange apple slices in the pan, placing them close to-gether vertically, with the slim-side down. Fan them around the pan and into the middle decoratively. In a small bowl, whisk to-gether sugar, cinnamon, nutmeg, allspice, and cornstarch. Sprinkle this mixture over apples. Gently fold over the extra crust so that it creates a two to three-inch rim around the inside of the pan. Pleat the edges so the crust lays flat. Brush top crust with beaten egg mixture and sprinkle with turbinado sugar. Place on a baking sheet and bake for 30 minutes. Cover with aluminum foil and bake an additional 10–15 minutes, or until crust is golden brown and apples are tender. Let cool in the pan for 10 minutes. Remove from pan while tart is still warm and cool completely.

To make the butterscotch sauce: In a small saucepan melt butter over medium heat. Stir in brown sugar and bring to a simmer, stirring constantly until sugar has dissolved. Stir in cream and salt and bring to a boil, stirring constantly for one minute. Remove from heat and stir in the vanilla. Serve warm apple tart with a scoop of vanilla ice cream and a generous drizzle of warm butterscotch sauce.